DON'T FENCE ME IN

HEATH DANIELS

Published by ITO Press

Cover Design by Monkey C Media
monkeyCmedia.com

Printed in the United States of America
ISBN: 978-1-7328812-3-5

Library of Congress Control Number: 2020907505

BOOKS BY HEATH DANIELS

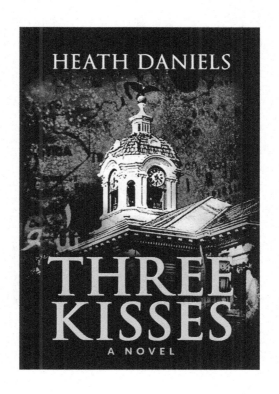

Visit HeathDanielsBooks.com for news of upcoming books.

List of Characters
In alphabetical order by first name

Aaron Benavides—staff attorney, U.S. Attorney General, New Mexico District

Adam Culbertson—explosives expert, FBI Operations Center, Quantico, Virginia

Adriana Cho—attorney, federal public defender, Albuquerque, New Mexico

Andrew Branson—U.S. Border Patrol headquarters executive, Washington, DC

Bijan Ahmadi—senior diplomat, Iranian embassy in Mexico

Bradley "Brad" Spencer—friend of Yusef; PhD student, University of Minnesota

Brenda Jackson—senior staff attorney, U.S. Attorney General, El Paso Division, Western Judicial District of Texas

Brock O'Neill—expert on issues of public demonstrations, FBI Operations Center, Quantico, Virginia

Carmen Cisneros—FBI agent, El Paso Field Office

Carter Kuykendall—FBI agent, El Paso Field Office

Charles Goodnight—head, FBI El Paso Field Office

Curtis Griffith—judge, U.S. federal court, Alpine Division, Western Judicial District of Texas

Delmar Armstrong—leader of the American Civil Liberties Union (ACLU) in New Mexico

Dwight Peters—private attorney and federal public defender, Alpine, Texas

Eric James—CIA agent, Washington, DC, area

Elliott Davidson—U.S. federal judge, New Mexico Judicial District

Emiliano Gonzalez—immediate past U.S. Attorney and head of El Paso Division, Western Judicial District of Texas

Imad Fladallah—Lebanese Hezbollah operative in Mexico

Ivan Petrov—mid-level diplomat with the Russian embassy in Mexico assigned to Ciudad Juárez

James Cunningham—investigator, U.S. Postal Service Operations Center, Washington, DC, area

Jared Cramer—senior agent, FBI Headquarters, Washington, DC

Jay Hodges—deputy sheriff, Hudspeth County, Texas

John Holmes—U.S. Attorney for Western Judicial District of Texas

Khan Nguyen—staff attorney, U.S. Attorney General, El Paso Division, Western Judicial District of Texas

Kuang-Sik, Ri—senior diplomat, North Korean embassy in Mexico

Leroy Russell—itinerant oilfield and construction worker

Marcus Porter—news producer for BBC America

Martin Bedingfield—staff attorney, U.S. Attorney General, Alpine Division, Western Judicial District of Texas

Nisrine "Nizzy" Maktabi—medical doctor; wife of Yusef

Omar Abu Deeb—best friend of Yusef, Professor, University of North Carolina

Otto Wildmann—statistician, NASA, Holloman Air Force Base, New Mexico

Peter Richardson—FBI agent, Las Cruces resident agency, New Mexico Field Office

Robert Andrews—head, Las Cruces branch office, U.S. Attorney for New Mexico

Robert Davis—attorney, head, U.S. Attorney General, Alpine Division, Western Judicial District of Texas

Roger Chen—senior attorney, U.S. Attorney General Headquarters, Washington, DC

Roosevelt "Rosie" Jordan—head, FBI Operations Center, Quantico, Virginia

Sara Shaito—toddler-age daughter of Nisrine and Yusef

Susana Tate—deputy head, U.S. Attorney General, El Paso Division, Western Judicial District of Texas

Vladimir Mikhailov—senior diplomat with the Russian embassy in Mexico

Woodrow Dawes—itinerant oilfield and construction worker

Yusef "Yusey" Shaito—deputy U.S. Attorney General, Western Judicial District of Texas; acting head, El Paso Division; husband of Nisrine

PROLOGUE

PROLOGUE

PROLOGUE 1

Mid-morning on a hazy, smoggy, sunny day typical of Mexico City, Ivan Petrov, a mid-level diplomat assigned to the Russian Embassy in Mexico, entered the office of Vladimir Mikhailov, a more senior diplomat. The two men exchanged collegial embraces, then Ivan said in Russian, "Vladimir Evgenevich, you want to see me before I go back to Juárez?"

Vladimir chuckled and replied in Russian, "Did you come down here to celebrate *Cinco de Mayo* holiday with us, Ivan Aleksandrovich? I'm surprised you didn't stay in Juárez for the celebrations."

They continued to speak in Russian. Ivan chuckled once again. "You know there's not much celebration here in Mexico for *Cinco de Mayo*, including Juárez. It's all the Mexicans in the U.S. looking for an excuse to party and celebrate their heritage. There'll be parties in El Paso across the river, but not much in Juárez on our side of the border. The ambassador's office contacted me and asked me to come down today and for the weekend. When I showed up in his office, I was sent here."

"Yes, I know," Vladimir replied. "After the ambassador agreed to this project, I'm the one who wanted to see you. I asked them to contact you to be here today and maybe the weekend. With the *Cinco de Mayo* celebrations, what few there may be in Juárez, the Americans who watch you won't pay too much attention to your coming down here. The Mexicans and the Americans both know you are our unofficial consul in Juárez monitoring the American military at Fort Bliss and the White Sands missile range just across the border. They know we know they know, so it's no big deal. They spy on us in Kaliningrad and other places also. But we don't want to give them a hint of what we want you to do now. So just keep to your spymaster stuff, but quietly go find us a place for this next project."

"What's that?" Ivan asked.

"We're going to dig a tunnel from Juárez to El Paso," Vladimir replied. "We need you to find a place in Juárez to begin digging."

"*Wha-a-a-t?*" Ivan blurted out. "You're going to dig a tunnel under the river?"

"No!" Vladimir said, and got out a blown-up copy of a map of greater El Paso and Ciudad Juárez. "Look here. In northwest El Paso the border between the U.S. and Mexico turns west and follows a line across land. See?"

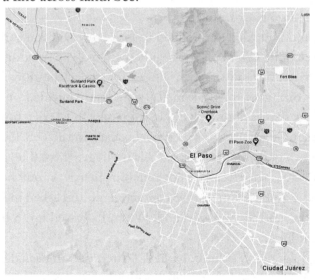

Map of El Paso and Ciudad Juárez (Map data ©2020 Google)

"Yeah," Ivan replied. "Bordering New Mexico. There's nothing of interest out there that we monitor."

"It's still El Paso and some suburbs; they are suburbs, even if they're in a different state," Vladimir Mikhailov replied. "State lines don't seem to mean much. And it's all part of Juárez on your side. The main road going west in Juárez is right next to the land border. That's where we want you to start looking for the Mexico end of our tunnel."

"What the hell do you need a tunnel for?" Ivan Petrov smirked. "Going into the drug smuggling business? People smuggling?"

"Get serious, Ivan Aleksandrovich," Vladimir almost shouted. "Of course, no drugs, and far away from any drug smuggling activity. People smuggling, maybe, but not illegal Central Americans and Mexicans. It could be smuggling people the other way, from the U.S. into Mexico."

"You have me totally confused!" Ivan stated. "Why in hell would you want to smuggle them into Mexico?"

"Come on now, Ivan Aleksandrovich," Vladimir said. "Get your head away from all the spy stuff you do. You know we have secret operatives all over the place in the U.S., supposedly in academic exchanges, on student visas, and all of that. We might need to get them out without drawing much attention. If they run into our embassy in Washington or one of our consulates in the U.S., the whole world knows about it and all hell breaks loose. We needed something like that to get Maria Butina out before she got caught."

"Yes, I suppose so," Ivan replied. "I hadn't thought about that."

"And," Vladimir continued, "we can get people and supplies in and out easily and quickly without drawing attention."

"Huh?"

"You know we're creating chaos in the U.S. so their whole notion of a so-called democratic society and supposed global leadership will collapse," Vladimir replied.

"Like manipulating the mid-term elections next year, the way we did in 2016?" Ivan suggested.

"No, no! You really are living in your own little spy world. Plenty of others are involved in influencing elections. They don't involve us here in Mexico. We're creating disturbances by various means—if you get the drift—for longer-term chaos and collapse. We need to get people in there and, er, supplies, and back out again quickly. They'll never figure out people and things are coming from Mexico."

"OK, now I think get it. But why Juárez? Wouldn't it be simpler and easier if it were some remote place out in Sonora on the border with Arizona?"

"No, no," Vladimir said. "You still don't get the point. We need to be in a big city, or cities, so people just blend in with crowds on either side. Juárez, as you surely know, is about two million population, and the El Paso metropolitan area over one million. More important, we need access to public transportation and a road network. Both El Paso and Juárez have big airports and passenger train service. Bus service too. Good roads for private cars."

Ivan muttered his assent.

Vladimir continued, "We considered Sonora and Arizona as plan B, but it's a long way from the border to Tucson and an airport; not as good transportation. And, of course, Tijuana and San Diego are pure madness and not even worth considering."

"Yeah," Ivan answered. "So, what is it you want me to do?"

"Find us some construction sites," Vladimir replied as he held up the map again. "This road goes right by the border fence on the Mexican side right in the city of Juárez. Find us a place where we can build something."

"Construction site?" Ivan asked. "Why construction? What are you building?"

"Well, it could be an existing building that needs extensive renovation or expansion," Vladimir continued. "It has to be someplace where we wouldn't draw attention to ourselves when we have crews digging and hauling out lots of dirt. You'd have to supervise the crew, or someone in your operation do it."

"Where would a construction crew come from?" Ivan asked. "Am I supposed to find them also?"

"No," Vladimir replied. "There are plenty of Syrian refugees in Mexico looking for work. Many of them are sympathetic to us. We can get Hezbollah guys here, too. They build plenty of tunnels and know what they are doing. Lebanese can enter Mexico with no problem. Also, lots of Venezuelans have fled to Mexico, mostly for economic reasons. There are a few opposition people among them, but the Venezuelan government has managed to insert some of its operatives also. These operatives are supposed to keep their eyes on the refugees and opposition people, but they're willing to help us too."

"At least they speak the same language." Ivan smirked.

"Yeah, they can communicate," Vladimir replied. "But Venezuelans have a different accent, so we have to be careful about who could hear them talking. If they are construction workers, no problem. The unemployment rate is low in Ciudad Juárez, so people wouldn't find it unusual to have Venezuelan workers. We couldn't allow them out on the U.S. side speaking with a Venezuelan accent, even if we could get them there. Too many local people there are U.S. citizens but speak Spanish. They would get suspicious and might report them. The local Hispanics in the U.S. are not on our side."

"Oh, OK. Anything else you want me to do for this project?"

"You could find someplace where we could dump all the dirt. Most of the dirt would have to be hauled out into Mexico and dumped here," Vladimir replied. "We also have to have someone ask around to find out what we might have to do to get building permits, utility connections, and all of that."

"Do you know where the tunnel would come out on the U.S. side?" Ivan asked. "What's happening over there?"

"I don't know directly," Vladimir Mikhailov said. "You know I can't travel there. We have operatives there who are keeping me informed. You must know about some of them in your spy work."

"I would? Who?"

"You monitor the White Sands Missile Range and Holloman Air Force Base next to Alamogordo, New Mexico," Vladimir explained.

"You know we have joint space programs with the Americans, and there's lots of space stuff there."

"We don't pay much attention to the space program," Ivan said. "Just the military."

"You also heard me say we have academic visitors and persons on student visas," Vladimir continued. "There are universities there where we have some operatives."

"Are you going to construct something on that side also?" Ivan Petrov asked. "Surely you aren't going to use these operatives as construction workers."

"We have it covered, we think. We're going to pretend to build a mosque, assuming we can get a building permit. Iranians are working with us and there are Iranian-Americans in the U.S. sympathetic to us. They're going to claim they need their own Shia mosque in El Paso; the only mosque there is Sunni. They'll claim it will all be volunteer work by them. Put up a big fence around the construction site and take their time until they have to carry away the last few loads of dirt."

"Who else is in on this?" Ivan asked. "You said Syrians, Iranians, and Hezbollah, maybe Venezuela."

"Just them and the North Koreans," Vladimir replied. "The North Koreans can't do any ground work because they'd be too easily recognized; besides there are none in the U.S. We coordinate it all here in Mexico City where Venezuela, Iran, and North Korea have embassies. Usually we just happen to show up at the same restaurant at lunch time and are "surprised" to see each other. Hezbollah is not here, of course, but we have our ways of contacting them."

"You've got my head spinning, but count me in. Sounds fun, and of course, worthwhile. Anything to get the fucking Americans to crumble."

Vladimir smiled. "Maybe tomorrow we can just happen to meet some Iranians for lunch."

They continued to talk for a while until Vladimir had to tend to more urgent business before the weekend.

PROLOGUE 2

Wednesday, November 28, 2017
San Antonio, Texas, USA

It was mid-morning on a warm, sunny day, typical of late fall in South Texas, when Yusef Shaito entered the office of John Holmes, U.S. Attorney for the Western District of Texas, one of the largest, if not the largest, judicial districts in the U.S. in both population and geographic size. Yusef was the deputy U.S. attorney for the district. He focused primarily on human and civil rights, and was viewed as one of the nation's experts on hate crimes. He took the position almost three years previously after exemplary service in the U.S. Attorney General Headquarters in Washington, DC. He was in his early thirties and stood five feet nine inches with slightly curly black hair and a trim build.

John Holmes was fairly new in the position, having been appointed three months earlier by the Trump administration and confirmed by the U.S. Senate. He had been the deputy in another U.S. judicial district and recently moved to San Antonio with a promotion. He was of average height and build, about five feet ten inches, with neatly trimmed brown hair. He was in his middle forties, young for a senior position. Both Yusef and John were professionally dressed with suit, dress shirt, and tie, their suit coats hanging in their offices.

Yusef and John had developed a good working relationship during the relatively short period John had been on the job, but they were not close and remained mostly professional in their interactions. Yusef immediately took a seat, not feeling a need to wait until asked.

After pleasantries, John said, "First of the year we need you to move to El Paso temporarily."

Yusef, stunned, blurted out, "What? Move to El Paso? Now?"

"Yes. As you know, Emiliano is retiring early to go into private practice, leaving a big vacancy at the top. Lots of things are going on in the El Paso area, and a good defense attorney, especially one with previous experience with the AG like Emiliano, would be in demand and do well."

"What about Susana? She's number two there and doing a good job."

"Yes, she seems to be doing a good job. But, if we promoted her, even temporarily, it would leave another hole. Things are shorthanded there anyway, and we don't have authority to hire right now. Besides, just between you and me, Susana's a great number two, but I'm not sure if she has the personality and style to take over, even if just temporarily. You are forceful but unassuming, and they all like you and respect you."

"Thanks for the compliment," Yusef said. "You know I focus on human and civil rights. Drug trafficking and immigration are not my thing, and that's what they have a lot of there."

"I know. When I was there to get to know them, Gerard was taking the lead in handling drug issues and doing very well. He can keep on handling the drug cases under you. The other staff all deal well with immigration issues. As you're no doubt aware, it's human rights and civil rights issues that are becoming much more important with migrants from Central America. El Paso doesn't have strength in that area. With you in charge, we'll have that covered. You'll still be in charge of human and civil rights for the whole district, but you can handle that from El Paso just as well as you can from here."

"You know I'm Muslim," Yusef continued. "This administration doesn't seem to like Muslims, to put it mildly. How would they react to my being there? I can keep a low profile here, which I would likely do Muslim or not. But head of a division is higher profile."

"In the first place, they likely would never find out. There's no reason to inform them, and positions like this are not monitored at the level of the administration. If for some reason it were discovered and someone objected, there are enough Muslims in Congress to make a big enough fuss about it. Besides, the mere fact that the administration must have approved of my appointment here, doesn't mean I agree with every position that's being taken."

"From the way you put this, it sounds like I have no choice."

"I wouldn't put it quite that way. But, yes, we really do want you there soon, temporarily."

"How soon?" Yusef asked. "You said after the first of the year."

"Yes, very soon after the first of the year," John replied.

"We have a young child," Yusef said. "I wouldn't want to be away from her, but I suppose my wife and family could go with me."

"Yes, I remember you have a little girl," John Holmes said. "Trust me. From my experience, it's much easier to move with children that age than older. I suppose your wife is able to move with you, with her work."

"Maybe you remember that she's a medical doctor," Yusef replied, "an OB/GYN. She's beginning to see patients again after the baby. This is such a surprise that we obviously haven't had a chance to discuss it. And we're in the process of buying a house, but I guess that has to be put on hold."

"We are too," John said, "now that our house back in Milwaukee has sold. Have you made any offers yet?"

"No, not really," Yusef said. "Say, I suppose we'll get moving expenses paid. What about per diem being away from home?"

11

"Yes, for sure, moving expenses," John answered. "I'm not sure about per diem if you set up a household there. Also, I'll try to get you a salary bump over this."

"OK," Yusef said. "You keep saying temporary. How long is temporary?"

"That I can't say," John replied. "We intend to take our time to fill the position permanently to make sure we're getting the right person to head the division there. El Paso, because it's right on the border, is shaping up to be one of the most important divisions in the whole country. Maybe not like San Diego, but I'm sure you get the idea."

"Yes, I can see that."

"And, just between you and me," John continued, "the Attorney General would have to be consulted on hiring someone permanently in a potentially high-profile position like this. We're not too sure we want to get the current AG involved."

Yusef thought, *Maybe I should contact Roger and see what he knows*, reflecting on Roger Chen, his supervisor, mentor, and colleague during the years he worked at the U.S. Attorney General headquarters in Washington. Aloud, he said, "That could be a year or more if he lasts through the mid-term elections."

"Yes," John said. "It depends on who replaces him, too. You know we can't be too political, but we can't ignore realities."

Yusef stated, "As anyone here in the district office and out in the divisions will tell you, I'm not at all political and avoid political interaction as much as possible."

Then he stood to leave, saying, "Thanks for the surprise. Maybe I'll leave on time to go home and drop the surprise on my wife."

Later, barely into the evening, Yusef drove his 2015 BMW 3-series sedan into the garage of their rented house in north San Antonio, a neighborhood of moderate-sized homes for professionals. He parked next to the 2000 E-class Mercedes sedan driven by his wife, which had been given to her a few years ago by her father, a well-to-do Dallas businessman who distributed sporting and athletic goods and supplies. He entered the house to find his wife, Nisrine Maktabi, relaxing reading a medical journal while his toddler-age daughter Sara amused herself nearby. Nisrine, in her early thirties, stood revealing a shapely, well-proportioned athletic body reflecting years as an Olympic runner. She was about five feet seven inches and had short, stylish black hair, brown eyes, and features reflecting the Arab ancestry of her parents, who were Lebanese immigrants. She was dressed casually, well groomed.

Nisrine and Yusef greeted each other affectionately. Then Yusef went to pick up Sara, who was excited to see her father. Sara had the same brown eyes and black hair of her parents.

While holding Sara, Yusef turned to Nisrine and said, "I have to move to El Paso."

Nisrine, startled, started to ask why, but Yusef interrupted to recount his conversation with John Holmes. He concluded, "You haven't really started your practice again, so maybe we can all go as a family."

Nisrine stood quietly for a few moments, thinking about what to say, then smiled and said, "That sounds great. You know we both liked El Paso when we were there on our honeymoon. It's a lot like Lebanon. I can practice there just like I can in San Antonio; it's in Texas where I have a license. There must be lots of women in need of an OB-GYN, especially with the refugees."

Yusef was quiet for a while and said, "I'm surprised. I was expecting you to be upset. You're so attached to San Antonio after being here so many years, medical school and all."

"Yes, I am attached to San Antonio. "But adventure is nice too. And the mountains there are so wonderful, just like Lebanon. Here, let me take Sara and feed her and maybe put her down early. There's some food laid out to make for supper. You know I'm not much of a cook, but we'll have something."

"Let me change clothes quickly." Yusef said. "Then I can start preparing whatever it is."

Later that evening with Sara asleep, they sat cuddling on the sofa and Yusef said, "I would have to drive out there alone and find us a place to live. Then fly back to get you and Sara."

"That'd work," Nisrine added. "We can give up this house, put our furniture in storage, rent furnished in El Paso if we can, then buy a house we really want when we come back."

"Maybe we should think about buying another car, too," Yusef said. "Maybe an SUV. Your old Mercedes is great, but it's seventeen years old. They don't last forever."

"I'm so attached to it now," Nisrine said and smiled. "It wouldn't be the same without it. That's the only car I've driven, except yours, of course, on occasion."

"We've got a lot to think about and deal with," Yusef said. "No need to do it all tonight. Thanksgiving is past, and we don't get involved with Christmas. We have time to work out the details."

They continued to cuddle and watch television, then went to bed to continue cuddling and love making.

PROLOGUE 3

Wednesday, January 3, 2018
El Paso, Texas, USA

On a chilly day—winter can be cold in the mornings in the high-altitude Chihuahuan desert—Yusef arrived at the empty office he would be occupying in the office of the U.S. Attorney General's El Paso Division in the Richard C. White Federal Building at the edge of downtown El Paso. He was bundled for the cold weather in a heavy coat he had brought from Washington but seldom wore in much-warmer San Antonio. He was dressed professionally with a suit, white shirt, and tie.

Richard C. White Federal Building, El Paso, Texas

While he was in his shirtsleeves, unloading items from boxes onto an empty desk, Susana Tate, the number two U.S. attorney for the El Paso Division, knocked and came in saying, "Hello, Yusef, welcome. I'm really glad to see you here."

She was in her late fifties with medium brown, graying hair, styled short and just below her ears. She was about five feet four inches and dressed in a solid red wool winter dress for the season, wearing matching ruby earrings.

Yusef was fumbling over the best words to apologize for having usurped her position when Susana Tate said, "It's good that you got here so soon to provide continuity at the top, just a couple of days after Emiliano left."

Yusef's fumbled words came out, "I'm a bit surprised at your attitude. I was afraid you'd think I was usurping your position to move up and take over, even if temporarily."

Susana Tate immediately stated emphatically, "No way, José!" using an old cliché. "With all that's going on, I would have tried to take early retirement before taking the position."

Yusef, stunned by the forcefulness of her response, curious, and worried, motioned for her to sit and pulled up a chair for himself. He said, "You seem concerned. What's going on that I need to know about?"

After sitting, she began, "Anti-Latino harassment is beginning again, and it's our government that's doing a lot of it. And we're expected to represent the government's interests."

"You mean harassment of immigrants caught in the country illegally?" Yusef asked.

"No, no!" Susana stated. "I have little sympathy for those who are trying to jump the queue to get here. I'm talking about Latinos who are citizens, born here, often from families who have been in the U.S. for generations. You must have plenty of Latinos in San Antonio. They aren't experiencing any of this?"

Yusef, surprised, said, "This is new to me, or at least I haven't heard about it. Maybe the media haven't picked up on it. And yes, there are obviously lots of Latinos in San Antonio, but I haven't heard of any harassment."

"Maybe it's because San Antonio's not right on the border," Susana answered. "Maybe you haven't had a chance to become aware that El Paso and Juárez have been essentially one integrated community for a few hundred years, even though the treaty ending the Mexican-American War in 1848 and the Gadsden treaty a couple of years later split the community between two countries. Only recently has a separate identity emerged because of tightening of border crossings.

"There was a recent NPR documentary broadcast nationally about Bowie High School right here in El Paso in the nineties. When you learn your way around the city, you'll surely notice that Bowie High School sits almost next to the border. It's a high school like any other American high school—Friday night football, marching band, senior prom, and all of that. But virtually all of the students are Latino; U.S. citizens, most of their families for at least a couple of generations; they're just like any American high school kids. In the1990s, the Border Patrol began to harass them on the school grounds when they were outside, or sometimes when going to and from school. They asked them to provide proof of citizenship."

Bowie High School, El Paso, Texas

"There's no requirement to carry proof of citizenship in the U.S.," Yusef interrupted, remembering his participation in the prosecution in a trial in Virginia in which one of the key witnesses was a naturalized citizen.

"That's right. And some of these kids were too young to have driver's licenses. In Texas, as you likely know, to get a driver's license for the first time it's necessary to produce proof of age, which is usually a birth certificate. That's not absolute proof of citizenship, but a good indication. Also some of the school staff, who are also virtually all Latino, were being harassed. There wasn't a huge amount of publicity, but finally the Border Patrol stopped after so many objections. I was away from El Paso in law school and not directly involved, but I sure heard about it."

"Interesting," Yusef commented.

"It's starting again," she continued. "Mostly by the Border Patrol, but some other groups are making waves. And the Border Patrol is part of our government that's acting under the perceived policy of the administration in Washington that is clearly anti-Latino— well, 'anti' lots of groups of immigrants, but especially Latinos. And we with the U.S. Attorney General are expected to represent the government legally."

"I've heard about DACA issues and dreamers," Yusef said. "Not in job-related work, but there's plenty in the media. Is this the issue?"

"No, not at all. Those kids at Bowie High School weren't dreamers. There might be a few dreamers in El Paso, but very few. Any dreamers here would likely have come from other parts of Mexico, not Juárez. Mostly dreamers' parents would have moved on to Atlanta, Philadelphia, Chicago, and places like that. Remember that the definition of "dreamer" is someone brought to the U.S. as a young child by their parents and the children know only an American culture and lifestyle. Here, with the integrated community on both sides of the border—until recently that is— people would just go back and forth all the time and any persons brought here as children would be exposed to both sides of the border. I personally haven't had any problems. I'm not an obvious Latina, even though my grandmother was Mexican, and I don't have a Spanish last name. As you can surely imagine, there has been so much intermarriage through the years that many people with Latin ancestry are not obvious."

"Wow, I didn't realize all of this," Yusef said, "even though I live in San Antonio, which is mostly Latino. And, yes, San Antonio is not right on the border, which might make a difference. I wonder if our division in Del Rio is facing similar issues. I suppose I'll find out soon enough."

"I've spouted off enough," Susana added. "I'll gladly support you while you deal with these things, but just don't get me involved condoning government harassment of Latinos."

"Fair enough."

Just that moment, Emiliano Gonzalez walked in, stopped, was startled at seeing the office occupied, and immediately apologized. "Sorry, I didn't know you'd be here so soon, Yusef. I just stopped by to get the last few things I left and look the office over carefully for something I might have left behind."

Emiliano Gonzalez was in his sixties with average build and about five feet nine. His graying hair had been black at one time. He was dressed casually but smartly.

"No problem," Yusef said and stood to shake hands. "If I may, I'd like to spend time with you so you can fill me in on what's going on here. Susana just gave me some possibly unsettling news."

"Sure," Emiliano said. "I'm not so busy with clients yet and have time on my hands."

"Thanks."

"If you'd like to visit this afternoon before you get too involved in things here, you could stop by," Emiliano added. "My office is nearby, close to the Federal Building and the Federal Courthouse."

Emiliano gave directions to his office and left with pleasantries to Susana Tate.

Susana said, "I should go back to my desk. I have plenty of work to catch up on after the holidays, and you need time to settle in."

They said goodbye, and Yusef resumed moving things into what was his new office.

Later in the afternoon, Yusef went to Emiliano Gonzalez's office, where Emiliano was still organizing his law books and other office things. After greeting each other with handshakes, Yusef told Emiliano about his conversation with Susana and asked for confirmation.

"Yes, unfortunately it's true," Emiliano said.

"If I may ask, is that what motivated you to leave?" Yusef asked.

"That's a good part of it," Emiliano replied. "Like Susana, I didn't want to deal with the prospect that government employees, my government, would be harassing people and I would be expected to represent the government. But also, seeing it might be coming, I suspected there would be people who were being harassed who would need legal representation. With my background, I thought I could take early retirement from the government and develop a good practice to last me until actual retirement."

Maybe not very lucrative, Yusef thought. *But he does seem to have a nice office that couldn't be cheap.*

As though reading Yusef's mind, Emiliano stated, "Some of the work will be pro-bono, legal aid, or reduced fee, but Latinos in El Paso fill the entire socio-economic spectrum, and many will pay fair, but not outlandish fees."

"If I may ask again," Yusef continued, "are you being harassed yourself because you are Latino with immigrant ancestry, or do you expect to be harassed?"

Emiliano smiled and said, "In the first place, my ancestors are not immigrants. They have lived here since Spanish colonial days and were living here in El Paso in 1845 when Texas became part of the U.S. They didn't immigrate; the border changed. I'm sure I'll get some harassment, but the Border Patrol and others know better than to try anything on me."

"I studied American history in school, of course," Yusef said, "but we didn't go into a lot of details about these kinds of issues of when and how the border changed."

Emiliano continued, "But, yeah, things could get dicey around the office, and I'm ready for a change anyway. You've surely heard of Alberto Gonzales, the AG for a while under President George W. Bush."

"I was still in school when he was AG," Yusef replied. "But I heard about him later, especially in law school. He was required to resign under pressure for getting involved in political matters, from what I recall."

"Well, he did get involved in what appear to be some questionable things. We might never know the full extent. But the fact that he's Mexican-American influenced a lot of the negative pressure from outsiders on him, and he was born in San Antonio. His parents were immigrants, though. My position as head of a division office was not as visible as the AG of the United States, of course. And, the position is protected from political pressure, supposedly. But certain persons could make life uncomfortable for someone with a Spanish name and ancestry, even if not really Mexican.

"By the way, we're not related. Maybe you know that Gonzalez is like Smith in English, about the most common last name of Spanish-speaking people. He spells his name with an "s" at the end, though, not with a "z" like my family."

"I've heard of a fair number of people with that name," Yusef said. "I'm the son of immigrants, first generation American. Legal immigrants that is. There was some harassment and bullying when I was in school, especially over my name, but there were enough of us Lebanese that we avoided most of it. For sure, I don't want to get involved in any harassment of persons just because of their ancestry."

"Yes, there are lots of Arab Muslims around Detroit," Emiliano said. "You must be one of them."

"Yes, I'm Shia Muslim. Say, could I come see you when I get better settled into the job and maybe discuss the status of some of the cases? Of course, Susana can fill me in on a lot, and I don't want to keep you from your practice."

"Sure thing," Emiliano replied. "Just call to see if I am free, but I'm not exactly overwhelmed with clients right now."

They exchanged goodbye pleasantries and shook hands, and Yusef left to go look at advertisements for homes for rent.

PROLOGUE 4

In the late afternoon, Yusef was talking to Nisrine on the telephone. They had talked every day about Yusef's frustration in not being able to find a place to live, among other things. Today, after talking about the latest with Sara and other family topics, Yusef said, "Finally, I think I may have found a place. It's an old house; it must have been built in the 1930s, but it's nice, in a good neighborhood where professionals live. We'd be the youngest people living in the neighborhood, but not out of place for a lawyer and a medical doctor. They want a one-year lease, which might not be so bad. It looks like I'll be staying here a few months, at least. It's not too difficult to get out of a lease if we're actually moving. I learned that in law school, but I don't know much about Texas laws."

"Sounds good," Nisrine said. "Tell me more about it."

"It's brick and well landscaped like some of the older houses in San Antonio," Yusef began. "Three bedrooms; actually two and a half bathrooms, which is rare for a house that age. There are hardwood floors throughout, which is typical of houses like that; like the one we have in San Antonio. We'd have to bring our oriental rugs with us, or else buy some cheap fakes here."

"Mama said we'd have to take the rugs with us, or else find someone to use them," Nisrine said. "Oriental rugs can be damaged by staying rolled up in storage. What about furniture?"

"It's completely unfurnished, except there's an old refrigerator and a gas range. No washer or dryer. We'd have to rent furniture or move what we have."

"Maybe it's not a good idea to leave the furniture Jason had made for us in storage," Nisrine said. "Maybe move it just like the rugs."

"I can contact him and ask," Yusef replied. He reflected on his good friend Jason Henderson, a furniture designer who had supplied Yusef and Nisrine with furniture items he had designed after he displayed them at the national furniture market in Dallas. "Maybe he wants to design some more for us to use in El Paso, but it might not be as easy to get them from the market in Dallas to El Paso. It seems we'll have to move some things anyway, like the rugs and Sara's bed. I'll contact a moving company, or maybe see about renting a U-Haul."

"We could buy baby things there easily," Nisrine offered.

"I'll check out what's here and prices," Yusef responded. "Maybe I need to rent a U-Haul trailer. I can check into that, too. I suppose we could pull it behind the old Mercedes. It's certainly big enough and sturdy enough to pull a trailer. I'll go get it checked out and serviced before we leave. I can do that when I get back to San Antonio."

"I can—" Nisrine began.

"Maybe you and Sara should fly and meet me here," Yusef interrupted. "I'll check schedules and airfares. As soon as I know dates, I can make a reservation for you two—"

"YUSEY STOP!" Nisrine screamed into the phone. "You're treating me like I'm incapable of doing anything. Just like a Lebanese man who has to take care of *everything*."

"Huh?" Yusef said.

"You still have a lot of your Lebanese cultural baggage from growing up in Dearborn. I know that, and I'm willing to tolerate a lot, but this is going too far. I'm capable of doing lots of things. I'm intelligent enough to be a medical doctor, after all."

"Of course, you're intelligent enough. I just wanted to make it easy for you."

"Bullshit. You don't need to make it that easy. I'm your wife and mother of your child, after all. Look, I know what's happening. I'm Lebanese too. Even though I didn't get the cultural baggage growing up in Dallas with very few other Lebanese around, Baba tried to rule the roost. But Mama would have none of it after a while. She slowly took over lots of things and Baba came to appreciate it all. I'll bet your father was in charge of everything!"

"Yeah, I see your point," Yusef said. "I was just responding and not thinking. Lots of stress. And, yes, my father did everything, but my mother was able to do lots of things behind his back. You know my family situation. No need to go there now."

"We do need to discuss things and decide who does what, so everything gets taken care of and nothing is overlooked because we assume the other is doing it," Nisrine began. "I can do lots of things here in San Antonio, like take the car for service and see if it'll make a long trip. Also I can check out U-Haul. We'd have to rent a trailer here in San Antonio, anyway."

They continued to discuss things that needed to be done and agreed to talk over the next few nights when Yusef was not so stressed.

BOOK 1

DIGGING
A TUNNEL

CHAPTER 1

Monday, September 17, 2018
México, DF, México

Shortly before 1 p.m., Vladimir Mikhailov and Ivan Petrov were together again in an upscale restaurant for lunch. Vladimir opened the conversation, asking in Russian, "Did you enjoy all the parties yesterday for Mexican Independence Day, 16th of September, Ivan Aleksandrovich?"

"Mexicans do know how to party, especially on their Independence Day," Ivan replied, also in Russian. "Not as good as the Russians, of course, but they do a better job of it here in the capital than in Juárez where I am. I'm sure there were some good parties in Juárez, too, like always, especially with Americans coming across the border to join in."

"And, of course, there was the diplomatic reception we had to attend last night," Vladimir added. "Maybe it was a bit more subdued with all the diplomats there."

"What an interesting coincidence to bump into Bijan Ahmadi from the Iranian Embassy," Ivan said with a wink.

"And Ri Kuang-Sik from the North Korean embassy," Vladimir added. "They'll "coincidentally" be here for lunch and be "surprised" to see us. There aren't too many good restaurants open today; the day after a major holiday on Sunday is still a legal holiday."

"Hopefully the Americans aren't following me," Ivan added.

"Likely not," Vladimir said. "They expect you to visit our embassy from time to time, and they no doubt saw us together at the diplomatic reception last night. Maybe they're too hungover to keep following you around the city. We're here to fill you in on what happened to the tunnel you found a location for. Good job. Of course, you had to back off, with the Americans and Mexicans following you all the time."

"Yeah, but once the Hezbollah guys were in place with the Syrian workers, I could rely on indirect news. I managed to keep abreast of what was going on. It was a brilliant idea of theirs to make that old shop I found into a Chinese herbal shop with massage and expand it so we could use it as a construction site."

"That was the North Koreans' idea," Vladimir said. "The man and woman running the shop are low-level functionaries from the North Korean embassy here. The locals wouldn't know that they're not actually Chinese. Most can't tell the difference between Koreans and Chinese just by looking at them."

Just that moment, Ri Kuang-Sik came in, made a point of asking the host to show him to an empty table; then, seeing Vladimir and Ivan seated at table with empty spaces, he pretended to be surprised to see them and asked in English if he could join them. Vladimir and Ivan welcomed him to the table and proceeded to discuss small talk in English, the language all had in common.

Shortly afterwards, Bijan Ahmadi from the Iranian Embassy arrived in the restaurant in the company of a young man and went through the same pretense of asking for a table in an increasingly crowded restaurant. Vladimir, noticing them walking around with the host looking for a table, stood, waived his hand, and said in English, "Please, come join us."

Bijan, also speaking English, introduced Imad Fladallah, indicating he was from Lebanon and visiting for the holiday. All subsequent conversation was in English. They all looked at menus and exchanged small talk, aware that waiters in an upscale restaurant like this would understand at least a small amount of English. Orders were taken, drinks were brought, and idle conversation ensued until the food arrived and they began eating.

Bijan indicated that Imad had supervised the overall tunnel project operating from the Mexican side, then said, "Mr. Kuang-Sik here was also very instrumental in finding the young couple of Koreans to run the Chinese herb shop," using the Middle Eastern custom of a title before a given name.

Kuang-Sik chuckled and said, "We had to do a lot of research and educate ourselves on Chinese herbs so we could act like we actually know something and are legitimate. It took some effort to find sources of supply. Now that the tunnel is complete, we can get some things from the U.S. and smuggle them in. There are plenty of Chinese herbs on the market in the U.S. We also had to give the lady some massage training so she can act like she's legitimate."

"Will she be giving happy endings?" Ivan asked and laughed. "Maybe I can stop by and have a good excuse to actually see the site."

"No, no," Kuang-Sik answered. "We might get more actual customers that way, but we need to be careful and not have the police coming after us for having a "house of ill repute," shall we say, or even worse, one of the Mexican Mafia wanting to get a slice of the business. But with proper arrangements, maybe something could be arranged for you to visit and actually get a massage if someone is actually trailing you."

"I'll take you up on that," Ivan said with a smile.

"Imad here did a really good job of overseeing the job and doing some digging himself," Bijan interjected. "Let's hear him tell about it."

Imad began, "The site you picked, Mr. Ivan, was great, close enough to the border but not right on it. Even though that main road goes right by the fence, it would have drawn a little suspicion if we were too close. I could actually walk up to the fence at night and talk to the guys working on the other side to coordinate with them. The old store you found was ideal. We could fix it up and make it bigger. We built a fence around the back so not too many could see what we were doing. The biggest problem was finding some place to dump the dirt, but this was at the edge of the dessert so we were able to spread it out.

"One problem was that we had to dig really deep immediately to get under the border. The border fence is built on a concrete base that is about two meters deep, we were told. Also, there's a major railroad line that runs three meters or less from the border fence; it's the main line between the east and west of the U.S. and gets lots of traffic. We didn't know how the heavy traffic would affect the tunnel, so we went really deep."

Vladimir interrupted, saying, "We can take care of that railroad line in due time."

Imad continued, "There's always the issue of the infamous border wall if it ever gets built. Will the construction of it cause our tunnel to collapse?"

Vladimir and Ivan laughed. "Don't hold your breath over a border wall," Vladimir said. "We have ways with dealing with that also."

Ivan asked, "What about the U.S. side?"

Bijan replied, "I had to supervise that one from a distance, but we have good operatives in the U.S. Imad was there talking to them through the fence sometimes. After the tunnel was connected, he went over himself. Let him tell you."

Imad reached into his pocket and pulled out a small piece of paper and said, "Look, a Texas lottery ticket I bought myself. There's a shop right on the state line, the Texas side, that sells those and other things." He passed the piece of paper around the table.

He continued, "Some of the operatives on that side, who are also Shia, found this piece of land and convinced the owner to sell a small plot. We probably paid too much, but there were no good alternatives from people who were willing to sell. It's on a side road immediately behind a convenience store but just off a main road, McNutt Road. It's in Texas, too, immediately on the state line. We had to get a building permit from the city of El Paso, but all the utilities are from the City of Sunland Park in New Mexico. It took a little bit of convincing El Paso authorities why we needed to build another mosque, since there already was one in El Paso. Some were concerned that the property would be taken off the tax rolls because mosques, like churches, don't have to pay property tax. We had to convince them that we're Shia and the other mosque is Sunni. We emphasized strongly that there are many different types of Christian churches in El Paso and three type of Jewish synagogues, so why couldn't there be more than one Islamic mosque? Finally, after they realized we had done our homework, they gave in, but they wanted to know why we were in such a remote location. We convinced them that it wasn't remote, just off a major highway, the CanAm highway, with easy access from I-10. They also realized that even though it would take the land off the property tax rolls, it might increase the value of the other property around and generate more business for the convenience store and increase the overall tax revenue for El Paso City and El Paso County.

"Anyway, we put a big black plastic fence around the lot and told the authorities that we would be doing the work ourselves because of financial reasons and that it would take a while to complete. Fortunately, there are no neighbors to observe, other than in the convenience store, and they don't care—it might bring more business to them. We ended up with a small prefab building that we convinced them would be a temporary mosque. We have a big oriental rug on the floor like all mosques have. Of course, it covered the opening to the tunnel."

"Does anyone live there?" Ivan asked.

"Yes," Imad answered. "We had to bring guys in from other parts of the U.S. to actually do the work; there were not enough Iranian sympathizers in the El Paso area. We fixed up a place to live with a bathroom which can also be used to wash our feet before prayers."

"What are we using the tunnel for now?" Ivan asked.

Vladimir replied, "We're not doing much now. We could have used the tunnel, if it had been ready, to get Maria Butina out as soon as we knew the Americans had gotten onto her. Maybe there'll be another person like her in the future. I'm not involved in the plans being discussed in Moscow and Washington, which is understandable. They just tell me and I tell you what we need to do here, like get someone on a flight from Juárez to here and then out of the country."

"You told me that we're going to use this tunnel to create chaos in the U.S.," Ivan commented.

"Oh, that we will," Vladimir said. "The details haven't been discussed with me yet."

They continued in conversation for several minutes and then retired to their respective embassies for a time-honored Mexican tradition of siesta.

CHAPTER 2

Monday, November 19, 2018
El Paso, Texas, USA

When Susana Tate approached the door of Yusef's office, he motioned her to come in and sit. Saying it was a holiday week he asked, "What do you have planned for Thanksgiving?"

She replied, "Lots of family, big turkey dinner, you know, all the trimmings. And yours?"

"It'll be kind of quiet and uneventful. At first, we thought my wife's parents might come from Dallas, but in the end they decided to stay home. My wife's brother will go back home to bring his girlfriend and likely fiancé. We don't know all that many people here, yet. My wife is a medical doctor, you know, working for public health. There were a couple of students from the medical school here she has worked with. We've invited them for dinner. My wife and I are not much in the kitchen, but we'll manage to prepare the basics."

Coming to the point of my stopping by, Susana said, "The staff want to know if we'll have a Christmas party this year."

Yusef, taken aback, responded, "Why shouldn't we?"

"You're Muslim. Muslims don't celebrate Christmas. Some thought you might not want to celebrate with an office party, now that you're in charge of this division."

Yusef pondered a moment and said, "It's true that we Muslims don't celebrate Christmas with gift giving, big parties, decorations, and all of that. We have our own celebrations where we exchange gifts.

You know I took time off for the Eid al Fitr and Eid al Adha. Our celebrations are lower key. But we certainly don't object or interfere with Christians when they have their celebrations. Also, our holy Q'ran talks about the holy conception of Mary and the birth of Jesus, the last great prophet before Mohammad. Go ahead and plan what you would normally do. I wouldn't want to be included in the planning, but I'd attend. Please remember that Muslims don't drink alcohol, but there seem to be plenty of Christians who don't drink either."

Susana said, "OK. I've always thought we overdid it a little in the past. Maybe I can tell them to tone it down a bit."

She stood to leave, but Yusef asked her to stay. He then said, "You've no doubt heard about the little boy from Honduras who crossed the border with his father in a remote part of New Mexico, was sick and brought to El Paso in an emergency air lift, and almost died. He seems like he'll make it, now. Lots of claims are being thrown around that the U.S. Border Patrol was negligent and contributed to his near death."

She replied, "Yes, it's all on the news."

"What if legal claims are made against Border Patrol and the government. I suppose we'd have to defend the government and its employees? What could be our role in this?"

"We've never faced a situation like this before here in El Paso," she said. "Maybe some other divisions have had to deal with alleged misconduct by government employees."

"It may just be a matter of time until someone does make both a civil and criminal claim against the government for things that are happening at the border and ending up right here in El Paso," Yusef said.

"Well," Susana said, "first the FBI has to get involved. But I take your point. We don't want to be totally unprepared."

Yusef continued, "I certainly don't condone illegal immigration, people trying to get ahead of the queue. My parents immigrated to this country legally, as did all the Lebanese Shia in Dearborn where

I was born and grew up. But, when you have death or near death due to action or inaction of government employees, then it becomes an issue of basic human and civil rights."

"Yes, I agree. We might be expected to defend U.S. government employees who are charged with violating human rights. I said before that I'm concerned with the growing anti-Latino sentiment that I don't want to get involved with. This particular situation is not anti-Latino *per se*, and indeed some of the Border Patrol personnel are themselves Latino. But it sure is a developing mess that we need to be prepared for. It's unclear whether we would be involved in this particular case. The border crossing was into New Mexico, and there are conflicting claims as to whether it was legal or illegal. The alleged neglect would have been in New Mexico; they did take humanitarian action to get him to El Paso, so there would be no criminal or civil acts in our division, because we're in Texas."

"Yes, but these state lines and federal judicial districts are arbitrary," Yusef added. "It might be a good idea to touch base with Robert in Las Cruces. He and I only talked briefly before. I can call him later. But what about those mothers with their children sitting on the bridge coming into El Paso from Juárez, just waiting to apply for asylum? They're sitting on the Mexican side, but it wouldn't take much for them to jump a few feet and be in the U.S. There's no fence on that bridge."

"You have good points," she replied. "I'll start looking into it and have some of the staff look into it also. Maybe have Khan look into it," she said referring to Khan Nguyen who had been hired fairly recently as a staff attorney. "His grandparents and lots of others fled Vietnam seeking asylum to avoid violence and settled in Texas, even though they did enter the U.S. legally and were immediately granted asylum. They were Asian and met some resistance from authorities and local people, but these people are Latinos. Maybe there's some bias against Latinos *vis a vis* Asians. I could sit here all day and speculate on that."

With that, she took her leave.

After a few moments, Yusef connected on Skype with Robert Andrews, head of the Las Cruces Branch Office, U.S. Attorney for the District of New Mexico. After preliminary greetings, Yusef summarized his recent conversation with Susana Tate, concluding, "The boundary between our divisions is arbitrary and cuts through the greater El Paso community. With things heating up, maybe we should visit so as not to get bogged down in jurisdictional issues."

Robert replied, "Yes, I agree. You know that our small office handles only criminal issues. Anything else is with the district office in Albuquerque."

"When we met briefly before, I got that idea," Yusef said. "So far, I haven't had occasion to explore the practicalities."

"We haven't completely sorted out the practicalities ourselves," Robert said. "Traditionally, we dealt exclusively with criminal issues related to drugs and illegal immigration. Now with the increase in asylum seekers and other issues like the little boy you mentioned, we may need to revisit the situation. Say, why don't I get in touch with Blake in Albuquerque and we could all have a meeting. Maybe lunch. Or, after I talk to him, maybe just you and I have lunch."

"Sounds good to me," Yusef replied. "Do you have any day or time in mind?"

"Mondays are usually pretty good for me," Robert said, "Maybe next Monday, December 3. I need to get down to the El Paso suburbs that are in our district from time to time anyway. I know a great restaurant that's on the state line; the state line runs right through the middle of the restaurant. How would that sound to you?"

"I've heard of that restaurant, the State Line is the name, but haven't been there. I hear it's mostly barbecue and very good. So long as there are alternatives to pork, it sounds great to me."

They continued for a few more minutes, saving more substantive conversation until the following week.

CHAPTER 3

Friday, December 21, 2018
El Paso, Texas, USA

Yusef arrived home shortly after 6 p.m. after having stopped for prayers and the sermon at the Islamic Center of El Paso. He greeted Nisrine affectionately and gave warm hugs to Sara. "How was your day?" he asked.

"Nothing special," she answered. "Seeing patients at the public health center and then stopping with Sara for Friday prayers at the Islamic center when women pray. You must've stopped for prayers on your way home, as usual. How was your day?"

"We're probably going to have a government shutdown," Yusef said. "I don't know if they want me to work or whether the office will be shut down."

"Last time you kept on working."

"Yeah, but last time it was just a few days and everyone knew the shutdown would end soon and we would get paid. This time we could go a long time without pay."

"We have enough to get by," she answered. "Why do you worry so much about money?"

"You can say that because you come from a wealthy family. I grew up in Dearborn where we got by, but we couldn't have survived if my father lost a paycheck. But maybe you're right; I might be influenced too much by my very modest upbringing. I'm concerned about some of the other staff. Some of them might not be so well off, although lawyers are fairly well paid. Some might just quit and go into private practice. There seems to be plenty of opportunity for private practice these days."

"I hope you do take the time off," Nisrine said. "You can stay home with Sara while I do some things. I can take her with me when I work at the public health clinic because there are child care facilities for the patients and Sara can stay there. You know I've been wanting to go to the Texas Tech medical school here and do some research. There's brand new research going on about how to treat pregnant women who come down with other conditions. All the research to date on how to treat these conditions has been done on women who aren't pregnant. We don't know what the complications might be if a pregnant woman is treated for something like a heart condition. We have to deal with some of that at the clinic. Poor women don't come to us until they have other serious illness while they're pregnant. I can't take Sara to the medical school library."

Yusef muttered agreement.

"Also, I might go out again to that detention facility right outside of El Paso in Tornillo for children who crossed the border illegally and were separated from their families," she added.

"What?" Yusef stated. "You're an OB/GYN, not a pediatrician."

"Yes, but there are teenage girls there who need examination and treatment," she continued. "Don't you remember the big controversy over the seventeen-year-old girl who was pregnant and wanted an abortion? She was impregnated in the most horrible way that could be imagined and really deserved an abortion. I don't do abortions, but have no moral objections to them. I can examine and treat them up to the point an abortion can be arranged. Also there are mature teenagers who have never had a gynecological examination. Sara couldn't go with me out there."

"OK, I suppose so," he said.

"Also, a group is considering putting together a team to go to Juárez to the small group of asylum seekers camped there. It's a much smaller facility than the one in Tijuana where a group of medical people from San Diego are going over to provide medical assistance. But still there are people there who might be in desperate need for medical care, including some women."

"But Mexico is a medically advanced country," Yusef interjected. "Americans go across the border all the time to seek medical care at much lower cost than here in the U.S. All you have to do is walk down the street in Juárez to see their clinics."

"Doctors there are too busy with their own practices they charge fees for," she replied. "They're not inclined to work for free to the very needy women there."

"Oh, OK," he replied. "We just have to wait and see how this shutdown plays out."

After a short pause in the conversation, Nisrine said. "Let's see what we have for supper.

During supper, Yusef commented, "Maybe we could go to the Inn of the Mountain Gods in New Mexico where we went on our honeymoon. Sara's big enough now that she can travel without having to bring lots of things for her."

"But It'll be too crowded with skiers and Christians celebrating Christmas."

"Maybe your parents could come visit; they couldn't come on Thanksgiving," he suggested.

"They don't like to travel in the winter," she said.

"You don't sound very enthusiastic about anything," he said.

"What I am enthusiastic about is furthering my career as a doctor," Nisrine replied. "There have been so many little opportunities that I couldn't do because of taking care of Sara or only doing things where she could go with me."

"Yes, of course. You do need to further your career," Yusef said. "Maybe we need to look into day care or a nanny."

41

"Maybe," she replied.

"No matter what, I won't work on the 24ᵗʰ, Christmas Eve," Yusef said. "You could go to the medical school library then."

"If it's open," she said.

With conversation at an impasse, they engaged in small talk until time to put Sara in bed, both with preoccupation over the uncertainty of the pending government shutdown.

CHAPTER 4

Monday, December 24, 2018
El Paso, Texas, USA

In the morning, Yusef said goodbye to Nisrine as she departed to spend the day working at the local public health clinic. Sara was with Yusef, who was not working because of the government shutdown. He played with Sara for a while, then put her in her room to entertain herself until she wanted more attention. Bored, he thought about reading a book, but first decided to turn on the television to get news from one of the national cable news channels.

The news announcer had just begun a new item with recognizable pictures of El Paso in the background that immediately caught Yusef's attention. The announcer began, "A bomb explosion destroyed a bridge on the main line of the Union Pacific railroad in Sunland Park, New Mexico, a suburb of El Paso, Texas. The bomb was detonated as a freight train passed along this busy cross-country rail route that carries freight between the eastern U.S. and west-coast destinations and major places along the route. The tracks are also used by two major Amtrak routes between the eastern part of the U.S. and Los Angeles. The train that detonated the explosion was a freight train, fortunately avoiding the risk to passengers on passenger train routes. Railroad employees operating the train were badly injured and are being treated in El Paso hospitals."

The television cameras changed to live scenes with police cars, rail cars on their sides, and the border fence in the near background.

The newscaster continued speaking. "The bomb had apparently been placed under a bridge over a shallow ravine and was triggered by the force of the first train passing over. Even though this is in the suburban area in the city of Sunland Park, New Mexico, literally in sight of downtown El Paso, Texas, there was little development in the immediate area and local people did not hear the explosion. The area is at the base of Mount Cristo Rey that has a large statue of Christ the King at the top, a very prominent El Paso area landmark that was built because of its location very near the point where the boundaries of Texas, New Mexico, and Mexico meet.

"The railroad tracks pass within ten feet or less of the international border fence. The noise of the explosion and train derailment was heard by persons in Ciudad Juárez, Mexico, who live very near the fence. When it was daylight, they came to explore and saw the train wreckage through the slats in the border fence. They notified local authorities, who relayed the information to the El Paso police department, which notified the Sunland Park police, who in turn notified New Mexico State Police. Few additional details are available at this time. Stay tuned for further news developments as they occur."

That could be a federal crime, Yusef thought, *disrupting a major interstate transportation route, but that one would be handled in New Mexico, in Robert's division. They'll have to bring in the FBI, who are working during the shutdown.*

Yusef spent the rest of the morning reading, entertaining Sara, and making lunch for the two of them.

Later, while Sara was taking a nap, he turned on the television again to the same national cable news channel. The announcer began, "We now go to El Paso, Texas, where agents of ICE, Immigration and Customs Enforcement, with no prior notice, dumped some 200 illegal migrants at the Greyhound Bus Station. Many adults and children were in the cold without adequate winter clothing because the space inside the bus station could not accommodate such a large number. ICE personnel provided no explanation for their action, saying words to the effect that because of the government shutdown, they had no means of dealing with these undocumented immigrants.

"Many of the immigrants attempted to board buses to keep warm, but were turned away because they had no tickets. Ticketed passengers seeking to travel for the Christmas holidays were disrupted. Eventually, the Greyhound company brought four additional busses for the immigrants to have a place to stay in relative warmth until further arrangements could be made. A local Catholic charity hastily made arrangements to accommodate some of the immigrants, and a local hotel was used to accommodate others. So far, U.S. Government officials have no comment.

"Next after a short break, we will return to El Paso for another developing story, the aftermath of a bomb set under the tracks of the Union Pacific Railroad main cross-country freight route."

What? Yusef exclaimed in his thoughts as the commercial break began. *This is what we feared. Government agencies and employees act illegally, and we at the AG are expected to defend them. These persons were supposed to be taken to detention facilities and held for deportation. They are already in the United States and some could make asylum claims, but they are still supposed to be kept in detention and not dumped on the streets in the winter. Allah knows I have little sympathy for those who come to this country illegally and try to jump the queue of those who enter legally, like my family. Still, they are human beings and deserve humane treatment. The judicial system is supposed to protect human rights, not defend the illegal behavior of the government.*

The television news resumed after commercials, with live cameras showing police around rail cars laying on the ground sideways, cargo spilling onto the ground, some railroad cars and cargo against the border fence. The announcer said, "Going again to El Paso, more details are emerging about the bomb attack on the main line of the Union Pacific Railroad just outside El Paso, Texas, in the suburb of

Sunland Park, New Mexico. The two crew members are in an El Paso hospital with injuries that are not critical, but which require hospitalization. New Mexico State Police have recovered remnants of the bomb that was attached to the underside of the bridge and was designed to be set off by the force of the train crossing the bridge. The bomb remnants were secured to be sent for forensic analysis in New Mexico State Police laboratories. The force of the bomb caused the bridge to collapse and the locomotive to fall into the shallow ravine. The force of the drop caused multiple freight cars to fall onto their sides, spilling contents onto the border fence with Mexico.

"Because of the proximity of the bombing to the border, police are exploring the possibility that the perpetrators may have thrown the bomb over the fence or were persons climbing over the fence from a well-developed neighborhood of Ciudad Juárez next to the fence. There is no indication of the ground having been disturbed as would result with the use of ladders. The mere throwing of a bomb would not have allowed the bomb to be attached to the underside of the bridge, which seems to be the case. Because of the possibility of the attack coming from Mexico, police in Ciudad Juárez have been contacted, and it is likely that the FBI will be brought into the case.

"Personnel from the Union Pacific Railroad headquarters in San Francisco are on the way to begin examination, clear the wreckage, and reopen this very busy line as soon as possible. Because of heavy holiday travel, they are having difficulty getting flights to El Paso."

Yusef thought, *FBI being brought in. Clearly a criminal act. It's in New Mexico so it'll be up to Robert to prosecute. Because of the government shutdown, his office likely isn't working either. I wonder how the FBI is affected by the shutdown—likely not at all, even though the Department of Justice is closed.*

Later that afternoon, Nisrine came home and greeted Sara and Yusef. When asked about her day, she replied, "Uneventful; just a few persons with minor issues aggravated by the holidays. I did volunteer to be on call for all the major hospitals in the city tomorrow in case they have emergencies with women needing an OB/GYN. The Christians who would normally be on call can take the day off to be with their families without risk of being disturbed."

"That's good of you." Yusef said. "Things are pretty boring here, just like all of our past Christmases. I can't think of anyplace I might volunteer as a lawyer on Christmas Day."

"And you need to be here to take care of Sara just in case I get called," Nisrine added. "What happened here?"

"Nothing, just a quiet day at home with Sara," he answered. "There was some interesting and potentially disturbing news, especially dumping the illegal immigrants at the bus station."

"I heard a little about it on the car radio," she replied. "I wonder if they would need an OB/GYN to tend to some of the women. Maybe I should contact them."

At that point, Sara was demanding attention and Nisrine rushed to her. The rest of the evening was spent in small talk and watching television to be updated on the news.

CHAPTER 5

Tuesday, December 25, 2018
El Paso, Texas, USA

Nisrine and Yusef slept late until Sara woke them wanting attention. Together they made a sumptuous breakfast with their and Sara's favorite breakfast foods, rather than the hasty cereal they usually had. After breakfast, Nisrine tended to Sara, helped her dress, then left her to play in a spare bedroom that had been made into Sara's play room. Yusef, with an additional cup of coffee, went to the family room and turned on the television to watch the news on a national cable station that had news broadcasts on Christmas morning.

The announcer was in the process of describing the death the previous day of an eight-year-old boy from Guatemala in the custody of Immigration and Customs Enforcement, ICE. The boy with his father crossed the border illegally at El Paso, Texas, and had been moved among different detention facilities. When an employee at a facility noticed the boy was sick, he was transported to a hospital in Alamogordo, New Mexico, where he was diagnosed with a cold, given a generic antibiotic and ibuprofen, and released back to ICE personnel. On the way back to the detention facility, the boy began vomiting, lost consciousness, and was immediately returned to the hospital, where he died a short while later.

Nisrine had sat next to Yusef during the broadcast. When the program went to a commercial break, Yusef exclaimed, "What!

Not again. A week after the young girl from Guatemala died here in El Paso. Only this time, it looks like government personnel are not at fault; it must have been the hospital in Alamogordo at fault. But why was he taken all the way to Alamogordo when there are more extensive medical facilities here in El Paso?"

"Poor thing," Nisrine lamented. "They need more medical personnel in those detention facilities. There must be some women in need of care, maybe pregnant ones."

"And how did they cross illegally here in El Paso?" Yusef continued. "There's a big, strong border fence to the west, and here in the main part of the city the river is well monitored and there is strong security at the bridges."

The news reporter continued, "Again in El Paso, ICE continues to dump hundreds of illegal migrants at a public park near the bus station and nearby restaurants. This time, local authorities were notified ahead of time so arrangements could be made to house them in local shelters. ICE says it is unable to cope with the number of illegal immigrants and has no choice but to release them."

"Again!" Yusef exclaimed. "Just turn them loose in cold weather with nothing to eat or drink. Now they are free to enter the country and do what they please and go wherever they want to. The president says they are rapists, gang members, and thieves— of course I don't believe that—but just in case, it's the failure of the government and this shutdown that would allow the criminals loose if there are any of them. We can't let people into our country ahead of legitimate immigrants who go through all the hoops, just like our parents, but we have to treat them humanely. I'm sure this will have ramifications for our division when—if—this shutdown ends and we go back to work."

"Those poor women," Nisrine added. "There must be some of them in need of gynecological treatment or pregnant. And here I am sitting at home with nothing to do until, maybe, some hospital calls."

With that statement, Nisrine got up to look after Sara, who was happily entertaining herself in her room while Yusef continued to watch television national news.

After the commercial break, the announcer continued, "Still in El Paso, the Union Pacific Railroad announced that crews were already working to salvage the cargo of the derailed train just outside the city in the suburb of Sunland Park, New Mexico. They were waiting for the arrival of heavy equipment, including cranes, to lift the locomotive out of the ravine. As soon as the locomotive and other debris could be moved, assessments will be made on repairs to the bridge and tracks on this, one of the most heavily traveled train routes in the U.S.

"In the meantime, trucks are being used to move backed-up cargo between Douglas, Arizona, and El Paso, there being no alternative railroad routes in the area. History buffs will remember that the Gadsden Purchase in 1868 was made to make this geographic area part of the United States for a southern transcontinental rail route. Amtrak has contracted with Greyhound Lines to transport passengers between El Paso and Douglas, Arizona, to provide continuing service until repairs can be made on the damaged bridge. The Amtrak station and the Greyhound bus station in El Paso share the same facility, adding to congestion in the station because of illegal migrants being dumped there by ICE."

Tiring of watching the news, Yusef found books to read and browsed through notes for pending cases his office was handling. Nisrine moved around the house aimlessly, with little attempt to do much other than care for Sara. Yusef prepared simple meals.

Much later in the evening, Yusef commented to Nisrine, "You seem unsettled about something."

"They didn't call me from the hospitals," Nisrine replied. "I've just been waiting to go deliver babies. Surely there are babies born on Christmas day."

Yusef answered, "Surely you're not the only one to have volunteered to be on call. It's pretty well known that Jewish doctors volunteer for duty on Christmas day and El Paso has a large Jewish community. Be pleased that no serious cases emerged that need additional care."

"Yes, I know, Yusey," she said. "Still I want to be of help to those who really need me."

The rest of night was spent with Nisrine listless and Yusef engaged in books and watching some television specials previously recorded to be broadcast on Christmas day.

Thursday, December 27, 2018

Yusef was at home with Sara while Nisrine worked because she had said it would be a busy day again right after Christmas and best that Sara stays home. Yusef followed his usual routine of watching television news and reading, bemoaning the fact it was too cold to take Sara outside to play. Newscasts in the morning gave updates on ICE continuing to release illegal immigrants in downtown El Paso, the death of the young Guatemalan boy, and the bombing of the railroad bridge, but with no additional significant facts.

In the afternoon, watching television again, he heard that a court decision that day by a judge in federal court had required that the government immediately begin hearing asylum claims despite the government shutdown. The government had argued that because of the shutdown, its lawyers were forbidden from working except in humanitarian emergencies. The judge stated that these were humanitarian emergencies and that asylum hearings must begin immediately.

Yusef thought, *Asylum hearings. That involves us. We certainly have enough asylum seekers here in El Paso. This is not my area of expertise. As head of the division, I've just been letting those qualified in the subject handle the cases. I'd better go to the office soon, even if I am on furlough, and educate myself; maybe inform our staff working on asylum that they need to come to work, without pay. Maybe Monday, even if it is New Year's Eve. I don't think it would be a good idea over the weekend. I'll check with Nisrine tonight and see what she thinks is the best day for me to go and for her to take care of Sara.*

CHAPTER 6

Monday, December 31, 2018
El Paso, Texas, USA

After breakfast, Nisrine got herself and Sara ready to go to work at the public health clinic. Yusef said he would be willing to drive them because of the snow and ice on the roads. "I don't need to be at my office until about ten, and I won't be there long. I just need to talk to Susana about this asylum situation. I can easily pick you up."

Nisrine responded, "What? You think I'm not capable of driving in snow and ice?"

Yusef said, "Well, I did grow up in Dearborn and learned to drive there where there's plenty of snow. I just thought I'd offer."

Nisrine said, "Dallas does get snow too, on occasion, and even worse, black ice. Maybe I haven't had as much experience as you have, but I'm not helpless."

With that, she gathered Sara and left. After showering and dressing in nice casual clothes, Yusef watched television news, which reported severe winter weather over a large portion of the country, with New Mexico being hard-hit as well as El Paso. Continued news reported no progress in ending the government shutdown, with a continued impasse over border-wall funding. Finding nothing new of interest, he went to his office early for his meeting with Susana Tate.

Upon arrival, he unbundled his coat in his office and went to the small anteroom where coffee-making facilities were located. While coffee was brewing, he noticed a light in an office down the corridor and went to investigate. Upon seeing Yusef at the door of his office, Khan Nguyen sat up at his desk, startled. "What brings you here on New Year's Eve?" Yusef asked.

"Nothing else to do, so I thought I'd come in and finish up some of the things I had going when I left for the holidays," he answered.

"You know we're forbidden from working during the shutdown."

"Well you seem to be working," Khan retorted.

"Yes, we've been ordered to work on asylum issues as a humanitarian emergency; maybe you've heard." Yusef replied.

"Yes, so I thought it would be OK to come into the office now, even if I'm not working on asylum," Khan said.

"How much do you know about asylum?" Yusef asked.

"Not a lot, but we touched on it in law school," Khan answered. "I've been looking up some on my own since I've been here because it's been in the news so much. My grandparents were granted asylum here when they fled Vietnam. I've been grateful and interested."

"Good for you. Maybe keep on doing research. We could assign you to a group that's looking at the issues. Say, I'm making coffee. Come join me if you like. Susana will be here later to discuss what we should do in preparation for resuming asylum hearings."

When Khan stood, he was about five feet six inches, slender with nicely trimmed straight black hair and brown eyes. He was clean shaven and had the Asian features of his Vietnamese ancestry. He wore clean blue jeans and a simple, stylish sweater over a solid blue shirt. They poured cups of coffee and went to sit in an adjacent break room.

"How was your trip home for the holidays?" Yusef asked.

"It was OK," Khan answered. "Nothing special. I just hung out with family and the few friends I have left in my home town. We went to church on Christmas Eve, and Christmas day, too."

Oh, yeah, the Vietnamese refugees who fled for their lives when the Communists took over the whole country were Roman Catholic, Yusef thought. He asked, "What is your home town? I know you're from Texas somewhere."

"Seadrift, a small fishing town on the coast, south of Houston," he replied.

"You went to UT Law, I recall," Yusef said.

"Yes. After living with extended family while I went to the University of Houston for undergrad, I felt the need to break away from the Vietnamese community and went to UT Law rather than stay in Houston for law school."

I can identify with that, a little bit, Yusef thought. *At least I didn't have to live with other Shia Lebanese in Ann Arbor and was able to make other friends.* "Have you ever thought about private practice, especially with this shutdown?" he said.

"I don't have the money to set up a private practice right now, and I wouldn't know where to do it," Khan replied. "I tried private practice a little bit in Austin right after I graduated, but mostly did public defending work. About the only way I could go into private practice would be in some Vietnamese community, and I don't want to do that. What about you? Any ideas for private practice?"

Yusef pondered a moment and said, "It would be about like you. About the only way I could get started in a private practice right out of law school would have been among the Shia Lebanese community in Dearborn. The U.S. Attorney General recruited me heavily and I felt it was the right thing for me. I could make a name for myself in the government. For right now, I can't imagine any private practice opportunities, so I'll just have to stick it out during this shutdown. Maybe a federal judgeship someday, but that's so far into the future I can't think about it now. You know we were put onto you to hire you because of your public defense work for some persons tried in Austin by the Austin division."

"I strongly suspected that's why I was approached and was asked to apply to the El Paso division," Khan said. "I was defending the three Somali guys as the public defender. Say, do you have any idea how long this shutdown will last? I could have financial problems if it goes too long. I have car payments to make. Maybe I shouldn't have bought a nice new car. My rent isn't that much, so I can probably hang onto a place to live for a while."

Yusef said, "With all of the turmoil at the border, especially right here in El Paso, I can't imagine it would be too long. There would be too much political fallout. But then I'm not into politics at all except to vote. Do you have a big celebration planned tonight for New Year's Eve?"

"No, not at all," Khan replied. "I can't afford it. And besides, I don't know enough people here to approach about celebrating. I've met a few Vietnamese, mostly through people at church, but they are here primarily in some military capacity, and we don't have much in common."

"Yeah, I can imagine." *Sounds like me in Washington until I was fortunate enough to meet Omar and we became roommates,* referring to his best friend Omar Abu Deeb. *Through him I met Frank and Paco, and Brad and Jason. Imagine three practicing Christians, one atheist or agnostic, and all gay. Maybe we should invite Khan over sometime, maybe tomorrow. I'd have to ask Nizzy. That wouldn't expand his social circle, but there were good times when Roger and Lisa invited me, and me and Omar, over for dinners from time to time.*

At that moment, Susana Tate walked in. They sat in small talk a few minutes while Susana had coffee. Then Khan returned to his office while Yusef and Susana went to Yusef's office.

Once at his desk with Susana in his office, Yusef mentioned Khan's interest in asylum and asked, "What do we usually do with asylum cases? When something has come up, I've usually referred them to you."

"We have a couple of persons who deal with that part time when issues come up, but no full-time effort," she replied. "It looks like we might have to ramp things up now."

"That's the way we dealt with things at the district office and in the San Antonio division," Yusef added. "I was too busy on other things to be involved. I'll need to get in touch with John in San Antonio to see what's going on. I presume he'll be back at work in the next few days."

They continued to discuss other issues, including the death of the two children in ICE custody, the dumping of some 1,000 illegal migrants in El Paso under inhumane conditions, and the bomb explosion on the Union Pacific tracks. They concluded that other than the asylum cases of the immigrants who were released, there was little else for them to do because they were forbidden to work except for humanitarian emergencies. Also, other than the migrants dumped in El Paso, the other cases would likely fall under the New Mexico district.

Later that afternoon at home, Nisrine and Sara returned, Nisrine very tired from a busy day at work. Yusef prepared a simple supper for them. When he asked about inviting Khan the next day, Nisrine said to wait and see. Right now, she was too tired to think about entertaining. After supper and with Sara in bed, they sat and watched television listlessly when Nisrine said she needed to go to bed and wished Yusef a happy new year, if he were staying up to watch the new year come in. After an affectionate kiss, she went to bed, leaving Yusef alone. After a short while he thought, *To hell with it. No need to sit up bored just to watch the new year on television. Besides, the festivities in Times Square have already happened two hours ago in the Eastern time zone.* He then went to bed.

Tuesday, January 1, 2019

Nisrine slept late while Yusef woke up to tend to Sara, who needed attention. After a simple breakfast, Sara was sent to her play room.

Yusef sat drinking coffee and turned on the television news. The announcer said, "Now we go to New Mexico, where in the early morning hours a bomb damaged a Border Patrol checkpoint on U.S. Highway 54 just north of the small village of Orogrande, New Mexico, between Orogrande and Alamogordo, New Mexico. A person on a motorcycle driving down the southbound lanes of the four-lane divided highway, where there are no border patrol barriers, slowed down and used some device to propel a bomb across the median up to the edge of the Border Patrol checkpoint in the northbound lanes. There was little structural damage. Border Patrol personnel were only slightly injured but were unable to contain the chaos that ensued from the large amount of traffic driving northward in the early morning hours after New Year's Eve. Because this is the major highway northward from the heavily populated El Paso metropolitan area to Alamogordo, there was heavy traffic due to of late-night celebrators. Separately from the bomb, a rock with the note 'F*bleep* ICE baby killers, take that' was also propelled onto the Border Patrol area.

"Border Patrol, operating with a skeleton crew because of the government shutdown and because of their injuries, were unable to give chase to the motorcycle. New Mexico State police and Otero County sheriff's deputies were called to the scene, but arrived too late to pursue the motorcycle. Cameras that monitor vehicles in both directions were able to get a vague description of the motorcycle, but the license plate was too small and partially covered with snow and mud to reveal an identification. Additional personnel working without pay were brought in to keep the station open and functioning, despite a damaged building.

"More details will be given as the investigation continues. Now, after a break, we go to Washington where the White House, Capitol Hill, and all other government facilities are quiet."

What the fuck is going on? Yusef exclaimed to himself. *Attacks on U.S. government property are certainly an issue that the AG will have to deal with. Again, it's in New Mexico and Robert's division.*

Yusef turned off the television and picked up a book to read. The rest of the day was spent with little significant activity.

U. S. Border Patrol Checkpoint near Orogrande, New Mexico

CHAPTER 7

Thursday, January 3, 2019
El Paso, Texas, USA

In the mid-morning after saying goodbye to Nisrine and Sara, Yusef leisurely watched television news, thinking, *It's too early to have additional news on the criminal investigation in Phoenix of the abuse of children at a detention facility. Interesting it's the county, not the state or FBI, that's investigating. Apparently, they don't see a federal issue. I can't imagine El Paso County investigating the huge site here at Tornillo. The one in Arizona was discovered by the local newspaper. Does the* El Paso Times *have the resources or inclination to do that? This detention situation is getting bad. Unfortunately, we'll surely get involved sometime at our office.*

When Yusef arrived at his office in the late morning, he went to make coffee, discovered the coffee had already been made, and saw Khan's light on and door opened. With a cup of coffee in his hand, he went to Khan's office and said, "Care to join me?"

Together they went to the breakroom, where Yusef asked, "How was your New Year's?"

"Pretty uneventful," Khan replied. "I went to church for New Year's mass and then the church had a New Year's Eve party afterwards. There were mostly older people, or older than me. I just went home shortly after midnight. What about yours?"

"We were just like old fuddy-duds," Yusef said, chuckling. "My wife went to bed early because she was tired from work. My daughter was already in bed. I couldn't see any point in staying up, so I went to bed too."

"She's a doctor, from what I recall," Khan said. "Your wife, that is."

"Yes, an OB/GYN," Yusef answered. "She works for the local public health clinic. My daughter's just two and a half."

"Sounds good," Khan said.

"Well, balancing two careers is sometimes challenging," Yusef added.

After a short pause, they began discussing asylum issues based on what Khan had found in his research. After a while, close to noon, Yusef said, "Let's go have lunch somewhere."

Khan replied, "I brought my lunch today. I really have to economize because of no pay for the shutdown."

Yusef thought, *Maybe I should do that too. We're not hurting financially, but Nizzy's pay is just a pittance.* He said, "I'll buy your lunch today. Next time, I'll bring my lunch too."

Khan agreed, and they went to a small restaurant that caters to the business community in downtown El Paso. While they were eating, Yusef asked, "Apparently you don't have a girlfriend to keep you busy here in El Paso; any girlfriend back in Austin or back home?"

Khan smiled and said, "No. I was just too busy with studies to develop any relationships. I had plenty of friends around law school, some who were women, but no one in particular."

"Sounds like me when I was in school," Yusef said. "I met my wife after I moved to San Antonio. Women in Washington were not that appealing, but luckily I had a roommate who was a best friend and some really close guy friends."

"There were Vietnamese girls back home and in Houston who were interested in me," Khan said, "but they were just interested in having a lawyer husband to make them look good and support them in a good style."

"I can't identify with that personally," Yusef added, "but I know what you mean. It was really lonely the first year or so I was in

Washington. Then I met Omar and we became roommates and close friends, and through him some others; no lawyers among them."

"Yeah, I had a couple of really close friends in Austin, but they were lawyers and moved on after law school," Khan said. "Where are your friends now? Still in Washington?"

"Omar is in North Carolina; he's a professor of Islamic Studies at the University of North Carolina. Also, he's a part-time imam; that's a Muslim clergyman, in case you didn't know."

"Oh, very impressive," Khan said.

"Two others are in Minnesota," Yusef continued. "One is a furniture designer and the other a PhD student in Middle Eastern studies. The other two are still in the Washington area. They all came to our wedding."

"Great, nice to have friends like that," Khan Nguyen said.

They continued in small talk for a short time and returned to their offices. Yusef went home in the afternoon before Nisrine and Sara arrived. After removing his winter coat, he relaxed and turned on the television.

The news announcer began, "We return to the El Paso suburbs to the Santa Teresa border crossing in the New Mexico suburbs. This morning, two men arrived and stood in front of cars passing through the border station into the U.S. They were dressed in some type of an official-looking uniform and wore hoodies that covered their head, barely exposing their faces. They appeared to be Caucasian, typical of Anglo-Americans. Apparently, if a car had license plate from the U.S., it would be waved through. If the car had a license plate from one of the Mexican states, they held up big signs that said in Spanish 'Go Back' and 'No Mexicans here.' The video footage you see was taken by a passenger in a car trying to cross in the chaos and is not good quality. It is possible to see signs that say 'REGRESA' and 'NO MEXICANOS AQUI.'

"Some incoming motorists attempted to drive around them, trying to avoid hitting them. Others did cross over the median strip to return to Mexico. Yet others just stopped and blocked traffic, creating chaos. The Border Patrol tried to make them leave, but did not have authority to arrest and detain them on U.S. territory. The Border Patrol called the New Mexico State Police, but traffic chaos continued for several minutes. When the State Police were seen arriving in the distance, the disrupters got onto their motorcycles and sped away northbound. It took the state police a few minutes to make a U-turn, but the persons on the motorcycles turned off to the east on a desert path heading in the direction of El Paso."

Oh, God, what's going on now? Yusef thought.

The news anchor continued, "In Los Angeles today, when the new House of Representatives in Congress was sworn in, members of a group of protestors marched in front of the office of Congresswoman Bertine Lagos, as they did in front of local congressional offices nationwide. Two persons, it is not sure whether they were men or women, appeared in hoodies to throw smoke bombs into the crowd of supporters and had signs saying 'F*bleep* Progressives.' The crowd dispersed in the smoke, only to reassemble later. The two throwing the smoke bombs and carrying signs had disappeared."

What's going on in this country? Yusef thought.

The rest of the day was spent with Nisrine and Sara around the house, not doing anything special.

CHAPTER 8

Sunday, January 6, 2019
El Paso, Texas, USA

On a leisurely Sunday morning, Sara was playing, Nisrine read medical journals and medical books, and Yusef watched television news.

The news announcer said, "Now we go to Midland, Texas, where a major bomb explosion destroyed facilities at a major oil refinery and terminal for oil pipelines. A note hurled onto the scene read, 'Stop polluting our air and stop climate warming or you will get more of this." Some persons on night security detail were injured and have been hospitalized. Fortunately, no deaths were reported. More details as they become available."

Yusef thought, *Oh my God. Midland's in the Western District. If this becomes a federal issue, the Midland Division might be involved. It probably won't affect me, because my specialty at District is human and civil rights. Hopefully, it won't spill over onto the El Paso division here.*

The news anchor moved on to the next story. "In the San Ysidro neighborhood of San Diego, California, on the border with Tijuana, Mexico, tear gas, smoke, and force were used by Border Patrol agents to stop would-be immigrants climbing the border fence, carrying children, allowing children to fall onto the U.S. side. Teenagers and young men wore heavy jackets to protect themselves from the razor-sharp wire on top of the fence. Fifteen persons were detained, but no details are available about where they were detained."

Not again! Yusef exclaimed to himself. *Of course, they shouldn't be climbing the fence and just letting children drop. But teargas and smoke? The Southern District of California must have its hands full, and with asylum cases too. Hopefully things won't get so bad here, but the way things are going, they could. The New Mexico District will be busy too. If things get worse here, maybe I should contact the people in San Diego for advice and guidance. They certainly have a lot more experience than I do.*

Okemah, Oklahoma, USA

In the middle of the day, Woodrow Dawes and his nephew Leroy Russell were listless, sitting watching television, high on various substances. Woodrow was in his fifties with long shaggy graying brown hair and a beard that hadn't been trimmed in ages. Leroy looked to be in his thirties with equally long shaggy brown hair and a long brown shaggy beard. Both men were about five feet ten inches with a paunch and bodies showing long-time neglect.

Woodrow said between sips of beer while watching television, "Damn Meskins tryin' t' get into this country; got too many of 'em as it is."

"News says they're Central 'mericans, not Meskins," Leroy responded.

"Who gives a fuck; they're all Meskins to me," Woodrow stated. "We need to go down there to El Paso or wherever 'tis and lynch 'em. That's what we done here in Okfuskee County for people we didn't want here."

"Yeah, but that was way back when no one gave a shit about lynchin' undesirables," Leroy said. "Today they'd fry your ass."

"Nah, not if you know whatcher doin'. Besides, they're just wetbacks; no one really gives a shit."

"So how we goin' to pay for a trip to the border?" Leroy asked. "Ya know we don't have enough gas to get us 'round the block."

"We c'n borrow some gas or steal it. Go down there and get some jobs in the oil fields around Midland. Y' know, I used to work in oil fields 'round here 'til all the oil played out."

"I don't know shit about oil field work," Leroy said.

"Don't mean nuthin'," Woodrow said. "They need lots of help, so they'll find somthin' fer ya."

"Midland, ain't that the place that got bombed this mornin'?" Leroy asked.

"Yup, that's where all the oil's at. On the way to the border where the Meskins is."

"When're we goin'?"

"Sometime next week, I s'pose. "Maybe get some odd jobs 'round here to get a little money, that is if the Meskins don't beat us to 'em. Damn all the Meskins comin' in here, workin' the farms, and takin' work away from us decent folks."

"Yeah, can't make decent money anymore," Leroy said. "I might hit up Mom for some. But, yeah, gotta get outta here. No decent work, girls ain't puttin' out no more."

"Well you knocked that one up," Woodrow said. "Ya wouldn't do nothin' to help her out, get a 'bortion. What happened to her? Leave town?"

"Yeah, I guess," Leroy answered. "Family prob'ly sent her off somewhere. She's just a two-bit whore, anyway. Ain't even sure it was mine."

"Ain't that the way with most of the girls you fuck?"

"Yeah, just warm holes to dump my load in. Go down to the border and find lots of Meskin whores. That's all they're good for."

"Maybe pills are cheaper there," Woodrow said. "That's where they come from."

They continued the rest of the afternoon until they passed out from too much alcohol and other substances.

CHAPTER 9

Yusef came to the office in the late morning after a leisurely morning at home alone, thankful there was not much additional upsetting news. When he arrived at the office to get coffee, he saw Khan's light on and went to say hello and tell Khan that he had brought his lunch.

Khan was startled, hurriedly closed a law book he was reading, and was obviously distraught. "You don't look so good," Yusef said.

"It's OK," Khan said.

"You're obviously troubled over something," Yusef said. "Is it something in that law book? What is it you're looking at?"

Khan whimpered, "Sexual assault."

Yusef, stunned, said, "What? Surely you're not being accused of sexual assault. You don't have to tell me unless it's something that involves your work with someone who committed or is a victim of sexual assault."

"No, it's personal," Khan said, his voice lowered. "The priest at church yesterday, and last Sunday, pressed his hand against my crotch in a way that was unmistakable, but subtle so that no one else could see it. Two weeks in a row made it pretty sure what he was doing. I can't go to the Bishop; he'd just cover up. It's been all over the news how the church protects its own."

"The Attorneys General of Pennsylvania and Illinois have taken action against priests accused of sexual assault who the church has covered up," Yusef stated. "I doubt that the Attorney General of Texas has the inclination to do that, but that's not what you want to hear now."

Khan slumped with his hands over his face, sobbing, and saying, "This isn't the first time. When I was a teenager, a priest back home abused me."

Yusef instinctively went and put his hands on Khan's shoulders, hastily went to close the door, and returned to sit next to Khan and put his arm around his shoulder.

"That may have made me gay," Khan said between sobs. "I don't want to be gay. You wouldn't want me to be here if I'm gay. And now it's happening again. I just don't know what to do."

Yusef pondered a moment and then said, "First, as for your position here, it makes no difference whether you're gay or not. What you do in your private life is of no concern to us."

"Are you sure?" Khan asked through sobs.

"You're a damned good attorney, Khan, and that's what matters. From all indications, you are ethical, considerate, and a good colleague."

"Thanks," Khan said, his sobbing continuing.

"But, that's not what made you gay, if indeed you are," Yusef added, remembering conversations in which his friend Brad had expounded at length. "It doesn't work that way. The abuse might have made the situation worse, more traumatic, but something like that can't change the way you're made."

"What?" Khan said, his sobs subsiding. "But the church says—"

"This is not my area of expertise," Yusef interrupted. "You remember those close friends I said I had in Washington? They're gay. Three of them are practicing Christians, one Catholic like you. It might be good if you could talk to them, Brad especially. He's in Minnesota now, so it would have to be on the phone or by Skype.

And Paco, he's still in Maryland, he's the one who's Catholic. You might talk to him too."

"Really?" Khan asked, his tears now subsided.

"When you feel you're ready," Yusef said, "Let me know. I'll make a contact for you. But it's up to you when you feel like it. I won't say anything to them until you're ready. And, of course, I won't say anything to anyone here in the office. Maybe you should consider going to another church, too. In a city as big as El Paso, there should be lots of Catholic churches around."

"Yes, there are," Khan replied. "It's just this one is close to me and I can walk to it. There's at least one other out by Fort Bliss. That's where some of the other Vietnamese go that I mentioned."

Yusef removed his arm and said, "You can talk to me any time, but be assured that this is strictly personal and nothing to do with work in the office. It's up to you."

"Thanks," Khan muttered.

Yusef said, "Say, let's have lunch. I brought mine too."

The rest of the day was uneventful. In mid-afternoon Yusef drove home after stopping to say goodbye to Khan in the office. On the way home, he heard on the radio, "Postal inspectors and the FBI are investigating envelopes with bombs inside that were sent to conservative news outlets and conservative news sources. Included in the packages was a note saying 'Fake News.' No one was injured when the envelopes were opened because mail rooms were very vigilant after bombs were mailed by a Trump supporter from Florida in the summer."

The announcer gave the names of the organizations and locations and continued, "The packages were all mailed from the Seattle area. Apparently, they were sent from a self-service station where postage could be paid by machine and the packages dispatched without being handled by a postal employee at a counter. The envelopes had a return address of a dispatch company in Point

Roberts, Washington. Point Roberts is part of suburban Vancouver, Canada, at the tip of a peninsula that sticks into Puget Sound and a small portion is in the United States, not connected by land to other parts of the state of Washington. There is no indication that the packages were actually sent from Point Roberts. More details when they become available."

Holy shit! Yusef exclaimed silently. *Now what?*

The remainder of the evening was spent quietly with Nisrine and Sara.

CHAPTER 10

Wednesday, January 9, 2019
El Paso, Texas, USA

Yusef left for his office in mid-morning after hearing yet another television news report: "Overnight, bombs were set off just outside the offices of the Texas state branch of the NRA in Austin and the Colorado state branch in suburban Denver. Attached were messages saying 'You kill school kids now take this.' Security personnel were injured and are recovering in hospitals. More details when they are available." Yusef thought, *Not again! This could land in the Austin division, or maybe Austin police and state authorities will handle it. The Austin division does a good job, but because it could involve civil rights, I might be called in.*

Once in the office, Yusef noticed that Khan was around. He went to Khan's office and said, "Coffee?"

Over coffee, Yusef asked, "How've you been? I've just popped in a couple of times and didn't look for you. There was nothing needing my attention."

"Better," Khan answered. "I went to another church on Sunday. It was just a regular mass. Say, maybe I should talk to your friend. I've been feeling more and more that it might be good for me."

"I'll get contact details for you," Yusef said. "His name is Bradley Spencer, Brad. I'll contact him right now and tell him to expect a call from you. I know him well enough to know that he's very willing to talk to people like you. He did it a fair amount at the church he attended in Maryland."

"Oh, really?"

"Yes, he's really good at that," Yusef continued. "He gets lots of satisfaction, too, knowing he can be of help. I think some of the guys he counseled at his church were former Catholics."

"What church is that?" Khan asked.

Yusef thought a moment and replied, "Metropolitan Church, or something like that. A gay-friendly church."

"The Metropolitan Community Church?" Khan offered. "I heard of it in Austin, but I didn't associate with any gay people there, or at least I didn't know they were gay."

"We can have lunch, if you like. I brought my lunch today. I'll have contact details written down then."

"OK, sounds good."

"Also, it looks like the courts will run out of money on Friday during this shutdown," Yusef said. "There's no real reason for you to keep coming in until we call you. Maybe go someplace interesting."

On the way home, Yusef heard the news on the car radio, "One of the mail bombs that were sent a few days ago from Seattle exploded today in the mailroom of Bedford Media Group, a group of right-wing conservative media outlets, at its headquarters in Ventura, California, in the Los Angeles metropolitan area. The mailroom had not been notified to be careful about opening large envelopes, not expecting conservative outlets to be a target after the previous attacks on perceived progressive media. One person was injured, and extensive damage was done to the mailroom. More details when they come in."

What the fuck? Again and again! Yusef thought. *What's this country coming to?*

When Nisrine came home, after affectionate greetings, Yusef said, "Maybe we should go somewhere this weekend or next week if you can get off. It looks like we're completely shut down after Friday. Courts are closed."

"Oh, I'm on call this weekend," Nisrine replied. "Some women are in danger of premature labor and might need me. I wouldn't want to get off with all of this going on and they might be needing me."

The subject was dropped and the rest of the night was spent uneventfully.

BOOK 2

DISCOVERIES

CHAPTER 1

Friday, January 11, 2019
Quantico, Virginia, USA

Roosevelt "Rosie" Jordan, Chief of Operations at the FBI Operations Center on Quantico Marine Base along the Potomac River south of Washington, entered a small conference room he had reserved for a mid-afternoon meeting. He was a large man, African-American, with well-groomed "salt and pepper," mostly black hair. He was dressed in the FBI "uniform" with a white dress shirt and nondescript red tie; his navy-blue suit coat hung on a hanger nearby. He had asked for a meeting with a senior postal inspector and experts in his center on explosive devices and protest demonstrations. Very soon, Adam Culbertson, the explosives expert, and Brock O'Neill, the demonstrations expert arrived, both in "uniform" wearing white long-sleeved dress shirts and ties. They were followed soon by James Cunningham from the U.S. Postal Inspector operations center in nearby Chantilly, Virginia. He was dressed in a charcoal gray suit with dress shirt and tie. He removed the suit coat and sat to join the others.

After introductions, Rosie began, "This is informal. It seemed to be a good time to meet and maybe get ahead of some things. James can tell us the latest on the mail bombs. That might involve us here at the FBI, but you in the postal inspection are very capable of handling things for yourselves. There might possibly be a connection with the other events that are happening around the country all of a sudden. Adam, can you fill us in?"

Adam reported, "Yesterday there was a bombing at the Metropolitan Community Church in Dallas and this morning at the Ebenezer Baptist Church in Atlanta. There were notes about 'fags go to hell' in Dallas and 'black churches burn in hell' in Atlanta.

"James?" Rosie signaled him to begin.

"We're gathering the envelopes with the bombs and messages inside that were sent through the mail so we can compare them and do extensive forensics," James began. "It's almost certain they are identical and have the same types of bombs in them; all mailed at the same time. The couple that were sent to the DC area are already in our labs being analyzed. We're told that the bombs look a little unusual, but we need to get the others here to compare."

"Thanks," Rosie said. "Our labs and facilities are open to you, if needed. You know that."

"Anything new on the other bombings, Adam?" Rosie asked.

"Many of them are not federal issues, yet," Adam added. "Maybe they won't be. The latest two you mentioned in Dallas and Atlanta could be federal hate crimes if local authorities call us in to investigate. If there's a connection, it would be strange because they are attacking both right and left politically, although mostly on the right."

"The same thing seems to be going on in the few incidents of crowd harassment and demonstrations," Brock added. "Both right and left. The one against a congressman could be a federal issue. The demonstration right on the border at the Border Patrol checkpoint in New Mexico is almost certainly a federal issue, the one where perpetrators were holding signs saying Mexicans return to Mexico."

They continued to discuss the details of each situation and concluded in time for the men to get home before heavy rush hour traffic.

El Paso, Texas, USA

In the evening, home alone, Khan was sitting at his computer connected on Skype with Bradley Spencer, who could be seen with brown-blonde, slightly curly, longish hair, blue eyes, and a few-days' beard representing the current style. After preliminary greetings, a slightly nervous Khan said, "Yusef Shaito said you counsel gay Christians."

Bradley Spencer replied, "Call me Brad. I'm not a regular counselor or anything like that, but I have talked to guys a few times. What would you like to know?"

"And please call me Khan. What did Yusef tell you about me?"

"Very little other than you would like to talk to someone about being gay and Christian," Brad replied. "You know Yusef, a very proper ethical lawyer. He says very little. How do you know him? He did mention something about through work."

"I'm a lawyer too," Khan replied. "We work in the same office. Yusef is the head. You must know where he works."

"Yes, U.S. Attorney General," Brad replied. "I knew him when he was at the headquarters in Washington. Then he moved to San Antonio, and now he's temporarily in El Paso."

"Yes, that's right," Khan said.

"Are you gay?" Brad asked. "Or trying to figure it out?"

"I guess I'm trying to figure it out," Khan replied. "I was abused by a priest when I was a teenager. I told Yusef that I thought that might have made me gay. He said that it doesn't work that way and referred me to you, saying he got his information from you."

"No, it doesn't work that way. We are born gay. Events like being abused, especially by a priest, might cause lots of issues to come out; might make you more vulnerable. It might have repulsed you; might have traumatized you. I could go on and on, but this is getting beyond my area of expertise. There are qualified counselors who can help you deal with trauma, or repression, or other issues.

I don't know of anyone in El Paso. I might possibly find someone who is qualified that you can contact by phone or Skype."

"I can't say I was traumatized," Khan said. "Nor repulsed. It happened a few times and it kind of felt good, but deep inside I knew it was wrong and I made him stop."

"Good for you," Brad replied. "Having sex with someone in a power position over you, male or female, is never healthy, even though it might have made you feel good at the moment. How old were you, if I may ask?"

"I was fourteen."

"OK, so you were in puberty and could orgasm."

"Yes."

"We're not going to pursue any details, because that's not what you're calling about. This is a very common situation, unfortunately. Momentary pleasure, then lingering regret; especially if it happened more times. You aren't unusual or weird, not in the slightest."

"Thanks, I guess," Khan replied. "I was always ashamed. I thought it was just me and tried to block it from my memory."

"Sadly, you are not alone at all," Brad continued. "There are hundreds, if not thousands, just like you, all afraid to say too much, feeling they are the only ones, and they don't tell anyone."

"Er, OK, I guess," Khan said. "But the church says being gay is wrong, a sin."

"Not all churches."

"But the priests say that the Bible says homosexuality is a sin," Khan replied.

"How can they say that?" Brad asked. "They abused you homosexually, yet say it's a sin. That is the ultimate in hypocrisy. And, whose sin is it? Yours or his?"

"Er, I don't know," Khan said.

"Where in the Bible does it say it says that it's a sin?" Brad asked.

"I don't know," Khan replied. "Catholics don't read the Bible much. We just rely on the priests to tell us what it says."

"Yes," Brad smirked. "I've heard that so many times. And Catholics aren't the only so-called Christians who say homosexuality is a sin, but no need to go into those details, at least not now.

"We have a fair number of former Catholics in churches I've attended. In our churches we do read the Bible. I can go over verse by verse and item by item where some of these churches say homosexuality is a sin and refute them in detail. We really don't have time here and now, but anytime you want to explore further what the Bible actually says, let me know. For right now, just remember that Jesus said 'Love your neighbors as yourself.' He didn't say love your heterosexual neighbors as yourself.

"Also, in the gospel of John, Jesus said 'for God so loved the world;' He didn't say God so loved the heterosexuals in the world. Then Jesus followed that with 'God did not send his son into the world to condemn the world,' yet these persons are using the Bible to condemn gays. I could go on and on, but maybe that's not what you want to hear now."

"Well I haven't specifically focused on the Bible very much, but you have me thinking maybe I should," Khan said. "What church to you go to? Yusef said something about the Metropolitan Community Church. I've heard of it. A gay church."

"That was when we lived in Maryland," Brad said. "Here in Minneapolis we attend a predominantly gay congregation of the United Church of Christ, the UCC. I grew up in the UCC. It's the only mainstream Protestant denomination that's formally open and accepting of homosexuals, other than the MCC of course. The UCC is mostly a northern church. You might not have them in Texas."

"I can look and see," Khan said.

"Hey, I'm not trying to convince you to change churches," Brad said. "There are gay Catholics who are still practicing Catholics. Our good friend Paco Mendoza is Catholic."

"Yusef mentioned someone with a name that sounds like that," Khan replied.

"But more than that," Brad said. "It's OK to be gay. You asked me specifically about being gay and Christian, and I hope we covered that, at least a beginning. But more than that, if you are gay, God made you gay for a reason. If so, God wants you to be someone and do some things that a gay man can do best. You can begin the process of finding out for yourself if you're gay and what the reasons might be...."

"How do I do that?" Khan asked.

"No one thing in particular, Brad answered. "Just be open and waiting for the ideas or feelings to come to you. Prayer and meditation can help, but then prayer and meditation help life in general. Being open and accepting of yourself as a gay man, if that's the case, can be a big first step. Hey, it took me a long time to come to the point that I am gay, so there's no reason why it shouldn't be a long time for you if you are gay. Maybe you can start the process, and, I don't mean full time. Maybe Yusef told you I'm getting a PhD in Middle Eastern studies focusing on the Arabic language and culture. I'm a linguist by background, specializing in Arabic. But God made me gay to set an example for other gay men. I even did some of that when I had a student exchange in Jordan."

"Oh, wow, you really have gotten around," Khan commented. "I've barely gotten outside of Texas and, now, a few times to New Mexico. Maybe you've detected that I'm Vietnamese, second generation in the U.S. The Vietnamese I come from stick to themselves and stay in Texas pretty much. I'm the first to break away and go to law school, and now end up here in El Paso."

"That sounds like my partner, Jason," Brad commented. "He's from Virginia. I dragged him all the way here to Minnesota where I grew up. He's a freelance furniture designer and can live almost anywhere. Also, I lived in New Mexico for a few months while I was recuperating, and he spent a fair amount of time with me there. It's too long of a story to tell now. Ask Yusef to tell you sometime.

He and his roommate Omar came to visit us in New Mexico, in Ruidoso. We had a big reunion with Frank and Paco."

"I've heard of Ruidoso since I've been here in El Paso," Khan said. "I haven't been there. I spend too much time working."

"You should go, sometime," Brad said. "Not in January, because it's too cold there unless you're into skiing. Here, I'll call Jason. Say, there are some nice spas in New Mexico, hot spring spas. Maybe that would help you in the process of learning whether you are gay and what it's like."

"You mean gay spas?" Khan said. "I'm not sure I'm ready for that yet."

"No, just regular hot springs that appeal to everyone," Brad said. "I didn't go to any because I was still recuperating in bandages. I can't say first hand. But, no, not gay places. You'll know if and when you're ready to get involved in more gay activities. Just follow your instincts and feelings. Don't rush it."

"OK," Khan said.

A slender man, about five feet eleven, with steel blue eyes, red-brown hair, goatee, and a long ponytail came in front of the camera. "This is Jason, Jason Henderson, my fiancé, I suppose I should say. We're going to get married one of these days when we have time to do it right, now that same-sex marriage is legal. It never really was an issue here in Minnesota, and the UCC will gladly marry us."

Jason Henderson waved and smiled, "Pleased to meet you. Any friend of Yusef, or Joe as we used to know him, is a friend of ours. Your name?"

"Khan Nguyen," he answered. "It's Vietnamese."

"I've never known Vietnamese before," Jason said. "Maybe when Brad here gets his head out of books and finally gets that PhD, we can meet sometime."

"Sure," Khan said.

They continued a very few more minutes in small talk and then said goodbyes.

Khan thought, *Yes, get away for a while. A spa sounds nice. I've been doing only busywork at the office, and now they don't want me to go there while the shutdown is going on. I've heard people talking about Faywood Hot Springs, not far away in New Mexico. Maybe I need to check it out.*

Khan continued to browse his computer for a while and then went to bed.

CHAPTER 2

Saturday, January 12, 2019
Faywood Hot Springs, New Mexico, USA

Shortly after noon, Khan arrived at Faywood Hot Springs after a little less than a three-hour drive, including a stop for a quick bite to eat at a fast food place in Deming, New Mexico. He paid the daily admission charge at the gate and was directed to a place to park. *This place is really rustic*, he thought. *Just a little gravel parking area off to the side of a dirt road. There are the signs pointing to the pools.*

He was wearing a long-sleeved shirt and upon getting out of his car, he put on a light weight jacket; it was a typical sunny day for southern New Mexico in the desert with mild temperatures for winter. He picked up a towel and bathing suit, not really knowing what to expect inside and started walking. As he continued down the narrow path through pine trees and bushes, he came upon a big fenced area with a gate. Once inside, he saw signs for 'clothing required' and 'clothing optional, no one under 18,'. Both signs were on gates to other enclosed areas with high fences. He first went into the area for clothing required and saw a fairly small hot springs pool with lots of children playing. Thinking, *This isn't the place for me with lots of noisy, active kids*, he left and entered the clothing-optional area. *Well, it does say optional. I can still put my bathing suit on.* Inside he saw three rectangular-shaped pools, one large nearby, and two smaller off to the side. They were simple rock and concrete pools that fit with the rustic atmosphere. A large group of men and women of all ages were in the large pool, with only a couple of people in each of the two smaller pools. Once inside the area, he looked for a changing room. Finding none, he did notice individual piles of clothes and towels under trees and bushes and by the several benches. He thought, *Gee, all of those people are naked and don't seem to care. Maybe I should just take my clothes off and cover myself with my hands and go in with them.*

He methodically took off his clothes, carefully turning his back to the crowd. He then walked with his hands covering his groin to an edge of the large pool where there were not so many people. Slowly he slipped in, turning himself to face the pool wall. After a moment, noticing that his genitals could not be seen in the moving water, he turned to face the crowd. Most of the people were moving around the pool randomly in small groups or individually, engaging in seemingly friendly conversation. Soon a group was around him. At first, he was quiet but responded to brief conversations. They mentioned where they were from. Some were just passing through on nearby Interstate Highway 10 and knew about the place for a break from travel. Some were from El Paso and Las Cruces, coming for the day. Because there were camping facilities, RV parking places, and bunkhouses for rent, some came for a few days' getaway. Khan opened up and mentioned he was from El Paso and that this was his first time here.

As the crowd drifted around in the circulating warm water, a tall man, about six feet, drifted into the group. He looked to be in his mid-thirties, with blond, wavy hair trimmed to medium length, blue eyes, and a trim but not particularly muscular body. He and Khan exchanged brief glances, then the blond guy was brought into the conversation. The blond man mentioned he was from Alamogordo and worked at Holloman Air Force Base.

As people drifted around, often casually bumping into each other, the blond man pushed against Khan's naked hip underwater. Khan felt a tingling sensation and thought, *I wonder what that's about*. Within a few minutes, the blond man and Khan were next to each other, hips touching in the jostling group. The man asked Khan, "What do you do in El Paso?"

"I'm a lawyer," Khan answered.

"Oh, what kind of law?"

"Criminal."

"Oh, you defend all those people crossing the border with drugs and doing criminal things," the blond man said, chuckling.

"No, I prosecute them," Khan replied. "I'm with the U.S. Attorney General, El Paso Division. I was a public defender in Austin before I joined the U.S. Attorney General, so I know the defense side also."

"I was just teasing," the blond man said, "with all the news we hear about criminals flowing into this country."

"I figured you were kidding," Khan said smiling. "There is some of that, but there is plenty of other criminal activity going on, unfortunately. Most are pretty mundane crimes with plea bargains and guilty pleas. But still we need to have an attorney present. Are you in the Air Force?"

"No, I work for NASA at its operations on the base. It's easier to say I work at Holloman than to go into details about NASA."

More people drifted around, and the blond man and Khan drifted apart and were involved in idle conversation with others. Soon Khan and the blond man were closer together. Khan asked, "Do you come here often?"

"Fairly often," the blond man answered. "It's not far; and when the stress at work builds up, it's good to come here, commune with nature, and soak."

"What more specifically do you do?" Khan asked.

"I'm a statistical analyst, a numbers geek," the blond guy answered. "Staring at numbers all the time can get to me; make me want to get away."

"I can imagine," Khan replied. "Same here. My head is buried in law books if I'm not actually meeting with other lawyers or I go to court. But now with this shutdown, I'm not supposed to be in the office. They haven't taken my key away or changed the locks, but it's pretty clear I need to stay away. And the courts are supposedly shut down too.

"Oh, you're affected by the shutdown too. Same with me. The base is open, but NASA is shut down. I was essentially told to wind up what I'm working on and stay away."

"Say, what are those other two pools?" Khan asked.

"They're progressively hotter," the blond man answered. "The water here comes out of the ground pretty hot. They have to cool it down for the main pool, but they have the two smaller pools for those who like to scald themselves."

"Maybe I'll try the next one up," Khan said.

"I'll join you," the blond man said.

Khan got out of the larger pool, careful not to expose himself and covered his mid-section with his hands. The blond man came behind him making no attempt to cover himself. Once in the warmer pool, the blond man again moved close to Khan, touching hips under water, ostensibly so he could hear better with the noise in the distance. Khan again felt a tingling sensation, wondering what it was about, but dismissed feelings from his mind.

With no one else in the pool at the moment, the blond man asked, "Are you originally from El Paso?"

Khan answered that he was originally from the Texas coast south of Houston, giving brief details about his background. "And you?" he asked.

"I'm originally from the Chicago area," the blond man replied. "German ancestry since about the 1800s; thoroughly Americanized by now."

"There are lots of Germans around central Texas," Khan said. "I ran into lots of them when I was in Austin. They seem to have adapted very well to Texas and are just regular Americans, except for their Oktoberfests."

"I've heard of Germans in Texas, but never got to that part," the blond guy said. "I've been to Houston a few times, NASA headquarters, but never got out and about in the state. Oh, El Paso of course, but that doesn't seem like Texas."

"That's what I hear all the time. El Paso is so remote that most Texans don't even know it's in Texas. My family were first pleased I was moving somewhere else in Texas, but then upset when they learned it was so far away."

"My family couldn't understand why I moved to this godforsaken desert, but I love it now that I've been here a while," the blond man said. "I love the wide-open spaces, the mountains, the desert and all of its beauty. Sometimes I go up to the mountains close by; Ruidoso, if you've ever heard of it. Sometimes for a show or just to hang out in the cool mountain breeze, especially in summer when it's beastly hot in Alamogordo."

"I've heard of Ruidoso," Khan said. "I just talked to a friend of my boss who lived there for a while."

"You should go," the blond guy said. "Maybe I could meet you and show you around."

"OK. Say, maybe I should try the other pool. It's hotter, you say."

Was that a rebuff? the blond man thought. "OK, I'll join you if you like," he said.

"OK," Khan replied.

They walked to the hotter pool with no one around, Khan only partially covering himself with his hands. Once inside, the blond man moved closer but not touching, wanting to be cautious. He asked, "Do you have girlfriends in El Paso that keep you tied down? Or back home?"

"No, not at all," Khan answered. He explained briefly what he had told Yusef. "I don't have much of a social life in El Paso. Too busy working and also it's not that easy to meet people." Hesitating, he continued, "What about you?"

The blond guy gradually moved closer, touching, and noting that Khan Nguyen did not react, continued to touch him hip to hip. "I have a few guy friends that I hang out with and go places sometimes. They mostly like to find women, but without too much luck in an Air Force community, they like to hang out with me. Mostly, I like to come places like this alone."

"This last hot pool is a little bit too much for me," Khan said. "Maybe I should get out now."

"Would you like to come join me in my cabin?" the blond guy asked.

"Cabin?" Khan said.

"Yes, they have two rustic cabins for overnight guests," the blond guy replied. "And some bunkhouses for large groups. Mine is the one here in the clothing optional area. We don't have to get dressed."

"Er, I guess so, for a little while," Khan said. "I've had enough water for a while. I'm about to turn into a prune."

When they got out of the water, both naked, Khan did not immediately try to cover himself. The blond man stuck out his hand and said, "Otto Wildmann."

"Khan Nguyen," he answered, shaking hands.

"Very nice to meet you, Khan," Otto smiled and put his hand on Khan Nguyen's shoulder.

"I'll go get my clothes and towel," Khan said.

"OK," Otto replied. "I'll meet you there by that bench where the trail to the cabin starts."

Khan picked up his towel and clothes, met Otto, and walked to his cabin, holding his towel and clothes in front of him, shivering in the cold air.

Once inside the cabin, Otto shut the door to keep out the cold air, then put his arms around Khan's shoulders and tried to kiss him. Khan turned his face and backed away as much as he could, saying, "This is the first time I've done anything like this." *Well, there was the priest back home,* he said to himself, *but this seems so different. Brad did say to follow my instincts and not think about it too much.*

"Oh, sorry," Otto said. "Sorry if I'm too forward. I thought you might be gay too. Are you?"

"Er, yes, I think so," Khan answered. "But I'm just now beginning to realize it. I don't know what to do."

"That's all right," Otto said as he backed away slightly. "I'll not push things. You're nice and I like you."

Khan hesitated a moment, then said, "That's OK. I like you too. Just be patient and gentle." He moved closer and put his arms around Otto, pulled him closer, then Otto kissed Khan, who returned the kiss. Otto led Khan to the bed, which was already folded out from a couch from Otto's having slept there the night before.

After awkward but intense sex, both Khan and Otto slowly got out of the bed. Otto said, "We'll have to go back into the pool to clean off. There're showers around here somewhere, but I don't use them, and not too many others seem to use them either. The water is hot and constantly flowing from the hot springs. Nothing like a hot bath."

"OK," Khan Nguyen said as he grabbed his towel.

They both walked back to the main pool and splashed around a short while, then returned to the cabin to dry. Once at the cabin, Otto said, "You want to go for dinner? There are no places here, but some back in Deming. Nothing special. Denny's and the like."

"Denny's is fine." Khan replied. "Then maybe I should head back to El Paso before it gets too late."

"Why don't you spend the night here? Just take one car."

Khan hesitated, thinking, *Brad did say just follow my instincts. I don't have any reason to go back, except church. Maybe I can find a late mass somewhere.* "Er, OK, I guess. You know I said this is my first time like this."

"That's OK," Otto said. "We'll take it slow. It's just that I'm enjoying being with you."

"I'm enjoying being with you too," Khan said. "It's just all new to me."

They decided to go in Otto's car because he knew the way. While eating, Otto asked, "What types of things do you do in El Paso socially? Or for entertainment?"

"Not much," Khan answered. "Go to movies sometimes; read books; watch TV. Back in Austin I had friends around the law school that I would hang out with, go to movies, occasionally bars. With the big university, there was always something to do. There's UTEP in El Paso, but so far, I've not run across anyone from there. Besides, I'm getting too old to hang with the college crowd."

"What kind of movies?" Otto asked.

"No particular type," Khan said. "Just something that I find interesting. I definitely don't go for the adventure, violence, action types. Recently, I saw *Bohemian Rhapsody*. It was great. And just now it won the Golden Globes award for best picture."

"I saw that too," Otto said. "I loved it! Rami Malek was great, and sexy. What types of books?"

"Almost any kind of fiction, especially mystery," Khan said. "Especially with a legal theme like John Grisham. You're doing all the asking. What about you? You say you go to El Paso some."

"Yeah," Otto replied. "Not so much in the summer in the blazing heat. Sometimes I go with friends, straight friends like I mentioned, to a concert. I go to movies, sometimes with them, sometimes alone. There are some classic old movies at the Alamo Drafthouse. I saw the *Rocky Horror Picture Show* there. Some gay movies too."

"I've never seen a gay movie, I guess," Khan answered. "Well, I guess *Bohemian Rhapsody* is a gay movie."

"El Paso has a fabulous art museum," Otto continued. "Have you ever been there? I go and take my sketch books to draw things. I like to draw desert scenes too."

They continued in small talk, getting to know each other, then went back to Otto's cabin for a night of more, less awkward, sex.

Sunday, January 13, 2019

Khan and Otto woke up lazily the next morning, lingering in bed for more sex. Khan said, "It's time for breakfast. You want to join me? I suppose it's back in Deming. I'd enjoy spending a little more time with you over breakfast, but I guess I should go back to El Paso."

"Yeah, sure," Otto said. "I'd like to spend more time with you too. I should probably go back to Alamogordo today, too, although there's no reason to go to work tomorrow."

"Same here," Khan said. "No work today, but I should try to find a church somewhere this afternoon."

"What church?" Otto asked. "I thought Vietnamese were Buddhists."

"Not the group who were chased out of Vietnam when Ho Chi Minh took over. We're Catholic."

"I grew up Catholic too," Otto said. "Since I've been in Alamogordo, I haven't found a church I feel comfortable in, so I rarely go. I hear there are a couple of churches in Las Cruces that have gays; Unity Church of Las Cruces is one. But I'm too lazy to drive 70 miles for church."

They took quick dips in the pool and then dressed, and Otto packed his few belongings to return home after breakfast.

They drove to Denny's in Deming in separate cars. While eating, Otto said, "It sure would be nice to see you again sometime."

"Yeah, I'd like that," Khan replied. "You said you come to El Paso sometimes. Anytime soon?"

"No specific plans, but we can look into that and see what's going on. There's almost always something going on in El Paso. But, say, why don't you come to Alamogordo? You said you've never been there."

"No, I haven't," Khan replied. "I've heard that Ruidoso is nice, but I am not a skier and it would be cold and snowy. But yeah, maybe Alamogordo sometime. What's there?"

"There's the White Sands," Otto began explaining, "but it might be closed because of the shutdown. The New Mexico Museum of Space History is well worth a visit."

"I've heard a lot about the White Sands," Khan said. "I'd really like to see it."

They continued discussing things they might do. Otto said, "Here, let's exchange contact details." He found a paper napkin and wrote, "Otto Wildmann," his phone number, email address, and Facebook address, saying, "That's 'Wild-' rhyming with 'filled,'" you heard me say. And I can be a wild man too."

"I'll bet," Khan said smiling. He wrote his name, phone number, email address, and Facebook address on another napkin.

When they were finished, they walked to the parking lot slowly, reluctant to part company, and exchanged a hug and a kiss out in the open, got into their respective cars, and left.

CHAPTER 3

Tuesday, January 15, 2019
Quantico, Virginia, USA

In the late morning, Rosie Jordan opened another informal meeting with James Cunningham of the U.S. Postal Inspection Service, along with Adam Culbertson and Brock O'Neill. "Thanks for agreeing to come over here, James. Sorry you have to drive a little way, but with the government shutdown, we can't be sure that other places would be secure. What can you tell us about your findings so far?"

James began, "We're about to complete our forensics and are getting some interesting results. The envelopes used to mail the bombs are not the same size as we use here in the U.S. They are basic manila envelopes like we use, but they had metric measurements that are used in almost all of the world except the U.S. You'd have to have a keen eye to notice the difference. We're still doing analysis of the paper used to make the envelopes, as well as the notes inside and other wrapping material. We're pretty sure the origin is not from the U.S."

"The return address was from a suburb of Vancouver, Canada, that happens to stick just a tiny bit into the U.S.," Adam offered. "Maybe the packages originated there."

"That, of course, was a thought," James said. "The explosive material is not something that's allowed in the Canada, or in the U.S. for that matter. We're not experts in analyzing the explosive material and are pleased that you'll do it for us," gesturing to Rosie. "From what we've been able to learn, this type of explosive is used in much of the world, but not here nor Western Europe. Besides, the packages were actually mailed from the Seattle area and processed by the main mail distribution center there, not from that little community next to Canada."

Adam stated, "The explosives in the devices we've been able to look at are not available in the U.S., Canada, or Western Europe, like you said, but are available in plenty of other places in the world. The rest of the items are pretty basic. Maybe we should go back and check for metric versus American measurements. When we get your items, we can do more comparisons. Maybe possibly bring in INTERPOL."

"Brock, anything new on your end?" Rosie asked.

"The demonstrations stopped," Brock said. "There must be a reason, but so far nothing comes to mind. We're still trying to see if there's any connection among the various demonstrations because they have conflicting opposite messages as to motives; as we said, some right-wing political, some left wing."

James added, "So far, we've not found anything else suspicious in the mail. We don't always make it public when we do find something unless a recipient makes it public."

"Sorry to have brought you together for such a short meeting," Rosie said. "We could go to lunch in a few minutes. Our lunch room for senior staff is still operating."

They continued discussing details and small talk through lunch, and then all went back to their offices.

México, DF, México

Ivan Petrov was in the office of Vladimir Mikhailov at the Russian embassy in Mexico City. They exchanged pleasantries in Russian and continued conversation in Russian, Vladimir beginning, "At least it's warmer here in the capital. You've had some cold weather up north there in Juárez."

"Yes, we had some snow, but it melted fairly quickly," Ivan replied. "That, plus the government shutdown in the U.S. slowed down some of our work, although the U.S. military hasn't shut down and we still monitor a lot."

"The shutdown has caused us to back off our activities to infiltrate and create chaos," Vladimir said. "Our operatives have to be able to take direct flights to and from El Paso, as you know, and with chaos in the airports it's too much of a risk that they might be delayed and raise suspicion. Besides, some of the fringe groups might start protesting and creating chaos independent of us. They're doing some of that already, protesting the shutdown. But it's still too cold in most of the U.S. for spontaneous protests by other groups."

"That's what I thought; you're not flying people around," Ivan said, "although you know that I don't monitor your activities all the time, on purpose. You want to keep me out of day-to-day activities for security reasons."

"Yes," Vladimir said, "plus this shutdown is creating enough chaos as it is. We don't need to stir up a lot more, at least for the moment. Maybe we can find some places our operatives can go to by road that are close enough to get to and back to the tunnel in one day."

"You know that the Border Patrol is briefing President Trump on tunnels they're finding in California, saying that building a wall won't help, "Ivan added.

"Yes. Trump just blew it off and didn't care. He's so fixated on his wall. We're not concerned about being detected, at least not now. We can control him, if necessary. You know we're purposely not sending drugs and undocumented people across, except for some of our operatives of course, but not large numbers that could draw attention to hordes of illegals in the El Paso area that aren't coming through regular border entry points. We don't get media attention that might force Trump to do something irrational. We do have a task for you, though."

"OK, what's that?"

"We have a very high placed businessman settled in North Carolina; he's very close to Putin's inner circle. He runs legitimate businesses in the U.S. and does a lot of money laundering. He's got himself in lots of trouble because he tried to hire someone to murder another Russian who he claimed is having an affair with his wife. He was arrested and jailed. With some tricky work with an American lawyer who works for us, he was able to get out on a million-dollar bail with home confinement and an ankle bracelet.

"We need to get him out of there. Maybe have one of our operatives drive him to an airport where he can get a direct flight to El Paso. We might have to wait until this shutdown is over. Atlanta is the most logical airport for a direct flight. We can't take a risk that someone would recognize him, waiting for hours in a security line. Even worse, that a flight might be cancelled or rebooked so he can't get a direct flight. We have operatives who can pick him up at the El Paso Airport and take him to the mosque. What we need you to do is arrange someone to get him out of Juárez and to an airport. Take him to Chihuahua City. If his name is found on a manifest from the Juárez airport, it could cause too much attention to be focused on Juárez. There's enough attention focused on Juárez as it is, with your spy activities there."

"How do I do that?" Ivan asked. "You know I'm followed almost constantly."

"Not you personally, Ivan Aleksandrovich," Vladimir said. "You have people working for you. One of them can pretend to be a truck driver making deliveries. That herb shop and spa will obviously need deliveries from time to time."

"If he goes by road to Chihuahua, how do we get him past the government twenty-kilometer checkpoint? You know Mexico doesn't have a control right at the northern border, but at a checkpoint twenty kilometers inland."

Vladimir handed over a medium-sized envelope saying, "Here's another Russian passport for him with a Mexican visa."

"Konstantin Leonidov," Ivan said, after opening the envelope.

"Yes, that's him. We thought it best to use his actual name. Check out the situation at those checkpoints. If necessary, hide him under something in the back of a truck. Also, Mexicans are not beyond taking bribes. It's probably best to give them a nice tip anyway. He'll be carrying a large amount of cash with him, so you have to keep that in mind as you make arrangements."

"OK," Ivan said. "You know I'll do what I can. How will I know when to send someone to the herb shop to pick him up?"

"We'll get signals to you like we have before."

"We have an even greater problem coming up, just to give you a head's up."

"What's that?" Ivan asked.

"At some point we need to get his wife out of there, also," Vladimir said. "If she falls into the hands of the Americans, she could tell a lot that we don't want her to tell. She and her husband are not on good terms, to say the least; in fact, they're pretty hostile. She might tell some things just for spite. We have to find some way to get her out of there and into Mexico involuntarily. That might be messy, but you would likely be involved."

"You know I specifically avoid messy situations," Ivan said. "They could jeopardize my intelligence gathering."

"We'll worry about that when the time comes," Vladimir said. "Come, let's go to lunch. Same place we usually go. Just in case we meet our Iranian or North Korean counterparts like we did before, absolutely nothing about this to them. They might find out if we need assistance from some of their operatives at the tunnel, but not now."

Ivan agreed and they went to the restaurant. After a while, indeed Bijan Ahmadi arrived and was invited to share a table. Conversing in English using very well-chosen words, they discussed their successful activities to create chaos in the U.S., including mailing letter bombs, demonstrations, and carefully selected bombing

DON'T FENCE ME IN

targets. Ivan said, "I've heard of all of those on the news, of course. I suspected we were behind it, now it seems I'm right."

Lunchtime conversation continued on other topics, then all went their separate ways, Ivan and Vladimir returning to the Russian Embassy.

El Paso, Texas, USA

In the late afternoon, Khan received a text message from Otto, asking to go onto Skype. Khan immediately answered back, and both connected on Skype. Both were at home, idle, because of the shutdown.

After preliminary, very friendly greetings, Otto said, "I'm thinking about going to El Paso tomorrow to buy some more art supplies. You want to meet me, have dinner, and go to a movie? It'd have to be an early movie so I can get back to Alamogordo before too late."

Khan smiled and said, "Sure, but why don't you stay overnight with me? You don't have work to go to, and neither do I. Unless you have something else planned."

"No, not at all," Otto replied. "That'd be fun," he added with a wink. "We could hang out and do things on Thursday."

"I'm not so sure that going out for dinner would be such a good idea for me financially," Khan said. "I can make dinner here for us. I'm pretty good making Vietnamese food. Sorry to be a wet blanket, but I didn't have time to accumulate too much savings, not anticipating the shutdown."

"Sounds good to me," Otto said. "I've never had Vietnamese food before. I can help you buy groceries."

"That's not necessary, Khan replied. "You can buy the food when I come to Alamogordo. If you cook, that is."

Otto smiled and said, "I do OK in the kitchen. I've learned to dabble in New Mexican food since I've lived here."

Both smiled and said, "It's a date." Khan gave his address for Otto's GPS. They agreed to meet in mid-morning and go from there.

CHAPTER 4

Wednesday, January 16, 2019
El Paso, Texas, USA

Otto arrived at Khan's apartment building and sent a text that he was in the parking lot asking what to do next. Khan promptly left his apartment and got into Otto's car. Otto leaned over to give Khan a quick kiss. They drove to an art supply store in the large shopping complex around Cielo Vista Mall, not far from Khan's apartment. After buying art supplies, Otto suggested they look around the mall. After a short while, not finding anything of interest, Otto said, "How about lunch? I don't want to strain your budget, but Jason's Deli is close and the mall has a food court."

Khan replied, "Jason's Deli is OK. I've eaten there a few times, and it's not too expensive."

Over lunch, Otto said, "Once we get back to your place, I'd like to draw you, if you're willing, of course. I'm just now beginning to draw people, not limiting myself to landscape and other objects."

Khan agreed. Once back in his apartment, Otto showed Khan where to sit to be drawn. When Otto showed him the finished product, Khan exclaimed, "That's great! You got my Vietnamese features just right. Can I keep it? I'd like to frame it and hang it over there."

"Sure thing," Otto replied. "I'll draw another one just for me to keep. Now, I've always wanted to sketch someone nude. Would you take your clothes off and sit there? Don't worry, I'm not going to draw your dick and that part of the body."

Khan hesitated just a moment and said, "OK. But you have to get naked too."

When Otto finished, he showed his work to Khan who stated, "That's great! Can I have that one too? You can draw another one any time." He gave Otto a kiss and, observing that both had become aroused, led him to the bedroom.

After quick showers, Khan dressed partially and went to the kitchen to begin cooking. He removed the wok and got out the fresh pork he had chopped in cubes. Otto, also partially dressed, asked if he could help, so Khan gave him vegetables to chop. Khan started rice cooking and prepared the other food: pork stir-fried with lots of chopped garlic, cabbage, and green beans, plus hot Asian peppers and a few spices. He also chopped fresh pineapple and papaya.

Otto said, "This is really spicy. Is all Vietnamese food spicy like this?

"A lot is," Khan replied. "Is it too spicy for you?"

"No, not at all," Otto replied. "Mexican food is spicy too, as you know, and I love it. Authentic New Mexican food is not quite so hot and uses green peppers instead of red ones. After all the bland German food some of my relatives made, this is a nice change. I can taste cinnamon. You use cinnamon in food like this?"

"Yes," Khan answered. "You've heard the term 'Saigon cinnamon.' That's where it originated."

"Where do you get all of these ingredients?" Otto asked again.

"Lots in regular supermarkets," Khan replied. "There are also some Asian supermarkets that sell lots of things, like pickled vegetables."

"Yeah, I suppose El Paso would have supermarkets with bigger selections than in Alamogordo," Otto said.

They put leftover food away and cleaned the kitchen, then Otto said, "We don't really need to go to a movie tonight and spend money. I need to cut back too, until I can see what this shutdown will do. Maybe just sit here and watch television."

"Sounds good to me."

They retired to the couch and sat cuddling, partially clothed, watching TV. Otto said, "One thing I'd like to do is draw pictures of a border fence if there is one anywhere near here. There's so much hype about border fences and walls, I'd like to see one and draw a picture."

Khan replied, "There must be some fence near here, because the bomb under the railroad tracks was just outside of El Paso and next to a border fence. I'll check it out on Google Maps before we go to bed."

Later, when they were ready for bed, Khan turned on his computer, looked at Google Maps, and said, "There, it looks like New Mexico highway 498 goes right down to the border in Sunland Park. That might be where the fence is. Take Sunland Park Drive off I-10."

They undressed, went to bed for more passionate sex, and eventually went to sleep.

Thursday, January 17, 2019
Sunland Park, New Mexico, USA

After waking to another round of sex, showering together, and a quick breakfast of cereal and toast, they drove in Otto's car to a point on New Mexico Highway 498 in Sunland Park, New Mexico, a suburb, that ends very near railroad tracks and the border fence.

"That must be the main line of the railroad that was bombed a few days ago," Khan said. "The bombed bridge must be a little farther away; can't see it from here."

"Too bad trains won't be running by," Otto said. "It could be interesting to show a train running right next to the fence."

Otto got out his drawing materials and started sketching while Khan stood by taking pictures with his phone, trying not to distract Otto. Soon another car approached; it was apparent that it was a police car. An officer got out and started walking towards Otto and Khan. He appeared to be in his early twenties, of medium height,

U.S.-Mexico border fence and Union Pacific mainline
railroad tracks in Sunland Park, New Mexico.

about five feet eight, with brown hair, and had Hispanic features. A
holster with a pistol was strapped around his hips.

When he was closer to Otto, the police officer said, "What do
you think you're doing?"

"Drawing pictures of the fence," Otto answered.

"Why do you want to do that?" the police officer asked.

"I like to draw interesting things," Otto answered. "Border fences
are in the news."

"Maybe he could sell it to some news media," Khan offered.

"Put your hands up and slowly use one hand to get out and show
me your ID," the police officer demanded.

"Wait!" Khan shouted, having meanwhile changed his telephone
camera to begin recording video and audio. "He doesn't have to
show you anything. U.S. citizens are not required to carry ID and
show it on demand in a public area unless there is some criminal
activity, and there's none of that here."

The police officer turned to Khan and stated, "Who do you think you are? You his lawyer?" Meanwhile Otto dropped his art materials, got out his phone, and began recording.

"No, not his lawyer," Khan stated. "But I am a lawyer!"

"Oh, some ambulance chaser looking to defend illegal border crossers that he's trying to set up by finding breaks in the fence?" the police officer stated.

"That insulting comment is right here on my phone, in case you didn't notice," Khan stated. "And for your information, although it's none of your damned business, I work for the U.S. Attorney General."

"Since when do they have Chinese working for the Attorney General?" the police officer smirked. "Setting up things to bring more of your Chinese drugs in?"

Increasingly angry, Khan stated, "For your information, I'm a citizen of the U.S. born here. My grandparents are from Vietnam, if it's any of your damned business. As for what I do, I specialize in human and civil rights, including the civil right to be on public property, a public roadway, minding our own business."

The police officer turned to Otto and asked, "Where are you from? Is that your car with New Mexico plates?"

"None of your damned business," Otto answered.

"I can just run your plates and find out when I get to my car," the police officer said.

"Go right ahead," Otto said. "I have nothing to hide."

The police officer then removed his pistol from the holster and started walking towards Khan, saying, "OK, smart ass, drop that phone."

Khan moved closer to get the drawn pistol on the video and then up to get the officer's name tag. He asked, "What's your full name, Officer Ortiz?"

"I don't have to fuckin' tell you," Officer Ortiz stated. "Now drop your phone."

"So what are you going to do if I don't, shoot us?" Khan said. "You'd better kill us, or all hell will break out for you if you leave us injured without our phones. Even if we're dead, our bodies will be found and you could still be in big time trouble."

"Er," Officer Ortiz fumbled his words, "just give me your phones and I'll leave you alone."

"Like hell, Officer Ortiz," Khan said. "The phones are staying with us. Now leave us alone. You have as much right as we do to be on a public road, so stay as long as you like and watch us being law-abiding citizens."

"What are you going to do with those things you have on your phone?" Officer Ortiz asked.

"Nothing, if you leave us alone and quit harassing us," Khan said. "Otherwise I can easily call 911 and he can too, and get another officer out here. Then we can turn our phones over to your chief, maybe the New Mexico State Police, or even the FBI."

Otto started pushing buttons on his phone as though calling 911.

"Either shoot us, or leave us alone," Khan stated.

"OK," Officer Ortiz said. "I'll leave you alone this time. You'd better be careful when doing suspicious things around the border."

"We'll do just that," Khan replied. "Exercising our civil rights to be on public property minding our own business lawfully."

Officer Ortiz returned to his car, hastily turned the car around, and sped away.

"Wow, you really handled that well," Otto said. "I couldn't imagine you'd be so aggressive."

"Comes with being a lawyer," Khan said. "I learned to be aggressive when I was a public defender. I had to be. Everyone in this country has a right to a vigorous legal defense in court. Some of those accused have such weak cases that the public defender has to be very aggressive just to maybe sway one juror. Fortunately, as prosecutors, we don't have to do that so much. But we do have to know how to read people, and I could see that he was getting scared that he had gone too far."

"Are you going to turn him in with these recordings?" Otto asked.

"No, not unless something else comes of this," Khan replied. "He'd likely lose his job and he probably has a wife and kids to support. He had a wedding band. Maybe, hopefully, he'll learn how to behave next time."

"It figures, all the good-looking ones are married, even if he is an asshole," Otto said. "But wow, you really are observant if you saw a wedding band. I'm freaked out. Let's get out of here."

"Nah, go ahead and finish your drawing. Nothing more will happen."

Otto picked up his materials and continued drawing for a while, then said, "That's it for today. I suppose I should get going to get back to Alamogordo before dark. Say, I saw that Border Patrol checkpoint on the highway to Alamogordo that had been bombed. It was closed off with apparently some construction work going on to patch up the damage. But the Border Patrol is still there checking all vehicles. Maybe I should draw that too, if I wouldn't be harassed again."

As they got into his car, Otto said, "It's past lunchtime and I'm getting hungry. Suppose we ought to stop somewhere?"

"There's leftover food at home that won't take much time to heat up," Khan replied. "It'd be nice to have you hang around some more, but I don't want to keep you from getting home before too late."

"OK," Otto said.

While they were driving back to his apartment, Khan said, "You're really good at those drawings. You should hire yourself out to TV networks or stations to draw pictures of the action, like those that are shown all the time on TV when cameras are not allowed in courtrooms."

"Really?" Otto exclaimed. "You think I'm that good?"

"Yes, for sure," Khan said. "I've seen a few of them and yours are as good as any."

Otto blushed and said, "Thanks."

"When our courts are ever open again, I might see if we can call you in as an illustrator," Khan said. "But, by then, you'd likely be back to work."

"I can pretty much set my own hours," Otto said. "We can see."

Back in Khan's apartment, they ate a warmed-over lunch and returned to the bedroom for a final quickie. Before leaving, Otto said, "This was great. I sure hope we can do this again soon."

"Sure, I'm up for it," Khan said. "Anytime you want to come back to El Paso, especially during this shutdown, let me know. I don't mind going to Alamogordo, either, but maybe not in cold weather with things shut down."

They finished with warm affectionate hugs and kisses, and Otto slowly left.

CHAPTER 5

Saturday, January 19, 2019
El Paso, Texas, USA

On a lazy winter Saturday morning, Yusef was watching the national news on TV after having spent the morning reading law books. Nisrine was reading medical journals while Sara played. The weather outside was too cold for much outside activity.

The television news anchor said, "Last night protestors blocked entrances to the Inn of the Mountain Gods, an upscale resort hotel and casino on the Mescalero Apache reservation in Otero County, New Mexico, up the mountainside from Alamogordo, New Mexico. Protestors carried signs saying 'Indians go away; this is white man's land now.' Security guards called tribal police and attempted to apprehend the protesters, but they jumped into a car and sped away, driving into the nearby community of Ruidoso and becoming lost on local roads. Cameras recorded the action, but license plates on the car were not visible. About an hour later, bombs exploded, blocking the parking garage entrance and exit, not allowing cars to leave. New Mexico State Police are investigating. More details will be reported later as they are known."

Yusef exclaimed, "Look, someone just bombed the place where we went on our honeymoon!"

Nisrine came to the room dressed to go out and said, "What's going on? Bombings all over the place. What's this country coming to?"

"Chaos, and this damned government shutdown too," Yusef added. "Did you hear the government is shutting down the refugee camp for teens at Tornillo, just outside El Paso?"

"Yes," Nisrine answered. "They won't need me to go there any more to examine some of the teen girls. Hopefully they can find a good OB/GYN where they're going."

"There are other detention camps around here, not just for teens," Yusef offered.

"They're in New Mexico, and I don't have a license to practice in New Mexico."

"Oh, right. I didn't think about that."

"Maybe I should get one," Nisrine said. "It depends on how long we'll be staying here."

"Damn, I wish I knew how long," Yusef said. "El Paso's a nice place to live, but so is San Antonio. And here I'm doing two jobs. They sure don't seem to be in a hurry to get a replacement here for head of the division. It's sure not going to be me on a permanent basis. Head of a division just isn't my thing. It's much better being first deputy focusing on civil and human rights."

"Yes, I want to get back to San Antonio again and set up my practice," Nisrine said. "But the people here really do need me."

"With this shutdown, everything is up in the air, and now they're saying it might last until February," Yusef said. "I suppose I could try to call John in San Antonio and see what's going on, but he's probably not working either. I'm getting bored just sitting here reading law books and paperbacks. Maybe I need to find the local library; also see what they have for kids Sara's age."

"I've got to go," Nisrine said. "The medical school library's open on Saturday, and I'm not working unless they call me in. I need to keep learning more about pregnant women being treated when they have some other serious medical condition."

"Tell me what you learn," Yusef said. "What about lunch?"

"I'll just get something on campus," Nisrine said. "Maybe you and Sara would like to go shopping for something for dinner today and tomorrow."

He stood to kiss her goodbye and returned to the television.

The news anchor returned saying, "Breaking news: We are just now learning that letter bombs were sent to the GOP House leader to his office in Bakersfield, California, and to his Washington office. Other letter bombs are reported to have been sent to local addresses of other Republican leaders of Congress in the Washington area. Enclosed were notes saying, 'Support Congressman Kenny Buford, true American nationalist.' The notes were apparently in response to the recent vote in the House of Representatives led by Republicans to disapprove of Congressman Buford's racist comments. Envelopes were identified and carefully opened by postal inspectors who are being paid during the shutdown. Postal inspectors indicated that the envelopes were mailed from a self-service center at an unidentified post office in the Albuquerque, New Mexico, area. More details will be given as they become known.

"Meanwhile, Oregon Senator Jeff Merkley has released copies of documents that indicate that the Department of Homeland Security has been planning a policy of separating children from parents at borders and detaining them in separate detention facilities for several months. These allegations will be investigated by Senate committees. Members of the House of Representatives have indicated an intention to investigate as well. We have not been able to independently verify these reports, but if verified, they represent major, possibly criminal actions against Homeland and Human Services personnel."

What the hell! Yusef exclaimed to himself. *Lots of those separations are right here. Our office could really be busy if this damned shutdown is ever over.*

The rest of the day was spent uneventfully, with Yusef's taking Sara with him shopping and looking for public libraries, noting that several had Legos and other activities for children.

Meanwhile, Khan spent a lazy Saturday morning attempting to amuse himself. He thought, *It sure would be nice to be with Otto again. Last time he contacted me. Now it's my turn to contact him.* Khan sent a text message saying, "It sure would be nice to be with you again this weekend."

Moments later, he received a text message that said, "Would be great. Right now, I'm driving. Will call when I can."

A short while later, Khan received a phone call. After preliminary greetings, Khan said, "Oh, you're up there drawing the bomb damage. Why that?"

(pause)

"A series of pictures about bombs and disruption. Sounds interesting."

(pause)

"Yes, I can meet you there tomorrow. About what time?"

(pause)

"OK, after I eat lunch, say about 12:30. No place to eat there. And yes, stay overnight with you."

(pause)

"Looking forward also. I'll let you get to your drawing."

Khan spent the rest of the day mostly bored, browsing online and reading.

Sunday, January 20, 2019
Orogrande, New Mexico, USA

In the early afternoon, after a quick bite of lunch out of his refrigerator and coordinating times with Otto, Khan drove north from El Paso on U.S. Highway 54, a four-lane divided highway. He passed through the Border Patrol checkpoint that had recently been bombed. It was about fifty miles north of El Paso, just a few miles north of the small village of Orogrande. There he got a glimpse of Otto in the median between the two lanes. He drove to the next crossover, made a U-turn and returned southward, parking

113

on the median where he could see Otto drawing. Otto motioned him closer, gave him a quick kiss, and asked him to stand by just a few more minutes. While standing, Khan took pictures of the construction to repair the bomb damage and observed a long line of railroad cars passing on the east side of the highway.

When he was finished, Otto joined Khan, showed him the picture, and said, "Border Patrol personnel tried to make me leave, but I used your line about civil rights to be in a public place. It worked."

Khan smiled and said, "Good for you. Say, those trains passing by seemed like a main line. There were box cars from all over, including from Hamburg, Germany. That must be the main line of the railroad that goes through El Paso and next to the border fence we saw."

"I suppose so," Otto said. "Railroads play a big part in some of the places here. I'd guess that Orogrande was a railroad town at one time where they took on water or coal in the old days. Sometime when you can come back and stay longer, and the weather's better, I'll take you on a historic tour of Lincoln County. The county seat is a very small town, Carrizozo. The county seat was moved there because it was on the railroad and a big water stop. Now it's just a small artists' community. It's an interesting little town, though. Follow me to my place, or I'll just give you the address for the GPS. I want to draw you again when you get there."

Alamogordo, New Mexico, USA

Khan and Otto met outside his modest house and walked in together. Once inside, after taking off jackets, Otto said, "Welcome to my little house."

"This is your house?" Khan asked.

"Yes, I bought it about four years ago when interest rates were so low," Otto replied. "I was tired of living in apartments that I couldn't fix up the way I wanted to. As it turns out, my monthly payments are about the same as rent."

"Good for you," Khan said. "Maybe one day I can do the same, especially if it looks like I'll stay in El Paso."

"Please make yourself at home," Otto said. "I'll start the beans cooking for dinner. Maybe take your clothes off so I can draw you."

After undressing, Khan looked around the family room at drawings framed and hung on the wall. "All of these are yours," Khan exclaimed. "I recognize the style."

"Yes," Otto replied. "Once these beans are started, I'll show you the one I did yesterday."

"The one at the casino on the Indian reservation?" Khan asked. "The one where protesters had a sign about 'This is white men's land now'? Yesterday a group of high school kids from a Cincinnati suburb harassed a Native American in Washington, although news today said that a small group of black extremists were harassing the kids."

"It's still division and hate," Otto answered. "I wanted to draw that one too, but the scene wouldn't stay on television long enough. I'm tentatively calling this series 'Illustrations of Division' or 'Illustrations of Hate'; I haven't decided which yet."

"Both sound good," Khan replied.

When Otto finished his two drawings of Khan, he showed them to him, who said "Great; as good or better than the ones you gave to me."

Otto kissed Khan, led him to the master bedroom where he too undressed and they spent time in bed.

After a short time, they returned partly dressed to the family room and kitchen, where Otto prepared the rest of the dinner.

Khan commented, "So this is New Mexican food."

"Yes," Otto replied. "It's based mostly on green chiles, not red like in Tex-Mex. A lot of Mexican food in El Paso is New Mexican because it's still the same region."

"This sure is good," Khan said. "I don't eat out much, all by myself, so I haven't eaten much Mexican food in El Paso. I ate plenty in Austin, though."

After dinner and cleaning the kitchen, they sat on the couch watching television and cuddling, then going to bed.

Monday, January 21, 2019

Otto and Khan slept late, showered, and had a leisurely breakfast. Otto drove them to the New Mexico Museum of Space History and dome theater like they had planned. They were pleasantly surprised that admission was free to furloughed federal employees.

After the museum, Khan commented, "That's a fabulous museum. Thanks for taking me."

"My pleasure," Otto replied.

New Mexico Museum of Space History, Alamogordo, New Mexico

As they were driving down one of the main streets leading from the museum to the center of the city, Khan said, "That building says 'Deutsche Schule.' It looks like a modern building, not like the historic Deutsche Schule in downtown San Antonio dating from the early days of German settlement in Texas."

Deutsche Schule, Alamogordo, New Mexico

"There's a German air force base here, and they need a place to send their kids to German-speaking schools for when they are transferred back to Germany," Otto said. "They keep a low profile so not many know about it. Americans know about U.S. bases in Germany but it doesn't occur to them that the Germans might have a base in our country."

"I certainly didn't know about it," Khan replied. "Why would the Germans need an air base here?"

"It's pilot training," Otto replied. "Some people say jokingly that it's better for the student pilots to crash over the uninhabited White Sands than over the Black Forest. The German Air Force is on Holloman Air Force Base, where they have a building with a German flag and also flight facilities. I heard that the Germans are going to close their base sometime soon."

"Interesting," Khan said.

"When this damned shutdown's over, I'll take you there when we can go to the White Sands; the base is on the way," Otto added. "There's not much to see on the base, but I can show you where I work."

They went to Otto's house for a late lunch, time in the bedroom, and relaxation. Eventually, Khan said he should be going back to El Paso. They agreed they wanted to meet again soon, maybe late in the week or weekend, so long as the shutdown continued.

CHAPTER 6

Friday, January 25, 2019
México, DF, México

At lunchtime in an upscale restaurant frequented by the diplomatic community, Vladimir Mikhailov from the Russian Embassy was having lunch with Bijan Ahmadi of the Iranian Embassy and Ri Kuang-Sik of the North Korean Embassy, who "coincidentally" all happened to appear at the restaurant at about the same time.

Kuang-Sik commented in English, the common language they all spoke when together, "Now with the shutdown about to be over, I suppose our operatives will be back in action in the U.S."

Vladimir replied, "Yes, if the airports and flights stay back to normal, we can start sending people to places where there are direct flights to and from El Paso so we can get them back through the tunnel if necessary. You know we've sent persons to a couple of places they could go by road and get back to El Paso in just a few hours, but there aren't too many places we could go without drawing attention to ourselves. In a way, the shutdown played into our hands and created more chaos. It might be good if another shutdown comes back; it upsets people more when they start creating chaos on their own."

"It seems things are going well for us," Bijan said. "There's chaos all over the U.S."

"Yes," Vladimir replied. "People are beginning to protest and create chaos all on their own. You saw that group of high school boys in Washington harassing the old Native American. Also, maybe you heard, the FBI caught a group of young white guys in upstate New York who were planning to attack a small community of black Muslims who follow a Pakistani leader in a rural part of upstate New York."

"Too bad the FBI didn't catch them after the attack," Bijan said. "If they were following a Pakistani, they must be Sunni. That's just for you here at this table. My government has reasonable relations with Pakistan, a neighboring country, even if the Pakistani government has suppressed Pakistani Shia."

The remainder of their lunch involved idle conversation focusing on the evils of the U.S.

Quantico, Virginia, USA

In the early afternoon, Rosie Jordan opened a meeting at the FBI Operations Center with James Cunningham of the postal inspection operations center, Adam Culbertson, in-house explosives expert, and Brock O'Neill, in-house expert on crowds and demonstrations. "Welcome. Too bad we didn't know the shutdown would be lifted next week, at least for three weeks, when we arranged this meeting. But we're here, so we might as well begin. James, what do you have for us?"

James began, "The last set of mail bombs, the ones mailed from Albuquerque with a return address for the Taos Pueblo Native American Reservation, were just like the first set mailed from Seattle. They were the same envelopes with metric measurements and the same explosives not available in this country. Again, they were mailed in a metropolitan area where there are many post offices with self-service counters."

Adam added, "The explosives from the last set that was mailed from Seattle match the explosives that were used in those bombs that were set off in several places, including at that Border Patrol checkpoint and Native American casino in New Mexico. They were both in southern New Mexico and not far from where the letter bombs were mailed from Albuquerque. As we know, this type of explosive is not available in the U.S., but it can be obtained in lots of countries. Is it a coincidence that the mail bomb explosives and the other bomb explosives are the same?"

"We're getting the idea that maybe they're not intended to cause lots of damage, but just to explode and create confusion and chaos," James said.

"Same here," Adam agreed. "The bombs set off in New Mexico, Dallas, Austin, Atlanta, and Denver could have caused a lot more damage and killed people, but they seem to have been placed to do minimal damage and avoid people but create a lot of disruption. That's not really a terrorist *modus operandi*."

"The demonstrations we're looking at are all pretty mild," Brock said. "One of them was in far southern New Mexico, too, right on the Mexican border next to El Paso. Some of the other demonstrations like the high school kids in Washington, seem to be just to get attention, and are pretty mild. The kids' demonstration was pretty spontaneous. This has us confused too. We just intercepted a plot to attack a black Muslim community in a rural part of New York state that seems totally unconnected.

Rosie said, "Some of these events were in the Southwest, not very far from the Mexican border. Heaven knows, there's enough turmoil over border issues and Mexico is one place those explosives are available. Maybe there's a connection with Mexico. Maybe we should bring the CIA and Department of Homeland Security into our deliberations."

The others agreed. The next several minutes were spent discussing more details. They agreed to meet again when more developments were apparent and dismissed in time for James to return home before rush hour.

El Paso, Texas, USA

Khan was sitting at home reading, trying to keep from being bored, when he received a text message from Otto saying, "Looks like shutdown over. Want to Celebrate? Skype?"

Once connected on Skype, they exchanged brief greetings. Khan said, "With the shutdown gone for only three weeks, I might not be up for much celebrating, and we won't get paid until Thursday. But yeah, it'd be great to be with you again. What do you have in mind?"

Otto replied, "Nothing particular in mind. It would be nice to be with you. One possibility would be to meet in Las Cruces and go to Old Mesilla if you haven't been there. It's nice and historic. There's a nice old square."

"I've heard of Old Mesilla, but never been there. Some have said there are nice restaurants there, but I can't go for a fancy restaurant right now."

"There's a nice coffee and sandwich shop right on the corner of the square that's reasonably priced. Mostly we'd be going to the area for the ambiance."

Khan replied, "I've been reading a lot of history while I've been so idle and bored. That square is apparently where the Gadsden Purchase treaty was signed. The last territorial expansion of the U.S., unless you count Hawaii. The U.S. sort of forced Mexico to sell this little piece of ground so a railroad could be built. That must be the main line of the railroad we saw right next to the border fence."

"Yes, I sort of remember something like that from history."

"Yeah, Otto, I'd meet you there tomorrow morning. Would you like to come back to El Paso with me for dinner and stay overnight?"

"I was just going to suggest that. I'll stay with you and help buy the groceries on the way."

They continued to talk for a short while to finalize arrangements.

CHAPTER 7

Saturday, January 26, 2019
Stanton, Texas, USA

Woodrow Dawes and Leroy Russell were in a small "efficiency" apartment in an old "apart-otel," combining the features of an apartment and motel, at the edge of town on the old highway through town before Interstate Highway 20 was built around the town. The building and units were old and dilapidated, but they served the needs of low-income working-class people who needed longer accommodation than overnight. The unit had two rooms, a combined sitting and kitchen area, and a bedroom with two double beds. Woodrow was sprawled on the sofa while Leroy sat at the table drinking beer. Both had taken various types of drugs, but Woodrow was not very high yet.

Woodrow said, "We gotta get outa here. My back's killin' me. I can't take enough pills anymore to get rid of the pain. I should've known better than to take that back-breaking job in the oil fields outside of Midland."

"What'd we live on then?" Leroy asked. "At least I got a job payin' half decent, even if it is just manual labor. And we found this place to live here in Stanton; prices too high in Midland."

"Yeah, this shitty place to live," Woodrow said.

"No worse than that place you was livin' back in Okemah," Leroy said.

"I don't know how long my back'll hold out with the work they got me doin'," Woodrow continued.

"Take some days off to let it rest," Leroy replied. "I can work. You c'n always get back on when your back is better. Plenty of jobs; they need people. We gotta have somethin' to live off."

"Gotta get me some more pills," Woodrow said.

"Say, when're we goin' t' lynch some Meskins?" Leroy asked. "Plenty of 'em 'round here."

"Ain't enough trees," Woodrow said. "B'sides, with this damned back, don't think I'm up to it, 'specially in cold weather."

"Well y' know I'd do it," Leroy said. "Just tell me what to do."

"Maybe when weather's better," Woodrow said.

"Now I gotta go get me some pussy. Ain't had some in a few days and my balls is achin'."

"Yeah, I bet," Woodrow muttered.

"Why ain't you getting any pussy, Uncle Woody?" Leroy asked. "Y' ain't gay or nuthin' like that."

"Didn't y' know that ever since I hurt my back and had t' take them pills, I can't get it up any more," Woodrow replied.

"Oh, didn't know that," Leroy said. "Guess I just didn't pay attention, not livin' in the same house with you back then. I know you used to get a lot. You were known all 'round Okemah as the ladies' man."

An hour or more later, Leroy arrived back at the little apartment with a young white woman, about five seven, with unkempt mousy brown hair, slim body, dressed in jeans, a flannel shirt, and a well-worn winter jacket. She and Leroy sat at the small table drinking beer and taking a couple of different types of pills. After several minutes, Leroy stood, took the young woman by the hand and led her to the bedroom, not bothering to shut the door. He hastily pulled her shirt off her, pulled down her jeans and panties, pulled his pants off, climbed on top and pushed himself into her; she let out a gasp. After several thrusts, Leroy screamed and then pulled out, spent. He jumped off the bed and began dressing while she slowly got up and dressed herself. He went back into the other room, and she followed. He gave her some pills and motioned her to the door.

"Ain't cha goin' t' drive me back?" she asked.

"I ain't in no condition to drive, bitch, ya just have to walk," Leroy replied.

"It's too damned cold to walk that far," she replied.

"Here, take a damned cab," he said and gave her ten dollars, then shoved her out the door.

He went to the refrigerator and opened another beer, popped some more pills, and sat for a while. After a short while, he looked out the window, suddenly stiffened, then shouted loudly, "Uncle Woody, wake up! We might have to get out of here quick!"

Woodrow groggily said, "Huh? What's up?"

"That bitch must've been hitchhikin', or maybe flagged down a passin' pleess car. She's talking to 'em and getting in the car with 'em. She has pills on 'er."

"Oh, shit!" Woodrow said and passed out again.

CHAPTER 8

Monday, January 28, 2019
El Paso, Texas, USA

In the morning at home after breakfast, Yusef checked email messages on his phone. He had an email message from the office of the U.S. Attorney for the Western District of Texas in San Antonio saying that all could return to work. He called the administrative assistant for the El Paso division to ask if she could come to work that morning and asked her to inform the staff that they could return to work the next day, Tuesday, and that they could wear casual clothes, if they liked, for informal discussions. He also called Susana Tate to see if he could meet her later in the morning.

Later in the morning, when he was in the office, Yusef greeted the administrative assistant who had arrived earlier then went to Susana's office, who had also recently arrived. "It seems we have three weeks before another shutdown, so maybe we should try for orderly closing of pending items, not abruptly like before," he said.

"There must have been lots of unfinished business that just got put aside," Susana agreed.

Yusef asked, "How do you think we should go forward? I'm sure that it's not just going back to business as usual."

"Well, one thing is to contact the FBI and see what cases they might have to hand over to us. They weren't shut down."

"Who should we contact? Yusef asked. "I've met some of them, but I don't know who specifically would be best for this."

"I've dealt mostly with Carter Kuykendall," Susana answered.

"OK, I can contact him, or maybe you might be willing if you know him," Yusef replied. "I'm not trying to shove work off onto you, though. If you contact him, I'd like to meet him."

"I'll gladly contact him. Then maybe we should get a status report from each of our staff."

"Yes, I had thought about that. As you know, I called a meeting for everyone tomorrow. We can start the process of status reports. And I suppose we need to contact the courts to see when they'll be operating again and what they have on their docket."

Susana concurred. "They might not want to schedule anything that can't be handled quickly; just focus on plea bargains and the like. Our people can give input on that."

"I haven't dealt directly with the courts here," Yusef said. "You know that courtroom trial isn't my long suit. This might be a good opportunity for me to get in touch with them. With all the protests and bombings going on, including mail bombs, things must be getting really busy for the FBI, and eventually for the AG."

"Yes. Some are right here in the El Paso area. Demonstrations at the border crossing and bombing of the railroad tracks, not to mention the bombs next to Ruidoso."

"Those are all in the New Mexico District, thankfully," Yusef added. "They'll have their hands full, I'm sure. I'm surprised we haven't had more right in El Paso. I suspect we'll get something, unfortunately. We need to be prepared."

"And there's that force-feeding of detainees by ICE agents," Susana added. "Civil and human rights groups are protesting and threatening lawsuits. That would be in your area."

"I've been thinking of putting Khan as lead in asylum cases," Yusef said. "He's neither Anglo nor Hispanic and might have an advantage there. Plus, his grandparents had asylum and he's done research in the area. I wouldn't want to be perceived as advancing him too fast ahead of more senior staff."

"They just might be pleased to have responsibility taken away from them," Susana said. "Asylum cases can be messy. Maybe wait and see what cases are coming up. With the courts closed, the asylum courts might take a while to get up and running."

Yusef and Susana continued to talk for several minutes. Yusef went to his office to see what work he needed to catch up on before meeting with the staff the next day. When he went to the breakroom for coffee, he noticed some office lights on, indicating some staff had come to work today. He stopped to visit individually with each one briefly and tell them about a meeting the next day. He noticed that Khan was in his office and did likewise. Yusef said, "If by chance you brought your lunch today, we could visit more. Nothing official, but just catching up."

"Yeah, sure," Khan said.

Later, over lunch, Khan asked Yusef what he did during the shutdown. "Stayed at home with my daughter some," Yusef answered. "We went to a public library where she could play with things and begin to read children's books. Just dull things of an old married man."

Khan chuckled and Yusef continued, "Other times, reading novels. I even started reading more about Texas law. I figured since I have been here a few years, it might be useful to know what Texas law is like. You surely know more about Texas law than I do, going to law school in Texas."

"Well, yes," Khan answered. "Texas has some interesting quirks, but not too far out of the mainstream. It basically follows the English common law like most of the other states, with some Spanish law thrown in. Louisiana follows French law, as you likely know."

"Yes, we learned that in law school, but we didn't go into details. What did you do during the shutdown?"

"Just stayed at home and read a lot; brushed up on Texas and U.S. history," Khan replied. "History has always been one my favorite subjects."

"Mine too," Yusef said.

"I needed to keep what little savings I've been able to accumulate," Khan added. "I did go to Faywood Hot Springs once, and also to the New Mexico Museum of Space History in Alamogordo." He thought, *Maybe I shouldn't tell him just yet about Otto, but then he has gay friends who are in relationships and is understanding. But, no, straight guys wouldn't go out of their way to tell about new girlfriends, so no need to say anything now that Otto and I have been together for just a couple of weeks.*

"Oh? What was the museum like?" Yusef asked. "I've never been there, but I've driven through Alamogordo a couple of times when we were at the Inn of the Mountain Gods next to Ruidoso."

"The museum was fabulous," Khan replied. "I want to go back. And the Inn of the Mountain Gods; isn't that the place where there was a bomb explosion?"

"Yes, same place," Yusef confirmed. "Shame; nice place."

"If this shutdown is ever over for good, I want to go there," Khan added. "And when the weather is a little warmer."

They continued discussing history and related topics a few minutes, and then Yusef asked, "I don't know if I should bring this up, but have you heard or read that the Catholic Church authorities in Texas are requiring that all of the dioceses in Texas provide a list of all priests who have been accused of sexual abuse and make the lists public?"

"I read something about that, but I didn't feel like exploring details," Khan said. "It's still painful, but I'm getting over it."

"I just wanted to say that if you do follow through to see if the priest who abused you is on the list, then feel free to report him if he is not there already," Yusef added. "This is strictly a personal matter for you, and I certainly don't want to influence you one way or another, but I wanted to reiterate that it would not affect your job here one way or another."

"Thanks," Khan replied. "Maybe I'll look to see if he's on the list. My family might not like to know about his abusing me, but so be it."

When Khan returned to his office and looked at his phone, he saw a text message from Otto saying, "Are you working like I am? Want to celebrate with a movie this weekend? Skype tonight?"

"Sounds good," Khan wrote back. "I'm at work too. Skype tonight."

A few hours later at home, they connected on Skype. Khan explained that he was still cautious with money, but yes, they could celebrate with an evening at the movies Saturday. They agreed that Otto would come on Friday night and stay over Saturday night, spending the whole day Saturday together.

Tuesday, January 29, 2019

With the legal staff crowded into a conference room, Yusef and Susana were in front where Yusef began, "Thank you for coming and thank you for your patience during the shutdown. We're having this meeting so we can discuss things quicker than meeting individually and save long emails. Much of what we have to say is what you likely already know, but bear with us. With another shutdown possibly coming in three weeks, hopefully we can get things to a good stopping point in the cases you are working on, and not have to quit abruptly like we did before. No doubt you have a lot of catching up to do. Please be assured that we don't expect you to put in overtime to get to good stopping points. Do what you can in normal business hours. After a brutal shutdown with no pay, you deserve good working conditions.

"You know we've asked you to stop by my or Susana's office to give a brief summary of what you are working on. Nothing elaborate, just a brief idea. We've already reached out to the FBI to ask for cases that they might want to turn over to us in the near future. Some of you have been working with the FBI and might be able to tell us too. Also, we've reached out to the courts to find out what might be on their dockets in the next couple of weeks, now that the courts are up and running again. Again, some of you have direct contacts with the courts and can let us know. Feel free to come see Susana or me anytime today."

Yusef them went around the room to ask for comments or questions. After limited discussions, they dismissed. Yusef went back to work and enjoyed a lunch over idle chatter with Khan and others who brought lunch.

CHAPTER 9

Friday, February 1, 2019
Mexico, DF, México

In the mid-morning, Ivan Petrov came to the office of Vladimir Mikhailov at the Russian Embassy. "Welcome back, Ivan Aleksandrovich," Vladimir said, speaking Russian. "Good to have you back for a weekend, even if it's not a holiday this time. How are things in Juárez? Staying warm?"

Ivan chuckled and said, all conversation between the two in Russian, "A little warmer these days, but still winter. Fortunately, no more snow. You want to see me?"

"When we have lunch, we can just "bump into" Bijan Ahmadi and Ri Kuang-Sik and catch up on what's going on with activities up there through the tunnel," Vladimir Mikhailov said. "Plus, I really want to thank you for your work to get Konstantin Leonidov through the tunnel and on to Chihuahua City to get a flight here. We got him on a flight to Moscow without drawing too much attention. The Americans might have caught on by now, but so far, we haven't heard anything publicly about his disappearance. We went to some lengths to mislead them. We put his ankle bracelet on an employee at his house, a Russian operative of course, who had to wear it for several days so it seemed like Konstantin was still there. We smuggled him out in a laundry truck and then took him to the Atlanta airport, where he got a flight to El Paso. As you know, our operatives met him at the El Paso airport and took him to the tunnel, where your people got him at the other end. We don't know what happened from there, but he got here and safely onto Moscow on Aeroflot flights without too many questions being asked."

"He was a pain in the ass to deal with," Ivan added. "He resented being made to crawl through the tunnel and being hidden under cargo in a truck through the 20-kilometer checkpoint on the way to Chihuahua City. He seemed to think that because of his important position, that he shouldn't have to deal with such indignities."

"Yes, he was like that here," Vladimir said. "He threatened to report us directly to Putin. We said go right ahead. We did him a huge service getting his ass out of there and to safety. Typical of those oligarchs who think they are so special just because they are close to Putin. We're not worried about what Putin finds out. The ambassador sent word ahead what kind of an asshole he is.

"Now we have to worry about getting his wife out of there before the Americans get hold of her and she starts telling them things we don't want them to know. You know that husband and wife now hate each other, and she would probably do almost anything to get revenge on him. I think I told you that you might be involved in that one, too. Maybe we can trick her into coming voluntarily. If she can't be tricked, then we might have to do some drastic things like forcing her to fly on a charter flight with one of our staff to a private airport near El Paso. Online, we found a private airport in Santa Teresa, New Mexico, close to the tunnel. Maybe you can possibly find out more about it.

"But that's where the problems begin. How can we force her through the tunnel involuntarily? Then how can you get her to Chihuahua City involuntarily? Not to mention, forcing her onto a flight to Moscow on Aeroflot that has an intermediate stop in Madrid where she could get off. Those are not your problems; we have to come up with solutions, but you might be involved."

"Surely there's some way to get leverage over her and make her go voluntarily," Ivan offered.

"We might try to work with her family and use them to get her to cooperate," Vladimir said. "That's up to the people in Moscow. We just do what we are ordered to do. And, by the way, the Iranians and North Koreans don't need to know anything about this, so nothing at lunch today."

"OK," Ivan said.

"One more thing," Vladimir added. "There was a demonstration in El Paso a day or two ago when young men marched in front of the food stamp office with signs and chanting 'Mexicans go home' and 'No benefits for immigrants.' Media speculated they were soldiers from Fort Bliss because of their hair styles and appearance, although some of them wore those 'Make America Great Again' hats that cover their heads. They were also shouting 'USA.' There has been no further news. Do you know anything?"

"We've picked up some things from monitoring Fort Bliss," Ivan replied. "The commander wants to keep it quiet. He's trying to find out who it might be. He has put out word through the units that any soldiers caught will be subject to court martial. He's checking with the legal staff about issues with soldiers' First Amendment rights versus prohibitions against their being involved in partisan political situations."

"This fits right into what we are trying to do, create enough chaos so that people will demonstrate on their own and eventually bring the country into chaos and collapse," Vladimir said.

"I'll keep you informed."

"We may not want to bring this up with the others at lunch, either, unless someone asks. It has gotten only a brief mention on the news," Vladimir stated. "Let's go to lunch."

A short while later in one of their usual restaurants—they varied restaurants in the diplomatic district from time to time so as not to draw too much attention to their meetings—Vladimir and Ivan were looking at menus when Ri Kuang-Sik and Bijan Ahmadi, each separately, joined them. After ordering and while eating, they conversed in English. "It looks like you're getting active again," Kuang-Sik commented, addressing Vladimir.

"With the shutdown ended and airports operating fairly well, we sprang into action," Vladimir replied. "Thanks to you, Bijan, we're able to use a couple of your people to go to different locations at the same time."

"You're welcome," Bijan replied. "The sooner we can get the U.S. to collapse, the better. But some of the incidents were not in places where there are flights and not close to El Paso, like some remote places; in Arkansas, I think."

"Yes, local people are doing things on their own, just like we expected they would," Vladimir stated. "After a while, there will be so many local demonstrations and bombings that we will have accomplished what we wanted."

"But aren't the authorities getting suspicious?" Kuang-Sik asked. "After a while they might connect the dots, so to speak."

"So far, we haven't heard of anything," Vladimir said. "We have our sources who let us know what's going on."

"But it can't go on indefinitely," Bijan offered.

"Yes, we know," Vladimir replied. "But we're not there yet."

"Are we going to fill in the tunnel?" Kuang-Sik asked. "Maybe we can find some other good uses for it, especially now that the Americans are trying to get cozy with North Korea."

"That's an interesting question for the future," Vladimir said. "Decisions like that will surely have to be made in Moscow and Pyongyang, not in Mexico City."

"Maybe our friends in Beijing could find some good uses too," Kuang-Sik offered.

"Let's not get carried away, now," Vladimir said, chuckling.

Lunch finished with mostly small talk and other diplomatic issues involving the group.

CHAPTER 10

In the afternoon, Rosie Jordan opened a meeting with Adam Culbertson and Brock O'Neill and other lower-ranking staff. "Lots has been going on, so let's start with you, Adam. You can speak up too, Brock, because the things you monitor overlap."

Adam began, "Let's review briefly the events we talked about before. There was the bombing of the mainline railroad tracks in New Mexico just at the edge of El Paso. Then the bombing of the Border Patrol check point north of El Paso in New Mexico, near a little village of Orogrande. The motives are unclear, especially for the railroad tracks."

"And a demonstration at the Border Patrol port of entry at Santa Teresa, New Mexico," Brock interjected. "No bomb, though. This one was telling Mexicans to go back to Mexico."

Adam continued, "I'm not sure I have the right order, but there were mail bombs from Seattle about a congressman. Then demonstrations at a congresswoman's office and a bomb in the Los Angeles area. Bombs at churches in Dallas and Atlanta, the first claiming to be anti-gay and the second anti-black. Also bombs at NRA state offices in the Denver area and in Austin that were anti-gun. Maybe we need to get a map to plot all of these and add the latest ones."

"Grace, maybe you can get going on a map for next time," Rosie said to one of the staff members there.

"There was the demonstration against a Native American in Washington by high school students from a Cincinnati suburb in Kentucky," Brock interjected again, "but that seems to be spontaneous and unrelated to the others."

Adam continued, "Things were quiet for a short time when the shutdown began, but then there was a bomb at a casino in New Mexico about 120 miles north of El Paso, and signs saying that this was white men's land. Then there were letter bombs from Albuquerque about a congressman. The interesting thing about all of the bombing incidents is that the explosives were all the same and not available in the U.S. Also, as we mentioned, the envelopes were not from the U.S. There must be a connection, although the stated motives are sometimes completely opposite. Not only that, the bombings seemed designed to get attention and do a little damage, but not take any lives. It all gets even more weird in the latest ones that I can tell you about. Maybe we should pause for a minute and I can take questions if we need to review anything, before I begin telling about these latest ones."

"Quick coffee break," Rosie said.

When they returned, Adam continued, "Again, these might not be in order. The most spectacular event was during the Superbowl in Atlanta. Two persons protested with signs saying things to the effect that football kills and maims young boys and should be banned. Somehow, they managed to get past security and left a bomb to go off later next to a ticket booth. Again, little damage, bombs seemingly designed to make a statement and using the same explosive material.

"Then there were almost simultaneous bombs set off, one in Oakland at a gay-lesbian center in the stairway leading to the center, which is on the second floor, and statements that gays are sinners destroying the country. The second was at a church in Houston that had received media attention for conducting gay conversion therapy with a sign saying words to the effect of 'Burn in hell for destroying gay lives.' The contradiction is very suspicious. The bomb materials are the same and not from the U.S. It's like they are trying to be confusing by taking opposite sides and just create confusion and chaos.

"There was a bomb set off at the MGM Hotel in Las Vegas—you remember, the site of the mass shooting—with a sign saying words to the effect of 'This is what you get for harboring mass murderers.' Again, no one dead, and not a lot of damage. Same explosives as the others.

"You have likely heard of the demonstration at Disney World in Orlando with signs saying 'Turn around and don't spend money on such decadence.' Apparently, a bomb was left at one of the entry booths that went off later; again, not a lot of damage, no deaths, and the same type of explosive.

"About the same time there was a bomb at the Bureau of Indian Affairs building in Phoenix with a sign saying words to the effect of 'White man go home and leave us alone.' This contradicts the bomb at the casino in New Mexico saying 'This is white men's land.' Also, in San Antonio there were protest signs around the Alamo saying words like 'Remember the Alamo' and 'Mexicans go back home.' Another bomb was set to detonate later. In both cases, the same type of explosive material not available in the U.S. was used.

"The two most perplexing cases are seemingly unrelated crude bombings in Berryville, Arkansas, and Corinth, Mississippi, on different days. In Arkansas, dynamite bombs were set off at a Spanish-speaking Baptist church with signs saying words to the effect of 'Mexicans go home' and 'Quit taking our jobs.' In Mississippi, it was at a Mexican restaurant on the main highway. Signs said 'Mexicans go home and take your foul food with you.' In both cases, local authorities said it was most likely local men from out in the countryside who live on the fringe of society, who are largely unemployable but believe Mexicans are taking jobs and opportunities away from them. Not only do the two seem unrelated, the explosives were basic dynamite that can be bought anywhere in the U.S., not like the others, and not like each other.

"That's all I have for now, but we are waiting for the next shoe to drop," Adam said.

Brock added, "There was a very recent demonstration in downtown El Paso where a group of young men marched, many wearing 'Make American Great Again' caps, in front of the office where people line up to get food stamps. They carried placards saying 'Mexicans go home,' and 'No taxpayer benefits for immigrants.' The demonstration was broken up by local police. There's media speculation that it was a group of soldiers at Fort Bliss, one of the nation's biggest military posts right in the city of El Paso. Local police pointedly did not turn the investigation over to us and seem to want to keep things quiet. All of this would be consistent with the demonstrators' being soldiers. So far we can't find out any more."

"If it becomes an issue, maybe we can get DIA involved," Rosie offered. "But for now, maybe let it ride. Anything else?"

One of the staff spoke, saying, "During the break we found a map and marked the locations. It's not very good, but for now we can see the locations where bombings and demonstrations took place. Except for the places in Arkansas and Mississippi and the casino in New Mexico, all are next to major airports."

"Thanks," Rosie said. "Grace, what can we make of this?"

She began, "Activity started again after the shutdown ended and airports began operating normally. There might be some pattern to this particular group of airports. I would guess there would be direct flights between all of them. Maybe we can narrow the nexus of activity to one of them."

"El Paso seems the closest airport to the largest number of the incidents, so maybe we should focus on the El Paso airport," another staff person added. "But, then, El Paso is in the news with President Trump speaking there on Monday. I don't want to jump to conclusions."

"Good point, Caleb," Rosie said. "Maybe we need to spend some time analyzing flight patterns and times and see if we can come up with something. Why don't you and Grace start looking into things and come back for another meeting as soon as you come up with something. Anything else? If not, let's get back to work and meet again soon."

CHAPTER 11

Thursday, February 7, 2019
El Paso, Texas, USA

In the middle of the morning after clearing away emails and other items waiting for him, Yusef went to Susana Tate's office, asking, "Do you have a minute?"

When she invited him in, he began, "You sure were right about anti-Hispanic sentiment emerging here in El Paso. You no doubt have heard about the protest at the food stamp place."

"Yes," she replied. "Let's just hope it doesn't spawn more."

"So far, no one has been arrested, so maybe we won't need to get involved in prosecution. It certainly seems like it would be a federal hate crime if something does come of it."

Susana replied, "Media speculation is that it's soldiers from Fort Bliss. When soldiers have been involved before in small things, the military takes care of it and does not want the FBI or us involved. I don't know if that's the case in this situation, but that's what past experience indicates. The media here tread pretty lightly when military from Fort Bliss are involved because Fort Bliss is such an important part of the community, economically and otherwise. If it turns out that non-military were in the crowd, we might see something."

"Maybe it was that way in San Antonio, too, with so many military there," Yusef said, "or at least I wasn't aware of any events involving military in human and civil rights issues."

"Yes," she agreed, "the military tends to take care of its own unless it's something really egregious. I suppose it is best that way. We surely have enough on our hands without military issues in federal courts."

"On another matter," Yusef said, "You've heard of the caravan just across the border from Eagle Pass. That's in the Del Rio division and doesn't involve us here in El Paso directly, but in my other role as deputy AG for the district, I might be called on if Del Rio faces something it would refer up to district."

"Yes, I heard of it, but I didn't pay much attention," she replied. "We've had very little interaction with Del Rio in my time here. A very few times, the Alpine division has been in touch with us because their division comes right up to the El Paso county line and things can spill over; especially with the El Paso suburbs spilling over into their area."

"I could probably send someone from San Antonio to Del Rio if need be," Yusef continued. "I talked to the Del Rio division on the phone and they just might need some help if there are human rights allegations with the caravan people. It seems that most of them want asylum. There are not enough asylum judges yet, so it might not be an immediate issue. Anyway, the thought occurred to me that we could possibly offer someone from El Paso to help because we're familiar with border issues and San Antonio is not. What do you think?"

"You seem to be developing a good rapport with Khan, and he's developing in the human and civil rights area," she offered. "Besides, as you just said, there won't be any asylum cases any time soon." *He was professional enough to ask my opinion*, she thought, *but I'm sure Khan is who he had in mind all along. I can readily go along with him on this issue.*

"Yes, good idea," Yusef replied. "Plus, he's single and wouldn't have family issues to worry about, although we're not supposed to take those factors into account." *Good, she made the suggestion herself. Now I don't have to.* "I'll check with him later today."

They continued to discuss other issues, including the upcoming rallies of President Trump and Beto O'Rourke in El Paso. Susana commented, "The two Republican senators from Texas and other state officials will likely be right here with the president this time. They don't give El Paso the time of day, otherwise. They don't seem to think we're in Texas and that we vote."

"Yeah, it seems that way the little time I've been here."

"I don't want to single out the Republicans, either," Susana continued. "Democrats have ignored us also, that is, until Beto came along."

"I stay out of politics as much as I can," Yusef replied, "but of course I pay attention to who I want to vote for. Beto certainly made a stir all over Texas, it seems."

Yusef returned to his office to continue working on pending issues. At lunch time, he invited Khan to join him. After eating over small talk, Yusef said there would likely not be much asylum activity for Khan to be involved with, but that he might possibly be sent to the Del Rio division in case something were to develop in the area of human and civil rights because of the migrant caravan at the border. "It's far from certain," Yusef explained, "and likely not on short notice. This is just an advance notice in case you get involved in something really long and complicated and can't break away readily."

"Thanks, I appreciate it," Khan replied. *And here things have been going well together with Otto every weekend. Wait, there are great places to visit in the Big Bend area. I stopped there when I drove here from Austin. Maybe Otto and I could spend time there together on the way to Del Rio if I go.*

As if by psychic means, Khan found a text message from Otto saying, "Monday I want to go to the Trump and Beto rallies to draw. Skype tonight?"

Khan answered, "Yes."

Later that evening on Skype Otto explained, "Maybe I'll work part of the day Saturday so I can take Monday off, maybe part of Tuesday too. You know I can set my own hours, mostly. It'd be great to be with you."

"Yeah," I'd like that," Khan replied.

"Here I am inviting myself to your place; hope you don't mind," Otto added. "Hopefully you'll be able to spend time in Alamogordo when it's warmer and there are things to do here."

"No problem," Khan said. "What do you have in mind?"

Maybe I'd come Saturday evening; it depends on how long I want to work. We could spend all day Sunday together; maybe we can go to the art museum if you haven't been. There are good things to draw there. I can find things to do on Monday if you have to work. Then the two rallies on Monday night. Come with me to the rallies if you can. They'll be over late, so maybe it's best to stay Monday night with you and back to Alamogordo on Tuesday morning."

"Sounds like a plan," Khan replied. "I'm not sure if I could take off work on Monday; for sure I'd have to tell someone. On Saturday, I can cook up some food so we don't have to go out unless we really want to. Even with the shutdown over, at least for another week, I still need to watch pennies."

"Great, we can keep in touch to work out more details."

"And, yeah, the art museum," Khan said. "I haven't been there yet."

"El Paso has a great art museum," Otto said. "I like to go there and just draw. Always nice to have good company."

Khan explained briefly what Yusef had said about going to Del Rio and that maybe they could go to the Big Bend area. "I'll tell you more over the weekend."

They exchanged goodbyes affectionately and returned to their usual night time activities.

Tuesday, February 12, 2019
El Paso, Texas, USA

In the mid-morning, Khan and Otto were saying goodbye affectionately after sleeping a little late following the two rallies the previous night. Khan had told his office he would arrive late.

"You really should try to sell your drawings to some media outlets," Khan commented. "Maybe there are some who don't have the resources to have sent a live crew down here."

"I wouldn't even know where to start looking to sell them," Otto replied. "I just enjoy what I'm doing."

"Or put them on display at the art museum," Khan added.

Otto chuckled, and said, "Maybe. Now I have to go. Thanks for a great weekend, as usual."

"And thanks to you for showing me the art museum," Khan replied.

With one last passionate kiss, they said goodbye, Otto left, and Khan began to dress to go to the office.

CHAPTER 12

Saturday, February 16, 2019
El Paso, Texas, USA

Woodrow Dawes and Leroy Russell woke up late in the morning in a shabby two-room mobile home they had rented in a mobile home park on the far east side of El Paso along Montana Avenue, U.S. Highway 62, the Carlsbad Highway. Both were hung over from the previous night of beer and drugs. Leroy stumbled to the bathroom.

When he returned, he cursed, "Damn fuckin' whore bitch gave me the clap. Now I gotta go find some doctor or public health place to give me a shot. Back home, I'd just drive down the road to Wewoka where the quack doctor gave shots when needed. Damn, in a big city like this, who knows where to go? Guess I'll have to take off work on Monday and see."

"It's such a shitty job in construction, maybe just quit," Woodrow said. "Maybe you'll learn one day to use rubbers."

"No way," Leroy replied. "Takes away all the feeling. 'Sides, we don't have money for shit much less buy rubbers. Can't even pay the rent and pay for the pills. Wonder if they'd give me a shot free for the clap."

"They'll likely kick us out of this trailer, so maybe just go back to Oklahoma," Woodrow said. "B'sides pills here are too damned expensive."

"With what to pay for gas?" Leroy said. "We came here to lynch Meskins. Maybe lynch this bitch for infectin' me."

"Ain't no trees here to lynch someone on," Woodrow said.

"Just tie her up and dump her in the desert," Leroy stated. "Same thing. Where'd you put that rope we had ready?"

"'Round here somewhere," Woodrow replied.

"You hunt for it while I go find her," LeRoy said. "Need some breakfast first if we do some serious work lynchin'."

After about an hour, Leroy returned with a young woman who he brought into the trailer. There he and Woodrow bound and gagged her and put a noose around her neck. They carried her in the back of their battered old pickup truck some thirty miles east of El Paso on highway 62, well into the desert.

Cornudas, Texas

Leroy was driving east along U.S. Highway 62 at 80 miles per hour when he put on the brakes and came to a screeching halt. Woodrow, who had been drowsing, shouted, "What the hell?"

"There's a tree," Leroy stated. "Over there on the other side of the road." He hastily made a U-turn and parked under a tree limb. "Let's get her out and string her up."

Woodrow strained to help Leroy tie the rope around the woman's neck and then around a limb of the tree. Then they drove quickly away back towards El Paso, leaving the woman dangling from the tree, noose around her neck.

Within a few minutes, a newer pickup with accelerating speed drove by the tree. The driver saw the woman hanging from the tree limb, screeched to a halt, and backed up. He hastily got out of his vehicle, grabbed the body and pushed it upwards, loosening the stranglehold. He awkwardly used his cell phone to call 911, described the circumstances, and was told that assistance was on the way.

147

After several minutes, a deputy sheriff of Hudspeth County arrived and immediately went to the scene. The man holding the dangling body said, "Please take over and hold her for a little while. My arms are about to give out. I don't want a sudden jolt to kill her. She seems to be unconscious but alive."

The deputy, wearing a name tag that read 'Hodges,' started holding the legs, asking what was going on. "I was driving towards El Paso, accelerating after having slowed down through the little village of Cornudas back there. I saw her and knew I needed to do something. When it seemed she was still alive, I just grabbed her legs and held her up and called 911."

"Very good of you," Deputy Hodges replied as he held the dangling woman. "I'll need to contact the sheriff's office and emergency services, but first we need to get her stabilized. Maybe I should drive my patrol car underneath so she can stand on that and take off some of the pressure."

"The roof of my pickup is taller. Let me drive underneath while you hold her," the passing motorist said.

After some careful maneuvers, the woman's body was standing bent over on top of the pickup truck roof. Deputy Hodges went to his car to radio the sheriff's office, then returned saying, "Emergency services are on their way. The ambulance has to come from Dell City so it might take a while. I also asked for them to get something from the fire department to cut the rope. What more can you tell me?"

The driver of the pickup truck introduced himself, produced identification, and replied, "Not much. I've told you as much as I know. I just saw what seemed to be a live body hanging, so I wanted to do what I could."

"Really good of you," the deputy answered, and introduced himself as Jay Hodges. "It looks like some signs are hanging from her neck too. Any idea what they say?"

"No, I couldn't read anything from the angle where I was standing," the pickup driver replied.

"Are you in a hurry to get anywhere?" the deputy asked. "We're using your truck, but maybe we could maneuver the patrol car into place if you need to go. I have your details if we need to contact you."

"I need to get into El Paso before too late, but no extreme urgency," the driver said. "I'm a little bit curious about how she is and what'll become of the situation."

The passing motorist waited several minutes until emergency crews arrived, cut the rope, and removed the woman who was confirmed as alive but unconscious. He then drove on to El Paso.

Signs saying "No Meskins here" and "Full of the clap" were seen hanging on the woman. The ambulance rushed her to the Texas Tech University Medical Center emergency room in El Paso with the deputy following. He contacted the Hudspeth County sheriff's office in the county seat of Sierra Blanca and was told to remain in the hospital until some initial assessment of the woman's condition was made.

After a couple of hours, the deputy was told by an emergency room physician that the woman was alive and comatose, in critical but stable condition. "She could come out of the coma in a few hours or a few days," the physician said. "But some persons have remained in this condition for months, if not years." When this information was relayed back to the sheriff's office, the deputy was told to return to his regular territory in the northern part of Hudspeth County. The local sheriff had a cooperation agreement with the El Paso County sheriff and the El Paso Police department to monitor the woman's condition and report as soon as she became conscious, and possibly take any statements.

BOOK 3

FOLLOW
THROUGH

CHAPTER 1

Monday, February 18, 2019
Quantico, Virginia, USA

In the mid-morning, Rosie Jordan opened yet another meeting with Adam Culbertson, Brock O'Neill, and lower-level staff members, "It seems we have lots to cover, so let's get started. Adam."

Adam began pointing to a large map on a screen. "Here's a map we constructed with the help of Caleb and Grace. These are the points where incidents have occurred, all but two close to major airports, including two that have happened over the weekend; I'll get to those shortly. As before, we considered the bombings in Arkansas and Mississippi to be random events, maybe inspired by the others, but otherwise with no common characteristics to the others. As you can see, there are direct flights among all of them. What's interesting is to consider the pattern of direct flights to and from El Paso. This, combined with the evidence of the bomb-making materials' not being available in the U.S., but available in Mexico, is drawing more and more attention to El Paso as being the nexus of these bombings and letter bombs. I feel obliged to comment, though, that with all the media attention being drawn to El Paso, we have to be cautious. Still, Grace was able to compare the times of the actual bombings with direct departing flights to El Paso. There's a match; the direct flights from the various cities to El Paso were within three to four hours of the events, giving ample, but not excessive time for perpetrators to get from the sites to the airport for flights back to El Paso.

"As mentioned, there have been two more incidents over the weekend. Both were about the same time, so it seems that more than one person or group was involved. On Saturday, in Fort Worth, a bomb was placed just outside a synagogue with a note that says 'Jews will not replace us.' It detonated when there were no activities inside the building, again seemingly designed to draw attention, but not harm persons. The perpetrators could readily go to the Dallas-Fort Worth airport where there are a few direct flights to El Paso.

"About the same time, two persons, bundled for the cold, approached a police station on the south side of Chicago with signs reading 'Cops kill blacks.' A bomb was left surreptitiously outside to detonate later, again designed to draw attention, but not do serious harm. An interesting aspect is that surveillance videos showed that the men might have been covered in blackface. In both cases, the explosives were the same as in all others, not available in the U.S., but available in Mexico. Also, in both cases, the timing was convenient for the persons to take direct flights back to El Paso.

"Let me stop here for a moment to see if there are other comments or questions."

Rosie asked, "What do you make of the blackface, Adam? Why is it important to note this?"

Adam replied, "The forensic people are examining face pictures caught on surveillance camera. They were not very good. Some possible reasons are that they wanted to disguise their faces enough so if caught on surveillance camera they would not be readily recognized. Or maybe they wanted to pretend to be black to add to the pretense of avenging killings of blacks; or possibly play into people's outrage over condescending blackface used by non-blacks. The forensic people tentatively think they are not the faces of black men, but not necessarily Caucasian. They'll get back to us."

Rosie said, "Thanks, Adam. Do you or others have any notions about how the explosives could come into the U.S.? If the nexus is in El Paso, I would think it could be fairly easy."

Adam answered, "There are four ports of entry in the El Paso area. Hiding small amounts of explosives in cars or trucks crossing could be relatively easy, not to mention on trains or buses. We're not sure to what extent Border Patrol personnel have the capability to search for explosives."

"It seems we need to bring Customs and Border Patrol people into this discussion," Rosie said. "I'll get onto that for our next meeting. We should bring in the El Paso field office, too."

"Maybe also the New Mexico field office in Las Cruces," Brock added. "Some of the events were in New Mexico, even if in the El Paso suburbs."

Rosie concurred, "Good idea. Who would be wanting to create this kind of chaos in our country? There's no indication that Mexico is attempting to disrupt things in the U.S.; Mexico has too much at stake in our stability. Yet, if the persons and explosives are coming from Mexico, that opens up a whole new dimension."

Brock said, "Russians have obviously tried to affect our elections and disrupt our democracy. I wouldn't put it past them to try something like this."

"That's an interesting possibility," said Rosie. "But why would Russians want to infiltrate from Mexico? We definitely need to bring headquarters into this. Maybe the CIA and possibly the DIA as well. Does anyone have anything else to add?"

When no one spoke up, Rosie said, "Let's all get back to work. I certainly have things to do, getting in touch with these various places."

CHAPTER 2

Thursday, February 21, 2019
Quantico, Virginia, USA

In the mid-morning, Rosie Jordan opened up yet another meeting with Adam Culbertson, Brock O'Neill, and lower-level staff members from the operations center. He introduced Jared Cramer, a higher-level agent from FBI headquarters in Washington who specialized in international issues; Eric James, a senior operative from the CIA; and Andrew Branson with the Border Patrol headquarters in the Washington area. On screen, a secure Skype connection had been made with Carmen Cisneros, a senior agent in the El Paso FBI field office, whose responsibilities included liaison with other FBI units.

After introductions, Rosie began. "Adam and Brock, why don't you begin with a summary of what we have discussed so far. All have been briefed individually, but it could be good to make sure we all have the same background."

After fairly long briefings with maps and other information, Adam added, "As you surely know, there have been two more recent incidents. One is a brief demonstration and bomb left to detonate later at the Asia-Pacific Cultural Center in Tacoma, Washington, with signs that said 'America for Whites' and 'Orientals go home.' Then in Phoenix, there was a demonstration in front of an abortion clinic with signs of 'Baby killers,' and a bomb set to denotate later.

Both cases had the explosives that could have come from Mexico and allowed convenient return flights to El Paso."

Brock added, "There have been several demonstrations all over the country; none seem to be directly related to these events, but the overall mood to demonstrate may have been inspired by the chaos. I hasten to add, though, that in the current political environment, there is ample cause for demonstrations without these events."

Carmen Cisneros said, "When we first heard from you, we went into action and verified those flights. We need to get access to flight manifests to see if there are names that might suggest someone or someones of interest, especially if the same names pop up a few times. For that we need court orders. We've started the process. Some of the airlines, like Frontier, have just a token presence in El Paso. With the majors, we have good relationships. You there in the operations center could also help with the court orders when we need to contact the airline headquarters."

Andrew spoke up. "It's certainly possible that the explosives could have been brought across border points of entry inside private cars or trucks, hidden under vegetables in a truck, or even in a train or bus. We can't catch everything at the border. But there would be some risk for them to use this way to get explosives in. On a random basis, we do pick vehicles for thorough checks. There's always a chance they would be caught, but not necessarily traced to these perpetrators."

"Maybe they're using some other means of getting things across the border," Eric offered. "We see news reports all the time of tunnels under the border."

"That's always possible," Andrew replied. "But we have helicopters patrolling the border in the El Paso area 24/7, with infrared at night. There hasn't been any sign of large numbers of people surfacing, nor any drug activity."

"If this is just a very few people, you might not detect much activity," Eric commented.

"That's a possibility," Andrew replied. "We can certainly explore more. But so far, the activity seems to be limited to explosives and possibly a few people. Who in Mexico would want to infiltrate the U.S. to do that kind of disruption?"

Jared said, "You mentioned the possibility of Russians. We keep a close watch on Russians in this country. After the Russians were caught with interfering in our elections, I can't imagine they would run such an operation from somewhere in the U.S. If they did, why El Paso, when there are so many other places?"

Eric said, "Maybe the Russians are running the operation from Mexico. They have an operative in Ciudad Juárez, immediately across the border from El Paso. He's sort of an unofficial consul named Ivan Petrov whose role is to spy on us at Fort Bliss, the White Sands Missile range, and Holloman Air Force Base, all in or near El Paso. The Russians know we know he's there. We spy on them also at places like Kaliningrad. This is modern spy craft. Maybe he's involved in getting people and explosives into the U.S. The Mexican government knows he's there and knows we watch him. We don't watch every move, like when he goes shopping. I personally don't monitor him, but I can make some inquiries and report back."

Jared added, "Now that this possibility has come up, that might explain what happened to one of the persons we had under indictment out on bond, a Russian oligarch. He managed to slip away, and we couldn't trace him. He showed up later in Russia. Maybe he got a flight to El Paso and slipped into Mexico, and from there, onto a flight to Russia. Maybe we can check flight manifests from these places. Maybe we need to coordinate with the Mexican federal authorities. They do cooperate with us from time to time."

Andrew added, "The Mexican federal police were present and helped with the caravan that arrived at the border at Piedras Negras, directly across from Eagle Pass, Texas. We didn't have direct contact with them, but they showed they were willing to help keep the people from crossing the river illegally. Maybe we need to reach out to them some more."

Carmen Cisneros added, "If we're seriously going to look at a tunnel as a possibility, we need to bring the New Mexico field office into this. We work with them a lot because their territory includes the El Paso suburbs. If indeed there's a tunnel, it would have to be into the New Mexico suburbs. Within our territory of El Paso County, there is only a river border; and a tunnel under a river, while not impossible, can be very tricky. Plus, it would have to run from highly urbanized Juárez into equally highly urbanized El Paso. It's difficult to hide construction and get rid of dirt."

"It seems we have a lot of work laid out for us," Rosie said in closing. "We will be having more meetings when we have more information, most likely soon. If any of you want to stay for lunch, I would be pleased to have you join me in my private dining room."

CHAPTER 3

Thursday, February 21, 2019
El Paso, Texas, USA

An intensive care nurse in the Texas Tech University Medical Center noticed the patient who had been brought to the emergency room the past Saturday was beginning to stir. The patient was connected to IV tubes, which limited her movement. Following instructions, the nurse immediately contacted the El Paso Police Department, saying that the person they were interested in might have begun to come out of a coma. Meanwhile, the nurse sought to comfort the patient and speak gently to establish how lucid she was.

"Where am I?" the young woman mumbled.

"Don't strain yourself to talk, hon," the nurse said. "Take it slow and easy. You're in the University Medical Center ICU."

"Oh, what for?" the patient asked.

"You were brought here Saturday afternoon to the emergency room passed out and remained in a coma until now," the nurse explained. "Now don't strain yourself, but we'd like some basic information from you. Also, police want to get some information from you, but anything can wait until you're better. Just tell us what you can. Can you give us your name?"

"Sheila Gomez," the patient mumbled.

"Is there someone you'd like us to notify that you're here?" the nurse asked. "You didn't have any identification on you."

"Uh, maybe my mother," the patient answered. "But she don't care much what happens to me."

"Let me get something to write with," the nurse said. "I'm sure the police will want to know."

When the nurse returned, she said, "The policeman is here. Let me get the name of a contact person and then I'll show him in. I'll be just outside if you need me. Again, don't strain yourself. Just push the call button if you don't feel like talking anymore."

Officer Dwayne Perez of the El Paso police department came into the room, introduced himself, and began, "The nurse gave your name, Sheila Gomez. Is that correct?"

She nodded, and the officer continued, "You were brought here by emergency services from Hudspeth County. This is their case, and a deputy sheriff from there will be here soon. We're just handling things for them until he arrives. Are you from Hudspeth County?"

"Hudspeth County? Where's that?"

"It's the next county east of El Paso," The officer answered. "You must not be from there. Where are you from?"

"I live in El Paso," she replied.

"The deputy will want to know why you were in Hudspeth County," the officer said. "Can you say something about that now?"

"Don't remember."

"What do you remember?"

The patient was clearly straining to remember and said, "A guy I was with before found me and wanted to take me to his place again to do some things and give me stuff."

"What stuff?" the policeman said.

"Stuff, you know," she said.

"OK, drugs. Do you mean in exchange for sex?" the officer asked.

"No, not in exchange for sex," she said. "Just gave me some things." Then hesitating, she added, "Do you mean, did we fuck? Yeah, the first time, not this time. It was just for fun and not in exchange for somethin'."

161

"What do you remember about this last time you met?" the deputy asked.

"I sort of remember that when we got inside the trailer, he grabbed me and then an old man started tying me up with somethin'," she said. "I must've passed out then."

"Can you describe him, and maybe his vehicle?" the officer asked. "The deputy from Hudspeth County will want to know if you could identify him from a picture or in person."

"Maybe," she answered. "He was a man like any other man, about as tall as you, long brown hair."

"Anything distinctive about him?" the officer asked.

"You mean his thing?" she asked.

"Oh, no, nothing like that," the officer answered. "Maybe distinctive facial features, facial hair, clothes. But wait until the deputy gets here. This is all up to Hudspeth County where you were found hanging."

"Huh?" she said. "I was hangin'?"

"Yeah, lynched," the officer said. "The sheriff's deputy should tell you more about it."

At that point, the nurse gently pulled the curtain away and said, "The other officer is here. But first I need to check the patient now that she's regained consciousness."

"You gotta give me some stuff," the patient said. "I'm hurtin' bad."

"What kind of stuff?" the nurse asked.

"Y' know, stuff, pills, what doctors give for pain," the patient replied.

"I'll make a note for the doctor to check on you when he does his rounds," the nurse said.

Outside the drawn curtains, out of earshot of the patient, Officer Perez introduced himself to Deputy Hodges, deputy sheriff in Hudspeth County, and explained what he had learned from the patient. He concluded, "Sounds like she might be on opioids or something similar. She's asking the nurse for something."

The nurse came out and said, "you can come in now, but not for long. She seems to be in pain and fading."

Deputy Hodges introduced himself to the patient and said, "Your name is Sheila Gomez, I believe."

The patient nodded and mumbled something like "Yes."

May I ask how old you are?" the deputy continued.

"Twenty-nine."

"Officer Perez said you don't recall what happened in Hudspeth County. What do you recall?" Deputy Hodges asked.

The patient stammered, "They beat me up, tied me up, and dumped me in the back of a pickup truck. Don't remember anything after that. What happened to get me here?"

"You were tied and hung from a tree," the deputy began. "You'll no doubt find out more later when you're better recovered. For now, just the basic facts. Could you identify the two men who did it? Officer Perez said there were two."

"Yeah," she said, "An old guy I didn't get a good look at. The younger guy had been with me before. I could sort of identify him."

"Officer Perez gave me a quick description; we can get more from you later," Deputy Hodges said. "Anything distinctive about what he was wearing?"

"Just some sloppy jeans and a flannel shirt," she replied. "And, some old cowboy boots that he had trouble getting off and back on when he undressed."

"Did you get a name from him?" the deputy asked.

The patient hesitated, then said, "Leroy, or somethin' like that."

"What can you say about the pickup truck?" Deputy Hodges asked.

"Kinda old, beat up, kinda dirty, black. Oklahoma plates," she said.

"Did you notice the make, by chance?" he continued.

"No, sorry," she said. "All old pickups look alike."

"Can you remember where he took you and then tied you up?" The deputy continued. "You said you had been there before."

163

"An old dirty trailer," she said. "In a trailer park."

"Can you tell us where it was?" the deputy asked. "Maybe show us when you get out of here?"

Somewhere way out east on Montana," she said. "Not sure if I could find it again on my own,"

That makes sense, he thought. *Montana Avenue is the highway that leads to Cornudas where she was found.* "There was a sign around your neck saying no Mexicans here," he said. "Are you Mexican?"

"They call me that, so guess so," she answered.

"Were you born in Mexico?" the deputy continued.

"No, born in El Paso," she answered.

"Your parents born here?" he asked.

"Mama, was," she replied. "Don't know who my daddy was; Mama don't, neither."

Maybe I shouldn't ask about the other sign that says she has the clap, gonorrhea, he thought. *Maybe I can ask some of the medical people. This might be enough for now.*

"Thank you for your information," Deputy Hodges said. "We'll be back in touch with you again when you're better. For sure we want to catch the guys who did this to you."

"OK," she mumbled, and turned to drowse.

When the deputy found the nurse, he thanked her for her cooperation and commented on the sign implying gonorrhea. The nurse said that she would make a note for the doctor. The deputy left to report back to headquarters. As he drove away, he thought, *Maybe I can find that trailer park; I drive right along Montana on the way out of town.*

Later as he drove along, he saw an old mobile home park on the east side of town and drove inside and around. *No pickups with Oklahoma plates, but they might be away working. This sure looks like it might be the place. We could ask the El Paso police to keep an eye on it.*

About an hour later, he arrived at his duty station near Dell City in the northern part of Hudspeth County. He filed a report with the sheriff's office in the county seat of Sierra Blanca. He also entered data in a database of shared information about pending cases. *Oh, here's a similar case, from Stanton, Martin County. Same name and pickup with Oklahoma plates. Hopefully they'll pick up on my post. We'll contact them if anything else happens here.*

CHAPTER 4

Saturday, February 23, 2019
El Paso, Texas, USA

About nine in the morning, Khan stirred in bed next to Otto after a night of restless sleep. He thought, *Otto must've noticed how restless I am. It's time to tell him, especially now that the Archbishop of Houston is calling for legal action against priests who are accused of sexual abuse. Am I up for taking legal action? What would my family think? Yusef seems to be OK with it. Maybe after breakfast I'll tell Otto. I can start the coffee and get things ready; maybe he'll be up soon.*

After breakfast they were sitting cuddling on a couch in their underwear. Khan explained his former abuse by a priest when he was a teen and that now there was some outreach to have him take legal action against the priest.

"Criminal or civil?" Otto asked.

"Could be both," Khan replied. "The statute of limitations might have passed for criminal. I need to look more into Texas law on the subject."

"What's keeping you back?"

"I guess I'm too Vietnamese. What would people think? I'm pretty sure that the division chief here, my boss, would be OK with it. He's the one who said it was OK for me to report the abuse when information was being gathered. He also encouraged me to be more open about being gay and that it wouldn't be a problem in the office. He even put me in touch with one of his long-time very good gay friends."

"Sounds good."

"There's more to the situation with my boss and his gay friend to tell you about sometime, all positive. For now, it's mostly, what would my family think?"

"Wouldn't they be concerned that you would be getting justice for being abused?"

"They don't know yet. There's still a mentality, especially among the older ones, that sexual victims bring it on themselves."

"Oh, yeah, but who really cares about what they think any more?"

"Maybe the biggest thing is that they are so indoctrinated with Catholicism that they would view this as an attack on the Holy Catholic Church and on God. It would bring shame on the family if one of their family members were responsible for doing something like this," Khan said.

"Growing up Catholic, I can sort of identify with that," Otto said. "But German Catholics are not all that devoted to the church these days. But consider yourself. Even under Catholicism, and especially what the Pope is saying these days, abused persons need justice. To hell with your family. Your first obligation is to yourself, not to them."

"Yeah, you're right. I need to think about it more and talk to my boss first chance I get." Khan gave Otto a big hug and kiss, saying, "Thanks. You've helped a lot."

"We're here for each other," Otto said. He returned the kiss and led Khan back into the bedroom.

In the afternoon, Leroy Russell was naked in bed with a young woman after they had taken some pills. Woodrow Dawes was drowsing on the couch. Almost immediately after his orgasm, Leroy heard a big thud in the other room. He jumped up without dressing and walked to the other room to find Woodrow on the floor after rolling off the couch. The woman, baffled, followed, still undressed.

"What the fuck's going on?" she asked.

"Looks like he passed out," Leroy said. "Help me lift him back up on the couch. I gotta call 911."

He fumbled to find his phone in the other room, called, and left details for an ambulance. He hastily pulled on underwear and pants. Returning to the other room, he said, "You gotta get dressed; amb'lance'll be here soon."

She hastily got dressed and said, "So how 'm I s'pposed to get home?" she asked. "Ain't y' goin' to take me?"

"Can't," Leroy answered. "Can't leave Uncle Woody alone."

"So, what'm I goin' to do?" she asked. "I sure ain't walkin' in this cold weather. B'sides it's a long way."

"Get Uber," Leroy said.

"Ain't got no money," the woman replied.

"Here," Leroy said, giving her a ten-dollar bill. "All I got."

"Gimme some pills, then," she said.

Leroy went to the other room and returned with a bottle, poured a few into her hand, and set the bottle on a table.

At that moment, a loud knock was heard on the door, and a loud voice said, "Police, open up."

Leroy quickly went to the door, saw an El Paso police officer in uniform with a name tag 'Garcia', and said, "Supposed to be amb'lance comin', not po'lees."

"Emergency services are on their way," the police officer said. "Police always come on calls like this. Please let me see the person."

Leroy stood aside and motioned to Woodrow on the couch.

Officer Garcia examined Woodrow carefully, saying, "Don't see the need for immediate CPR. Wait for emergency services." *Looks like he's dead already,* Officer Garcia thought, *but I don't want to tell them that.*

"Can you tell me the name of the person on the couch and your relationship to him?" Officer Garcia asked. "When he gets to an emergency facility, they will attempt to find some identification, but it can help if you could tell me now."

"My uncle, Woodrow Dawes," Leroy answered.

"You all live here together?" Officer Garcia asked.

"Him and me do," Leroy answered, becoming a little nervous.

"May I please see your identification?" Officer Garcia asked. "Both of you."

Leroy pulled a wallet out of his pocket and showed his driver's license to the officer, who said, "Leroy Russell, you're from Oklahoma."

"Just moved here," Leroy answered.

The woman dropped the ten-dollar bill and a handful of pills on the table, fumbled inside a coat laying nearby, and got out a wallet showing her driver's license. *Looks like drugs and prostitution, and cheap at that,* Officer Garcia thought. *I bet there are plenty of other drugs here. When emergency services are here and I get some backup, I can search more. I'm sure there's probable cause.* He pulled out his portable radio, pushed the button to call for backup, and hastily left a voice message saying, "send a woman."

The woman reached to pick up the money and the pills, but the officer said, "Don't touch those. As soon as backup arrives, those will be taken as evidence."

Leroy lunged at the officer, attempting to distract him while the woman collected the pills and money. The officer took out his pistol and said "Stop."

Seeing the pistol, Leroy stood back and the woman withdrew her hand. The officer continued, "Alana Graves and Leroy Russell, you are under arrest. You have the right to remain silent," continuing with the well-known statement of Miranda rights. "We would have found the pills anyway when the backup gets here and we do a search."

"You can't do a search 'cause we ain't done nuthin'. B'sides, I gotta go with Uncle Woodrow and see what's with him, and she's goin' with me."

"We most certainly can search," Officer Garcia said. "You have the right to have your own attorney or the court will assign one to you. Your attorney can explain your rights. For now, stand back out of the way. It's in your best interest not to say anything. My body camera is running and is recording what you say."

After a short while, they heard the noise of the emergency vehicle arriving and a knock on the door. Waving his pistol, Officer Garcia pointed to Leroy and said, "Let them in."

An emergency medical technician entered and was directed to Woodrow Dawes on the couch. "He just collapsed," Leroy said.

When the EMT checked for vital signs, he said, "Looks like we're too late, but we have to get him to the hospital to check everything properly. I'll get my partner."

While the EMT went to get his partner, Leroy, still high, rushed to Woodrow, shook his body saying, "Wake up, Uncle Woody, you can't leave me now."

The two EMTs returned. Leroy, faced them, trying to shield them from putting Woodrow on a stretcher. One of them gently started pushing Leroy out of the way; officer Garcia came to help the EMT, grabbing Leroy and pulling him aside. In the commotion, Alana Graves tried to run out the door. Officer Garcia yelled "stop!" putting his hand on his pistol, moved to the door to block her exit.

Eventually, the two EMTs loaded Woodrow onto a stretcher to maneuver him through the door and into the emergency vehicle. One of them said, "You can meet us at University Medical Center emergency area."

Woodrow rushed to the door to attempt to go to the emergency vehicle along with Woodrow and the two EMTs. Officer Garcia blocked the door again and said to the EMT persons, "These two aren't going anywhere except to the police station when backup arrives. They are under arrest. Tell the people in the ER to check for drugs. They probably would, anyway."

After some minutes of awkward silence with Officer Garcia, Leroy, and Alana inside, the noise of police cars was heard. Two officers, a man and a woman, arrived. Officer Garcia explained briefly to them that he had arrested the man and the woman and that he would give more details at the police station. Alana and Leroy were handcuffed after they had their winter coats on. The

170

police officers managed to put Alana in the police cruiser the two newly arrived in. Leroy was put in Officer Garcia's vehicle.

While outside, Officer Garcia noticed an old black pickup truck with Oklahoma plates. "That must be yours," he said to Leroy. Leroy grunted something the officer took as affirmative. *We'd better make a note of this license plate number too,* Officer Garcia thought. He took pictures of the pickup truck and the license plate.

All departed for the police station where Leroy and Alana Graves were booked and put in cells until they could notify attorneys. Officer Garcia entered the arrest data along with driver's license and license plate information into the data base. *Two pending warrants for persons with very similar stats,* he said to himself. *One in Hudspeth County right next to El Paso, attempted murder. Another in Martin county, rape and drugs. Pretty serious stuff. Better get the other authorities notified right away.*

CHAPTER 5

In the late morning Eastern time, in order to accommodate participants in the Mountain time zone, Rosie Jordan convened another meeting with the same people as before, including Carmen Cisneros from the FBI El Paso field office, plus a new participant, Peter Richardson of the Las Cruces, New Mexico, resident agency of the FBI's Albuquerque field office, both on secure Skype connections. He began, "We have lots to cover, so, Brock and Adam, maybe you begin and fill us in on things you are monitoring.

Adam Culbertson began, "There has been only one bombing incident, you likely know about, a brief demonstration in Houston at the Chancery of the Roman Catholic Archdiocese of Galveston-Houston, with a bomb set to go off later. Again, minimal damage like the others, apparently designed to create chaos, not death or serious damage, same explosives as the others, and with convenient time to get a flight to El Paso before the bomb went off. The two demonstrators had placards that said 'Priests abuse children' and 'Down with the church.' This came right after the Archbishop called for criminal investigations of priests and bishops for their roles in clergy sexual abuse, so it's unclear what the motive is, other than, as I said, to create a disturbance."

Brock O'Neil reported, "There have continued to be protest demonstrations, big and small, all over the country, including some in places where there has been cold weather. In addition, there has been an increase in petty protests, including persons writing notes on restaurant bills that they do not tip Mexicans, and similar things. These protests seem mostly spontaneous and not orchestrated by any of the persons we are following. Still the chaos created by the general atmosphere no doubt contributes to the spontaneity. The biggest thing is the arrest of a Coast Guard officer who was discovered to be a white supremist with an arsenal of weapons and to have made death threats against members of the media and some Democratic party presidential candidates. Again, there's no apparent link to the activities we're following, but again it's possible that all the chaos and disturbances created an atmosphere in which he felt more emboldened."

"Questions? Other comments?" Rosie asked.

Jared Cramer spoke, "With respect to that Russian oligarch who disappeared and resurfaced in Russia, we did some more inquires here using some of our airline contacts. He was on a flight from Atlanta to El Paso. We also checked with our Mexican counterparts. They let us know, very confidentially of course, that he took a flight from Chihuahua City to Mexico City. He must have taken an Aeroflot flight from Mexico City to Moscow; they don't have the means to check passenger lists on Aeroflot.

"He could possibly have crossed the border in a car or just walking; there's not a significant border check by the Mexicans directly on the border, but there are cameras. Instead, their check points are twenty kilometers inside the country. Still this must have been an organized effort for someone to meet him in Ciudad Juárez and take him to Chihuahua City. Also, there would have to be some effort to conceal him past the twenty-kilometer check point, and some sort of valid ID, like a visa, to get on a plane in Chihuahua City. The Russians must have something organized to pull this off."

Eric James from the CIA concurred and said, "We inquired about the travels of Ivan Petrov, their spy in Ciudad Juárez. He has taken a few trips to their embassy in Mexico City, which would be expected. We don't monitor the Russian Embassy in Mexico City; the Mexican government would not appreciate that. But we have expressed our suspicions to them. They have agreed to cooperate, but Mexico wants to keep good relations with Moscow, so they have to be careful. There are a few other Russians involved in spy activity in Ciudad Juárez under Ivan Petrov. We can't monitor them all. The Mexican government would not appreciate that, either, but we did inform them. They might be more interested if indeed there is a tunnel like we think there might be; we didn't tell the Mexicans about a possible tunnel because we would not want a premature detection and disclosure."

Peter from the Las Cruces resident agency said on Skype, "When we first heard about the possibility of a tunnel, we checked with the city government in Sunland Park, New Mexico. Any tunnel under a fence would have to come out in Sunland Park on the U.S. side; it's a river border in Texas. Sunland Park authorities know of no places close enough to the fence to be a tunnel entrance that have been changed or modified lately. No evidence of any dirt dumped. We didn't go down there to examine in person. The city government there should be reliable, though."

Carmen of the El Paso field office interrupted and said, "Wait. I sort of recall that there must be a tiny piece of Texas that is southwest of the river. There's a major road there that's one of the ways to go to the racetrack that's barely in New Mexico where gambling on horse races is legal. I remember one time seeing a convenience store with a sign saying the Texas Lottery is available there. The store is just past the bridge over the river. It must be in Texas in order to have the Texas lottery. The state line follows the original river bed, but the river has been put in a channel a few hundred feet away. This is almost exactly where Texas, New Mexico, and Mexico have borders that meet. There might be some place in there where a tunnel opening could be built out of sight. We can go there from our field office and look. It's only about five miles or less away from our office and close to downtown El Paso."

"Sounds like a good idea," Rosie replied. "With all these new discoveries centering around El Paso, maybe we need to send someone from the operations center to assist. We don't want to get in the way of you in the El Paso field office, though."

"I'm sure we could use as much help as you can offer. We're not experienced in international intrigue nor tunnel situations," Carmen said. "I need to tell my boss about your offer. He'll likely contact you."

Peter said, "We definitely could use some help. We have a fairly small staff and a big territory to cover all along the border. We certainly get enough illegal border crossing and drug issues, but nothing that would involve Russian interference"

Rosie said, "We're making progress. We'll keep meeting as soon as we have something more. We'll let you know."

With that, he closed the meeting and said local people could join him for lunch in his private dining room.

El Paso, Texas, USA

Meanwhile, Yusef took a Skype call from Charles Goodnight, head of the FBI field office in El Paso. After preliminary greetings, Charles said, "We've just had a case turned over to us, three cases actually. If I may, it would be good to have your preliminary assessment for when they go to court."

"Sure," Yusef replied. "That's what we're here for. Do you want to tell me, or have me read something?"

"I can send it over electronically on a secure connection, if that's OK with you," Charles Goodnight said. "Then we can discuss later on Skype or on the phone."

"Sounds good," Yusef said. "I'll check for an incoming file and let you know when I'm ready to discuss."

They said goodbyes and disconnected.

Later in the afternoon, they connected again. After pleasantries, Yusef said he had read the file once and continued, "I'd have to read it more times and maybe do some research, but I can see the basic points and can discuss it with you. How did you come across the case?"

"Hudspeth County wanted to give it to us quickly, saying it's a hate crime, which is federal, attempted murder," Charles explained. "It's a drug crime too, which can be federal. Hudspeth County is sparsely populated other than the El Paso suburbs spilling over in a couple of places. It really does not have resources and is very pleased for us to take it on. The other two cases with the same defendant are state crimes but could be federal because of drugs. It made sense for all three to be combined into one prosecution and let us have it. Martin County does not have big resources, either. The third case is in the city of El Paso. They have plenty of resources but are always busy. They didn't mind having their case consolidated with the others and turned over to us. We also got the preliminary cause of death for Woodrow Dawes, fentanyl overdose. There's no indication it was suicide or homicide; he was just a heavy drug user. Lot of the stuff coming across the border, you likely know, is laced with fentanyl."

"I see," Yusef said. "What crimes do you think we should focus on if it goes to prosecution? Drug issues? Rape likely does not fall into a hate crime category, but there is the hate crime for the attempted murder in Hudspeth County. That seems to be the motive they used to want to turn the case over to you."

"The hate crime might be the hardest to prove," Charles said. "He claims that his uncle is the one who did it, and his uncle is dead. The drug possession, and maybe drug dealing, might be more straightforward. But you are the prosecutors. Like many FBI agents, I have a legal background, but I'm not actively involved in prosecution."

"As a minimum, he could be prosecuted as an accessory to attempted murder, which could be a hate crime," Yusef said. "There seems to be little difficulty proving intent with a sign around her neck. Proving intent is one of the biggest obstacles in a hate crime."

"Yes, I understand."

"But that doesn't keep us from pursuing the drug charges at the same time," Yusef added. "You know I have two jobs, one the human and civil rights specialist, hate crimes, for the whole district, and acting head of the El Paso division. I don't want my primary specialty to push this toward the hate crime."

"Understood. But it's good to explore issues before we turn things over to you and the courts. And also, maybe we can see what additional investigating we need to do."

"If we focus mostly on the hate crime, it would have to be in the Alpine Division," Yusef added. "Hudspeth County, where it occurred, is in the Alpine judicial division, even if it is right next to El Paso. Martin County is in the Midland Division. And of course, El Paso is here in the El Paso division. I could check with Alpine and Midland to see what they think. The courts here in El Paso are pretty clogged. One consideration might be where we can get a speedier trial. But maybe we can get a plea bargain before that. It looks pretty straightforward, but one never knows."

"Yes, don't clog up the courts," Charles said.

"Also, it would be good to learn more about what public defenders are like in these places," Yusef added. "I don't have much courtroom experience, but I can ask."

They continued to discuss the case for a short time and then disconnected. Both went back to work.

CHAPTER 6

Tuesday, March 5, 2019
El Paso, Texas, USA

In the morning, Yusef spoke briefly on the phone with Robert Davis, head of the Alpine Division, U.S. Attorney for the Western Judicial District of Texas, then went to Skype to connect with him. After pleasantries, Robert said, "You decided that this trial of Leroy Russell will be in our division, it seems. We have some questions and concerns."

Yusef said, "It wasn't me who made the decision. I'm just the deputy for the district. John, the district AG, decided. I supported the decision all the way and gave him the input he wanted. If we want to include a hate crime element, it has to be in your division there in Alpine; that's where the hate crime occurred. The drug issues could be tried anywhere. Also, you know, I called both you and the Midland division, and I'm in charge of El Paso temporarily, to ask about workload and other things. We all have our hands full, but Alpine seems to be the least busy. Another factor is your relative isolation; it might be a little off the media radar scope. Of course, we support media coverage, but with all the political chaos going on, maybe we don't want a lot of publicity about lynching Hispanics."

"Oh, I understand," Robert said. "We're willing to handle the case, but we need some guidance. We've dealt with plenty of drug-related issues, but hate crimes are something we don't have much experience with. You're the district's hate crime expert."

"Well, yes, that's why I got the position for the whole Western District," Yusef replied. "I'm always ready to help. What more specifically would you like?"

"Things to look for and watch out for. How best to build a case for the hate crime, and not get bogged down in drug issues, although the drug issues are important. Also, we need help on relevant case law, although we can certainly start doing research on our own."

"Yes, those are definitely issues, and what we at District are here to help with," Yusef replied.

"Is there any possibility you could come over here sometime before the trial and help?" Robert Davis asked. "Maybe even be here for the trial."

"That's something we often do, visit in person," Yusef said. "But you know I have two jobs now, one as acting head of the El Paso division. That might keep me close to home, but certainly I'd do whatever I could." *Wait, this might be something for Khan. I have to check with Susana first, of course.* "I might be able to send someone from El Paso to help. Can you tell me what juries are like there, especially how would they react if we had an Asian-American prosecutor? He's third generation American and from Texas, Vietnamese, for what difference that would make."

"The population is about fifty-fifty Anglo and Hispanic," Robert Davis answered. "Very few if any Asians. Juries are generally Anglo, but some younger Hispanics who are voters are in the pool. There are lots of mixed Anglo-Hispanics who have been here for generations, so it's difficult to categorize potential jurors. It would be difficult to predict how they might react to an Asian prosecutor. We just don't have Asians here, except for a few Chinese restaurants."

"Maybe he could just work behind the scenes and let your local prosecutors take the lead," Yusef said. "It's too soon to make definite plans about his coming. I need to ask around the office here. What are public defenders like there? It looks like this defendant wouldn't be able to hire his own attorney."

"Public defenders here are mostly local attorneys who aren't too busy in their own practice and take public defense on the side," Robert Davis replied. "Most don't have criminal experience other than maybe traffic issues. They limit themselves to real estate, wills, and things like that."

"Maybe we could get a plea bargain," Yusef suggested. "It looks like the defendant doesn't have much of a defense to present, except maybe for the attempted murder charge versus a charge as accessory based on the claim it was his dead uncle."

"I'm pretty sure that a public defender here would go along with a plea bargain," Robert Davis said.

"It likely will be a while until the defendant is brought before a judge there," Yusef said. "The U.S. Marshalls would have to transport him there from El Paso and that can take some days to arrange."

Robert concurred. They continued in a brief discussion and said goodbye, agreeing to keep in touch.

Yusef then went to Susana Tate's office, waited to be invited in, and began, "You know the Leroy Russell case that the FBI talked to us about; the one where the defendant is in jail here in El Paso?"

She responded affirmatively. "John, the district boss in San Antonio, decided it should be assigned to the Alpine division," and continued with details he had just discussed with Robert Davis. "Robert just called me and wants my help in dealing with hate crime issues. He wants me to come visit. If I were still in San Antonio at the district office, I would probably feel obliged to go. But now that I'm also acting head of El Paso, I have plenty of work here and would just as soon not have to travel. Also, I admit, with a young daughter and wife at home, I'm not up to travel much anymore. If I do end up going, that means you would be in charge for a few days, if that's OK with you."

"Yes, of course, you can count on me," Susana Tate stated. "But you've been grooming Khan on civil and human rights issues so maybe he could go. According to what the Austin division told us when we hired him, Khan had good courtroom skills when he was public defender there."

Here again, she reads my mind, Yusef thought. "I'll mention it to him when I see him next, maybe later today," he replied. They discussed things in the office for a few more minutes, then Yusef returned to his office.

Yusef later went to Khan's office after having had a casual small-talk conversation over lunch with others present. "We may have another traveling assignment for you," Yusef began. "This time to the Alpine Division. So far things seem to have settled down around Eagle Pass, so there's no need for you to go to Del Rio, at least not right away." Yusef continued to tell Khan about the cases being consolidated against Leroy Russell in Alpine and the information he had obtained from Robert Davis.

Alpine, Khan thought. *I stopped there and spent a day in the area on my way moving here.* "I remember Alpine," he said. "Nice place. I spent time there when I was driving to El Paso to take this job. It could be good to go back." *Hey, maybe Otto could go with me, just for a weekend,* he thought.

"So, you've driven it," Yusef said. "I was going to say that you'd have to drive, most likely. The nearest airport is Midland, over two hours away. It would be only a little bit farther to drive straight there from El Paso. I rented a car and drove from Midland when I made courtesy visits to both Midland and Alpine a couple of years ago when I first got the job. It's really a nice area to drive though and visit. People in the Alpine Division are very nice."

"Say, do you think we might arrange it to include a weekend?" Khan said. "It might be good to invite a friend to spend a weekend there with me."

"Possibly," Yusef replied. "It's too soon to know exactly when. We have to wait, among other reasons, until the U.S. Marshals take the defendant there from El Paso."

"There hasn't been a good opportunity to tell you, yet," Khan began. "I've been dating someone, another guy, for a couple of months. He's from Alamogordo. We spend almost every weekend together, and a weekend in the Alpine area could be good."

"Good for you," Yusef said. "Of course, it's none of our business who you date. Other staff members don't disclose details of their personal lives. Brad did tell me that he had a good Skype visit with you, but didn't go into details. He's too professional for that."

"Yes, it was Brad who sort of gave me courage," Khan said. "It was that same weekend that I met Otto. Brad said I should follow my instincts, that I would know when the time was right to start dating. I did follow my instincts, and the rest is history, so to speak. We don't know how far it will go, but for now, things are good."

"Really good to know," Yusef said. "Brad and Jason keep threatening to visit, especially with Jason going to the Dallas Furniture Mart a couple of times a year. But so far, no visit yet. If my wife and I are still in El Paso when they do visit, for sure you'll be invited to meet them."

"Say," Khan continued, "Otto's an amateur artist. He sketches people and events. He's good. When this case goes to trial, maybe he could sketch for the news media. Cameras are not allowed in our courtrooms."

"Interesting," Yusef commented. "Jason is an artist too, so far he's amateur. He does a different kind of painting than sketches. If they ever come visit, maybe Jason and your friend would like to meet and share experiences. Back to the topic at hand, maybe it could be an idea for your friend to make sketches for the media in the courtroom in Alpine. When I was talking with Robert Davis this morning, we said we might try to keep a low media profile. We don't want too much publicity, to keep from inspiring copycat lynchings of Mexicans."

"Good idea," Khan agreed. "So far, almost everybody associates lynchings with blacks. People forget there were lynchings of Mexicans too, especially here in Texas back in the thirties and before."

"Oh, I didn't know that," Yusef said.

"Not many do," Khan replied. "But we covered it in a Texas history class I had at the University of Houston."

They continued in brief discussions, then went back to work individually. Khan was eager to tell Otto about the possibility of a weekend in Alpine.

CHAPTER 7

Thursday, March 7, 2019
Quantico, Virginia, USA

In the late morning Eastern time, as usual to accommodate participants in the Mountain time zone, Rosie Jordan opened a meeting at the FBI Operations Center with Adam Culbertson of the Operations Center, Jared Cramer of FBI Headquarters, Eric James of the CIA, and Andrew Branson from the Border Control headquarters present in person. Carmen Cisneros of the El Paso field office of the FBI and Brock O'Neill, who had traveled to El Paso from the Operations Center, were on a secure Skype connection from El Paso. Peter Richardson from the Las Cruces agency of the Albuquerque FBI field office was also on secure Skype.

"We've had significant breakthroughs," Rosie said, "so let's begin. Carmen?"

Carmen displayed a detailed map on another screen, saying, "We think we've found the likely location of an opening in the U.S. for a tunnel under the border fence. It's right here in a small sliver of Texas southwest of the river and in the El Paso city limits. It's behind a convenience store that is right on the Texas side of the state line. There are no signs marking the state line, but there are large signs on the convenience store saying 'Texas Lottery, Play Here!' clearly indicating that it's in Texas. The likely tunnel opening is right behind the convenience store, inside a mosque that's under construction and surrounded by a tall, black plastic

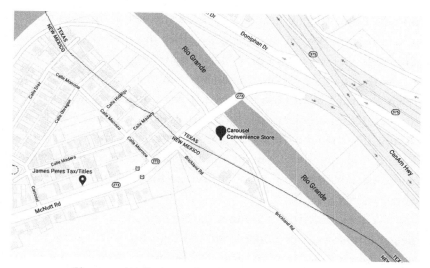

Close-up detailed map showing convenience store with
site of mosque behind (Map data ©2020 Google)

Carousel Convenience store directly on the state line
with New Mexico, selling Texas Lottery tickets

fence, typical of construction sites. We checked building permits
issued by the City of El Paso and found a permit for a mosque
at this site that would be built over time by the members. Our
inquiries with city authorities indicated there was a reluctance to
give a permit to them, but they did not want to be perceived as

anti-Muslim. The applicants convinced them that this was needed as a Shia mosque because the only other mosque in the area was Sunni. It was an fairly inexpensive, undeveloped plot of ground, but within half a mile of a major highway that allowed easy access from all over the El Paso area and, as we noted, easy access to the airport. Despite objections from anti-Muslim persons in El Paso, authorities thought the mosque might attract more people to the area, stimulating development and increasing property tax revenue, and especially bringing more customers for the convenience store and sales tax revenue.

"We were able to get some sonar equipment to see if we could detect a hollow space underneath and detect a probable route. The equipment was not very sophisticated, but we were able to trace what we think is a tunnel that goes right up to the border fence right next to a neighborhood of Ciudad Juárez called Anapra. The place where the tunnel likely goes under the border fence is in New Mexico, so Peter's agency in Las Cruces is involved. Because Peter's agency is about forty miles away, he couldn't come to investigate further on short notice. Therefore, Brock and I went in one of the old clunkers we keep around to drive and not draw attention to ourselves and drove into Ciudad Juárez to the Anapra neighborhood. As we have noted in this group before, there's no significant border control by Mexico right at the border, so we were able to drive in and around Juárez without drawing attention to ourselves; Texas and New Mexico license plates are commonplace in Juárez because this is one large, fairly integrated metropolitan area. There was control at the border coming back into the U.S., but we could both produce passports and be allowed in without difficulty. At the Santa Teresa land border crossing in New Mexico, there are much shorter lines for ordinary vehicles; it's primarily a crossing place for commercial traffic with trucks. You might recall that this was the location of a demonstration a while back with persons holding signs telling people that Mexicans are not welcome in the U.S. and to return to Mexico.

"While driving around the Anapra neighborhood, we found what appeared to be a fairly newly renovated Chinese herb shop and massage spa with a walled-in back area, typical of many houses and buildings in Mexico. This place could be the Mexican end of the tunnel. It wasn't right next to the fence, but close enough to get under the fence without a major effort. This is a semi-slum neighborhood of Juárez, and, on the surface, not a place to support a Chinese herb and massage spa. We couldn't use the sonar there, of course, and we didn't want to draw attention to ourselves by going inside or walking around the neighborhood. We don't think it's a good idea to notify Mexican authorities what we suspect, at least not right now. We'll get to that in a moment. One feature, though, is that the tunnel must immediately go deep, maybe with stairsteps. First it must go under a six-foot-deep concrete slab that the fence is built on. Also, immediately on the U.S. side of the fence, there's a railroad track. If there's much traffic on the railroad track, then the repeated vibration of the trains passing above could damage the tunnel."

Adam interjected, "Remember that the first bomb explosion case we were brought into was under a bridge for the main line of the railroad that passes right next to the border fence. The bridge was not next to the place that you indicate as the likely place for a tunnel, but maybe the bomb was placed not far away and designed to stop rail traffic for a while so it wouldn't affect the tunnel construction. The railroad built a temporary bridge, and trains must run very slow while crossing it. When they build a standard sturdy bridge, there might be some impact on a tunnel."

"What do you think is the next step?" Rosie asked. "Get search warrants to go inside the mosque and see if you can find the tunnel opening?"

Jared Cramer interjected, "Maybe not be so hasty. Is there some way you can surveil that mosque and get an idea of what's going on? Of course, we have to be careful about putting a mosque, or any other house of worship, under surveillance in the current political environment, much less get a search warrant."

Brock nodded and said, "That's what we thought here. We don't want to shut this tunnel down right away. It could be very useful to be able to see who is using it and maybe for what purpose. There doesn't seem to be any urgency to shut it down, which would be the case if it were being used to smuggle drugs or illegal immigrants. Or at least we need to observe a while to verify that there are no drugs or illegal immigrants. That's why we don't want to notify the Mexican government just yet. We wouldn't want the Mexicans to shut down their end too soon. But the people here in the field can't make those kinds of decisions."

Eric said, "That makes sense. I'll run it by the people in CIA headquarters who deal with Mexico, just to be sure."

Carmen said, "Ideally, we would put something at the top of that convenience store so we could look down on that mosque under construction. But that would require a lot of effort of getting permission from the building owner and the people in the convenience store knowing what we are doing. That might put us at too much risk of detection. We might be able to put cameras on utility poles nearby. Utilities are provided by the city of Sunland Park, New Mexico, even if the mosque is next to the state line in Texas. We could probably get them to go along without too much risk of being discovered. It would be very tedious to watch directly in person. This is an area where a strange car and people wandering around would draw attention. Peter's agency would have to be involved in that because it's in New Mexico."

Peter said, "Our agency and the Albuquerque field office stand ready to be involved. Sometimes state lines are just a nuisance. We appreciate Brock coming down here. All help is appreciated."

Anyone else?" Rosie asked.

Adam replied, "You have all probably noticed that there were two more bombings. One was the First United Methodist Church in Grapevine, Texas, right next to the Dallas-Fort Worth airport. Signs said, 'Take this, anti-gay Methodists.' There was the same type of explosives and all that. Convenient flight back to El Paso. Then there was another bomb in a corner of the Texas state capitol building, saying 'Down with Democracy.'" Again, the same explosives and other things. We suspect they are going to warm-weather sites here in mid-winter. Many other places with direct flights to El Paso have had some weather-related problems. Notable exceptions are Orlando and Atlanta. Maybe look for them next. Hopefully, you on the ground in El Paso might be able to discover more."

"That's our plan," Carmen said, and Brock affirmed.

"Others?" Rosie asked. "If not, let's be prepared to meet again on short notice. Now we can go to lunch, if you like."

CHAPTER 8

Monday, March 11, 2019
Alpine, Texas, USA

At 9:00 a.m., Judge Curtis Griffith, dressed in a traditional black judicial robe, opened the first day of trial of the case of *U.S. versus Russell* in the uniquely designed federal courthouse for the Alpine Division of the Western Judicial District of Texas, located north of the town in a desert environment with scenic views of nearby mountains. Judge Griffith was in his fifties and had served in this role for almost twenty years, having been appointed during the administration of President George W. Bush. The defendant had been arraigned in a routine court appearance the previous Friday, and a jury had been selected with only perfunctory examination by defense and prosecuting attorneys.

The defendant was sitting at the defense table dressed in jail clothing. Sitting next to the defendant was his attorney, Dwight Peters, dressed in a gray glen-plaid suit with muted hints of dark green, a light-yellow shirt, and dark olive-green tie. Dwight Peters was a local attorney who appeared to be in his late thirties or early forties. He handled mostly commercial transactions but served as a public defender in both federal and state courts when, on occasions like this, defendants could not afford their own attorneys.

Martin Bedingfield, a staff attorney with the Alpine Division of the U.S. Attorney for the Western District of Texas, was in his early

U.S. Federal Courthouse, Alpine, Texas

thirties. He sat at the prosecution table. He wore a blue polyester-wool suit, a light blue shirt, and a nondescript red tie. Next to him, Khan Nguyen sat wearing a navy-blue worsted wool suit with a white dress shirt and navy-blue tie. Khan thought, *I'm conspicuously overdressed here, but this is the only suit I have. It's good in El Paso, and also back in Austin. If I have more assignments like this, I might have to buy some more clothes; at least another suit. The impression attorneys make on juries is very important, and it's as important not to be overdressed as to be underdressed.*

Seated in the courtroom, as near to the front as possible, Otto Wildmann was dressed in khaki-colored Dockers Chinos and a plaid long-sleeved shirt covered with a stylish dark-brown sweater. He and Khan had arrived Saturday and were staying at the historic Holland Hotel, where the U.S. government has a contract for its official guests. His drawing supplies were at his side within easy reach. A few other persons were in the courtroom, apparently from local newspapers, there being no television stations in the area.

191

Holland Hotel, Alpine, Texas

Both Martin and Dwight gave brief opening remarks. Martin's comments indicated that the prosecution would present evidence and arguments that the crime of attempted murder was not merely a criminal act, but was a federal hate crime. Dwight indicated that the defense would challenge the credibility of all of the evidence.

Martin began by calling the first witness, Jay Hodges of the Hudspeth County sheriff's department, who was wearing his deputy's uniform. He was sworn in with a Bible and Martin led him through testimony describing coming upon the scene of a woman hanging from a tree after a 911 call from a passing motorist. He indicated that the woman was unconscious and had a rope around her neck, and described how he and the passing motorist arranged the motorist's pickup truck to take pressure from the noose on the victim's neck. When asked if he had pictures, the deputy removed his body camera that had pictures of the woman hanging with signs saying 'No Meskins Here' and 'Full of Clap.' The picture was shown on a large screen. Martin asked that the electronic file from the officer's phone be placed into evidence, which the judge ordered.

"Do you have any other evidence you collected?" Martin asked Deputy Hodges who answered, "We obtained a photo from the cell phone of the motorist that you can display."

Dwight stood and said, "Object, Your Honor. This is indirect, second-hand information, which is not admissible."

Martin immediately replied, "This evidence was taken by law enforcement in conjunction with an investigation. Therefore, it is admissible. If the court wishes, we can subpoena the motorist to have him appear in person to verify the photograph. He lives in New Mexico, so it would be more tedious with two states involved and would delay the trial."

Judge Griffith thought, *Dwight's not a criminal lawyer and likely hasn't come across law regarding evidence since he was in law school. Still, he might have a point if this case goes to appeal and things revolve around this one piece of evidence. No way this case will end up on appeal, so I'll just go ahead and overrule the objection.* "Objection overruled," the judge stated. "You can display the photograph and request that it be placed in evidence."

When the photo was displayed, it showed the same scene from a different angle, with the two signs visible. Otto busily drew the scene of the hanging woman and the two signs.

"Have you had any additional contact with the victim?" Martin asked. Deputy Hodges explained having met with her in the hospital in El Paso and gave details.

When Martin said that he had no further questions, Dwight began, "How do you know this victim is connected with defendant; or do you?"

"She gave us a name and a physical description of him and his vehicle," Deputy Hodges answered. "When he was arrested on other charges, a connection was made."

"You don't know from direct evidence, do you?" Dwight asked.

"No," Hodges answered.

"No further questions, Your Honor," Dwight stated.

"The court will be in recess for twenty minutes," the judge said.

During the recess, a young woman in a wheelchair who had entered the courtroom during the previous testimony, was assisted to the first row near the front.

When Judge Griffith returned, he called the court back to order and said, "Counselor, call your next witness."

Martin stood and said, "The prosecution calls Sheila Gomez."

The young woman stood from the wheelchair and with assistance walked to the witness stand, where she was sworn in using a Bible. Martin asked questions to establish her identity and that she lived in El Paso. He also established that she and her mother had both been born in El Paso. Then he asked, "Do you know the defendant; and, if so, in what capacity?"

"Met him first with a group of people," she answered. "He offered me some stuff if I'd go home with him."

"When was this?" Martin asked.

"Maybe 'bout four or five weeks ago," Sheila answered. "Was on a Saturday."

"When you say 'stuff,' you mean drugs?" Martin asked.

"Yeah," she answered. "Little white capsules that we get high on."

"So, you went home with him and got high on some substance," Martin stated.

"Sorta like that."

"Then what did you do?" Martin continued.

"He took me to the bedroom and we did it," she replied.

"You mean you had sex," Martin said.

"Yes," she answered.

"And after that?" he asked.

"He took me home," Sheila answered. "Said he'd find me again."

"Did you meet with him again, and when?"

"Yes," she answered. "Couple of weeks ago on Saturday. Offered me stuff to go home with him again."

"Then what?"

"Soon as we got inside his house trailer, he grabbed me," she began. "Said somethin' that Meskins deserve to be lynched 'cause I gave him clap. The other guy, the older one, grabbed me and choked me. I passed out and don't remember nuthin' after that."

"What's the next thing you do remember after that?"

"Wakin' up in the hospital, with a policeman from El Paso askin' lots of things."

"And after that?"

"That deputy sheriff who was just here come in and asked me a lot more. Told 'em what I could, which wasn't much."

"And since then?"

"They kept me in the hospital until I could do things on my own," she replied. "Then they put me in some rehab place to get me off the stuff. Still there until I got brung here."

"No further questions," Martin said and sat.

Dwight began, "You testified you were high, so how can you say you can identify the defendant?"

Sheila answered, "Weren't high when he picked me up both times."

"The sign around your neck in the photographs said 'Full of Clap,'" Dwight said again. "Does that mean, to you, that you had gonorrhea?"

"Don't give me them fancy words," she replied. "If I got the clap, it was from him."

"You just got out of the hospital," Dwight continued. "That must mean you would have been tested for sexually transmitted diseases, STDs. Do your medical records show you have any STDs?"

Martin immediately stood and said, "The witness's medical records are private and confidential and not subject to disclosure in open court. Furthermore, this information is irrelevant. Whether or not the witness has or had an STD does not justify a hate crime attack."

Judge Griffith stated, "Objection sustained. Counselor, you will not pursue this line of questioning."

Dwight continued, "You testified that you received drugs in exchange for sex, didn't you?"

Ms. Gomez started to say something, paused a second, and then became visibly angry. "I ain't no prostitute, if that's what you mean!"

"No further questions," Dwight said.

The judge said, "You may step down. Court is adjourned for lunch until 1:30."

"He's planting seeds with the jury, even if he is overruled," Khan commented to Martin while they went to lunch, Otto joining them.

After lunch, Martin called Officer Garcia of the El Paso police department, who described being in the defendant's mobile home in response to the defendant's 911 call about his uncle and the events that transpired, including the arrest of the defendant on drug possession and drug dealing charges, and Alana Graves on drug possession and prostitution. He stated that evidence would be used in local trials in El Paso for Alana Graves and that he could not disclose details here. He also described how a search of databases led to identification of the defendant and his vehicle in both the crime that was being tried right now and a reported crime in Stanton, in Martin County. As a result, Leroy Russell and Alana Graves had been arrested and detained on the spot.

Dwight had no questions.

Martin then called Nina Maxey, who identified herself as being from Stanton in Martin County. She described how the defendant had raped her and pushed her out the door of an apartment in Stanton, leading her to get a ride with police and report the rape. He also asked her if the defendant had given her drugs that were found on her when she was discovered by police. She replied that any drugs had been planted on her clothes while she was naked and trying to get away from the rapist.

"Isn't it true that the defendant gave you drugs in exchange for sex?" Dwight asked when it was his turn to question the witness. "You were both high on drugs you brought with you and had consensual sex."

Ms. Maxey hesitated and said, "I don't think I gotta answer that. Somethin' about a Fifth Amendment."

"No further questions," Dwight said.

"The prosecution rests, Your Honor," Martin said.

Judge Griffith said, "Court adjourned until 9 a.m. tomorrow. Defense, you can begin your case then."

Dwight stood and said, "The defense has no case to present. We move for dismissal because the prosecution has failed to prove a case, much less a hate crime."

"Motion denied," the judge stated. "Closing arguments will begin tomorrow morning."

After the trial, a thirty-something man dressed in casual clothes, carrying a note pad, rushed to Otto, introduced himself as Fred Dunlap of the *Alpine Avalanche,* and asked, "What media outlet do you represent? I saw you drawing."

Otto replied, "None. I just do this on my own because I like to draw."

"May I see what you've drawn?" Fred asked.

Otto showed him sketches of the woman hanging with the signs attached to her, and other sketches of some of the witnesses.

"Say, these are great," Fred said. "And you do this just for fun?"

"Well, actually I'm here with a friend, one of the prosecuting attorneys," Otto said. "He keeps telling me that I should try to sell them. So far, I don't know how to go about it."

"If you would give me that one of the woman hanging," Fred said, "I'll share any royalties with you. I have connections with the media who might like this."

"I wouldn't give it to you," Otto replied. "I want to keep it with my collection. I'll gladly draw another one for you. Let's find a place to sit where I can draw."

Meanwhile, Dwight was in whispered conversation with Leroy, the latter becoming agitated. Khan turned to Martin and said, 'Good job. You didn't need me after all."

"Are you in a hurry to get back to El Paso?" Martin asked. "If you can spare the time, I could use some help on the closing arguments, especially hitting the hate crime focus."

Khan replied, "I probably could, and I'd be pleased to offer what help I can, but a friend is with me—you can see him talking to that person, who is likely a reporter. He wanted to draw sketches of the trial. I don't know when he needs to get back to work. Drawing is a hobby with him. I can ask him; He'll likely go along with staying over."

Court officials led the jury out of the courtroom to go to their respective homes with instructions not to discuss the case. Leroy was led back to the county jail that houses federal prisoners. After brief discussion, Otto agreed to stay overnight while Khan helped with the closing arguments. He would wander the town on his own while Khan and Martin conferred.

CHAPTER 9

Tuesday, March 12, 2019
Alpine, Texas, USA

Shortly before 9 a.m., Martin Bedingfield and Khan were sitting at the prosecution table of the courtroom in the federal court house. Dwight Peters was sitting alone at the defense table. The jury was seated. Otto and a few others were sitting in the area for spectators. A very few minutes after nine, a court official announced that the judge had been detained in chambers and would be out shortly.

Judge Griffith, wearing his judicial robe, appeared and asked the attorneys to approach the bench, where he said, "I have just been informed by officers from the jail that the defendant was found dead in his cell this morning. There is no evidence of foul play. It's possible he could have suffered a heart attack or something similar. Or maybe an overdose of drugs. An investigation is underway to consider all possibilities, including murder, suicide, or accident. Formal announcements will be given later, after preliminary investigations. I will obviously need to close the proceedings."

The attorneys looked at each other, stunned. "Please take your seats," the judge said. When they were seated, the judge said to the court, "Due to the death of the defendant, the case is dismissed. More details will be provided at an appropriate time. Members of the jury, thank you for your service. You may go now."

Martin and Khan looked at each other, Martin saying, "This is a new one. I've never heard of anything like this."

"Me neither," Khan said. "Of course, I'm new, but I don't recall coming across any instances like this in law school. I've got to notify Yusef soon; I'm sure he needs to notify the district AG in San Antonio right away."

"I need to contact Robert right away, too; I'm sure he'll need to notify San Antonio also. In a small town like this, news travels fast so Robert might know already. Thanks for staying over to help with closing arguments, even though we don't need them now."

"My pleasure," Khan said. "And thanks for taking us to dinner last night. "I'd better check with Otto to see how soon he wants to leave. He seems busy now."

Martin and Khan each got out their cell phones and went off to the side to call their respective heads of divisions. Otto was talking to Fred Dunlap again. Khan, noticing they were shaking hands in farewell, walked to Otto. They discussed when they should leave and went to Khan's car.

Quantico, Virginia, USA

At 11 a.m. Eastern time, again to accommodate those in the Mountain time zone, Rosie Jordan opened another meeting at the FBI Operations Center with the usual persons from the Washington area and with Carmen Cisneros and Brock O'Neill in El Paso, and Peter Richardson in Las Cruces on Skype. "You have lots of information, Carmen and Brock, so please begin."

"We managed to get surveillance that I can describe in detail in a moment," Carmen began. "There appear to be two groups of two men who conduct the activities. Sometimes it's only two men going to a single location; sometimes two groups go to two different locations. They all seem to be men in their late twenties or thirties, average height and build, and seemingly Caucasian, although it's difficult to tell from the distance. They are definitely not black, but many Middle Easterners and Hispanics can easily look like Caucasians.

"They arrived at various times of the day, apparently depending on the time of the flight they were taking. The ones we saw, with hindsight, fit the times of flights to places where bombs went off. We've tentatively concluded they go through the tunnel, pick up bags with the bombmaking apparatus, and signs. They must assemble the bombs at the destination and carry components in separate small bags to avoid detection at security at the El Paso airport. We did not follow them to the airport, just in case we would be seen following them, but the times we saw them coincided with direct flights to Orlando and Atlanta. They did not come back to the mosque after the mission was complete. We conclude they must live in the El Paso area, at least temporarily, so they go straight home. They must have permission to be in the country legally, maybe even be U.S. citizens, or else they would not be able to board flights readily at the El Paso airport.

"For our next step, with your guidance, we would like to have the FBI field offices in the likely destinations to be on standby, go to the airport to look for persons carrying bags like those we saw in our surveillance, and follow them if possible, taking videos or using other methods of surveillance. We might also be able to wait for them at the El Paso airport when they return and follow them to see where they live."

Jared Cramer of FBI Headquarters said, "That sounds reasonable. The operations center can notify agents at the likely destinations, can't you, Rosie? We could send them pictures of the faces to look for."

Rosie said, "Yes, we can do that."

Carmen said, "It might be more distinctive to look for men carrying those two types of bags; the bags look unique. We suspect they would be using rental cars to get to the locations where they set off bombs, so maybe look around car rental counters. It's hard to imagine that this group, whatever it is, would have operatives in each of these locations."

"What should we instruct the agents in these locations to do when they find these persons? Arrest them?"

"Our thought is just to follow them, confirm their activities, hopefully take videos, and notify us when they return to the airport to get a flight back to El Paso," Carmen said. "A premature arrest in some place like, say, Seattle, might tip someone off. Besides, they would just have to be transported here to El Paso anyway. We can arrest them as soon as we have a larger body of evidence. What do you think? You people are the final word."

"You said you set up a surveillance routine," Rosie said. "Please describe it so we all get an idea."

Carmen began, "We discarded the idea of being on top of the convenience store; too many logistical problems and we might be detected. Peter from the Las Cruces office contacted the City of Sunland Park to allow us to put up surveillance equipment on utility poles. We could have made the contact ourselves with Sunland Park authorities, even if we are in Texas and the mosque is in Texas. Fortunately, even though our field offices follow state lines, we do not have to be rigid in observing field-office boundaries. Still, the Las Cruces office could let on to the city of Sunland Park that provides the utilities that the FBI in Las Cruces is looking at drug traffic and illegal immigration in the area without saying we're focusing on a mosque. It certainly would not be good optics if we were prematurely seen as watching mosques.

"The sensors are designed to notify our office if there's activity around the mosque. Someone in our office is on standby all the time, and we are only about two miles away. There's no need to monitor activity in person around the clock, because there are no flights in and out of El Paso after about midnight. We drive by occasionally, but not too often because we could easily draw attention to ourselves on that road. We can and do pretend to be customers at the convenience store from time to time and look around outside. We have to wary who goes inside so the convenience store clerks don't get too suspicious at seeing the same persons repeatedly. Of course, we dress very casually, even shabbily to fit the immediate neighborhood in Sunland Park, and we drive old clunkers we have confiscated. Sometimes we get old cars from Las Cruces to give us some variety. Any questions?"

After a pause to see if there were questions, Rosie closed the meeting, as usual welcoming people to stay for lunch.

CHAPTER 10

Friday, March 15, 2019
El Paso, Texas, USA

In the early evening, Yusef and Nisrine met at home after each had individually attended Friday prayers at the local Islamic center while the other stayed at home with Sara. Yusef asked, "Did you hear comments at the Islamic Center about the massacre of Muslims today in New Zealand during prayers at two mosques?"

"No," Nisrine replied. "During women's prayers, usually little is said; we just pray."

"It was mentioned during the sermon at the men's prayers," Yusef commented. "Some of the people at the office asked me, knowing I'm Muslim. The biggest thing is that the media immediately jumped on me, wanting to know what I think because I'm Muslim and in charge of the office. I can't just blow them off, so I agreed to give them a statement on Monday. I've got the weekend to develop a statement that expresses my annoyance at their focus on my being Muslim and that I should have an opinion about something that happened halfway around the world. They don't jump on Jewish staff in the AG network when something happens in synagogues or other Jewish venues worldwide."

"The people I work with probably know I'm Muslim," Nisrine added, "or must have heard me comment when asked, but they don't seem to remember or care. They just need me to work. I was going to tell you that tomorrow I have to go to some of the refugee camps, so Sara has to be home with you."

"Oh, OK," Yusef replied.

The rest of the evening was spent in normal activities, eating an evening meal, playing with Sara until her bedtime, relaxing, and going to bed early because Nisrine would get up early the next day to go to work.

Monday, March 18, 2019

At the designated time of 10:00 a.m., Yusef welcomed representatives of local media into the conference room of his office. He passed out and read his prepared statement:

As an attorney employed by the Attorney General of the United States whose primary focus is on human and civil rights, I condemn and express my utmost disgust at the wanton massacre of Muslims during Friday prayers in Christchurch, New Zealand. In addition, I express admiration for authorities in New Zealand who are moving forward to prosecute the case with the utmost respect for human and civil rights of the victims as well as respecting the rights of the accused. From all indications, New Zealand law respects civil and human rights at least at as high a level as we do in the United States.

At the same time, I reiterate my condemnation and utmost disgust for the recent wanton massacre of worshipers at a Jewish synagogue in Pittsburgh, Pennsylvania, in this country. My counterpart in the Western Judicial District of Pennsylvania is surely prosecuting the situation with full respect for the civil and human rights of the victims as well as protecting the rights of the accused. I am not involved in that case in any way and express my confidence in the judicial system of the United States, including the activities of U.S. Attorneys in all locations.

"In addition, I felt condemnation and utmost disgust for the wanton massacre of Christian churchgoers in Charleston, South Carolina, a couple of years ago. Likewise, my counterparts in the South Carolina District from all indications dealt with the situation with full and proper respect for civil and human rights of the victims and rights of the accused.

You obviously know that I am Deputy U.S. Attorney for the Western District of Texas, with a primary focus on civil and human rights. Also, I am the acting head of the U.S. Attorney's office of the El Paso Division of the Western District of Texas. You also must know that I am Muslim, and that is why you have chosen to approach me for comments on the massacre of Muslims in New Zealand. It is curious to me why you in the media focus on Muslim-Americans in important positions like my position here in El Paso. But you do not place a similar focus on Jewish-Americans in the U.S. Attorney General network with respect to the massacre at the Pittsburgh synagogue. Similarly, you do not put a similar focus on the numerous Christians in the U.S. Attorney General network with respect to the massacre in Charleston, South Carolina.

"Now I'll remain for your questions, but I must state that I will not answer any questions relating to political or policy issues. As an employee of the U.S. Government, I cannot ethically nor legally state my opinions on such issues."

One media representative asked, "How many other Muslims are there in the U.S. Attorney General network?"

Yusef answered, "I don't know, and I don't particularly care to know. It does not affect how I do my job. Religious affiliations are not a part of our public records, nor our private records for that matter. So far, no one has come forward to say that he or she is also Muslim. During the years I worked at the national headquarters in Washington, the subject was never raised by anyone, including the media. Some of my co-workers, especially supervisors, knew

I'm Muslim because I told them I would be away during Muslim holidays like Eid al Fitr and Eid al Adha. It was only when I arrived in San Antonio and the media interviewed me because I was the newly arrived Deputy AG for the Western Judicial District of Texas that I was asked about my religious affiliation. It's not secret, so I told them. The same thing happened here in El Paso when I became acting head of this division. Apparently, Texans feel it is important to know religious affiliations. In both cases, I insisted that my religion must not be emphasized because it has nothing to do with the nature of my work nor my qualifications for the position."

Another person asked, "You said that no Jewish person in the Attorney General network was asked by the media about how he or she felt about the massacre at the Pittsburgh synagogue. How can you be sure? Based on what you just said, how would you know if some other person in the AG network is Jewish?"

"Obviously I can't know," Yusef replied. "There were no public reports in the media I read, watched, or listened to that Jewish attorneys in the AG network were asked their reactions to the massacre in Pittsburgh. How would I know if someone were Jewish? Among co-workers, some might comment that they were not going to be at work because of a Jewish holiday. Also, very recently, the television news networks have featured former federal prosecutors. Some of them have bios on Wikipedia or similar places that indicate they are Jewish. Elie Honig is one example."

"Yet another member of the media asked, "With all the issues here at the border, how are they affecting your work and the work of the El Paso Division?"

Yusef responded, "I can't discuss any of our ongoing cases. All I can say is that we get criminal cases when the FBI turns them over to us just before they are turned over to the courts for prosecution. At that time, they become public records, which are readily available to you in the media. For civil cases in which we represent the interests of the U.S. government, they have been filed with the courts and are a matter of public record that you can readily access."

After a short pause, Yusef was about to express his thanks for the opportunity when one person raised a hand and asked, "Can you comment about Sharia law and a desire to introduce Sharia law in this country attributed to the new congresswoman from Minnesota?"

Yusef pondered a brief moment, then replied, "First, I am not going to comment about allegations related to a congresswoman because, as I stated, I will not comment on political issues. I can say that my personal knowledge of Sharia law is limited to vague memories of attending Islamic school on weekends when I was a young boy growing up in Dearborn, Michigan. In those studies, the things we learned were strictly informational, not any attempt to introduce Sharia law to the U.S. To my knowledge, there are no serious proposals to introduce Sharia law into the U.S. nor any desire among Muslim-Americans whom I know to introduce Sharia law here. From my limited knowledge of international law, there are countries with substantial Muslim populations that have secular legal systems; Turkey is one example. Despite the large amount of media attention about Sharia law in Brunei, it appears that Sharia law is not widespread, even in countries with large Muslim populations. It is inconceivable to me that anyone would seriously propose Sharia law in the U.S.

"In my professional life, I deal exclusively with English common law as it is practiced in the United States at the federal government level and I support its application. The features of the common law are what attracted me to the study of law and preparation for this profession in the first place. As you know, my primary focus has been on human rights and civil rights law, for which the common law is ideal to protect.

"In my private life, I am subject to the English common law of the U.S. and especially English common law of the State of Texas that has elements of Spanish law. I am personally very pleased with the elements of protection offered by the common law in our state. As many of you would know, the individual states of the U.S. are the sovereign entities, and the U.S. federal government has only those rights explicitly granted to it by the constitution. Human and civil rights that are my focus in my professional life are indeed among the rights protected by the U.S. federal government. I am not expert on the law of the State of Texas, but sufficiently so that I am very pleased with the legal protections my family and I are offered.

"This is likely much more than you wanted to hear from me, and I could go on and on. To return to your original question, Sharia law has very little interest or impact on me professionally or personally. Within the U.S. Attorney General headquarters in Washington, there are some who are familiar with Sharia law to some extent and who are consulted when the U.S. is involved in international legal issues when interacting with countries where Sharia law is practiced. If you want to pursue the issue of Sharia law further in the context of Islamic theology, I can refer you to a professor who is knowledgeable on the subject here in the U.S., in North Carolina."

After a period of silence from those present, Yusef said, "Thank you for your interest in the El Paso Division of the U.S. Attorney for the Western Judicial District of Texas. We are always open to respect freedom of the press and open ourselves to the media."

Some members of the media attempted to question Yusef individually, to which he replied, "There are no further comments other than what I have said publicly." He then returned to his office.

CHAPTER 11

Monday, March 18, 2019
El Paso, Texas, USA

Immediately after the media conference, when Yusef returned to his office, members of the staff individually and in pairs stopped by to congratulate him on his response to the media about the massacre of Muslims during Friday prayers in New Zealand. When Khan stopped by, Yusef said, "Stop by again when you have a moment. I just received a preliminary report about the death of the defendant in the jail in Alpine."

Later, when Khan returned to Yusef's office, Yusef said, "I'll send you the preliminary report by email, but here is the gist of it: The remains of the defendant were sent to the state medical examiner in Austin because he died in a county jail which is under the jurisdiction of the State of Texas. The cause of death was overdose of opioids and fentanyl."

"Not surprising," Khan interjected. "He has a record of possession of those drugs. But how did he get them in jail?"

"Unfortunately, there are lots of ways to get drugs in jails," Yusef replied. "Jail personnel are not beyond selling drugs for enough money. But, most likely, the persons themselves smuggle them in. One way is taping them to the inside of the crotch hidden by underwear and not visible without moving the genitals. Usually detainees are not required to remove underwear when searched. If he had been incarcerated before, he may have been aware of that fact."

"He had a record of prior arrests in Oklahoma, I sort of recall," Khan said.

"The preliminary report does not eliminate the possibility of murder," Yusef continued, "but it seems highly unlikely. There's no indication that anyone else in the jail at the time would have a motive for wanting him dead. The most likely situations are suicide and accidental overdose. There are cases on record of prisoners committing suicide in jail during a trial because they believed they would be convicted and sentenced to lengthy prison terms."

Khan added, "When the judge adjourned the court the day before, the defendant and his attorney, the public defender, were in a heated exchange. We speculated that the attorney was telling the defendant that he should try for a plea bargain and reduced sentence because the evidence was so strong."

"That would fit a pattern for the few instances I'm aware of, regarding defendant suicide," Yusef said.

"My friend who was drawing sketches of the key persons in the courtroom captured this heated exchange," Khan said. "I encouraged him to take time off work to go with me and sketch people and things in the courtroom in Alpine."

"That's right. You said you have a friend who's a courtroom artist." Yusef commented.

"Right now, it's just a hobby," Khan answered. "I'm trying to convince him to pursue the possibility more aggressively." Khan paused, pondering, and then added, "You remember I told you I have been dating someone. He sketches people and objects as a hobby. We spend every weekend together, so I could bring you his sketches from Alpine next week if you'd like to see them."

"Yes, it'd be interesting to see them," Yusef said. "He must live here in El Paso."

"No, actually, he lives in Alamogordo," Khan explained and then described briefly the work he does for NASA and that Otto has lots of flexibility in setting his work hours.

211

Yusef said, "Good for you that you've found someone. I look forward to seeing his sketches."

"Is there anything else?" Khan asked. "I interrupted you about the sketches."

"Only that the defendant's relatives in Oklahoma refused to claim the remains," Yusef added. "It seems they were glad he had gone away, and they wanted no more dealings with him."

"That seems to be the case with his uncle, the record showed," Khan said. "Sad that families feel that way."

"Yes, sad," Yusef concurred. "But in this profession, we see all sorts of human frailties. I'm sure you must have run across some things in law school, too."

"Yes," Khan agreed, and left to go back to work while Yusef continued his work for the day.

CHAPTER 12

Friday, March 29, 2019
México, DF, México

Ivan Petrov entered the office of Vladimir Mikhailov in the Russian Embassy in the late morning. The latter said in Russian, "Have a seat, Ivan Aleksandrovich. Good to see that you could come for a weekend."

"Good to be here, as usual, Vladimir Evgenevich," Ivan Petrov replied in Russian. All subsequent conversation was in Russian.

Vladimir handed over an envelope, saying, "Here are the documents for the wife of the oligarch; you got her husband out a while back. She'll be brought to a private airport near the tunnel and then will go to the herb shop, where someone will meet her and get in touch with you. She's to go to Chihuahua City like her husband and get a flight here, where we'll get her on flights to Moscow."

"OK," Ivan said.

"She's a pain in the ass to deal with," Vladimir continued. "We had to use threats against her family to get her to agree to leave the U.S. before she could give details to the Americans. As before, the people we're having lunch with today don't need to know about this."

A short time later they were having lunch with Bijan Ahmadi of the Iranian Embassy and Ri Kuang-Sik of the North Korean Embassy, whom they "coincidentally" met at lunchtime in one of the popular restaurants in the diplomatic area of the city. All conversation was in English, their common language. They engaged in small talk and pleasantries until after their food was delivered and they could be reasonably assured of confidentiality.

Vladimir began the conversation. "You've surely been seeing the news of all of our activities. With the weather improving, we can go into Chicago now. But have you seen all the chaos going on all over the U.S.? Demonstrations about Jussie Smollett in Chicago, a driver in a van plowing down people in Maryland, churches being burned in Louisiana, a woman in Oklahoma wanting to rid the country of all but whites. We can't take direct credit for all of these, but we keep the atmosphere stirred up for them to happen. Violence and chaos are all over the U.S."

"Isn't it time to slow down or stop our activities?" Bijan asked. "Our guys are getting tired and want to go back to California to what they were doing before."

"We're just getting started good," Vladimir stated. "If your two guys are getting tired, maybe we can rearrange things. Or maybe you have a couple of others to rotate in and out."

Bijan turned to Kuang-Sik and asked, "What about your people in the herb store and massage place? Are they getting tired of the activity too?"

"So far as we know, they are content and not eager to move on. Kuang-Sik thought, *these guys don't need to know that we got the two people there some sophisticated computer equipment, and they're gathering all sorts of intelligence information for us.*

"Tell your people that we really appreciate your good work," Vladimir said. "The U.S. will not crumble easily or quickly, but they are on their way down."

They continued in small talk for the rest of the lunch and parted company with warm handshakes.

BOOK 4

CONCLUSIONS

CHAPTER 1

Monday, April 8, 2019
Quantico, Virginia, USA

Rosie Jordan opened yet another meeting at the FBI Operations Center in the late morning, Eastern time, in order to accommodate participants in the Mountain time zone. The usual people were present: Adam Culbertson from the Operations Center, Jared Cramer from FBI Headquarters in Washington, Andrew Branson of Border Patrol Headquarters, and Eric James from the CIA. As usual, they were joined on Skype by Carmen Cisneros of the El Paso FBI field office and Brock O'Neill who was with her in El Paso, and by Peter Richardson of the Las Cruces FBI resident agency. Rosie said, "Before we get to what you want to talk to us about, Carmen, Eric has some information for you."

Eric James began, "You reported to the Operations Center that you had seen a car drive up to the mosque with a woman passenger. Both the driver and woman went inside and came back out after a while. The car drove with the woman to the international bridge in downtown El Paso. Fortunately, you had an FBI agent with a car who was able to follow them. The woman got out of the car, appeared to walk across the bridge, and the car turned around and went to the home of one of the persons you've been monitoring. We're supposing that she refused to go through the tunnel you suspect is there, so they took her to the bridge, where apparently there was some arrangement for someone to meet her on the other side."

International bridge to downtown Ciudad Juárez,
Mexico, from El Paso, Texas, USA

Carmen said, "Yes, that's right."

Eric continued. "Because Mexico was involved, the Operations Center immediately notified us and also notified their counterparts in Mexico. Thanks to your being on the ball and prompt reporting, that woman was found on a flight from Chihuahua City to Mexico City and immediately taken into custody for entering Mexico with false documents, including a Russian passport with a fake visa. To cut the story short, she's the wife of the oligarch who fled to Mexico a short while back and then on to Russia. She claims that she was tricked into going to Mexico and ultimately to Russia. She refuses to board a flight to Russia because she fears for her life there. She wants to return to the U.S., where she has a residence visa.

"When U.S. authorities contacted her in Mexico, she said she had information about her husband and his activities that she'd tell if she returns to the U.S. Maybe because the administration wants to placate the Russians, the Department of Homeland Security refuses to have her come back. It claims her U.S. visa is revoked because she used false documents to enter Mexico. Mexico will not deport her, or at least not right away, if her claim that she fears for her life in Russia is upheld. This doesn't have any immediate relevance for what we're dealing with today, but we wanted to let you know. We especially appreciate your quick action in notifying us immediately."

Carmen said, "Thank you."

Rosie said, "Thank you, Eric. Carmen, you asked for this meeting. Please go ahead."

Carmen began, "We're ready to make arrests. It's always good to get your concurrence and guidance. We have enough evidence from previous trips made by the suspects. Field offices in other locations we contacted were able to locate the suspects, make videos, and intercept bombs with the help of bomb disposal squads. We think it's best to wait until both pairs go away close to the same time. If we arrested one pair alone, word could get to the other. We'll arrest them when they arrive back to the El Paso airport, rather than following them home. Two of the people live in New Mexico; if we arrested them there, they would be brought to trial in Las Cruces. The AG in Las Cruces handles primarily drugs and immigration issues, so the arrest of two of these guys might strain their resources. We have all the evidence here in El Paso, so it's good to have all judicial activity in one place."

"We concur," Peter added. "We have good working relationships with the AG in New Mexico, but it's a relatively small operation. We're very pleased to cooperate with El Paso."

"Any questions?" Carmen asked.

Andrew asked, "If there is a tunnel, as we suspect, what will be done to keep a flood of immigrants from rushing through? Do we need to bring in the Border Patrol?"

Carmen replied, "At the earliest moment possible after the arrests, we'll appear before a federal judge in El Paso to get a search warrant to enter the mosque and confirm the existence of the tunnel. We will also attempt to find the opening in Mexico so we can go through channels to notify Mexican authorities. As for a rush of people flooding through, it will surely take time for word to get around, so we wouldn't expect a lot immediately. We have the mosque under constant surveillance and FBI agents on regular patrol. We could even call on El Paso and Sunland Park police if need be. From what we hear, the Border Patrol is spread thin at legitimate border crossings, so we might not want to spread them even thinner. But we can call in the Border Patrol if it appears lots of people will indeed try to go through the tunnel."

"That sounds like a well-thought-out plan," Andrew replied.

Jared said, "I presume you have this all coordinated with the other field offices where the suspects might travel."

Carmen replied, "We haven't explicitly told them that arrests are to be made, but we follow the usual procedures. When we notice they are leaving their homes here in the El Paso area and through the tunnel and back, presumably to go to the airport, we immediately check flight schedules and look for likely destinations. There are typically a few possible destinations, and we have to guess which destinations are the most likely. There are FBI field offices in all of the possible destinations, so we notify all of them. So far, the procedure has worked out well, and the other field offices have been very cooperative in collecting evidence and sending it to us. The Operations Center had set up this procedure, and it has worked out well."

After a pause during which there were no questions, Rosie said, "Thanks, all of you, for attending. Be prepared to meet again on short notice when the arrests have been made. Those of you here can join me for lunch if you like."

CHAPTER 2

Friday, April 12, 2019
El Paso Texas, USA

Shortly after Yusef was settled in his office to begin work for the day, he received a phone call from Charles Goodnight, head of the FBI Field Office for El Paso, asking if he could come over right away to give Yusef advance notice of a major case that would be referred to the AG very soon. Shortly, Charles and Carter Kuykendall arrived and were welcomed by Yusef with professional handshakes. Charles wore a navy-blue suit, white shirt, and a dark blue tie, the FBI "uniform." He was in his fifties, about five nine, fit, with graying hair, and looked distinguished. Carter was in is forties and of average height, about five ten. He wore a charcoal gray suit with white shirt and navy-blue tie, also the "uniform".

Charles began, "This is a high-profile case with major international implications, so we want to give you advance notice. Late yesterday, we arrested four men, two Russians and two Iranian-Americans, who have been using El Paso as a base of operations to fly to various cities, set off small bombs, and in general create disturbances. We'll provide you with detailed evidence, of course, when there's an arraignment and subsequent trial. Hopefully, we can stall and have an arraignment on Monday or Tuesday and give you as much evidence as we can then."

Yusef said, "That does sound like a big one. Thanks for giving us advance notice. As you know, I'm only the acting head of this division. I should bring in the associate director. Please wait a moment while I get her."

Susana Tate came in and exchanged greetings, having met the two from the FBI before. Charles repeated what he had told Yusef. Susana responded, "Yes, that is big. It'll bring even more publicity to El Paso. What are their motives; have you discovered yet?"

"Investigations are still going on," Carter said. "We suspect it's a continuation of Russian activity that began in 2015 to create chaos in the U.S. and bring down our democracy."

"But this time with Iranians?" Yusef asked.

"We're looking into that," Carter said. "Iranians and Russians are cozying up to each other, and Iran is upset over sanctions from the U.S. The two Iranians are U.S. citizens, born here. They must have been radicalized at some point. The FBI knows there are Iranian sympathizers among the Iranian-American community in this country."

"You'll arraign them soon," Susana said, "but it could be a while before any trial, especially on major cases like this."

"We'll certainly have someone at the arraignment," Yusef said. "We need to get in touch with our district office in San Antonio, and they'll surely contact our headquarters in DC."

"Our Operations Center is in touch with AG headquarters in DC also," Charles said.

Yusef thought, *I'd better contact Roger as soon as I finish talking with John,* referring to Roger Chen, his mentor and colleague when he worked at Attorney General headquarters in Washington, and John Holmes, the U.S. Attorney for the Western District of Texas.

Charles stood to leave, saying, "We have lots to do, so we'll leave you with the information now. We'll get evidence to you as soon as we can, and we'll keep you in the loop as we continue investigating."

Yusef and Susana said thanks and stood to shake hands with the two from the FBI as they left.

Yusef motioned for Susana to sit, saying, "We really have a situation on our hands. I'm grateful for your experience and guidance on how to handle it."

Susana nodded and said, "Thanks," while Yusef continued. "We need to send someone senior and experienced to represent us for the arraignment, someone the judge would know and respect. Maybe that could be you."

"I'd do it," Susana said. "I don't mind at all appearing in front of the judges here."

"And if they are arraigned individually or in pairs, who else?" Yusef asked. "I don't think it should be me. I have little courtroom experience, am younger, and the judges don't know me."

"What about Brenda?" Susana said, referring to Brenda Jackson, a more senior staff prosecutor. "I can tell her now."

"Sounds good," Yusef said. "We could probably look at the dockets and see which judges are most likely to be assigned to this case or cases."

Susana left, and Yusef immediately contacted John Holmes in San Antonio and relayed the information. John appreciated the early notice and that Yusef and Susana had made arrangements for the arraignment. John said he would have to contact the national office but suspected it had been notified by the FBI in Washington. They agreed to keep in touch.

Yusef then called Roger Chen. After describing the situation, Roger said, "With all that's going on in this country, especially here in DC, it's not surprising the Russians are up to something. It's not surprising it's in El Paso, either, the biggest city on the border and with a major airport. While I don't have any direct interest, I know you'll handle it well. Keep me informed."

Yusef then thought about who else he might notify, and suddenly Marcus Porter popped into his mind. Marcus was a friend from Virginia when Yusef helped prosecute a case in Roanoke, Virginia, and when Marcus was a young reporter for the local newspaper. Yusef thought, *It's been a while since I was in touch with Marcus. He's a nice guy, and I owe him a big favor over that incident with the flight in San Antonio. I bet he'd like a scoop, now that he's with BBC America.*

Yusef took out his cell phone, thinking, *I'd better call him on the cell phone so he recognizes my number.*

When Marcus answered with enthusiastic greetings, Yusef began, "Hey, I've got a scoop for you. It's been a while since we were in touch. I haven't told you that I'm now in El Paso as acting head of the El Paso division office. But first, what's new with you?"

(Pause)

"Oh, a promotion. Congratulations!" Yusef said. "You're living back in Virginia, closer to home."

(Pause)

"And now a little girl. Congratulations again!"

Yusef described the situation with the arrest of the defendants. "You can't quote me as a source, but I want to be sure you are one of the first to know. The local media here will be on it soon, but maybe you can beat them to it."

(Pause)

"Oh, you might come down for the arraignment," Yusef said. "That'd be great. And yes, El Paso is a great city, not appreciated as much as it should be."

(Pause)

"I've heard of a courtroom artist here that you might use," Yusef added. "No need to bring one. We can talk about details as soon as you can make travel arrangements. There's a nice hotel close to the courthouse; a historic old hotel that has been restored and is now open."

They continued in brief conversation, then concluded that Yusef would hope to see him Sunday.

Susana came to see Yusef in the afternoon and said, "It looks like the two most likely judges would be Richard Underwood and Francisco Salazar; everyone calls him Frank. They're both well-seasoned judges, appointed by George W. Bush a fair number of years ago. Frank can be cantankerous at times, but we have a good relationship with him."

"If this is like back in DC," Yusef responded, "The defendants would have the best hotshot defense attorneys they could find. I'll bet we get some of them down here on Monday. How would these judges react?"

"Hotshot lawyers from DC or wherever wouldn't faze them at all," Susana Tate answered. "They'd just as soon overrule them and hold them in contempt as they would any lawyers."

"It sounds like you and Brenda know how to deal with the situation," Yusef said. "Besides, it's just an arraignment. There might be follow-on actions dealing with release on bail and things like that, not to mention a trial. If this goes like the cases in DC, there will eventually be a plea bargain and guilty pleas to avoid trial, trying to get them off as light as possible."

"That's not what usually happens here," Susana Tate said. "These judges are pretty independent minded. Of course, if there's a guilty plea, they can't require a trial, but they might not go along with a light sentence."

"It's going to be interesting," Yusef said. "With your experience, we can work through this."

"Maybe we should bring all the staff together and tell them," Susana suggested. "It might not be good if they heard about this through the media. Should I round them up?"

"Sure, great idea."

After briefing the staff, Yusef called Khan aside to tell him about Marcus Porter's planning to be present for the arraignment, and asking if Otto might be free to make drawings.

CHAPTER 3

Friday, April 12, 2019
El Paso, Texas, USA

In the late afternoon, Yusef received a text message on his phone from Nisrine saying she was working late so he would have to pick up Sara. Later at home, Yusef fed himself and Sara. Nisrine arrived and gave both of them brief kisses, changed clothes, and started rummaging through the kitchen for something to eat.

Later when Nisrine came into the family room, Yusef confronted her. "What's going on, Nizzy? This is the second time this week you've told me to pick up Sara, and the third time lately. You know I like being with Sara and she appreciates me, but sometimes, like today, I have work to do. I wasn't able to go to prayers, and I suppose you didn't go either."

"You just have to understand that we are a two-career family and that you have to support me," Nisrine responded.

"Yes, I know," Yusef replied. "I've supported you all the way. But I need support for my career, too, and we had a huge event today that I'll tell you about."

"They need me, Yusey," Nisrine said. "They need me tomorrow, too. You'll have to keep Sara then, too."

"Tomorrow I have to spend some time working," Yusef said. "I'll do what I can from home and maybe take her with me to the office, but I do need to be there."

"They need me tomorrow, too," Nisrine repeated.

Yusef pondered for just a moment and said, "Who is the one who needs someone? Is it you who needs to be needed?"

Nisrine sat up and almost shouted, "What do you mean?"

Yusef replied, "I'm no psychologist, but we've seen enough in cases. There's being workaholic, or more likely codependency, the need to be needed."

"How can you be so cruel, Yusey?" Nisrine blurted out.

"That's not cruel," Yusef said. "I love you; Sara loves you. You're tearing yourself apart over your work. We want you back like before."

Nisrine got up crying and went to bed with no further communication.

Saturday, April 13, 2019

Nisrine woke up, still indifferent towards Yusef, and gave brief kisses goodbye to Yusef and Sara when she went to work. Yusef worked at home as best he could while entertaining and taking care of Sara. He did not go to his office, hoping to go the next day before he met Marcus at the airport. When Nisrine arrived home from work, she was visibly stressed but non-communicative. The rest of the evening was spent with all being tense and barely communicating. Sara, picking up on her parents' distress, was fussy and went to bed and to sleep with notable difficulty.

Sunday, April 14, 2019

After sleeping late and being awakened by Sara's needing attention, Nisrine and Yusef were less tense but still careful in their communication. When Yusef said he had to go to his office and then to meet Marcus Porter at the airport, Nisrine asked why. Yusef explained the arrests of the four defendants and that Marcus was coming to cover the arraignment. Nisrine showed only casual interest. Yusef left with a brief kiss to Nisrine and a warm hug to Sara.

In the mid-afternoon, Yusef met Marcus at the airport, took him to the historic Paso del Norte Hotel in downtown El Paso. Marcus was in the same age range as Yusef, early-to-mid-thirties, about five ten with blue eyes and slightly wavy brown hair, closely trimmed. He wore smart casual clothes for traveling, with a blazer and a tie in his carry-on baggage. At the hotel, Khan and Otto met them and discussed Otto's drawing during the arraignments the next morning; Otto was taking a day off work. Arraignments were scheduled at separate times to allow Marcus and Otto to go to both. Khan said he would be there with Yusef's concurrence.

Marcus said, "Maybe I can rent a car and go look at the place where the tunnel is to take pictures. At a supposed mosque, you said. Could one of you tell me how to get there?"

Otto said, "If the arraignments don't take too long, I could take you there. I have the rest of the day off, and it's just a couple of miles from downtown. Maybe Khan could go with us if he doesn't need to work the rest of the day."

Yusef said, "I'd gladly go with you too, but with all this going on, I'd better stay close to the office. Unless Khan has some urgent project, he could go." Smiling, he said, "We could make him our media contact for the day."

They continued in general chat for a while, then Yusef as well as Khan and Otto said goodbyes and left Marcus to have dinner and organize the next day.

When Yusef arrived home, Nisrine was sitting listlessly on the sofa while Sara played by herself in her room. Yusef gave Nisrine a brief kiss, saying he had met Marcus and that they needed to meet him the next night. "Maybe not make dinner here, but we need to do something with him after what he did for us in San Antonio."

Nisrine said, "I'm not sure I'm up for it." She then paused and broke out crying, saying, "I hate my job."

Yusef sat next to her, putting his arm around her shoulder, while she continued. "You're right. I needed to be needed on this job."

Between sobs, she continued, "They're so indifferent, like they don't care. Yes, medically they do everything right, but the other doctors and the nurses just don't seem to care about the women and the babies. Too often they just refer for an abortion. And for the women—and girls—too often the pregnancy is accidental. They just want confirmation that they're pregnant and sometimes just a referral for an abortion. Or just have the baby and get it over. You know I have no moral objection to abortion; sometimes that's the best way for all. But what about the joy of delivering a healthy baby to grow into a productive person? I thought if I kept trying hard enough, showing how much I cared for mothers and their babies, I would eventually get through to the other medical staff. Now I know it can never happen there."

Yusef pulled her closer to hold her while she continued, "I just want to go back to San Antonio where I can have my own practice. There I can serve women who have only limited means, but at least I can connect with them and help them deliver healthy babies. They appreciate that."

"You could just quit here," Yusef said. "You know we don't need your income, and your distress is really having a bad impact on all three of us. Maybe you could have some type of private practice here. Work part time for an established practice, not a public health clinic. Be available to provide backup for midwives, like you did in San Antonio."

Nisrine continued to sob, and added, "Definitely I need to stop, or at least slow down. I'm pregnant. Yesterday I confirmed it, although I had suspected for a day or two. Sorry I haven't told you until now."

"Oh, wonderful," Yusef said. "Great news!"

"When can we go back to San Antonio, Yusey?" she asked.

"For sure, I'd like to move back to San Antonio," Yusef replied. "I'm tired of working two jobs. But with all these issues at the border, and especially this latest set of indictments, they wouldn't move me anytime soon. I talked to Roger a couple of times. Headquarters is aware of the issues. They need to find just the right person to take my place here. Maybe someone from California who has dealt with these issues before. But let's not think about that now, and just make the best of it. I'm starved. What do we have for dinner?"

"Oh, Yusey, I was so upset and depressed that I couldn't fix anything."

"I'll just go see what I can find for us," Yusef said.

The rest of the evening they relaxed as best they could, watching television and trying not to occupy their minds, Yusef's anticipating a busy day on Monday.

CHAPTER 4

Monday, April 15, 2019
El Paso, Texas, USA

In the morning, Marcus Porter, accompanied by Otto, went to the two arraignments scheduled half an hour apart in the federal courthouse. They sat near the front while Otto sketched the defendants. Yusef sat farther back in the courtroom with Khan. The Russian defendants were represented by attorneys from a prestigious Washington law firm, and the Iranian-Americans by a law firm from Los Angeles with a firm name that had Iranian surnames. All pleaded not guilty, and the attorneys asked for release on bail. During their respective arraignments in which they represented the government prosecution, Susana Tate and Brenda Jackson each emphasized flight risks, especially being on the border and the ease of walking across the border bridge unimpeded. The judges denied bail and said that trials would be scheduled at later dates.

When the judge closed the last arraignment, Yusef told Khan he would see him in the office the next day and left, pointedly avoiding being seen publicly with Marcus and Otto lest he be thought to show favoritism towards a specific media outlet.

While defendants were being escorted out of the courtroom, in each case Marcus, along with local media representatives, rushed to the defense attorneys, holding out his cell phone to ask for and record statements. Both attorneys waved them away, saying that statements to the media would be given later.

Marcus then said to Otto, "I need to go to my hotel room and quickly upload your drawings and give my report. We didn't agree on how much to pay you, but I'll find out the going rate. I need to get this on air before the other national and international networks get it from local media. Please meet me in the hotel lobby in about twenty minutes."

When Marcus came to the lobby, Otto and Khan were waiting, Khan still dressed in his business suit. Otto was wearing the smart casual clothes he wore in the courtroom. Marcus said, "Now they can get this and your sketches on air this afternoon and definitely in time for the evening news; it's two hours later on the East Coast."

"Maybe we can see you on TV later today," Khan said.

"You won't see me, or even hear me," Marcus replied. "I'm a news producer, not a reporter. Producers just gather the news and develop it in a form to be presented before a camera. They don't like my accent," he chuckled. "I just develop what happened, and a reporter will read it and show Otto's drawings. The reports are usually repeated a few times because of being broadcast live in different time zones. When they have the trials, or some other significant event, they'll likely send a reporter down here with me and maybe a camera person, although no cameras are allowed in the courtroom. We'll still want your sketches, Otto. Be sure to give me contact details so we can send payment to you."

"OK," Otto said. "Say do we want to have lunch somewhere and then go show you the tunnel site?"

"Sounds good to me," Marcus said. "Where do you recommend? My treat."

"One place that's interesting and nice and a little expensive is a barbecue place called the State Line. The state line runs directly through the middle of the restaurant. It's close to the tunnel where we want to go."

After an ample lunch of traditional southwestern-style barbecue, they drove in Otto's car to the site of the supposed mosque and tunnel. As they approached, Khan said, "We're exactly on the state line. It's not marked, but that convenience store over there is definitely in Texas; it has a sign that says 'Texas Lottery Play here!'. The site for the supposed tunnel is directly behind, and surely in Texas also. The other side of the road is New Mexico, the city of Sunland Park. The state line follows the original course of the Rio Grande, which was very irregular. The river has been channelized in this area, but the state line still meanders. No doubt it's marked on some official map, but there's nothing here to tell us where the state line is."

As they approached the supposed mosque, armed El Paso police were outside. When they approached, one of the police officers stopped them and said they could not go any further. Marcus held out his press card and said he would like to ask questions. The police officer replied that the FBI would have a press conference later, but for now, no one but law enforcement was allowed on the property and that no further questions were allowed.

They stood back from the scene while Marcus took photographs with his phone, and Otto hastily got out his sketch pads and started drawing. After a while, Khan suggested they go to the point where the railroad came next to the border fence where he and Otto had been before.

After a short drive, they drove across the railroad tracks and parked where Khan and Otto had stopped before for Otto to make sketches and where they could see through the fence into the Anapra neighborhood of Ciudad Juárez. Marcus used his phone to take pictures from various perspectives. They noticed a car with New Mexico license plates parked off to the side and a man standing observing them. Khan and Otto remembered their previous visit when a uniformed police officer from Sunland Park harassed them, but this person was not wearing a uniform.

Soon the man started walking towards them. He was apparently in his fifties with graying, balding head with hair kept trimmed, wearing cowboy boots, jeans, and a flannel shirt. When he got closer, he said, "Be careful and don't get too close to that fence. Teenage boys on the other side climb the fence and throw objects at people who are too close." Extending his hand, he said, "Delmar Armstrong of the New Mexico ACLU. May I ask what brings you here?"

Marcus Porter held out his press card and said, "I've been in El Paso covering a major story, and my friends brought me here to this point to see the border fence up close. May I ask what is the interest of the ACLU?"

Delmar Armstrong replied, "There have been armed militias, civilian groups, monitoring the area, confining immigrants crossing the border illegally, and turning them over to the Border Patrol. You don't seem to be armed and aren't dressed like vigilantes. Not too many others come out here."

"That sounds very interesting," Marcus said. "Could you tell me more? Why is the ACLU interested?"

"There's some indication they're violating immigrants' human rights, kidnapping them, confining them against their will," Delmar replied. "We're not ready to talk to the media yet; we just started monitoring them. We've also turned it over to the FBI for investigation."

"Who in your organization would be willing to give me more information?" Marcus asked.

"That would be me, when the time comes," Delmar answered. "As I said, we're not ready to talk to the media yet, and I suspect the FBI wouldn't want to comment at this early stage in the investigation."

"Where could I find out more, then?"

"The group has a website, The United Constitutional Patriots. They operate out in the open and claim they are lawful. Maybe they would talk to you, and we could find out more when you publish it. They have a campsite just over there, out of sight. I don't know how they would react if you approached it, but there doesn't seem to be anyone there right now."

"Where do they find the immigrants here?" Marcus asked. "There's a big fence. I suppose some could climb over it. You said that teenagers climb the fence and throw things, but it's a big drop-off on this side."

"There's a break in the fence down that direction out of sight," Delmar said, pointing towards a mountainside. "The Border Patrol didn't think a fence was necessary up the mountainside because of the steep slope, but people found a way. The strip of land next to the fence on this side is U.S. Government property. This is New Mexico, where the U.S. Government kept the land for a short distance inside the border to be able to control what happens on it, install a fence, and all of that. Also, the Union Pacific Railroad owns the tracks and the right-of-way along each side of the tracks. Technically you would be trespassing if you walked too close to the railroad tracks. So far, neither the government nor the railroad is pursuing trespass, but they could." He wished them well and turned to walk away.

They walked to the campsite, where Otto drew more sketches and Marcus took photos before they returned to El Paso, Otto saying he needed to return to Alamogordo soon. They parted company, exchanging contact details.

Back in his hotel, Marcus located the website of the militia, left a message with a contact person, and waited for a response. Later he spent a relaxing evening with Yusef, Nisrine, and Sara, Nisrine still feeling stressed and depressed but sociable. During the evening, Marcus asked, "Khan and Otto are a couple, aren't they?"

Yusef answered, "It seems so. This is the first time I've met Otto, but Khan had shown me his drawings before. Khan and I are not close, but he's a very good attorney and brings a lot to our staff. Whether he's gay or not, makes no difference. You know from our wedding in San Antonio that we have gay friends."

The evening continued with general conversation, during which Yusef asked Marcus, "When are you going home to Washington?"

Marcus replied, "I just changed my booking to go on Wednesday. This seems like a nice city, and it would be good to explore more, maybe do a feature for viewers, now that El Paso is getting more news attention."

"Yes, for sure," Yusef replied. "The mayor said it's the size of Boston, yet the rest of the country doesn't know much about it."

"Also, I think I might have a chance for an interview with the head of the United Constitutional Patriots, the vigilante group that's operating in the suburbs, Sunland Park I think is the place," Marcus said.

"Oh, I haven't heard of that," Yusef said.

Marcus described his meeting with Delmar Armstrong of the New Mexico ACLU and that the case was being investigated by the FBI. "The group seems to be open and wanting media attention, maybe too much attention; but I can see if I can talk tomorrow."

"We haven't heard about it yet in our office," Yusef commented. "If it's operating in Sunland Park, the New Mexico field office of the FBI and the New Mexico district office of the AG would be involved in any prosecution. Even though Sunland Park is right next to downtown El Paso, it's in New Mexico. State lines are not rigid for federal organizations, as you would know in DC, Virginia, and Maryland. Still, we're not actively involved in what the others do. We do cooperate. Maybe we'll find out more if this becomes a bigger activity."

The rest of the evening was spent in general conversation, all enjoying the ability to catch up. Nisrine excused herself to go to bed early, while Yusef and Marcus continued to visit. Yusef took Marcus back to his hotel in time for a reasonable bedtime and for Marcus to view the evening news on BBC America as well as competing networks.

CHAPTER 5

In the early afternoon, Yusef sent a text message on his cell phone to Marcus asking, "Can you take a call?" Marcus immediately agreed.

Yusef called and said, "There's another scoop for you. The FBI contacted me late this morning to give advance notice that two North Koreans came through the tunnel from Mexico saying they wanted asylum in the U.S. The FBI suspects they might be spies, but so far there's not enough evidence to charge them with espionage. They turned them over to the Border Patrol, who put them in detention with the Central Americans while they investigate further. I've been on the phone with the AG for the Western District in San Antonio and Roger in Washington to notify them. I'm sure nothing has been released to the media yet, but I thought I'd let you know. Of course, you can't attribute this to me, but you seem to have your ways to get the story."

(Pause)

"Please let me know if you find anything interesting," Yusef said. "Hopefully, talk to you tomorrow before you leave."

Yusef returned to work, pondering about how to deal with this latest hot issue that might end up in federal court in El Paso and needing his attention. *We're going to need help if this turns out to be an espionage trial,* he thought. *Roger has a heads up, so he can help. Gotta keep John in the loop too.*

Quantico, Virginia, USA

In the mid-afternoon, Eastern time, Rosie Jordan opened a hastily called meeting; Adam Culbertson and Brock O'Neill of the Operations Center attended in person, and other frequent attendees all joined by Skype: Jared Cramer of FBI Headquarters in Washington, Eric James of the CIA, Andrew Branson of the Border Patrol headquarters, Carmen Cisneros of the El Paso FBI field office, and Peter Richardson from the Las Cruces FBI resident agency. Rosie said, "Carmen and Peter, you asked for this meeting. Peter, why don't you go first."

Peter began, "What I have is short, but we want to bring it to the attention of headquarters and the Operations Center as soon as possible. The New Mexico ACLU has discovered an armed citizens militia group operating along the border right outside of El Paso in the suburb of Sunland Park, New Mexico. It's rounding up illegal immigrants crossing through a gap in the fence and turning them over to the Border Patrol. The ACLU claims the armed vigilante group is violating human rights and kidnapping immigrants. The militia group, which operates openly, claims it operates lawfully by making citizen arrests and turning persons committing crimes over to law enforcement. The group has a makeshift camp right next to the border fence. We have just now begun our investigation. We'll certainly keep you informed."

Andrew added, "We've just been informed today by our agents in the area that this activity is going on. It's too soon to make any comments other than the fact that the Border Patrol does not condone any civilian activity to enforce laws at the border."

"Questions or comments?" Rosie asked. "If not, Carmen, please go ahead."

She began, "The most bizarre thing is that this morning two Asians, a man and a woman each appearing in their thirties, came through the tunnel speaking broken English saying they wanted asylum in the U.S. They claimed they're Chinese. We detained them and notified the Border Patrol. In El Paso, the Border Patrol has interpreters available for the most common languages because of the wide variety of people who try to cross the border there. A Border Patrol agent arrived soon and contacted an interpreter on the phone. The asylum seekers did not respond to any Chinese dialect. We determined that they spoke better Spanish than English, but not well. They admitted they are from North Korea and want asylum in the U.S. While a Korean interpreter was being located, in halting Spanish they claimed they had been working at the Mexican end of the tunnel and when Mexican authorities arrived that morning to investigate, they fled for their lives.

"A Korean interpreter was located who reported that they were attached to the North Korean embassy in Mexico City and assigned to work as disguised spa workers to monitor activities on the Mexican side of the tunnel. They seemingly had some naïve notions that Chinese or North Koreans would be welcomed as asylum seekers and that they could just go join other North Korean asylees in California, and even had contact details. The Border Patrol agent took them into custody and apparently sent them to a detention facility where asylum seekers from Central America are being held to await appearance before an asylum judge. We suspect they are spies, but until we have more information about them, we can't arrest them. Your guidance will no doubt be required about how to proceed next."

Andrew Branson with Border Patrol headquarters, said, "We were notified today as well about supposed North Koreans in custody there. This situation certainly has the potential for major international implications and must be handled carefully here at the highest levels. Certainly, we want to keep them in detention until we can determine what to do next."

Eric James of the CIA added, "Having spies operating at the Mexican border—the Canadian border too—is not unusual. We know the Russians have an agent in Ciudad Juárez spying on all our activities in the El Paso area, military, and other places, and into New Mexico. They know we know. We also spy into Russia at places I'll not mention, and the Russians know that we do. Spying by North Korea at our border is something new. For sure, we'll be looking into this, but we need to keep things quiet for a while until we see how things fall out. The administration's relationship with the North Koreans is, shall we say, tense at the moment, especially with Kim Jong Un going to Russia to meet with Vladimir Putin. Also, there's the possibility the North Koreans could detain someone to use as a prisoner swap in order to get these two back under their control, even though they say they want asylum. We don't want to go too far in speculation right now."

Jared Cramer of FBI headquarters said, "If North Korea is involved, that adds new dimensions we need to consider. When we look at all of the activities of the two pairs of Russians and Iranian-Americans you arrested, we're reminded of some of the tactics of the Russians to create chaos in general to bring down democracy, going back to 2015. This was before Russians started interfering with elections. Some of these recent incidents have targeted both sides of sensitive issues and just seem to be designed to create chaos, not support nor attack a specific position. For example, there were attacks on gay and lesbian centers while at the same time there were attacks on churches that supported anti-gay activities. Now it appears the attacks on both sides of the gay-lesbian issue were made by the same sets of people working together just to create chaos.

"Maybe the Russians are coordinating these attacks out of Mexico. We watch them very closely here. In Mexico, maybe they get the cooperation of Iran and North Korea, both of which have embassies in Mexico. It's much too soon to take specific action based on this speculation, but we might start the process, maybe be more observant in Mexico, but that needs the cooperation of the CIA."

Eric James said, "It is not unknown for us to observe diplomats in foreign countries, but obviously we have to be careful. The Mexicans would not be too receptive to our spying on diplomats in their country. But, if the foreign diplomats are taking advantage of Mexican "hospitality," shall we say, then Mexico might be more open to cooperate with us. As you know, Mexico has a new president. So far, he has been generally open to working with us, although there are some tensions on border issues. Certainly, we need to look more into things, now that you have brought these developments to our attention."

Jared added, "We have ongoing but limited contact with our Mexican counterparts. We notified them about the existence of the tunnel. Apparently, they investigated, and that motivated the North Koreans to flee. We need to contact them again. We'll notify you directly, Carmen. You, too, Peter, because you're so close to the situation. The Mexicans might contact you directly, which is OK with us. Just keep us informed."

After a lull in the discussion, Rosie asked if anyone had anything else to add. When there was no response, he thanked everyone for being present on short notice and closed the meeting.

CHAPTER 6

Tuesday, April 23, 2019
El Paso, Texas, USA

In the early afternoon Mountain time, Yusef sent a text message on his cell phone to Marcus asking, "Can you talk on Skype or take a call?" Soon they were connected on Skype, where Yusef said, "The local media want a statement from me about the attacks on Christian churches in Sri Lanka. I suppose they are reacting because I chided them on contacting me about attacks on Muslims in New Zealand just because I'm Muslim. Now they want comments on Muslim attacks on Christians. I told them I would give them a written statement tomorrow. I can't really blow them off, but this is getting annoying, with all we have going on here on border issues. In any event, would you let me read my statement to you and give me feedback before I release it?"

"Sure," Marcus replied.

Yusef read his prepared remarks:

Just as I condemned the attacks on Muslims in New Zealand, I condemn the attacks on Christians in Sri Lanka in the strongest way possible. The fact that the attack was by persons who call themselves Muslims and that I am Muslim does not affect my revulsion. Wanton destruction of property and taking lives is the extremist form of violation of human rights, regardless of religion. Moreover, the mere fact that persons call themselves Muslims does not mean they are. Islam does not condone destruction of property or murder under any circumstances, so these persons could not be viewed as Muslim. I am not a theologian, but I can refer you to a theologian, and you can surely find Muslim theologians yourselves.

Much the same thing could be said about Christians; just because people claim to be Christian does not mean they are. Christianity condemns destruction of property and murder equally as strongly as does Islam. Yet, among the earliest religious terrorists were crusaders marauding in the name of Christianity. Also, during the anti-civil rights terrorism of the 1960s, groups like the Ku Klux Klan identified themselves as Christian, while clearly they were not.

Hate crimes are sadly universal and to be condemned and prosecuted with equal fervor everywhere.

Yusef paused, Marcus pondered a moment, then said, "The first part is good, direct, and to the point. You should consider toning down or eliminating the second part about Christianity. The less scrupulous in our profession could seriously misrepresent it."

Yusef thought for a moment and said, "OK, I can think about it. I got this from the lady who was pastor at that Methodist church in Virginia a few years ago. You met her."

"Yes, I remember her. Very nice lady. She can get by with it speaking in front of her congregation, even if media were present. I'm sorry I wasn't there to hear that comment; it would have made a good story. You are a high-profile U.S. Attorney in a location under the microscope. Imagine a headline 'Muslim U.S. Attorney Claims Christians Were Terrorists.' How many would actually read the story, even if it were accurately written, to see the context of your comments?"

"OK, I see your point," Yusef said. "I'll tone it down."

Marcus continued, "I was going to contact you today, anyway. The attorney for that citizens militia group contacted me earlier today. He liked the way I developed news about their group and wants as much good publicity as possible. The leader of the group was arrested by the FBI and will be arraigned tomorrow in Las

Cruces. Because it's in New Mexico, I didn't know if you would know anything about it yet. Of course, I'm eager for any comment you have."

"I haven't heard of anything here, yet," Yusef replied. "We likely wouldn't unless it involved something in our division, and you say it's in New Mexico."

"Yes," Marcus said. "He was arrested on an old weapons-possession charge apparently somewhere in New Mexico. So far, there are no charges over his recent activities with illegal immigrants, which they steadfastly claim are legal. There isn't enough time for me to arrange a trip down there on such short notice. Besides, arraignments are routine events that take just a few minutes, so it could be difficult to justify a long trip. I did contact Otto, who was able to take time off work to get some sketches for me. Apparently, where Otto lives in Alamogordo is not that far from Las Cruces."

"I'd guess about seventy miles, a little over an hour," Yusef said.

Marcus continued, "I can't keep imposing on Otto to take time off to sketch, even if we're paying him. But this time, it works to our advantage."

Yusef concurred and said, "There's another reason I would've contacted you today. The FBI notified us this morning that they're opening the site of the tunnel to us and the press. We will be sending our prosecutors there to gather evidence for trials. No doubt the local media will be there too. If you could get here quickly, you should be able to take pictures and get information too."

"Wow," Marcus exclaimed. "Thanks for the tip."

"You're welcome," Yusef replied. "I told you once before back in Virginia that we in the AG are very aware of the benefits of a free press."

"I remember," Marcus said, "even though there are all the claims of fake news."

"You must surely realize, though, that we can't show favoritism to you," Yusef continued. "The local media would already know, and there's a good chance that the other national networks can find out very soon."

"Yes, I know," Marcus said. "I'll start checking right away on flight schedules. Too bad there are no direct flights from DC, but there are connections in Houston, Dallas, Atlanta, and Denver, I found out last time. As soon as I know something, I'll let you know. I can make my own hotel reservations this time, so you're not showing so much favoritism."

"This opening to us and the media is only on the U.S. side," Yusef added. "We don't know what the Mexicans are doing. As a free citizen, you can surely cross the border readily, travel around that part of Ciudad Juárez freely, and take a look at the building where the tunnel comes out, if nothing else. Maybe you remember that the North Koreans who want asylum claim it was a Chinese herb store and spa as a cover. You need to have a current passport, which surely you have."

"It's probably too late to arrange a reporter and photographer to come with me," Marcus said. "I'll just have to do what I can on my own. I'm not bad with a camera. I can't impose on Otto again."

"We might be able to get Khan free to go gather information for the prosecution at the same time you are nosing around," Yusef added. "We're always open to have media cooperate and go along with us. Of course, if another media outlet approaches us first, you might have to share Khan's attention. He wouldn't have a good official reason to go to Mexico, although as a free citizen he's free to cross the border and come back. I'm sure he has a current passport, although I haven't had occasion to ask him."

They continued to discuss logistics a few minutes, Marcus ringing off to begin making travel arrangements.

CHAPTER 7

Friday, April 26, 2019
El Paso, Texas, USA

In the early morning, Khan was having breakfast with Marcus near the El Paso airport before Marcus's flights back to Washington. While eating, Marcus said, "Thanks again for going with me while I covered the tunnel, even going to Mexico to get pictures over there, even if we did have to share the experience with CNN."

"My pleasure," Khan replied. "No doubt Yusef has emphasized to you the importance of good relations with the media."

"Thanks, also, for finding a Spanish interpreter on short notice for when I went to see the Mexican end of the tunnel," Marcus added.

"Again, my pleasure," Khan said. "There are plenty of people in El Paso who speak Spanish. Fortunately, I'm getting to know people at church and other places. Some would do favors for me, and of course like to earn a little money, especially UTEP students." *Maybe I shouldn't say gay places Otto and I go to sometimes,* Khan thought.

"My network is saying they want me to move here temporarily," Marcus said. "With all the things going on along the border, they want to have someone on the spot. My wife sure wouldn't welcome this, especially with a new baby. But, I guess it comes with the job, and I'm not ready to quit and look for something else now. Besides, the other major networks move people around just as much. In a city as big as El Paso, there must surely be some extended stay places where I could stay and not be confined to a single hotel room and eating out all the time."

"Yes, I stayed at a place like that when I first moved here," Khan said. "I'm pretty good at making my own meals. There are several extended stay places all over town. Let me know when you get ready to come here, and I'll see what I can find for you. And say, maybe you can come over for dinner and not have to eat your own cooking. I'm pretty good at making Vietnamese food."

"Sounds good," Marcus said. "Thanks."

"Maybe Otto can join us too," Khan said.

"That'd be good," Marcus said. "He's a really nice guy, and he's been very helpful in drawing sketches for me."

"I've been trying to encourage him," Khan said. "He's probably not ready to give up his day job, though."

"You spend lots of time together, it seems," Marcus offered.

Oh, does he know we're a couple? Khan asked himself. *Maybe Yusef told him.*

"Er, yes," Khan said. "Did Yusef tell you?"

"Yes," Marcus said, "but only after I asked him. Did Yusef tell you that I attended his wedding? There I met his gay friends, two couples. It seemed a fair thing to ask him about you two. But, hey, we're not going to out you on air, unless you want to be, of course. Pete and Chasten Buttigieg are basking in media attention, as you would well know."

Khan smiled and said, "Well, let's not get ahead of ourselves. Otto and I've been seeing each other pretty regularly for a couple of months now, but we're certainly not ready to discuss anything permanent. Living two hours apart kind of limits things."

"I suppose you'll be together this weekend," Marcus said.

"Yes," Khan answered. "I'm going to his place. Usually he comes to El Paso because there's more to do here. But, now that the weather is getting warmer, we want me to spend more time there.

There are lots of nice places in nature in that area, especially in the mountains. If you move here for a while, we can show you."

"Tell him goodbye for me, and thanks," Marcus said. "It's time for me to head to the airport. Thank you again for giving me a ride and joining me for breakfast. This is my treat."

Khan dropped Marcus off at the airport terminal, where they parted company with a warm handshake. Khan then drove to work.

When Yusef arrived at his office, he noticed a message from Roger Chen in Washington to connect on Skype or phone. Soon they connected on Skype. After preliminary greetings, Roger said, "Late yesterday we got a phone call from the U.S. Attorney for New Mexico asking for our assistance to provide guidance on human rights law. It's for the case involving the head of the civilian militia who was just arrested. I'm sure you are aware of the case."

Yusef nodded and indicated that he was familiar. Roger continued, "The militia leader was arrested on a firearms possession charge going back a short while. The ACLU is claiming human rights violations, kidnapping, and other charges with respect to the illegal immigrants the militia were apprehending. The office of the U.S. attorney in New Mexico doesn't have much experience in developing human rights cases and was asking for guidance. We could send someone from here, but not right away. I told him about you being close by in El Paso. You're very busy, I know, especially on the cases you just got, but maybe you could give some temporary assistance until we can get someone there from headquarters. The militia guy was arraigned in Las Cruces and is being held there. That's close to you. The case will likely be tried in Albuquerque because the federal court in Las Cruces is small and mostly handles drug and immigration cases."

Yusef replied, "Yes, Las Cruces is close; some would say just a far suburb. And, yes, I'm pretty busy. But we have a young guy here in the office who's developing expertise in human and civil rights law.

You likely remember when we hired him, Khan Nguyen from the University of Texas law school."

"Yes, I remember him, sort of," Roger said. "You contacted us when you learned he was looking for a position and had impressed the staff in your Austin division."

Yusef continued, "He could surely go to Las Cruces to give some guidance, especially if temporarily, or someone from Las Cruces could easily come here. Maybe I could have a little time to spare, especially if I don't have to travel. Albuquerque's another matter. Apparently, there's no good way to get there from here to Albuquerque except to drive, and that takes about four hours. But we can wait and see how the case develops."

"OK," Roger said.

Yusef added, "Maybe I should add that our focus is primarily on hate crimes, which are obviously human and civil rights issues. This case doesn't seem to have a strong hate-crime element, or at least not from what I've heard. I suppose one might stretch and say that the focus on illegal immigration is hatred of immigrants, but based on what I've heard, it's just a local group wanting to flout authority."

"You have a point," Roger said. "Right now, I just wanted to give you a heads up for when the New Mexico district might contact you."

"Thanks, I appreciate that," Yusef said.

"By the way," Roger continued, "this afternoon I'm going out to the FBI operations center to get the latest developments in the case of the four guys apprehended using the tunnel and flying from El Paso to set off bombs. You'll no doubt find out more as more facts become known."

Roger and Yusef continued to talk briefly, mostly with office gossip, then said goodbye.

CHAPTER 8

Friday, April 26, 2019
Quantico, Virginia, USA

Rosie Jordan opened yet another short-notice meeting of the task force dealing with the four persons who had been apprehended in El Paso for having set off bombs throughout the U.S. The usual group attending was joined by Roger Chen from the headquarters of the U.S. Attorney General. Rosie turned to Jared Cramer of FBI headquarters, who began, "The four suspects are in custody in El Paso and are not speaking to anyone but their attorneys unless something has changed. Carmen, have you heard anything?"

Carmen Cisneros said "No," then Jared continued, "The attorneys for the two Russians have suggested their clients might be willing to agree to a plea bargain and tell what they know; we're still evaluating their offer. Russians at their embassy in the U.S. and at the U.N. have denied any knowledge and involvement, which is to be expected. The two Russians were assigned ostensibly to joint U.S.-Russia space programs at Holloman Air Force Base in New Mexico. We've known for some time that Russians assigned to these programs were also likely involved in espionage and kept our eyes on them. The espionage was likely in our space program, so anything involving domestic terrorism was not something we looked for. The Americans they worked with have told us that they have been taking time away from the places they supposedly work for a couple of days at a time. The American co-workers, though, didn't think it sufficiently important to report it to us.

"All indications are that they were continuing what the Russians started in 2015 to create chaos in this country, with the goal to eventually bring down our democracy. This is over and above election interference. This time, though, they are doing it in conjunction with Iranians and North Koreans, both countries that have their reasons to disrupt the U.S. They're doing it from Mexico."

Eric James of the CIA interjected, "One of our people in Mexico City managed to see high level individuals from the Russian, Iranian, and North Korean embassies in Mexico having lunch at a restaurant frequented by the diplomatic community. Our person reported that there was a heated exchange, although the content could not be heard. It might have been their displeasure that we caught their people."

Jared continued, "We've known for some time that there are sympathizers for the current Iranian regime among Iranian-Americans in this country. Almost all of them have some family in Iran. Most of our effort so far has been focused on looking for money laundering because there are sanctions on almost all money transfers between the U.S. and Iran. This is the first we've known of Iranian terrorism within this country. The largest portion of Iranian-Americans live in southern California, and that appears to be where these two are from. We found California driver's licenses that match them. Recently, they ostensibly moved to El Paso and enrolled in El Paso Community College. There's no indication they're actually attending classes. So far, we're not getting any indication of plea bargains in exchange for information. Because they're natural-born U.S. citizens, deportation is not an option.

"The last item I have for you," Jared said, "is about the North Korean asylum seekers. Our Mexican counterparts notified us that they discovered sophisticated computer equipment left behind when they fled through the tunnel. They've invited us to examine the equipment, but understandably they will not let it out of the country. Next week we'll send our computer experts to examine it under the supervision of the Mexican authorities. Our Mexican counterparts have good computer skills so we should be able to learn some things. So far, they've indicated that the computers are connected to a Wi-Fi provider in New Mexico, which would make sense because the building is just a few feet from the actual border with New Mexico and close enough to make a connection. We don't know, yet, how sophisticated the two asylum seekers are in computer technology, but with the ability to go to and from through the tunnel, they could easily have gotten assistance from the U.S., including from the two Iranian-Americans now in custody."

Roger Chen said, "The Attorney General's office is certainly interested in developments, considering all the political implications. We keep in touch with the field, but, of course, the districts and divisions are free to pursue cases on their own. We're confident the Western District of Texas and the New Mexico District will be able to represent our interests adequately."

Carmen added, "We're in contact with the prosecutors in the AG division office in El Paso. They seem very competent, and we've turned over the evidence we have. The acting head of that division seems to be good too."

"Yes, he worked with us here in Washington for a few years," Roger added. "We have confidence in him as well."

Peter Richardson said, "We're in contact with the U.S. Attorney for New Mexico, too, over the vigilante group. The leader was just arrested, and we turned the case over to them. They're exploring human rights crimes."

"Yes, we've been in touch with them," Roger said. "I referred them to the acting head in El Paso. His specialty is human rights."

"There has been one recent development," Peter continued. "The vigilante group has been ordered to close their camp right against the border fence. They protested, saying it was on public land. The

Union Pacific Railroad said that the group was trespassing on their land to get to the camp and they would not allow the trespass. The City of Sunland Park and even the governor of New Mexico said that the camp had to go. It looks like the group will disband, especially with the leader in jail awaiting trial. Maybe it'll be sufficient to convict him on the possession of firearms crime and not be concerned about human rights violations that are seemingly more difficult to prove in court. That's up to the AG, of course."

Jared said, "We're focusing our attention here on these events all in and around El Paso. Domestic terrorism is increasing all over the United States. Maybe this activity operating out of El Paso is having some impact all over. We at FBI headquarters are certainly doing what we can to monitor all activities and look for possible connections. There's little doubt the Russians are behind this. As we're seeing, the Russians have their willing co-conspirators."

After a pause in the discussion, Rosie said, "There's a lot going on and it's happening quickly. I'm sure we'll be meeting again soon and on short notice. Thank you for your dedication and attendance today."

CHAPTER 9

Monday, April 29, 2019
El Paso, Texas, USA

Yusef had been sitting in his office several minutes, pondering, when Susana Tate arrived asking if she was disturbing him.

"No, I'm just wondering if local media will contact me for comment about the synagogue shootings in California like they did about the shootings in New Zealand and Sri Lanka. I'm thinking about what I might say this time."

"You likely won't get any media contact this time," Susana said. "Your previous comments were very specific about your views, very professional, and well done. They would surely expect the same from you this time. It wouldn't be very newsworthy."

"Is El Paso going to be next?" Yusef asked. "Anti-Semitism is on the rise all over the country. Anti-Muslim, too."

"There are crazy people everywhere, unfortunately," Susana said. "The biggest threat here is anti-Mexican, as they call the local Hispanics, like in that case with the lynching. There's no anti-Semitism in El Paso and never has been. Jewish people have been prominent residents of El Paso ever since the 1800s when non-Hispanics first started moving to Texas. There are synagogues and Jewish community centers here. I know some Jewish people professionally, and my children went to school with Jewish children and were good friends. I just can't imagine anything here except an outpouring of support."

"Oh, really, that many Jewish here?" Yusef asked.

"There are Jewish people all over Texas," Susana continued. "Maybe not as concentrated as in places like New York City, but substantial. Those of us who had to study Texas history—before they started watering down the courses—learned that the early Anglo-Americans who settled Texas brought with them an attitude of 'live and let live.' As a result, Jewish people came right along with them and have been well established ever since. From what I've gathered, there are substantial numbers of Jewish people in all major Texas cities."

"Jewish lawyers in San Antonio really helped us when we had problems with an airline," Yusef said.

"Oh, were you the Muslim couple who had to leave a flight to El Paso and then sued the airline for a big settlement?" Susana asked.

"Yes, that was us. We don't talk about it. I could tell you the details, but maybe another day. You must have something on your mind to come see me this morning."

"Yes. Just now I got off the phone with the attorneys in Washington for the two Russians. They don't seem to realize we're in the Mountain time zone, thinking all of Texas is on Central time. That likely indicates just how arrogant they are and just don't care. El Paso has been in the Mountain time zone ever since time zones were first established. They must not have bothered to look. They insisted that their clients should be allowed to give a plea bargain, a period of probation in exchange for cooperation, and be deported to Russia. They even gave veiled threats that if we didn't go along, the administration would intervene and make sure we complied."

"We saw some indication of that type of attitude when I worked for AG headquarters in Washington," Yusef stated. "Not specifically with respect to Russians, but by prestigious Washington law firms who have exaggerated views of their own importance. They might have some leverage with the judicial district for DC and the Eastern District of Virginia because they appear there so often. The U.S.

Attorneys for those districts were usually able to keep them at bay. The judges there are no pushovers, either. It seems to be a matter that they all know each other, interact frequently, and each pushes the limits as much as possible."

"The judges here aren't pushovers, either," Susana said. "Especially Judge Underwood, who'll be hearing the case I'm prosecuting."

"What cooperation are they talking about?" Yusef asked. "I haven't heard about any cooperation, but then I'm not following the case very closely."

"I haven't heard of any cooperation either. Maybe the FBI knows of something, but the FBI would normally tell us if there were any significant cooperation."

"We can call the FBI," Yusef said. "Or you can call because you are working closest with them. I can call, too, if a direct call from me would help."

"I'll call and get back to you," Susana said.

"What about Brenda and the Iranians?" Yusef asked. "Has she had any contact about plea bargains?"

"I haven't talked to her in a day or two," Susana replied. "I'll ask her and get back to you, or have her get back to you."

Several minutes later, in the late morning, Susana returned and said, "I just talked to Carter Kuykendall. The FBI has no indication of their willingness to cooperate and give information in exchange for a plea bargain. He said that Carmen Cisneros of their office has been attending Skype meetings with the FBI Operations Center, most recently on Friday, and the topic of plea bargains never came up."

"Roger Chen told me he was going to that meeting," Yusef commented. "He'd have told me if anything were discussed affecting these cases. They must be dangling the defendants' cooperation with offers of more information as a ploy to get them off light. Sounds typical of some Washington lawyers."

"Brenda said she had no contact with the lawyers for the Iranians," Susana added.

"If they want plea bargains to avoid the effort of a trial for them and save us the effort and expense of a trial, then we can consider the situation," Yusef said. "But you two are competent prosecutors, and I don't need to tell you that."

Susana returned to her office and Yusef continued the rest of the day dealing with issues that had accumulated.

CHAPTER 10

Wednesday, May 1, 2019
El Paso, Texas, USA

Yusef and Nisrine were going through their morning routines, eating breakfast, feeding Sara, and getting dressed for work, when Nisrine went to the bathroom suddenly with nausea. When she returned, she asked, "Yusey, can you stay with Sara for a while this morning? I've got morning sickness. I need to call and say I won't be in for work on time. I'm going to tell them today that I'm quitting, so being a couple of hours late won't matter."

"Go ahead and go back to bed," Yusef said. "I can stay here for a while. There's nothing pressing. I'll have to go to the office sometime."

"It's just morning sickness," Nisrine said. "I come across this all the time with women I treat."

In the early afternoon when Yusef arrived in his office, he found messages to contact John Holmes in San Antonio, the U.S. Attorney for the Western District of Texas. On Skype, after preliminary greetings, John said, "The Attorney General wants the two Russians you're prosecuting to be allowed to plea bargain, receive probation, and be deported."

Yusef was stunned for a moment. "What? You mean you want our prosecutors to accept their offer to plea bargain? What's this about an offer to cooperate? So far, the FBI says there's no indication they're offering to cooperate and provide useful information."

"Their attorney says that they'll give information if this plea bargain goes forward," John said. "After all the publicity about the Maria Butina prosecution, the administration doesn't want to upset the Russians further and wants to get this case over with as soon as possible, with minimal publicity."

Yusef, stunned again, exclaimed, "I swore an oath to serve the interests of the United States, not the interests of Russia!" After a moment of strained silence, he asked, "What about the Iranians? Are plea bargains expected for them too?"

"The administration wants to charge them with treason," John answered.

"What? What about equal protection under the law? I swore to uphold the constitution. They committed the same crimes as the Russians."

"They're U.S. citizens and can be charged with treason," John Holmes replied. "Russians can't be charged with treason."

"But does the law of treason apply? From what I recall about the law, treason is committing acts that specifically benefit another country, an adversary. From the evidence we've gotten from the FBI, their crimes were to create chaos in the U.S., not to benefit a specific adversary country. There are plenty of other crimes we can charge them with."

"The administration wants to charge them with the maximum," John said.

"But a jury has to accept the charge beyond a reasonable doubt," Yusef added. "Wouldn't it be a potential embarrassment if we focused on a charge we couldn't prove and the jury didn't accept it, when there are plenty of other crimes we could prove?"

"The administration wants a public trial covered by the media that shows we are as tough on the Iranians as we can be, especially now that we're enforcing sanctions on Iran worldwide. The AG will send prosecutors to El Paso to present the cases and show we're serious about prosecuting them to the maximum."

"That's not necessary. We have two very competent prosecutors assigned to these cases." Remembering a case in the Western District of Virginia in which the federal judge refused to add prosecutors from Washington headquarters to a case, Yusef added, "Besides, there's no guarantee the judges would accept additional prosecutors being added to the case. The judges here are experienced, and the two presiding over these cases are senior judges, appointed during the George W. Bush administration."

"This is what the AG wants, so I have to tell you," John said.

"John, I know you serve at the pleasure of the president, so you must show some deference to the AG. I'm not in that position. So long as I follow the oath I took and follow the law, doing my duties, I can't be fired. I'll consider what you said."

After a few more moments of awkward silence, they terminated the conversation.

Yusef sat bombarded with conflicting thoughts, wondering what to do next. *Should I just resign in order to maintain my integrity? What else would I do? I have a family to support and a new child on the way. Should I go along with them in order to save my job? But they can't fire me. They sure could make life miserable. What else could I do?*

I need to talk to someone. Nizzy has been more open to talk with, especially about her own career. Hopefully tonight, when we're both at home, we can talk. Omar and I used to have good talks when either one of us needed a listening ear. I can't talk to him now because he'd be busy at school. He's two time zones different, so maybe I can send him a text now and talk when he goes home and I'm still in the office. For now, for sure, I need to tell Susana and Brenda. Roger might have some insights, too.

Yusef went to Susana's office and asked Brenda to join them. He recounted his conversation with John Holmes, emphasizing the oath they had all taken. He said, "So far as I'm concerned, you are to continue using your best professional judgment on how to proceed. Do either of you know of situations where prosecutors came from Washington to take charge of the prosecution? Would a local judge accept adding a prosecutor from Washington to these cases?" Yusef described the case in Virginia in which the judge refused to accept from prosecutors from headquarters to join a case.

Susana said, "I've not been involved in cases in which outside prosecutors were present. You, Brenda?"

When Brenda said she hadn't, Susana continued. "I suppose if we specifically asked for a prosecutor to be added because of his or her expertise, a judge might allow it, but it's difficult to know what he might do in this case."

They continued to talk for a short time; then Yusef returned to his office, where he sent a text message on his cell phone to Omar, asking if they could talk when Omar went home for the day. Yusef then sent a message on Skype to Roger, asking if it would be possible to have a Skype conversation.

Soon Roger connected and after very brief pleasantries, Yusef recounted his conversation with John Holmes. Roger responded, "Your cases are getting lots of attention here at AG headquarters, as I suppose you can imagine. There is divided opinion. The highest levels that are closest to the administration want to handle the cases as John described to you. Those of us with career appointments on the professional staff take your position about our oaths, serving the interests of the United States, equal protection under the law, and all that.

"It's easy to see that they would put pressure on John, because he serves at the pleasure of the president. They certainly can't intimidate the whole AG network, including those of us here at headquarters. We're just keeping a low profile and avoiding direct conflict. It'll blow over when the media get hold of the situation."

Media, Yusef thought. *I need to contact Marcus too.* "Thanks for your input," Yusef said. "I'll let you get back to work. I feel better now." They said their goodbyes.

Yusef used his cell phone to send a text to Marcus, asking whether he could talk. After a while, they connected on the phone and Yusef told Marcus about the pressure from the administration. He added, "With your contacts, you can surely find someone in Washington who will corroborate this, but, of course, you can't attribute it to me."

After Marcus concurred, "Yusef asked, "Any more about your reassignment here to El Paso?"

(Pause)

Yusef continued, "Oh, now that you are aware of this attention at the top levels in Washington, you think you might get more information there than here on the border and not have to move. Makes sense. And of course, you want to be with your family, although we like to have you here."

They said goodbye, with Marcus especially eager to start contacting his sources.

Yusef spent the rest of the afternoon trying to focus on work, but his mind kept drifting about what to do next. In the late afternoon, when Omar was at home in North Carolina, Yusef and Omar connected on Skype. Yusef described the events of the day concluding with, "I wish I could just quit, but I have a family to support and another child on the way. Besides, I don't know what else I could do. I don't have connections to start a private practice, except back in Michigan, and for sure I don't want to go back there. Besides, the type of practice there would drive me crazy. Here in Texas, all local legal positions in the government are elected, and I don't have any political connections nor a desire to have any."

Omar replied, "Yes, of course. It's easy to see why you would be upset and want to get away. You're dedicated to justice and the rule of law, not political pressure."

"Thanks for the encouragement," Yusef answered.

"Be careful, though, about just cutting and running," Omar continued. "Think about the Prophet. He faced adversity in many forms from lots of sources, including authority figures. Yes, sometimes, he did leave, but more often he stood up to the challenges and persisted following the will of Allah for his life. Maybe you shouldn't be so quick to just quit."

Yusef pondered just a moment and said, "Yeah, maybe."

"But at the same time, don't avoid taking steps due to fear," Omar continued. "If it's Allah's will for you to be in private practice, the way will be open for you to succeed. Same with running for public office."

"Oh."

"Don't misunderstand," Omar said. "This is not to suggest you should follow these paths. Every part of your soul that I've been able to observe all these years shows that spiritually you are intended to be a prosecutor, one who upholds justice and the rule of law. But, still, let your choices be based on the positive, where you are destined to be, not fear of some unknown path."

"Yes, you're right," Yusef said. "As usual, you see right into me and show me the way to go."

"Ramadan begins on Monday," Omar continued. "As you know, it's a period of reflection and renewal, among other things. By the time Ramadan is over, you'll know what to do next. No need to rush things."

Yusef agreed. He and Omar continued to visit for several minutes, catching up on what was happening with each other, as would be the case with longtime best friends.

Yusef returned home earlier than usual, eager to talk to Nisrine. She arrived with Sara shortly afterwards. After affectionate greetings with both Sara and Nisrine, Yusef took Sara to her room to play. Upon returning to the family room, Nisrine said, "I did it; I told them I'm quitting."

"How do you feel about that?" Yusef asked, moving to put his arm around her.

"Mixed feelings, I guess," Nisrine said. "You know I love to deliver healthy, happy babies, and treat the mothers until they deliver. Some of the people there seemed pleased that I'm quitting.

265

It's like they viewed me as a threat, too competent, too dedicated to caring for people."

"That happens in the legal profession, too," Yusef said. "It's about finding the right niche where you can feel good about yourself because you're good at what you do. You can't always pick your associates, but sometimes you can avoid having to deal with those who feel threatened."

"I saw the doctor I want to take care of me and deliver this baby," Nisrine continued. "I approached her about part-time work, filling in when she's busy, or just being on call. She said maybe, that maybe she would treat me without charge in exchange for some of my effort. I told her that wasn't necessary because you have good insurance, but we're open to most any financial arrangement."

"That sounds good," Yusef replied. "I wish I could find something else after what happened to me today." Yusef described his conversations with John Holmes, Roger, and Marcus, and his quandary about what to do next.

Nisrine interrupted and said, "Well, you could go into private practice. We could go back to San Antonio and each have our practices."

He recounted the conversation with Omar, including reservations about private practice. "It could be just like you are experiencing, I would have situations the clients don't want to be in, looking for a cheap and easy way out, charged with petty crimes, messy divorces, being sued for spite. Right now, I still feel that I'm meant to be a prosecutor, and I'm a damned good one, especially at the supervisory level, focusing on human and civil rights. Ramadan starts Monday, you know. You can't fast, being pregnant, but I can and will. Maybe I'll just take a few days off work; I have plenty of vacation accumulated. When is your last day of work? Maybe we could go someplace like Ruidoso after that."

"Oh, yes, Yusey," Nisrine said. "I gave them two weeks' notice."

The rest of the evening they discussed possible plans and retired early after putting Sara to bed, making love for the first time in a while.

CHAPTER 11

Thursday, May 2, 2019
El Paso, Texas, USA

In the early afternoon in his office, Yusef received a text message on his cell phone from Marcus, then connected on Skype. After brief pleasantries, Marcus said, "Be sure and watch the news tonight. You'll find something interesting."

"You got them to admit that the administration was exerting political pressure on the Attorney General and down to the level of the judicial districts?" Yusef asked.

"Anonymous sources in the U.S. Attorney General's office, of course," Marcus replied. "After I uploaded the story and made sure we would run it first, I brought in other media. Newspapers like the *Post* and *New York Times* have their sources that are sometimes even better than mine. With more media outlets involved, the more publicity this will get, and the more credibility."

"They'll be onto me next for comment, I suppose," Yusef said.

"No doubt. But, of course, all you have to say is that you do not discuss ongoing matters."

I'd better alert Susana and Brenda, Yusef thought. *But I can't tell them directly and let them know I'm in touch with national media. Oh, well, I'll figure out something. Maybe wait until some media outlet approaches me.*

"Get this," Marcus continued. "One senior guy said something to the effect that isn't the Western District of Texas getting uppity, especially in El Paso, thinking that it's bigger and more important than the Southern District of New York."

Yusef pondered a few seconds, chuckled, and said, "Do the math, Marcus. The Western District of Texas is bigger than the Southern District of New York, both in population and geography. The Southern District of New York is pretty much confined to Manhattan Island. In the Western District of Texas, San Antonio, Austin, and El Paso together have a population of four million, not to mention all the other cities. But of course, no district is more important than another. Even the New Mexico district that's much smaller."

"Yeah," Marcus replied. "Typical East Coast thinking. But he also made snide comments that, the next thing, you'd be trying to deal with financial crimes like the Southern District of New York."

Yusef laughed and said, "Wouldn't you know we do have one. The FBI came to see me late this morning. You know those North Koreans who defected? Well, it seems that when the FBI got into their computer, they found out they were hacking bank accounts in the U.S. and putting the money into accounts belonging to them at banks in California. They're asking for asylum claiming they would be executed in North Korea for defecting."

"Really? I need to get on that one!"

"The FBI will likely turn this over to the U.S. Attorney for New Mexico," Yusef continued. "They were using an internet provider in New Mexico and they're in detention in New Mexico right now. The El Paso FBI office had been conducting the investigation because it's easier to cross the border from El Paso, and the FBI activity in El Paso is much larger with more expertise than their limited facility in Las Cruces. They'll likely be arraigned in Albuquerque and tried there, which is fine with us. We have enough to do here as it is."

"For sure, I need to get in touch with my FBI contacts here in Washington," Marcus said. "This might be ironic. They get asylum backhanded because the U.S. government wouldn't deport them to North Korea where they might be tortured or killed. But who knows what the administration would do?"

Yusef said, "It'll be interesting to see what'll happen, for sure."

"I've got to go," Marcus said.

"Thanks for telling me about tonight's news," Yusef responded.

They disconnected, emphasizing they would keep in touch.

CHAPTER 12

Sunday, May 5, 2019
México, DF, México

At lunchtime in an out-of-the-way restaurant, Vladimir Mikhailov lifted his wine glass in toast to Ivan Petrov, saying in Russian, "Welcome again on Cinco de Mayo, the Mexican holiday Americans like to celebrate, but the Mexicans just take in stride."

Ivan acknowledged the toast and said, all dialogue in Russian, "Thanks Vladimir Evgenevich. A pleasure to be here."

Vladimir continued, "It was exactly two years ago we met on Cinco de Mayo and started the tunnel project and created chaos. Thanks for all of your efforts, Ivan Aleksandrovich, making it successful."

"Successful?" Ivan asked. "But they got caught."

"Well, yes," Vladimir said. "But we started things in motion, and people and groups are now demonstrating and creating chaos all over the U.S. We didn't expect our people to keep going forever. Their FBI is too good for that. They caught us a little sooner than we would have liked, but things were still successful. The North Koreans defected and fucked things up. Hope we don't run into someone from their embassy anytime soon."

"But our people are arrested and will be tried?" Ivan asked.

"Not a big deal. We can get them off with a minimal sentence, like we did Maria Butina."

"What about the Iranians?"

"Who gives a fuck about the Iranians?" Vladimir replied. "They should have known there would be risks and not expect us to protect them."

"Oh."

"Say, Ivan Aleksandrovich," Vladimir continued, "the reason we invited you down here this weekend is to tell you we have another place for you to do your good work; you won't need to go back to Juárez."

"Oh?"

"The U.S. has known all along we have a spy there; you knew that," Vladimir began. "Now that the tunnel has been discovered and the North Koreans fucked up, they might come after you. Plus, they're devoting a lot of their military activity towards the border now, so there's not all that much activity for us to spy on that we don't monitor already in other ways. With the flood of Central Americans crossing the border, they're busy. All we have to do is keep working underground to keep the Central Americans flowing, and the chaos will continur."

"I'll need to go back to Juárez to pack my belongings," Ivan said.

"No need for that. We'll get them packed for you and send them where you're going next."

"Where's that?"

"Venezuela. At first, we thought about sending you to Guatemala and Honduras to keep stirring up the people to leave and go to the U.S., but that's under control. The biggest need is in Venezuela."

"Support the Maduro regime?" Ivan asked. "I hear it's crumbling."

"No, the Maduro regime is on its way out. It's just a matter of time. Of course, we're keeping the pretense that we're supporting Maduro. We need you to infiltrate the Guaidó supporters so we can slowly move in and use our influence with them."

"How soon will this happen, especially since you don't want me to go back to Juárez?" Ivan asked.

"You'll take the next diplomatic shuttle back to Moscow," Vladimir replied. "There you'll be briefed and given more instructions on what to do."

The rest of the lunch was spent discussing their activities and making general conversation.

CHAPTER 13

In the early afternoon Eastern time, late morning Mountain time, Rosie Jordan opened a meeting at the FBI operations center with the usual people attending either in person or by Skype. He began, "It looks like we're ready to put another situation to rest, although there are lots of peripheral issues and, on the border, lots of things will come up. Carmen, please go ahead."

Carmen Cisneros of the El Paso FBI Field Office, speaking on Skype, began, "The two sets of men we arrested have been arraigned and are in custody. Their cases have been turned over to the El Paso Division of the U.S. Attorney for prosecution. One interesting thing is that, as you know, the U.S. government confiscates property used in crimes, including the site of the would-be mosque and tunnel opening.

"Now a group of Shia Muslims in El Paso has come forward saying they were duped by Iranian-Americans from California and that it was actually they who bought the land, got building permits, and planned to build a mosque, until they were shoved aside. Now they want to continue to build a mosque out in the open and allow inspection. Ultimately, it's up to the U.S. Attorney to decide on that. An interesting element to that is that the head of the El Paso division is himself Shia Muslim and has no knowledge of a group of Shia in El Paso who want their own mosque. That's not our concern, though. No matter what, we'll seal off the opening to the tunnel so that it can't be easily reopened. It would take too much effort to fill it up with dirt. I'm sure Mexico will do something similar on its side, but we haven't discussed that with our Mexican counterparts.

"We have another item, but it's best to bring Peter from Las Cruces in on that. You know about the North Koreans who defected and asked for asylum." She explained details of the El Paso FBI field office going to Ciudad Juárez to examine the North Koreans' computer along with Mexican authorities, and the discovery of the North Koreans' hacking bank accounts in the U.S. and transferring money to their own bank accounts. "The case has been turned over to the FBI in New Mexico because they were in detention as asylum seekers in New Mexico and their internet connection was with a provider in New Mexico."

Peter Richardson began, "We immediately arrested them. They are confined in Albuquerque, and we turned the case over to the U.S. Attorney for New Mexico for prosecution. The U.S. Attorney General representative here should be able to speak more to the situation. As for the head of the vigilante group, he's also in custody in Albuquerque. The U.S, Attorney General representative can speak to his situation as well."

Roger Chen, with U.S. Attorney General Headquarters in Washington, immediately began, "We're in touch with the U.S. Attorney for New Mexico about the prosecution of the North Koreans. So far, there hasn't been any political issue come up, despite the ongoing tension with North Korea. For now, they are represented by the public defender.

"With respect to the case of the two sets of bombers apprehended and in custody in El Paso, you have surely been following the media attention about the administration wanting to let the Russians off easy and prosecute the Iranian-Americans to the fullest. After all the media attention, the U.S. Attorney General's office has "clarified" the situation. Soon, expect a public statement to the media that the U.S. Attorney General has full confidence in the Western District of Texas to be able to represent the interests of the U.S. government.

"With all the evidence we have, we're confident they can be convicted. So much so, that we strongly suspect the Russians will plead guilty in order to avoid too much evidence coming out in a public trial. They can receive reduced sentences because they have saved us the effort and cost of a trial, but they'll still receive substantial time in prison because of the seriousness of their crimes. We also suspect that, after a while, they'll be released on parole and immediately deported, but I don't want to speculate too much. By the time parole is considered, there could be a different administration with a different attitude towards Russia.

"With respect to the two Iranian-Americans, we suspect that they, too, will want to plea-bargain just to save themselves the effort of pursuing a pointless defense. It's too soon to speculate what kind of sentence they'll receive, but most likely it'll be substantial, and the chances of parole seem remote.

"For the head of the vigilante group, his movement has disbanded. We have a good strong case to convict him on the firearms charge; we don't see any benefit in pursuing cases based on human rights violations, which would be more difficult to prove. Because of his prior convictions, any sentence will likely be quite long."

Eric James of the CIA said, "This situation has demonstrated that we can work with Mexico on issues of interest to both countries, so long as we show them proper respect and don't publicize situations very much. Hopefully we can continue."

"Anyone else?" Rosie asked. "If not, thank you all for attending. Even though we're closing this situation, there will no doubt be other issues come up with all that's happening at the border. It's good to be part of a group in which everyone is working so well together."

With that, he closed the meeting.

BOOK 5

AND THEN...

CHAPTER 1

Saturday, May 25, 2019
Ruidoso, New Mexico, USA

Yusef woke up early, just before sunrise, to prepare himself a big breakfast before sunrise on this first full day in a vacation condo they had rented for a week. Nisrine woke up not long afterwards and made herself breakfast, not fasting because of her pregnancy. Yusef was idly watching news on television when Nisrine interrupted. "Oh, Yusey, I'm so glad we came here. The mountains are like in Lebanon, so peaceful, and so spiritually stirring. This is just what I need after quitting that stressful job. And for Ramadan too, even if I'm not fasting. We all need it. It's obvious you've been under intense stress and need to get away."

Yusef agreed and they sat in idle conversation for a few moments as the sun continued to rise over the horizon and the snow-covered mountain peaks, albeit the snow gradually melting. Nisrine returned to check emails at the dining room table where she had set her personal laptop computer.

Soon she said, "Yusey, Husey just sent an email," referring to her younger brother, Husayn Maktabi. "He sent more information about his wedding. You remember they set the date for June 8, right after graduation when he gets his Master's degree and she gets her Bachelor's, and after the Eid al Fitr. It's Saturday night to make it easier for their non-Muslim friends to attend."

"Yes, I remember," Yusey said. "We mentally made a note of the date. We can have a quiet Eid at home. We don't have many Muslim friends in El Paso anyway. I suppose we might invite some others to celebrate the Eid, but right now, I don't know who. The wedding will be in Lubbock, I recall. We should be able to drive there easily enough from El Paso."

"Yes, the wedding's in Lubbock," Nisrine replied. "Her family lives in San Angelo; her father's a professor there at Angelo State. They're originally from India. Just like we did, they want to have their wedding where their friends are. He says it'll be in a football stadium?"

Yusef laughed, saying, "A football stadium. Just right for someone getting a Master's degree in sports science and who's in the sporting goods business. But Texas Tech was in the NCAA basketball final game. Maybe they should have the wedding on the basketball court."

Nisrine laughed and continued, "He says it's a private club at the top of the football stadium, one side with windows overlooking the football field and one side looking at downtown Lubbock. He says there's a nice hotel nearby in walking distance for out-of-town guests. They live in student accommodation, so they wouldn't be able to accommodate anyone. I'm sure Baba and Mama will stay at that hotel. Most good hotels would have babysitters on call, so someone can watch Sara."

"Oh, OK, good." Yusef commented. "We should make reservations now."

"I can do that now while I'm on the computer," Nisrine answered. "I'll make the reservations in your name. The wedding will be a catered dinner like we had; they're copying us and having a little ceremony in public with Husey, her father, and the imam, not in a private room as in Muslim tradition."

"Sounds good," Yusef commented.

Nisrine returned to her emails while Yusef went to the balcony to look at the mountains in the distance, with the breeze flowing through the piñon trees. Sara came downstairs to join them and have breakfast. They spent a leisurely morning relaxing and unwinding from the stress of the recent past weeks.

In the early afternoon, Khan and Otto were sitting at an outdoor table in front of a taco stand in a courtyard in midtown Ruidoso that had shops around a square. They were having a light lunch after a big breakfast at Otto's house in Alamogordo that morning on this, one of the first really warm spring days in the mountains.

Khan said, "Thanks for bringing me here. This does seem to be a nice little town and the mountains are so nice; different from the mountains in El Paso. Of course, any time with you is good. I can hardly wait for weekends to see what we're going to do together."

"Me too," Otto said. "Weekends with you are what keep me going all week."

"I've been waiting for the right opportunity to tell you," Khan said. "I want to be with you all the time, not just on weekends."

"There is no right time," Otto replied, "or any time is the right time. I love you, Khan."

"I love you too," Khan said. "This is the first time I've felt like this, but it's real. But what are we going to do? We live almost two hours apart. El Paso is the only place I could work that's anywhere near. If there were good job opportunities, I'd move for you, but there just aren't. Besides, I love my job."

"I like my job too," Otto said, "but I'd consider moving for a good opportunity and to be with you. I work for the government. There are plenty of government jobs in El Paso, but I don't know how many there would be for an experienced statistician geek. I can certainly look."

Khan smiled broadly and took Otto's hand in his. Otto continued, "NASA has some activities in Las Cruces. I don't know what, but I can look there, too."

Khan said, "I'd gladly move closer to Las Cruces if that would let us be together."

At that moment, Otto saw Yusef, Nisrine, and Sara walking very near their table, having come out of one of the nearby shops. Otto said, "There's your boss with a woman and a little girl. It looks like they've seen us, so we can't just ignore them."

Khan looked up and said, "That must be his wife and little girl. I wouldn't want to ignore them; he's nice and knows you and I are close."

Khan waved to Yusef, Nisrine, and Sara. Yusef, already having noticed them, was walking to their table. Khan and Otto stood, Khan saying, "Please have a seat. Can I get you something to drink?"

Yusef replied, "We can join you for a few minutes, but nothing to drink, thank you. It's Ramadan and as you know, we're Muslim."

Introductions were made all around, then Khan said, "Yes, I know you're Muslim, but what's Ramadan that you just said?"

Yusef explained that Ramadan is an almost month-long period of fasting from food and drink during daylight hours, a period of reflection and spiritual renewal. "Maybe you noticed that I haven't been bringing my lunch to the office nor drinking coffee."

"I just thought you were busy," Khan said. "There is so much going on."

"Well yes, I have been busy," Yusef said, "But Ramadan, too, kept me away from the break room."

Otto commented, "We both grew up Catholic and that sounds sort of like Lent, except we just do without a certain thing, not entire meals and drink. It must be tough for a whole month."

Yusef replied, "Yes, it can be a challenge, especially when Ramadan is in mid-summer like it was a couple of years ago. Muslims follow a different calendar, so Ramadan is a little earlier each year."

"That's when we had our first dates," Nisrine added. "Iftars after a long hot summer day in San Antonio and fasting with no water."

"Iftar is the evening meal right exactly at sunset," Yusef explained. "We'd go to a restaurant, get water and place an order, then sit looking at our watches to know when to guzzle the water and eat right at the moment of sundown. Waiters and waitresses in San Antonio thought we were weird."

"I'll bet," Khan said.

"Say," Yusef said, "will you two be around at dinnertime? We could have iftar with you. Iftars are expected to be social occasions with others. If you're still around, we could join you."

Otto and Khan glanced at each other, then Otto said, "We were going to spend the rest of the day with me showing him the historic sites of Fort Stanton and Lincoln—you know, Billy the Kid fame. We'd probably be finished close to dinner time. No hurry to get back to Alamogordo, so long as it's before about eleven or midnight. What time would you have in mind?

Yusef answered, "Sunset is very close to 7:45 here in this part of the Mountain time zone. We could meet about 7:30. Do you have any places to recommend here in Ruidoso?"

Otto replied, "There's the buffet at the Inn of the Mountain Gods, you know, where the casino is. Right here in Ruidoso, Cattle Baron is good and has a good salad bar. There are lots of other restaurants in Ruidoso being a tourist town."

"We've eaten at the buffet a few times because that's where we've stayed before, including on our honeymoon. It's good, but maybe someplace different. There's a Cattle Baron in El Paso. I've heard it's good, but we've never been there. We don't go out too much with Sara."

"OK, Cattle Baron at 7:30," Otto said.

Nisrine said, "I'll take a rain check if that's OK with you. Your company would be good, I'm sure, but I'll likely be eating a little earlier. Pregnant women don't have to fast in Ramadan. We need to take care of ourselves and the baby we're carrying. I'm a doctor, an OB/GYN. I make sure my patients know how and when to eat properly so I need to follow the same for myself. Besides, that's a little late for Sara. She'd be getting fussy by then."

They continued visiting for a few more minutes. Then Yusef, Nisrine, and Sara continued to wander into the shops.

Shortly after 7:30, Yusef, Khan, and Otto were seated at a booth in the Cattle Baron restaurant, with Otto and Khan next to each other on one side and Yusef facing them on the other. After orders were taken, while they were waiting for the exact time for Yusef to start the salad and soup bar, Yusef commented, "You two look especially happy tonight."

Khan smiled and said, "We made a commitment to each other today. We can thank you, at least to some small extent. You referred me to your friend Brad. I talked to him on Skype and met his partner Jason. Brad told me to be open and go for it when I thought I met someone special. It was shortly after that, that Otto and I met each other."

Yusef smiled and said, "Glad I had some role in the process."

Khan and Otto continued to talk about how they were taking things very slowly and waiting for developments, especially living two hours apart, Otto maybe trying to get a closer job.

Khan then said, "Do you remember when I told you about the Catholic Archbishop in Houston wanting people to come forward and report abuse? Well, I did. So far there's been nothing else."

Otto commented, "Typical Catholics. Just making statements for show and not following through."

Khan added, "We both grew up Catholic so it's part of us, kind of hard to give up. But maybe we could be like Pete and Chasten Buttigieg who became Episcopalian."

Otto chuckled and said, "Let's not get too far ahead of ourselves. A lot's gotta happen before we settle down together, but the prospect sure feels good."

Khan said, "It serves no purpose for me to follow through on that sex abuse thing with the church. That was long ago. Now I'm in a good position personally and in a career I like, and with someone I care for and who cares for me."

"You two might not know yet," Yusef added, "but there's been a series of burnings of Catholic churches in El Paso. The FBI just reported it to us. They're investigating arson. We might have that case to prosecute as a hate crime. Hopefully, it doesn't affect the church you attend."

"I'm not that much of a church goer anymore," Otto said, except when I am with Khan in El Paso on Sunday."

The three of them spent the rest of the evening while eating in very enjoyable company, expressing a desire to get together again sometime, hopefully with Nisrine present.

CHAPTER 2

Friday, June 7, 2019
Lubbock, Texas, USA

In the late afternoon, Yusef, Nisrine, and Sara drove into the arrival area at the Overton Hotel after a leisurely drive from El Paso with a stop at Carlsbad Caverns National Park. With Sara at her age, they could not go into much of the caverns, but they made a note to come back when Sara was older and able to walk longer distances. Inside the hotel, they stood in line at the reception area waiting to check in. Nisrine commented, "Are all of these people here for the wedding? I wonder if Mama and Baba have arrived yet. I told them we'd meet them this afternoon. I'll send a text to them to say we're here, but maybe I should wait until we know our room number."

Soon, a woman appearing to be in her mid-thirties, about five eight with blonde hair and a stylish figure, walked out of an office behind the counter up to the reception area where people in line were waiting to check in. She was wearing a solid light-blue dress and a name tag that read "Elsie, Assistant Manager."

"I can help you over here," she said, motioning to Yusef, Nisrine, and Sara.

Yusef, who was nearest, stepped forward and said, "Shaito, we have reservations for three nights."

The assistant manager looked through the files and said, "Yusef Shaito, two persons and a child. You're Mr. and Mrs. Shaito."

Overton Hotel, Lubbock, Texas

Nisrine stepped forward and said, "I'm very pleased to be his wife, but actually it's Dr. Maktabi for your records."

The assistant manager looked at them and said, "Those names sound familiar, especially that you're a doctor. Are you friends with Frank and Paco? They visited us when we were at Fort Hood and said they were going to visit you in San Antonio, but here it says you live in El Paso. Mr. Shaito, they said you were friends from Washington and your wife is a doctor."

"Yes, that's us," Yusef replied. "They're Frank Reynolds and Paco Mendoza. They stopped by our home in San Antonio on their way to visit Paco's family in Mexico a couple of times and attended our wedding, too. We live in El Paso now."

Nisrine added, "Now I remember something they said, that you might move to Lubbock. It caught my attention because my brother was attending Texas Tech in Lubbock. We're going to his wedding tomorrow night. The wedding is in a private club in a football stadium, apparently very near here."

"Yes, that's the Red Raider Club in AT&T Jones stadium," The assistant manager said. "Just a block or two away. Easy to walk. You can probably see it out of the hotel window on an upper floor if it faces this side."

"We drove by it on the way in," Yusef commented. "I thought that might be the place."

Left: AT&T Jones Stadium, location of the Red Raider Club, Lubbock Texas;
Right: Entrance to the Red Raider Club in AT&T Jones Stadium, Lubbock, Texas]

"I'm Elsie Ferris," the assistant manager said. "My husband is Patrick Ferris. He's Lebanese, or Lebanese-American like you two are, apparently. He works as a research engineer at the research center here. And yes, when they visited us, we were considering moving to Lubbock so Patrick could get a research job and I could study hospitality management, which I did, as you see."

Yusef replied. "Frank and I talked quite a bit about Patrick, and I suspect Frank and Patrick talked about me. Our family roots are very different, but Lebanon's a small country and all Lebanese have some bond, especially ones like us who were born and grew up in a different country. From what I recall, Patrick's family is Christian and from the north of Lebanon. My family are Shia Muslim and from the south. I was born and grew up in Dearborn, Michigan, the largest concentration of Shia outside of Lebanon."

"My family is also Shia Muslim," Nisrine added. "They're from around Beirut, but I was born and grew up in Dallas. My younger brother just got his Master's degree in sports science from Texas Tech. His wife-to-be has been a student here, too."

"Yes, that's Patrick. He was born and grew up in Alabama; I'm from Ohio, though. I'll be sure and tell Patrick when I get home," Elsie said. "He might even want to come meet you tomorrow, if you're free, that is."

"We're going to the wedding tomorrow night," Yusef replied. "As family of the groom, not a lot is expected of us, so maybe we would have some time free during the day."

"We'll be spending time with my parents," Nisrine added. "We haven't made specific plans, so maybe we'd have time to meet him and visit a while. My parents could watch Sara while we visit with Patrick. First-time grandparents, you know. Can you check to see if they have checked in? Their name is Maktabi also."

Elsie replied, "Yes I know about first time grandparents. Our daughter was the first grandchild for both sets of our parents. Let me check if they've arrived." After a moment of checking the records, she added, "No, they haven't arrived yet. Here let me get you your keys so you can get settled."

Nisrine said, "We requested a babysitter for tomorrow night. Could you check to see if that's in order?"

"Yes, everything's all set," Elsie replied. "Enjoy your stay, and I'll leave messages for you about Patrick and his plans for tomorrow. I'm off tomorrow and can stay home with the children if he's free."

Monday, June 10, 2019
Mescalero, New Mexico, USA

After a leisurely drive across a mostly desert area, Yusef, Nisrine, and Sara arrived at the Inn of the Mountain Gods, where they chose to break their trip back to El Paso following a different route from the one they drove to Lubbock. As they drove along, they conversed from time to time, Nisrine saying, "That seems like a nice campus, and Lubbock's a nice city. Husey really liked it there, although I was too busy to go visit while he was a student. Maybe Sara would go there someday."

"Oh, you don't want her to go to SMU like you did?" Yusef said.

"Well, if she wants to," Nisrine replied. "She's not going to be a Lebanese princess like I was, who had to go to a prestigious school close to home to make her parents look good."

"No, for sure not," Yusef said. "As you know, I went to the University of Michigan because it was close and finances were tight, although it was prestigious and made my family look good. You know, boys are not Lebanese princes like girls are Lebanese princesses. Who knows what this next child will be? It sure was good of your parents to keep Sara while we met with Patrick. It was good to meet him after hearing about him all this time."

"Yes, he really is a nice guy," Nisrine commented. "Elsie's very nice too. In a way, it's too bad that Husey will move back to Dallas to take over the business so we won't be going to Lubbock anymore."

"There's the Lubbock judicial division of the Northern District of Texas," Yusef said chuckling. "Who knows, maybe there'll be a judgeship open there one day."

"Oh, don't say that, Yusey," Nisrine said. "You know we want to make San Antonio our home. Do you have any idea when we'll move back?"

"Yes, I know, San Antonio's home," Yusef replied. "As much as I like El Paso, and Lubbock seems nice, San Antonio is home. And for sure, I'd like to have just one job at a time. But with all the chaos and confusion on the border and in Washington, I doubt the AG is going to make any changes anywhere unless someone quits or dies. It might be sometime after the 2020 election before there's enough stability to consider personnel moves. This next kid of ours will most likely have to be born in El Paso."

"That's fine with me," Nisrine said. "There are good hospitals and facilities in El Paso, and my doctor is there, too. Besides, I'm not sure I'd be up for a move advanced in pregnancy."

Later when they were settled into their room, Nisrine said, "I'm so glad we decided to break our trip and stay here. This is one place I'll really miss when we move back to San Antonio. These mountains are so magical, mystical, spiritual."

"We can always fly back here for vacations," Yusef added. "Of course, with two children, it won't be all that easy for a few years, but this can be a great place for family getaways. Say, maybe we can see if Marcus and his wife would like to join us here for a long weekend soon. With the trial of those two sets of defendants, he'll surely be here covering the action."

"Yes, good idea," Nisrine said. "How is he? Any more on being reassigned to El Paso?"

"So far, he's putting them off by finding all sorts of scoops right there in Washington," Yusef answered. "No doubt he'll be back down to the border soon for short assignments. The other networks, the U.S.-based networks, are after him to go to work for them. He might make a move for a big salary jump. He certainly deserves to move up all the way."

"What are we going to do tomorrow?" Nisrine asked. "You said something about White Sands. I'm in no hurry to get back home to El Paso, but you likely need to go back to work. Besides, I think Sara is getting a little tired of traveling."

"Yes," Yusef replied. "Khan and Otto talked so much about the White Sands. I was there too, a few years ago when we all met at Brad's place in Ruidoso. It's the only place like it in the world. Then we can decide whether to go back to Alamogordo and straight down to El Paso, or maybe keep on to Las Cruces and then to El

Paso. And, yes, I probably should at least check in with the office. Along the border, who knows what might be going on?"

They spent the rest of the evening leisurely eating dinner at the buffet, reflecting on the great weekend with family and pondering what lay ahead for them.

CHAPTER 3

Sunday, June 23, 2019
El Paso, Texas, USA

Marcus Porter and his wife, Tiffany Porter, were relaxing with Yusef and Nisrine in their home after a simple dinner of food that had been ordered in. Sara was in her room playing for a few minutes before time for her to go to bed. Tiffany had come with Marcus on Friday to visit and explore the area before he would cover the courtroom appearance the next day, Monday, of the two Russians who had been arraigned on domestic terrorism charges. They had spent a weekend with Yusef, Nisrine, and Sara at the Inn of the Mountain Gods in Mescalero, New Mexico, exploring historical sites and natural phenomena in Lincoln and Otero counties. While in Alamogordo, they had lunch with Otto and Khan.

While Yusef was putting Sara to bed, Tiffany asked Nisrine, "When are you due?"

Nisrine answered, "In December, close to Christmas, although Christmas doesn't mean much to us Muslims."

Just as Yusef returned, Tiffany asked, "Are you hoping for a boy this time? Do you know yet? You know, we just had a girl, a little sister for our son who's almost three."

Nisrine answered, "It's a little early to reveal the sex. We'd just rather wait and see until he or she is actually born."

Yusef said, "For me, another little girl like Sara would be just fine. The stereotype of Lebanese men is that they have to have a son because men are supposed to take care of their parents, even if they're not the oldest child. We're not very Lebanese in that respect." *Now's not the time to tell them that my parents disowned me, but still expect me to take care of them.*

Nisrine added, "My brother and I—he's younger—have agreed that we both have equal responsibility to take care of our parents when the time comes, although they are pretty well off."

"Also, Lebanese men take the nickname of "Abou" plus the oldest son's name," Yusef added. "This is used by other men who really want to get close to someone and usually get a favor so they call him Abou something. We don't associate very much with other Lebanese, so it's not a big deal."

"Other Lebanese call my father Abou Husayn," Nisrine said, "but my parents don't associate with other Lebanese much."

"If we have another girl and no boys, then a daughter's name can be used," Yusef added. "I could be Abou Sara because she's the oldest. But since we don't associate with other Lebanese much other than Nizzy's family, I can't imagine anyone would do that. Husey's Americanized enough that he doesn't call me Abou Sara."

"Do you have names picked out yet?" Marcus asked. "Do you have any naming customs?"

Nisrine replied, "Growing up with names like Nisrine and Yusef, we had our share of teasing. We determined that our kids would have names that are good both as American names and Lebanese."

"If it's a boy, his name will be Omar," Yusef said, "after my very best adult friend. You know him from Virginia, Marcus. It's not really a common American name, but not all that weird, either."

"If it's another girl, we have a couple of names we're considering," Nisrine said. "It'll be something like Sara that can work both as American and Lebanese."

Marcus said, "Yes, I remember Omar. He's a great guy. Good to name a son after him."

After a brief lull in the conversation, Nisrine said to Tiffany, "Apparently you're not working. Do you plan to go back to work?"

Tiffany answered, "Not right away. I work mostly freelance as an advertising campaign developer. I can do that from home, if need be. That's what I did after our son was born. Also, Marcus doesn't work on a fixed schedule. Sometimes he can stay at home with the children for a few hours while I go into the office. What about you?"

Nisrine said, "I'm sure I'll be staying home for a while, especially while breastfeeding. My career as a doctor, an OB/GYN, is part of who I am, and I just can't give it up. Yusey and I agree to share parenting duties as much as we can. We want to move back to San Antonio as soon as Yusey's job will let us. I want to set up a private practice that I can pursue part time. My goal is to serve underserved women who are able and want to pay a little for their own care and not rely on public health. For sure, I won't make much money that way, but it can supplement Yusey's income and allow us to live comfortably.

"If you're free tomorrow, Sara and I would be pleased to show you around El Paso, shopping or some of the sights, although I'm not much of a shopper. There's a fabulous art museum and history museum here."

"That would be great," Tiffany replied. "Thanks for the opportunity. I was just going to sit in the courtroom with Marcus for lack of anything better. Do you suppose we could go to Mexico? I heard we can walk there."

Nisrine answered, "If you have your passport we could. Conditions at the border might be tumultuous with all the immigrants trying to get in, but so far, I've not heard of any issues with walking across and back. I haven't been there in a long time. There can be some interesting things to buy in some of the tourist shops just across the border, and also at the market, if we want to walk that far."

"Oh, it never occurred to me to bring a passport," Tiffany said. "Maybe next time. I'm sure Marcus will be coming back with all the activity going on at the border. Maybe he would let me tag along again if my mother can keep the children."

Marcus, who had overheard the end of the conversation, said, "With what we're hearing about appalling conditions in the children's camps, I'm sure I'll be back here to cover as much as I can. It's always good to have Tiffany come with me."

Yusef added, "Lots of attention seems to be on the facility in Clint, a suburb, just down the river to the southeast from El Paso. Our office isn't involved in anything yet, but I suspect it's just a matter of time."

"Maybe some of the other doctors I do volunteer work with would want me to go along," Nisrine added. "I'm sure that some of those teenage girls could benefit from a gynecological examination."

They continued in casual conversation until time for Marcus and Tiffany to return to their hotel.

CHAPTER 4

Monday, June 24, 2019
El Paso, Texas, USA

At 9 a.m., a courtroom in the federal courthouse in downtown El Paso was crowded with news media and other spectators, including Marcus Porter in his role as news developer and a reporter from BBC America who would appear on camera. A video camera operator was with them to make videos of the reporter after the court hearing; no use of cameras was allowed in the courtroom. Otto sat with them with his sketch pads to make drawings during the hearings that are shown later on the videos. Yusef sat in the spectator section near the front. Susana Tate sat at the prosecution table wearing a light-weight summer blue dress. Three attorneys from Washington sat at the defense table, along with two defendants. The three attorneys from Washington, all in their late forties or early fifties, wore dark, upmarket designer suits with white shirts and obviously expensive silk ties. The two defendants wore slightly down-market dark suits, white shirts, and ties.

The bailiff announced the case of the *U.S. versus Kozlov and Nikolaev*. Judge Underwood entered wearing a black judicial robe. He stood average height, about five ten, with a husky figure and salt-and-pepper brown hair. When he asked the prosecution to present its case, one of the defense attorneys asked permission to approach the bench. When the three attorneys for the defense and Susana Tate for the prosecution were in front of the judge, the oldest of the three attorneys for the defense said, "Your Honor, the defendants are willing to plead guilty to one count in exchange for a year of supervised probation, during which time they will cooperate with the U.S. government in providing information about the circumstances leading to this case. After that time, they will be returned to their home country of Russia."

Judge Underwood thought, *Do those high-powered Washington lawyers think we are pushovers here in the desert and are not aware of what's going on?* He said, looking at Susana Tate, "Counselor?"

Susana Tate said, "Your Honor, the prosecution is willing to accept a plea bargain on one count with a sentence at the low end of the sentencing guideline range, followed by deportation, in order to avoid a lengthy trial. We are not aware of any agreement to cooperate and provide information."

The lead defense attorney then stated, "Your Honor, arrangements have been made with the U.S. Attorney General in Washington for such cooperation to occur once the defendants are released on probation and are located in the Washington, DC, area."

Judge Underwood thought, *Does he really think that we here are that naïve; that we don't watch and read the national news? This is just a ruse by the administration to placate the Russian government and get them back to Russia. Typical of the administration, they think they can push the judiciary around to get their way. For sure, I'm not going along with it, but I'm committed to uphold the law. A plea bargain with a lesser sentence does make sense.* He turned to Susana Tate, saying again, "Counselor?"

Susana Tate stated, "Your Honor, we are in regular contact with the U.S. Attorney for the Western District Texas and the office of the Attorney General of the U.S. We are not aware of any agreement that was made to accept probation in exchange for cooperation." She thought briefly, *That's not a lie. Yusef said that the administration wanted a probation plea deal in exchange for cooperation but did not inform him of any specific plans.* "The document we submitted to you describes our concurrence with a plea bargain and sentencing at the low end of the sentencing range. It states that we have been in contact with the FBI that provided evidence of the defendants' crimes. The FBI, in consultation with its Operations Center, stated that it has sufficient evidence and that there would be no additional benefit from cooperation by the defendants."

Judge Underwood turned to the defense attorneys, saying, "May I please have your document in which you outline the arrangements you have made with the Attorney General of the U.S. and the nature of the cooperation to be provided by the defendants."

The lead defense attorney, fumbling for words, said, "Your Honor, we will provide the document next month when you schedule a sentencing hearing."

Judge Underwood thought, *What the hell! They're telling me when to schedule a sentencing hearing.* He replied, "Your clients should not be penalized by your lack of preparation. You have until 11:30 this morning to provide your arguments to me in written form; that's about two hours from now. For your information, under the law, I am the one who sets the time for a sentencing hearing, not you. Such a hearing will be at 1:30 p.m. today, after I have had an opportunity to read the documents provided by you and the prosecution."

"But, Your Honor, ..." the defense attorney began to protest.

The judge stated publicly, "Court is recessed until 1:30 p.m., at which time the defendants will offer pleas." He banged the gavel, rose, and went to his chambers.

The large number of news media present rushed to the defense and prosecution tables, Marcus and his crew going to the defense. One of the defense attorneys waved the media away, saying, "We're not in a position to comment now. The judge just imposed additional unreasonable requirements on us."

Susana Tate said to the media gathered around her table, "The El Paso Division of the U.S. Attorney General is always willing to cooperate with the media. We're not in a position to comment at the moment, but will schedule a press conference to which all will be invited after pleas are heard."

Yusef moved quickly to the nearest exit, pointedly avoiding Marcus and his crew. When local media saw him, he politely declined comment at this time and hastily left for the short walk to his office in the nearby federal building.

Otto waited patiently with his sketches until Marcus and his crew returned from the bench. Marcus said, "We need to find a place in the building to make a video of the reporter describing the session and upload it for immediate broadcast. We'll show your sketches, Otto. Please wait with me if you like; as you know, I don't appear on camera." They moved to a relatively uncrowded place in the corridor outside the courtroom where the video of the reporter and the sketches were live streamed to BBC America studios in New York.

Once the upload session was ended, Marcus asked Otto, "Is there a coffee shop nearby where we can hang out until court reconvenes?"

Otto replied, "I'm not familiar with downtown El Paso. If we could all cram into my car, I could drive you to some places out along Mesa Street, where there are coffee shops and places to eat for lunch."

Marcus said, "We have an SUV rental car so we can carry all of our gear. We could get into that, if you can show us where to go. Say, maybe you could take us to that place where we went before with the railroad tracks and the border fence. We could get video to upload later rather than the still shots I took back then. With luck, maybe get a video of a train going by on the main line of the Union Pacific. We have plenty of time to have an early lunch and get back here."

After a visit to the border fence and an early lunch at Jason's Deli, Marcus, Otto, the reporter, and the camera operator all returned to the federal courthouse early in order to get good positions near the front.

At 1:30 p.m., the courtroom was packed with spectators, including Yusef and other media personnel. When court was called to order, Judge Underwood asked counselors to approach the bench. The same older defense attorney approached, along with Susana Tate. The judge said, "The court will entertain pleas from the defendants. If the plea is guilty for one count, the court will pass sentence. Otherwise, a trial date will be scheduled."

Counsel for the defense said, "We will consult with our clients and return in a few moments."

After appropriate legal steps in which the defendants pleaded guilty, the judge stated, "Andrei Kozlov and Dimitri Nikolaev, based on your plea, the court finds you guilty of one count of domestic terrorism. You are sentenced to ten years' confinement in federal correctional facilities, after which you will be deported."

The defense counsel said, "Your Honor, we request the defendants' release on bail pending appeal."

The judge thought, *He can't be so stupid as to think that the Fifth Circuit Court of Appeals will hear this case after a guilty plea. He must be expecting this request to be heard by his actual client, the Russian government. I'll just have to go through the motions.* He said, "Prosecution?"

Susana Tate responded, "The prosecution rejects any possibility of release on bail because of the ease of leaving the jurisdiction of the court by walking across the border."

The judge said, "Request denied. The defendants will continue in custody until a suitable location for their continued confinement to serve out their sentence can be located. Court dismissed." *There's a federal prison right outside of El Paso in the suburbs in Anthony. Maybe the marshals will find a place there. Serves them right to be confined here in the desert a long ways from Washington so the Russian government would have to send people here to confer with them.*

With a bang of the gavel, he left the courtroom while media rushed to both the defense and prosecution tables. Marcus and his crew went to the defense table, knowing that statements from the prosecution would be forthcoming at a later time. Yusef, as before, left as quickly as possible, avoiding the media.

After the defense declined comment, Marcus rushed his crew along with Otto into the corridor, this time in order to upload a description of the afternoon's proceedings and Otto's drawings. As soon as they finished, the camera operator and reporter hastily said goodbye, stating they wanted to go to the airport to see if they could get flights back to New York right away. Marcus suggested Otto join him for coffee while they decompress from the day's activities, saying, "I'm not going back to Washington today. The next trial for the Iranians is Thursday. I'm tempted to just stay here. There must be all sorts of stories I could dig up here on the border, including the abuse of children in detention facilities right here in the El Paso suburbs. Frankly, I'm tired of airplanes. But then I really miss my wife and children."

Otto said, "I'd gladly join you. Maybe I could take you to some out-of-the-way places Khan and I go to sometimes. I'll meet him for an early supper and then go back to Alamogordo early. I'm going to have to work overtime the next two days to make up for the time drawing for you today and Thursday."

While seated in a nearby Starbuck's coffee shop near the historic plaza in downtown El Paso, Marcus and Otto engaged in idle conversation, among other things describing their backgrounds. Marcus described growing up in the coal mining community of Bluefield, West Virginia, eager to get out and explore the world, unlike most of his contemporaries. After a degree in journalism at nearby Virginia Tech, he started with the *Roanoke Times* in Roanoke, Virginia, the largest city in the area. There he met Yusef, who had participated in the prosecution of two cases in federal court for the Western District of Virginia. They formed a friendship that continued after Marcus was offered positions with BBC America in New York and now in Washington.

Otto described his background growing up near Chicago. "I was basically a numbers geek, not really socially inept, but content in my own little world. Being gay and reluctant to admit it contributed to my isolation. After a Master's degree in math and statistics, when I was offered a position with NASA at Holloman Air Force Base, I jumped. I fell in love with the desert and lifestyle. Now that I've met Khan, things are even better." He continued explaining that he might be looking for jobs in El Paso or closer so he and Khan could be together.

After continued idle conversation, they parted company, agreeing to meet again for the trial of the Iranian-Americans on Thursday.

CHAPTER 5

Thursday, June 27, 2019
El Paso, Texas, USA

At 9 a.m., again a courtroom in the federal courthouse in downtown El Paso was crowded with news media, including Marcus Porter in his role as news developer and a reporter from BBC America, along with a reporter who would appear on camera, and a video camera person accompanying him. Otto sat with them with his sketch pads. Yusef sat in the spectator section near the front. Brenda Jackson sat at the prosecution table. She was in her late forties, dressed in a light green summer dress. An attorney from Los Angeles sat at the defense table between two defendants. He appeared to be in his thirties and wore a dark, well-made suit, short of designer quality, along with a white shirt and tie. The two defendants wore slightly down-market dark suits, white shirts, and ties.

The bailiff announced the case of the *U.S. versus Pashang and Rouhani*. Judge Salazar entered wearing a black judicial robe. He was in his sixties, had graying black hair, and was about five feet seven and slender. When he asked the prosecution to present its case, the defense attorney asked permission to approach the bench. When he and Brenda Jackson were in front of the judge, the defense attorney said, "Your Honor, the defendants are willing to plead guilty to one count in exchange for a reduced sentence and supervised parole. We submitted a document for your review prior to this morning's session."

Judge looked at Brenda Jackson and said, "Counselor?"

Brenda Jackson said, "Your Honor, the prosecution is willing to accept a plea bargain on one count with a sentence at the low end of the sentencing guidelines range, followed by probation in order to avoid a lengthy trial. We also submitted a sentencing memorandum for your review."

"Very well," Judge Salazar said. "Please take your seats."

Then publicly, he asked the defendants to plead, to which they said "guilty." He continued, "Amin Pashang and Hamid Rouhani, based on your plea of guilty to domestic terrorism, I sentence you to ten years' confinement in a federal prison, followed by another ten years of supervised parole."

He then banged the gavel and said, "court dismissed," and returned to his chambers. Marshals escorted the defendants out of the courtroom to a detainment room from which they would be returned to jail and then to a federal prison. Yusef exited through the nearest door, pointedly avoiding Marcus and other media representatives.

The large number of news media present rushed to the defense and prosecution tables, Marcus and his crew going to the defense. The defense attorney said, "We will provide a written statement to the media shortly."

Brenda Jackson stated, "The El Paso Division of the U.S. Attorney General is always willing to cooperate with the media. We are not in a position to comment at the moment, but will schedule a press conference to which all will be invited."

As with the sentencing of the two Russians, Marcus directed the reporter and camera operator to a corridor in the courthouse, inviting Otto to join him. After uploading the reporter's description of the proceedings and Otto's drawings, Marcus said to Otto, "The crew will want to go to the airport to get flights back to New York as soon as possible. I'd be pleased to join you for coffee for a little while, but I might try to get flights to Washington today."

Otto said, "I could join you somewhere close to the airport or even in the airport itself, because that's on the way to Alamogordo. Maybe I should try to get back and get some work done today, especially if you want me next week in Albuquerque for the trial of the North Koreans. July 8, Monday, right after the Fourth of July holiday, you say?"

"Yes, at 9 a.m.," Marcus answered. "I'll have to fly in from Washington the night before."

"I'll have to get up really early," Otto said. "The only way to get there is to drive, and it's over three hours."

"Come the night before, if you like," Marcus said. "We'll pay for your hotel."

"Maybe Khan will be able to join me using the long four-day holiday weekend to explore northern New Mexico," Otto said.

They met in the airport coffee shop after a short while and visited more on idle topics until Marcus took a flight to Denver with a connection to Washington.

Later that night, Yusef was recounting to Nisrine what happened in the courtroom.

She replied, "Sounds good. Justice was done and you saved lengthy trials and media circuses. With all that's going on in the detainee camps, including right here in the El Paso area, in Clint, you must have plenty going on in your office."

"Yes, for sure," he replied. "There's talk of criminal charges against some of the employees."

"State charges or federal?" she asked. "If federal, then you would prosecute."

"Could be both state and federal," he answered. "Most likely federal with human rights violations. I haven't looked into what state law says on the subject. For something this high profile, the big guns would come down from Washington to handle the prosecution, but then the judges might not allow them. We'd be kept busy, for sure. In fact, we're pretty busy now. With a holiday coming up, we're all pushing ourselves. The Fourth of July is on Thursday; I told the staff to take Friday the fifth off. I'm sure we'll be swamped the week after."

"Say, what are we going to do on the Fourth?" Nisrine asked. "There must be lots of celebrations here, if it isn't too hot. I don't know if I could take too much heat, being outdoors when pregnant. Of course, like everyone says, it's a dry heat, not humid like San Antonio."

"A few years ago, when all of our group of friends in DC had a reunion in Ruidoso on the Fourth with the guys from DC, we went to a fireworks display at the Inn of the Mountain Gods. We could go there. Just a day trip, if we can't get a room."

"Let's do it," Nisrine answered.

The rest of the evening was spent in mostly idle chat before going to bed for an affectionate night.

CHAPTER 6

Monday, July 8, 2019
Albuquerque, New Mexico, USA

About 8:30 a.m., Marcus, along with his crew of a reporter, camera operator, and Otto, gathered early in a courtroom in the Pete V. Domenici Federal Building to get a good position close to the front, before the trial of two North Korean defectors accused of hacking bank accounts in the U.S. and transferring amounts to their personal bank accounts. Earlier, Marcus, Otto, and the crew had breakfast in their hotel to discuss their upcoming activities for the day. Otto and Khan had spent the long holiday weekend together visiting northern New Mexico. They were in two cars, one parked while they toured, so Khan could go home to El Paso on Sunday night for a busy day at work today.

With the courtroom full of people from media outlets, the defendants were seated at the defense table with Adriana Cho, a public defender, seated between them. She was a recent graduate of the University of New Mexico Law School, working public defense until she could find a suitable full-time legal position. She was diminutive, in her middle twenties with Asian features, standing about five feet two with short, straight, black hair. She wore a summer dress with muted floral designs.

Aaron Benavides sat alone at the prosecution table. He was in his middle-to-late twenties, recently hired by the U.S. Attorney for New Mexico, a recent graduate of the J. Ruben Clark Law School

Pete V. Domenici Federal Courthouse, Albuquerque, New Mexico

at Brigham Young University, which he completed after his mission trip in Bolivia for the Church of Jesus Christ of Latter-day Saints. He stood five feet eleven, with a slim body, dark brown hair, brown sparkling eyes, and features that reflected both his Hispanic and Anglo-American ancestry. He wore a mid-market light weight wool suit with white shirt and red tie.

A court-appointed Korean-language translator, a professor emeritus in linguistics from the University of New Mexico, sat near the defense table dressed in a well worn but clean and pressed suit with a light yellow shirt and a green tie with small designs.

The bailiff called the court to order in the case of the *U.S. versus Kim and Kwang.* Judge Elliott Davidson, wearing a black judicial robe, entered the courtroom. He stood five feet ten, had salt-and-pepper mostly dark brown hair, and appeared to be in his late forties or early fifties. He had been on the bench for about four years, having been appointed by President Obama.

When the judge called the prosecution to present its case, Adriana asked to approach the bench along with prosecution counsel. When they arrived, she began, "Your Honor, now I've had an opportunity to discuss the defendants' positions with them, first using my limited Korean with help from my grandparents, and then with the court-appointed translator. They speak only limited English and Spanish. They have been administrative staff with the North Korean embassy in Mexico, including computer-based communication and domestic duties, because the North Korean government does not trust locally hired Mexican staff. They were not diplomats. They were believed to be trustworthy and assigned to an herb shop and spa façade for a tunnel opening in Ciudad Juárez that went under the border fence to El Paso. This element of their background has been well covered in the media and need not be covered here.

"They were not aware they were committing what would be considered serious criminal activity in the U.S. by hacking bank accounts to transfer money to themselves. Such activity is commonplace among North Koreans. They had the naïve notion that they would be welcomed as asylum seekers in the U.S. because they are North Korean and would be allowed to join former North Korean asylees in California.

"Now they believe they will be abducted by North Korea and returned to North Korea for execution if they are returned to Mexico. They are also very concerned they would be abducted and executed if released in the U.S. The upshot is that they would plead guilty in exchange for being confined to prison in the U.S. for some period. They feel safer in a U.S. prison than elsewhere. A more detailed description of the defendants' position is in the document we submitted to the court. I've had a brief preliminary discussion with counsel for the prosecution, who also has a copy of our document."

The judge looked to Aaron Benavides and said, "Counselor?"

Aaron said, "I've talked briefly with counselor and discussed the issue at higher levels in our office, including with the U.S. Attorney for New Mexico. We are willing to accept guilty pleas and have the court impose a sentence within the sentencing guidelines range. We have prepared a sentencing document to that effect."

Judge Davidson pondered momentarily, then said, "I'll ask the defendants to plead formally. Then I'll review your comments and pass sentence in the early afternoon. Please take your seats."

When the attorneys were seated, Judge Davidson asked, "Chaewon Kim and Daehun Kwang, how do you plead?"

Adriana spoke briefly with the defendants and motioned for the court-appointed translator to translate the judge's question. The defendants replied to the translator who in turn said, "The defendants plead guilty."

The judge continued to ask, "Has your attorney explained to you the type of sentence and length of confinement you would likely face in a federal prison?"

Adriana looked at the defendants and also the translator, who translated the question. When the defendants answered, the translator said, "She explained the conditions. They are willing to accept any length of incarceration."

The judge then spoke publicly. "The court is recessed until 1:30 p.m., at which time sentence will be passed."

While the judge was walking to his chambers, he thought, *This is a new one. Their crimes are pretty small for financial crimes. Normally, they would get a sentence of just a couple of years or maybe only supervised probation. With all the political uncertainty over North Korea, I just couldn't turn them loose so quickly and put them at danger of abduction and execution by the North Korean government. There'll be a new administration in 2025, maybe four years sooner, but within six years for sure. Maybe if I sentence them for seven years, that can keep them safe. They can always get attorneys to ask for release on parole sooner.*

While the marshals escorted the defendants to a holding room, the media present all rushed to the defense and prosecution tables. Both attorneys declined comment and quickly left.

Marcus suggested coffee and an early lunch. Otto commented that he was unfamiliar with the area, but surely they could find something.

When court reconvened at 1:30, Judge Davidson said, "Chaewon Kim and Daehun Kwang, based on your guilty plea, I find you guilty of theft. You are hereby sentenced to seven years in a federal prison. Court dismissed."

Media representatives rushed to both the defense and prosecution tables. Adriana said that any statement would be given later by the public defender's office. Aaron gave a similar statement that a public press conference would be called by the office of the U.S. Attorney for New Mexico.

While he gathered his papers and documents, Aaron thought, *Adriana sure is attractive and a good attorney. From all indications, she's not married. I wonder if she has a boyfriend? I've got to find some way to get to know her better and maybe ask her out. I wonder what my family would think about me dating an Asian girl. I'm getting ahead of myself, though.*

While Adriana gathered her belongings, she thought, *Aaron sure is cute, very professional also. He's not wearing a wedding ring. Does he have a girlfriend? How can I manipulate things to get him in a social setting to find out more? He went to Brigham Young law school. Does that mean he's Mormon? What would my family think if I dated a Mormon? But I'm getting ahead of myself.*

Marshals escorted the defendants out of the courtroom to be returned to jail cells, pending transfer to prison. Marcus rushed his crew, along with Otto, to a relatively empty corridor to make a video of the reporter describing events, to be uploaded along with Otto's drawings.

The camera person and reporter left quickly to go to the airport to attempt to get flights back to New York. Marcus said he would not return until the next day and invited Otto for coffee and maybe dinner.

Otto replied, "It'd be good to drive back to Alamogordo tonight, but I could spend some more time with you just so long as I get home by a reasonable bedtime."

While sitting in a coffee shop, Marcus said, "This is an interesting city, what I've seen of it."

Otto replied, "This is only the second time I've been in Albuquerque; the first was a few years ago, shortly after I moved to New Mexico just to see what the state was like. El Paso's a lot closer to me, quite a bit bigger, and has a lot more to offer. And safer too."

"Yes, I've heard that El Paso is the second safest city in the U.S.," Marcus said.

Albuquerque's OK," Otto said, "but Santa Fe, the capital just a little bit further north, is much more interesting and historic. It really is part of the Land of Enchantment. Albuquerque's just a big city. Sometimes people in Albuquerque think they're the only place in New Mexico that's important and forget about us in places like Alamogordo."

"It's been great working with you, Otto. This seems to wind up all the events coming from that tunnel situation. I'm sure there'll be other things coming out of the border where I can use your sketches again. With all the attention given to the appalling conditions in the border camps and congressional visits, I'm sure I'll be back to El Paso often and to the Lower Rio Grande Valley."

"It's been a great experience for me, too, Marcus. Some extra income helps."

"Other networks have been after me to join for pretty good increases in income," Marcus said. "I'll probably jump, now that this is behind me. One condition is that I get to pick my own illustrator; and that would be you, if I'm anywhere near where you can travel."

Otto said, "Other media outlets have approached me too. I consider myself to be freelance, so I might go for them also. For sure, if I have to make a choice, I'd go with you. I don't think I'm ready to give up my day job just yet, so anything I'd do would have to be pretty close to the El Paso area."

After a brief lull in the conversation, Marcus asked, "What did you and Khan do for the Fourth? You said you were spending a long weekend together."

"We toured northern New Mexico," Otto answered. "Santa Fe; he had never been there before. Also, a rustic area, Jemez Springs. Then Taos and all of that area."

"You're always welcome to come visit us in Washington," Marcus offered. "Maybe not so soon after the Fourth of July holiday this year, but it'd be a pleasure to show you all the sights."

Otto smiled and said, "Thanks a lot. That'd be great. I know Khan would really like that. He's barely been outside of Texas and now New Mexico."

They spent several more minutes in friendly conversation until Otto said he needed to leave for the drive home. They parted company with a warm, friendly handshake.

CHAPTER 7

Monday, July 8, 2019
El Paso, Texas, USA

Yusef came home from work about 6 p.m., slightly later than usual, showing obvious signs of stress. Nisrine greeted him warmly and said, "Sit down; I'll get you a cup of tea."

"Let me go greet Sara first," he said.

"She's playing happily in her room," Nisrine said. "Just relax. She'll be very pleased to see you later."

When Nisrine returned with a cup of tea, Yusef said, "Thanks."

Nisrine continued, "You seem especially frazzled. Anything special going on?"

"No, no one thing," he replied. "Just lots of activity all related to border problems. In my other job as head of civil and human rights for the district, I'm getting calls from Alpine and Del Rio. They have their staffs busy with border issues with illegal immigrants and don't have big enough staffs to deal with hate crimes that are emerging. Fortunately, San Antonio, Austin, Waco, and Midland have enough staff that so far they haven't needed to contact me."

"This border situation is really getting ugly," Nisrine added. "Of course, I don't need to tell you that. The pediatrician I do volunteer work with went to the confinement center for children in Clint to offer his services but was turned away. Unfortunately, I wouldn't be able to be admitted either. Otherwise, I'd have to call you to take care of Sara; and with your work, that just wouldn't work out."

"Yeah," Yusef replied.

Nisrine continued, "I heard on the news today that the two North Koreans were sentenced to seven years in Albuquerque."

"Yes," Yusef said. "Khan mentioned it. Otto was with Marcus drawing sketches. We can surely watch the news tonight and see the sketches."

"Who knows how long this disaster at the border will go on?" Nisrine continued. "I was thinking about what we might do for the Eid al Adha next month. It's on a weekend, August 10 and 11. I had thought we might go to Dallas to celebrate with Mama and Baba; maybe Husey and Dima could be there."

"I don't think I could take time off from work to go to Dallas," Yusef replied. "Even if it's on a weekend, we'd have to fly on Friday and likely come back Monday. It just wouldn't be worth the effort to fly on Saturday and return on Sunday."

"Yes, you're right," Nisrine said. "Maybe they could come here. In this heat, though, I don't know if we would want to be roasting a leg of lamb."

"We could grill lamb chops outside," Yusef offered. "We might even eat out on the patio in the shade if it is not too hot. Other than lamb, there are no traditional foods. We could just have summery things."

"That would work," She said. "Say, Tiffany said she might like to come back with Marcus sometime. Maybe invite them. I'm sure there's enough going on here at the border to bring Marcus back."

"Yes, and maybe invite Omar," Yusef added. "He hasn't been here yet, and he's a friend of Marcus too. Omar is on summer break and not teaching summer school this year."

"Good, Nisrine said." Eid al Adha events are big gatherings. We wouldn't have room for all of them to stay over here in this house, but maybe they wouldn't mind hotels."

"We could even invite Brad and Jason and Frank and Paco," Yusef added.

"I could invite some of the people I've worked with," Nisrine said. "Especially that pediatrician I talked to today. He could bring his wife. Maybe you would invite people you work with."

"Well now that we're making this a big event, there could be Khan and Otto, of course," Yusef continued. "Maybe some others from the office. We'd need lots of lamb chops; it's not that much effort to cook a lot of them. There's a kosher butcher here in El Paso, so we could get halal. We'd have to order a long time in advance. We could have other food catered."

"It's over a month away," Nisrine said. "We can see how we might arrange this. I'll let Mama and Husey know; then we can let the other invitations fall into place."

At that moment, Sara came into the room and eagerly greeted her father. They spent the rest of the evening as a congenial family group, Yusef relaxing from the stress of the day.

CHAPTER 8

Thursday, July 25, 2019
El Paso, Texas, USA

Later than usual, about 6 p.m., Yusef arrived home. Nisrine was serving food to Sara and helping her eat. She had prepared a simple supper for her and Yusef. Yusef greeted each of them with a hug and kiss. Nisrine looked at him and said, "You look frazzled."

Yusef mumbled, "Yes; lots going on at work."

Nisrine cleaned Sara, guided her to her room to play, then returned, put her arm around Yusey, and said, "Do we need to have the same conversation as when you confronted me about needing to be needed too much?"

Yusef paused for a moment, a bit startled, then said, "Thanks for your concern. You care. But no, just the opposite. I'm needed too much and don't want to be needed so much."

"Oh?" Nisrine commented.

"It's the other job, the one I didn't leave behind when I moved to El Paso, point person on human and civil rights and hate crimes for the whole district. Now all the division offices, including San Antonio, Austin, Waco and Midland are looking to me for guidance. I do have expertise, but not on every issue. I have to do lots of research, analysis, and just plain guessing."

"Well certainly there are lots of human rights violations," Nisrine offered.

"Yes, for sure," Yusef replied. "But not necessarily all are crimes. It depends on exactly how the statutes are written and interpreted, and lots of this is new."

"I'm not a lawyer, of course," Nisrine added. "But I do know a little bit about the difference between criminal and civil law. If they're not criminal, wouldn't they be civil?"

"That's one of the issues," Yusef replied. "My expertise is criminal. I'm not completely ignorant of civil human rights issues, but it's not an area I've had to deal with. I'm being asked about civil law issues, and I have to do a lot of research and analysis. Plus, civil law is nowhere near as straightforward as criminal law. In criminal law, either an act is a crime or it isn't. Well, it's not all that cut and dried, but basically. For civil law there are lots of nuances and precedents, requiring lots of research, analysis, and just plain guessing. On top of that, lots of the allegations are against contractors, not the government itself, so the AG might not be involved. We have to dig, though, to see just how much U.S. government activity is involved."

Nisrine continued, "That young eighteen-year-old guy in far south Texas, a U.S. citizen who was detained in horrible conditions, is suing the government. It's not clear from the media whether it's civil or criminal. He's the one who was born in Dallas, grew up in Reynosa on the Mexican side, but now apparently lives in McAllen. Reynosa and McAllen are just across the river from each other, with a bridge connecting them. It's not quite like El Paso and Juárez, where the bridge goes from downtown to downtown, but they are close, and essentially one community."

"Yeah, one community like El Paso and Juárez, it seems," Yusef concurred. "It seems that it's going to be both civil and criminal against the U.S. government and government personnel. That one will be handled by the Southern Judicial District of Texas with headquarters in Houston. While I'm glad they have the headache, not me, similar future events could very well be right here in the

Western District. Susana predicted some of this when she said she wouldn't take the head of the El Paso division.

"Maybe I should get in touch with the people in Houston and compare notes. I probably have as much expertise as they do, maybe more, but they might know some things we don't, and vice versa. For that matter, maybe I should get in touch with the Southern District of California in San Diego and compare notes. I'm already in touch with New Mexico. They and Arizona don't have nearly as much activity, but maybe we all should communicate with each other. Now you see why I'm so stressed and why I'm needed more than I want to be needed. And I still have to run the office, although Susana helps a lot."

"Oh, Yusey," Nisrine said giving him an extra big warm hug and kiss on the cheek. "Why don't we go to Ruidoso and just get away from it for a day or two. Go tomorrow after you get off work. Go to Ruidoso where we can get a condo or B&B and make our own meals, not the fancy casino hotel."

Yusef thought a moment and said, "Sounds great. I've got Khan doing lots of the research for me. Maybe I could take off tomorrow afternoon and Monday and just spend the weekend there. I could say that I'm taking law books with me to do research where there's some peace and quiet, which would be true. I'd take some books and legal pads with me and continue my research and analysis. The temperatures here are over 100. I'll bet it's in the 70s or 80s in Ruidoso. Maybe we could go to Friday prayers in the early afternoon at the Islamic Center here. There's no mosque in Ruidoso or anywhere near that I know of."

"We can certainly check," Nisrine said.

"Say, did I tell you," Yusef interjected. "You know that the U.S. government took over that land where the tunnel opening was that had a phony mosque. Now a local group of Shia say they planned a mosque there all along; they were duped by other Iranians, and now they want to take the property and continue to make it into a Shia mosque. We're Shia and we haven't heard even the faintest word about other Shia in El Paso who wanted their own mosque. It must be some sort of scam. Because I'm head of the office, I might be expected to make a recommendation as to whether they get it. It's well known I'm Muslim and Shia; so no matter what decision I would make, it would look like I'm biased. I'll turn this over to John in San Antonio and let him make the decision."

"No, I hadn't heard of that," Nisrine said. "Good idea. The district office in San Antonio sure owes you for putting up with all the crap here in El Paso, so let them deal with some of the crap for a change. If we do go to Ruidoso, maybe Khan and Otto would be there. I told them I'd take a rain check on dinner. Maybe this weekend."

"I can ask Khan," Yusef said. "I'll need to talk to him tomorrow anyway if I go away while he's doing research for me. You know I avoid having too much contact with him in the office so not to appear to be too close socially."

"Let's have supper while it's still a little bit warm," Nisrine said. "You just stay here, I'll get it."

They spent the rest of the night relaxing after putting Sara to bed, anticipating the cool weather of Ruidoso.

CHAPTER 9

Saturday, August 3, 2019
El Paso, Texas, USA

In the mid-morning, Yusef was sitting on the couch listlessly watching news on television, his mind preoccupied with issues in his office due to the many border issues. Suddenly he sat up startled and almost shouted, "Nizzy, come here! There's an active shooter right now out by Cielo Vista Mall. Wait. Check on Sara first; she shouldn't see this."

Soon Nisrine joined him on the sofa, having said that Sara was playing happily in her room. They sat mesmerized for a few moments. Yusef broke the silence, "I wonder if any from our office are there and injured. I'd better check on them. I need to contact Susana first."

"I need to contact hospitals and see if I can offer to help," Nisrine said.

"Why you?" Yusef asked. "You aren't a trauma doctor."

"I've had basic medical training," Nisrine replied. "Besides, there might be some pregnant women."

"They're saying that all the off-duty personnel at the Texas Tech University Medical Center have just gone in to work without being called. They might not need someone today. Their biggest need might be tomorrow or the next day, when the seriously wounded have been stabilized, especially if there are pregnant women. I'm no medical expert, but that's just a thought. Besides, I strongly suspect that I need to go to the office soon, and someone needs to be with Sara. I can probably stay with Sara tomorrow, at least part of the day. Monday will no doubt be hectic beyond belief."

"OK, you're right," Nisrine said. "I'd better check on Sara again. She definitely doesn't need to see this."

Yusef found his cell phone and called Susana on her cell phone. When she answered, after very short greetings he said, "I'm checking on you to see if you or anyone you are close to is affected by the shooting at Walmart. Also, we likely need to talk about work things soon. We'll no doubt be involved, but mostly for now, I'm concerned about your well-being."

(Pause)

"Good to hear no one you know is involved," Yusef said. "Do you know about the others in the office?"

(Pause)

"OK, I just thought you might possibly have heard something," Yusef replied. "I need to start checking on people in the office, not only for their personal well-being, but also to be able to plan office workload in case some of them need to be out. I'll have to go to the office where all of their phone numbers are on file. I don't have them here."

(Pause)

"Oh, you'll join me? Good!" Yusef said. "I'll probably try to find a quick bite of lunch here and go fairly soon. Join me when you can."

They said goodbyes. Yusef told Nisrine of his plans and got her concurrence. After a quick lunch and a hasty shower and shave, he left for the office. Just in case he would meet someone with the media, he wore gray slacks and a short-sleeved white shirt. He grabbed a jacket and tie to carry with him just in case.

Yusef arrived in his office before Susana, turned on his computer to watch the events at the shooting scene live stream, located the list of personnel, and began calling He used his cell phone for those who had cell phones and would likely recognize his number, and used the office land line for others. He left messages for people to call him back.

After a short while, Susana came into his office dressed smartly but casually. He stood and greeted her. After a few brief pleasantries, he said that he had called a couple and left messages, and talked to two who did not know anyone involved in the shooting. He said, "If you like, you can start with names that begin with *N* onward while I continue to call the rest. I'll call Khan, though, because he's doing research for me on hate crimes and this might very well be a hate crime. The news is saying the shooter targeted Mexicans, apparently referring to Hispanics who may or may not be actual Mexicans."

"Yes, that's what I'm hearing," Susana said. "I'll go start calling, and discuss things with you shortly."

When Yusef called Khan's cell phone, the only phone Khan had, it rang several times, and Yusef left a message to call back on Yusef's cell phone. In just a very few moments, Khan called back. After short preliminary greetings, Yusef explained the reason for his call. After a short pause, he said, "Oh, you're at the scene. Is everything OK with you?"

(Pause)

"Oh, he's drawing sketches from the scene," Yusef said. "Maybe I can see them sometime. Now I have to call others. Good to know you an Otto are OK. Next week, we should talk more. All indications are that this is a federal hate crime, and you're doing a lot of research into the issue."

After another short pause, Yusef said goodbye and proceeded to call others.

When he finished calling others on his list and was pondering what to do next, Susana came to his office. She asked, "What did you find out?"

Yusef replied, "A couple know someone who was there, but no one close to them. I had to leave messages for some."

"Same here," Susana said. "It looks like our office is largely unscathed, but there are still those we haven't heard from. No doubt this will affect us and what we do here the next several weeks, maybe years."

"This will have a lasting effect on the whole community," Yusef said. "I know it would in greater Detroit, where I grew up, and the Detroit area is not a safe place like El Paso is."

"Yes, and an impact on the whole state of Texas," Susana stated. "It was good that the governor was here in just a couple of hours. I know I've been cynical about elected officials' paying only nominal attention to El Paso and only at election time, like in their minds El Paso is not really part of Texas. This time it's different, and I'm sorry I was so cynical. He's not even eligible for reelection. I'm sure other elected officials will be here soon enough."

"This will no doubt keep us busy. They're already saying it's a hate crime," Yusef said.

"Yes, the FBI is there on the scene," Susana said.

"You just reminded me," Yusef said. "Carter Kuykendall tried to call me when I was on my cell phone and left me a text message to call him. I'd better call him now."

Susana stood to leave; Yusef said, "No, stay. It might be useful for you to hear this."

Yusef called and as soon as he identified himself, he paused, then said, "Please repeat. There's a lot of background noise."

(Pause)

"Oh, you're on the scene," Yusef continued. "You want to bring me into the case as soon as possible because it's almost certainly a federal hate crime."

(Pause)

"Yes, I could come out there," Yusef replied. "I can understand you need to stay on the scene and can't come to our office. Right now, I'm with Susana in the office. I'll let you know when I'm on my way and you can tell me then where exactly to find you."

To Susana, he said, "You likely heard most of that. The FBI has been brought in and is investigating the shootings as hate crimes. They seem to have evidence that the shooter specifically indicated he is shooting Mexicans. Charles Goodnight wants to bring me into the picture right away, and he can't come here to this office right now."

Susana offered, "Whenever I've been in that shopping area, there have been lots of cars with license plates from Chihuahua. The dead might be literally Mexicans, although, as you know, people around here call all Hispanics "Mexicans," even the Hispanics themselves."

"International implications," Yusef stated. "That certainly will make it complicated for us. The news has also said that local authorities are pursuing capital murder in the state of Texas."

Susana replied, "Yes, and that almost certainly leads to the death penalty in Texas."

"The U.S. Attorney General has just announced he wants to bring back the death penalty for federal murder crimes too," Yusef commented.

"But it depends on who is actually prosecuting and whether there is a request for a death penalty, and whether a jury and the judge approve," Susana said. "But we're getting way ahead of ourselves. I might run into you out there. There's some kind of a memorial service that local clergy planned. I might go."

"A memorial service already?" Yusef asked.

"Yes," she answered. "The community, and especially the clergy, responded right away."

"If I am out there anyway," Yusef added, "I could go to a memorial service too."

"It'll be a Christian service," Susana said, "probably the Catholic Bishop and maybe some others. Is that a problem for a Muslim like you?"

"No problem whatever," Yusef replied. "I've been to Christian services before. Christians are 'people of the book' for Muslims,

Jewish too. All descending from our father Ibrahim, Abraham you call him."

"Good, maybe I'll see you there," Susana said. "We might need to be in touch tomorrow, also. Now I should go."

Yusef stood as she left, saying, "I'll need to give a statement to the media. Probably tomorrow. If I run into media today, I'll just make a short comment. Thanks a lot for your support. It's good to have you around for messy situations like this."

As Susana left, Yusef thought, *Media. I bet Marcus is right on top of this. I'd call him, but I'm sure he's using his phone for all sorts of things; and besides, I need to go.*

As if by telepathy, Yusef's cell phone rang, indicating the call was from Marcus. Yusef answered, "Hello, there, I'm just thinking about you this very minute."

(Pause)

"That's what I thought, you might be on your way," Yusef continued. "I don't know too much about hotels in El Paso except for those downtown by the office, and you want to be near the shooting site. Wait, the shopping area where the shooting took place is near the airport. There are all sorts of hotels near the airport. If you can hang on, I'm next to my computer—I'm in my office—I'll look and let you know. Just a moment."

Yusef laid his cell phone down, hastily did a hotel search for the El Paso airport, and then went back to the cell phone saying, "How about Holiday Inn Express. I could book one night for you and then when you get here, you can see what you want to do after that. If you can hang on just a little while longer, I'll use the land line to call."

Yusef laid his cell phone down again, used the land line to reserve a room for one night that night in Marcus's name, and gave his own credit card number to hold the reservation. He then returned to the cell phone, saying, "All set; Holiday Inn Express Airport in your name. I used my credit card. You can probably change to your credit card when you get there, or pay me later."

(Pause)

"You're welcome." Yusef said into the cell phone. "When you get to Dallas and know you're going to be on a flight to El Paso, call me again. I might possibly be able to meet you at the airport. No guarantees, but I'm going out to the site now to meet the FBI, and likely local media. Maybe at least I can show you where the site is, so you can find it yourself tomorrow. You know how to rent cars at the El Paso airport so I'll not worry about that."

They said a hasty goodbye, then Yusef thought, *Media are there, so I'd better put that tie on and have the jacket, even if it is 100 degrees. Gotta call Nizzy too.*

Yusef called Nisrine, told her about his plans, that he would grab something to eat while out, and concluded, "Don't wait up for me; I can't be sure how long I'll be gone, especially if I meet Marcus when he arrives."

(Pause)

"Love you; bye," he concluded.

Yusef went to the Walmart shooting site, met Charles Goodnight and Carter Kuykendall with the FBI, gave the media a brief statement that he was brought in because this is a hate crime, and said he would have a statement for the media the next day or two. He then met Marcus at the hotel he had booked and took Marcus to the site to show him briefly where it was located so Marcus could find it the next day. Both were exhausted—Marcus especially, being used to the Eastern time zone. They each went to bed as soon as possible, Yusef being careful not to wake Nisrine.

Sunday, August 4, 2019

Yusef slept later than usual, got up about 9:30 a.m., and walked into the family room wearing a robe. Nisrine was watching television while Sara was in her room playing. Nisrine began to stand to greet

330

him; Yusef motioned her to remain seated while he walked to her, bent over, and kissed her.

"You've been on TV all morning," Nisrine said. "News networks are showing your brief statement to the media."

Yusef gave a faint smile and said, "Yeah, I have to give a more detailed statement today. As soon as my head clears, I need to start preparing it. Are you going to go to any of the hospitals to volunteer today? I can probably prepare a statement here at home watching Sara, but at some point I'll likely have to go out."

"Apparently there are no pregnant women and they have an OB/ GYN on call," she replied, "so, I'll be here. Say, what are we going to do about the Eid al Adha? We can't have a festive party so soon after all this."

"We can't cancel, either, at this late date." Yusef replied. "Meat has been ordered from the butcher and flight reservations have already been made. Paco and Frank are traveling this weekend, I think. Paco has a job interview in Amarillo this coming week, from what I recall. Maybe I can call Omar and see what he has to say from the perspective of an imam. Maybe we could make it into a memorial and prayer service, a Muslim one."

"The victims are just now being identified," Nisrine said. "No indication that there are Muslims among them."

"That's OK," Yusef replied. "The service I went to last night was supposedly multi-faith although the clergy present were all Christian. Omar can pray for Christians—Jewish too if there were any there—they are all people of the book."

Yusef went to the kitchen to make coffee and get cereal for breakfast. He played with Sara, had idle conversation with Nisrine, and went to prepare his statement for the media.

CHAPTER 10

Saturday, August 10, 2019
El Paso, Texas, USA

Right around 12 noon, Yusef, Nisrine, and Sara greeted guests arriving for the Eid al Adha lunch gathering, Sara charming everyone with her precocious smile and demeanor. Nisrine's parents and Omar had arrived a couple of days previously and were houseguests. Yusef guided arrivals to the large covered patio, where shade made being outside tolerable in the dry heat of the Chihuahuan Desert where El Paso was located. A large selection of juices, soft drinks, iced tea, and bottled water was on a large table, with ample ice and large plastic cups. A large number of lamb chops was on ice and loosely covered, waiting to be grilled over a gas grill off to the side of the patio so as not to contribute more to the heat of the day. Because of the large Jewish community in El Paso, Yusef was able to order kosher lamb, which was also halal for Muslims.

Omar along with Nisrine's parents greeted arriving guests on the patio, tending to them while Yusef returned to the front door to continue greeting arriving guests. Young persons, including Yusef and Omar, wore shorts and t-shirts or loose-fitting shirts with collars; Nisrine wore a loose-fitting maternity dress. Some older guests, including Nisrine's parents, wore sleeveless summer dress or casual pants with summer shirts. All anticipated afternoon temperatures close to 100 degrees Fahrenheit, typical of August in this area of dry desert heat.

Paco and Frank had arrived two days earlier, among other reasons to go shopping in Ciudad Juárez. Paco had an upcoming interview for a nursing position at the Veteran's Administration Hospital in Amarillo; he was excited about the prospect. Frank, who would soon complete his dissertation for a PhD in International Relations, looked over job prospects near Amarillo.

Brad and Jason had arrived the day before. They had rented a car so that after church services tomorrow they could take a leisurely sight-seeing trip to Lubbock, where Brad had been invited to explore a post-doctorate position at Texas Tech as soon as he completed his PhD. Brad had met faculty in international studies from Texas Tech at a recent professional conference. Texas Tech faculty were impressed with the paper Brad presented and wanted to explore giving him a position.

Khan and Otto were mingling, Otto carrying his sketch pad to draw highlights of the occasion. He pointedly did not sketch people unless they asked him to draw them. Some were aware of his sketches on news reports and were pleased to get sketches of themselves or people accompanying them.

Brad and Jason connected with Khan and Otto and had instant rapport. While Brad and Khan discussed being gay and Christian, among other things, Otto and Jason had lively conversations about art and sketching. Otto was intrigued with furniture design and Jason was fascinated with Otto's sketching. Otto drew Jason from the side showing his pony tail and enough of his face showing the facial hair. He made drawings for Brad and kept one for himself.

Roger Chen had come from U.S. Attorney General headquarters in Washington to consult with the El Paso division over prosecution of hate crimes from the previous weekend's shootings and collaborate on other issues. His wife, Lisa, came with him for the weekend to attend the Eid al Adha gathering, being longtime friends of Yusef and Omar and having attended Yusef and Omar's Eid al Adha dinner in Washington a few years earlier. They were not put off by the heat, because Washington was more humid and often equally as hot. Their high-school-age children were old enough to stay home alone for a weekend.

Marcus mingled with the crowd; Tiffany had not come with him, preferring to wait until weather was cooler so she could go shopping in Ciudad Juárez, among other things. With all the activity at the border, she and Marcus were sure that Marcus would be returning frequently.

Susana attended with her husband. Brenda Jackson came with her daughter in high school, who wanted to know more about Islam. The daughter was immediately charmed by Sara and spent time allowing Sara to entertain her. A few others from Yusef's office were present, some with significant others. Some of Nisrine's medical colleagues attended, also some with significant others. All mixed and mingled congenially but somberly, so soon after the massacre of twenty-two innocents and several wounded right there in El Paso.

When all were gathered on the patio, Yusef got their attention and spoke briefly, explaining that Eid al Adha is the second major holiday of the year for Muslims, an occasion in which friends are invited to share a meal of lamb, recognizing that God told their father Ibrahim to sacrifice a ram rather than kill his son Ishmael. In non-Muslim countries, guests from all backgrounds, including Christian and Jewish would be invited for a festive meal. He continued, "With the horrible massacre of innocents almost exactly a week ago right here in our community and many wounded needing healing, we cannot and should not be festive. Still, we must honor tradition and share a meal. Now I ask my very good friend Omar Abu Deeb, a Muslim imam, to offer prayers for the deceased and for healing of the wounded."

Omar moved to the front of the gathering, began with greetings, and said, "Islamic prayers in this country are mostly in English because that is the language we have in common. We have ritual prayers in Arabic, the language of the Prophet, that I will not offer

today. Please join me silently, if you like, with your own prayers."
Omar then offered short prayers for the departed and healing, then
concluded, "Here is one prayer that I will recite that all Muslims
would know and use for any occasion when compassion and caring
are needed. Please join me if you know it.

In the name of God, the Compassionate the Caring
Praise is to God, the sustaining Lord of all worlds
The Compassionate the Caring
Master of the Day of Reckoning
You do we worship
And you we ask for help
Guide us on the straight road
The road of those whom you have given on them
Not those with anger on them
Nor those who have gone astray

The Muslims in the group joined, notably Nisrine's parents,
Husayn and his wife Dima. Brad joined also; even as a Christian
he knew Islamic prayers from his time as an exchange student
in Jordan and his studies. As soon as the prayer was over, Otto
sketched Omar from the side, not showing his face, but wanting
to show that a Muslim imam could wear shorts and a t-shirt. He
would not show others the sketch without Omar's permission.
Likewise, Marcus took photos of Omar, but also would not post
them without Omar's permission.

Yusef moved in front of the gathering and said, "Please get
your plates and start filling them. By then some lamb chops will
be ready. Enjoy."

Omar and Yusef moved to the large grill and began grilling
while the crowd continued to introduce themselves to each other
and interact. They filled their sturdy paper plates. Large quantities
of food, mostly salads and other cold food for the season, were on
the dining room table, most of which had been catered. Paco and
Frank had brought large fresh papayas and large avocados from

Mexico which were sliced and ready to be eaten. Fresh, extra-sweet, chilled Texas cantaloupes and watermelons were available for dessert. Middle Eastern flat bread and baklava sweets came from a pastry shop that served the Syrian Christian community that had been in El Paso for at least seventy-five years, and was popular with all in the area.

Lunch was finished with Lebanese coffee, for those who wanted coffee on a hot day. Soon the guests left in small groups, thanking Yusef and Nisrine for their hospitality. Marcus stayed behind, as did Brad and Jason, to help clean up, along with Nisrine's parents and Omar, who were houseguests. Later, with little desire for an evening meal, Yusef put Sara to bed. He, Omar, Nisrine, and her parents spent the rest of the evening in casual conversation, pleased that they had honored tradition while still being respectful of the tragedy in the community.

Monday, August 12

In the afternoon, Roger Chen was in Yusef's office, winding up his visit to collaborate on issues the El Paso division was dealing with and to say goodbye before heading to the airport. Roger said, "You're running a good operation here, especially with all the issues facing you here at the border."

"Thank you, and, yes, lots of issues," Yusef replied. "And now this hate crime for the shooter who's now in custody."

"That might not be too big of a challenge for you here in El Paso," Roger said. "There's a very good chance that a judge would grant a change of venue if the defense asks for it. It could be very difficult, if not impossible, to get an impartial jury here with all the public sentiment, not to mention that the jury pool would have a huge percentage of Hispanics."

"Yes, that could be," Yusef concurred. "The defendant has just been assigned a public defender from San Antonio. The court must

336

not have been able to find a public defender from El Paso who is willing to defend him, or maybe no one here is capable of giving a vigorous defense for personal emotional reasons."

"Most likely," Roger agreed. "The defendant might have a martyr complex. He surrendered willingly. Maybe he just wants to plead guilty and serve the rest of his life in prison. Hopefully they'll put him on a suicide watch."

"That's possible, too," Yusef said. "Still, there's enough to keep us busy for a while, not that we don't have enough work already."

"For sure the El Paso division is one of the most prominent in the country at the moment," Roger said. "You are getting lots of favorable attention, for sure. Maybe you're ready for a promotion to a district AG."

"No way José, to quote Susana." "District AGs serve at the pleasure of the president, and I'm not willing to take that risk. I'm content to stay as first deputy for the Western District of Texas, although having two jobs while head of the El Paso division is taking its toll. Unlike Susana, I can't take early retirement, so I'll just have to wait it out."

"We would surely like to have you in Washington again when a suitable opening is available for someone with your talents."

"I wouldn't reject that out of hand, like I would district AG," Yusef said. "Still, Nizzy and I really want to settle in San Antonio. To us, that's home. El Paso is good too, but not like San Antonio. Nizzy wants to have her own OB/GYN practice there. If I were to go to Washington again, she would have to start all over again and get a license in Virginia, Maryland, or DC, or maybe all three."

"We'll obviously be in touch," Roger said. "Either I or someone else from headquarters will be down here from time to time to collaborate. Not that we don't trust you to take care of things; all of you, and you personally, are really handling things well. Still, sometimes we have to collaborate on things in person."

"We understand."

"Thanks a lot for your hospitality," Roger continued. "Lisa enjoyed being with Nisrine and Sara yesterday. It was nice to see Sara; she reminds me of our daughter at that age. It was good to reconnect with Omar again and also meet all of the others."

Roger and Yusef stood to shake hands and say goodbye.

AFTERWORD

With appreciation to Cole Porter for his classic 1930s song that gave me the title for this book, welcome to the place where I tell some of the background for this book, my secrets, and give credit where credit is due. Also, acknowledgment to renowned actor Tony Perkins who chose this song title, and now my book title, to be engraved on the urn containing his ashes.

This is the fourth in a series of current-events historical fiction books featuring some of the same delightful characters in the previous books and some new ones. But, like the others, it's a story that is designed to be read alone without reference to the previous books. There are a few teasers thrown in to motivate you to read the previous books, if you have not done so already.

This is a work of fiction. As in my previous novels, some events I wrote about fictionally actually happened shortly afterwards, although not exactly in the form I had written about them. This story combines fiction with fact in fictional contexts. There is no attempt to actually separate fact from fiction; that much readers can do on their own. It gives me no pleasure whatever to write about a massacre of over twenty persons at the Walmart in El Paso, but I would be seriously remiss to omit this horrible event that occurred during the final stages of writing the story.

As soon as I finished getting *Judgment!*, the third book in the series, ready for publication, I began pondering on how to write my memoires. Then, suddenly the inspiration for this fourth novel popped into my head and began writing itself. It has been completed in record speed in order to appeal to readers who appreciate very current stories.

The setting had to be in El Paso, Texas, a city with a metro area population over one million, the largest city on the U.S.-Mexico border, but one that was not broadly known when I started writing; this was *before* President Trump conducted his first well-publicized campaign rally in El Paso. It also had to be a city with a major airport. Now, sadly, El Paso is well known worldwide, due to the horror of the massacre in August 2019. For many years, El Paso has been a cosmopolitan center of art and culture, great civic spirit, and consistently among the very safest cities in the U.S. As noted by the fictional Russian diplomat in Mexico, in addition to the one million population of the El Paso metropolitan area on the U.S. side of the border, another nearly two million live immediately across the border in Ciudad Juárez. As mentioned in the story, traditionally they were one integrated community for many years. It is my hope that, with *Don't Fence Me In*, the world will recognize the great attributes of El Paso beyond its great response to the horrible tragedy in August 2019.

The harassment by the U.S. Border Control in the early 1990s of students and faculty at Bowie High School in El Paso, who were almost entirely Hispanic, has been documented in the news media. At that time, a federal judge ruled that the Border Patrol exceeded its authority by demanding proof of citizenship for persons merely because they were Hispanic. As indicated in the story, many

Hispanics on the U.S. side of the southern border have been loyal, proud citizens of the U.S. for many generations, with few, if any, ties to what is now the country of México other than to visit as part of an integrated community. Many have ancestors who were living in the thriving community of El Paso del Norte on the north side of the Rio Bravo (now known as the Rio Grande in the U.S.) when the area was a Spanish colony. When the Republic of Texas joined the U.S. in 1845, these people found themselves in the United States, even though they had not moved. These ancestors were not immigrants; the border changed.

It is well-known through media reporting that Russia continues to attempt to create chaos in the U.S. to disrupt democracy. The specific means in this story, though, are fictional. I know of no specific means used by Russians other than those reported in the news media. Likewise, I know of no specific efforts of Russia to involve Iran and North Korea in these efforts, although cooperation of Russia and Iran and North Korea is reported in the media. The use of Mexico as a base for such activities is entirely fictional, although plausible.

Even though fictional parts of story were brought to a close by me because events related to the fictional tunnel were mostly resolved, other events in the story have continued. As widely reported by the news media, a private group has just completed construction of a fence on private land along the border to close the gap around Mount Cristo Rey, as described in the story. This private group who built the fence section is the same group described in the story as a private vigilante group that was detaining supposedly illegal immigrants. The arrest of the leader on unrelated firearm charges has been reported in the media.

The horrible massacre at a Walmart store near Cielo Vista Mall is sadly well known, as reported extensively by the media to this very day. The El Paso community has developed the slogan, *El Paso strong*. A large memorial continues to expand along the back side of the Walmart property. El Paso residents and visitors spontaneously add to it regularly. This memorial strip, some quarter mile in length, contains displays of artificial flowers, crosses, and the flags of the countries of nationality of the people killed in the massacre, Germany, Mexico, and the U.S.

El Paso Strong memorial to victims of Walmart massacre, El Paso, Texas

As in the previous novels, all characters are based on people I have known directly or indirectly, a large number indirectly. There are no stereotypes. Apologies, perhaps, to the fine people of Oklahoma if my characters Woodrow and Leroy appear stereotypical of your state. Both my parents and their extended families are from Oklahoma, so I am very aware of the fine people in that state. Nonetheless, there are people like Woodrow and Leroy from virtually every state. Oklahoma fit the story line best. Among other reasons, as this is being written, the State of Oklahoma has just received settlements from opioid manufacturers and has received a judgment against another opioid manufacturer for fraudulent promotion of opioids in the state. Oklahoma has one of the highest, if not the highest, rates of misuse of opioids, causing a public health emergency.

A few prominent politicians are mentioned by name, but do not have roles in the plot. Otherwise, the names of all characters are fictional and come from my imagination. Because they are common names—otherwise the story would not be realistic—there are surely persons with these names. If you have one of these names, please be assured that the characters in this story are not you.

As with my previous books, I claim no legal and medical expertise. All I know about how these two professions operate is from news media and very limited personal interaction. Apologies if I have seriously misrepresented proper legal and medical protocol.

Many dear friends and others contributed to this book. Some would not want to be mentioned by name, so I will not name any. You know who you are. With big hugs and kisses where appropriate, and many grateful thanks.

Enjoy the story and let me have your feedback, which is always welcome. If you have not done so already, enjoy the previous three books in this series.

—Heath

HeathDanielsAuthor@gmail.com

HeathDanielsBooks.com

DISCUSSION QUESTIONS

Please use these discussion questions for your book reading groups, or yourself. Feel free to supplement with additional questions and/or comments. If you like, let me know your additional discussion questions so I can add to the list.

Email me at HeathDanielsAuthor@gmail.com.
    —Heath Daniels

1. As with my other books, this story is historical fiction based on current events. How effectively have current events involving Russian attempts to create chaos in the U.S. and other current events been presented?

2. The story presents factual current events along with fictional events with no attempt to separate fiction from fact. How effective is this juxtaposition of fact and fiction?

3. As with the previous books, inspirations are to write to entertain as well as to inform and foster tolerance,

acceptance, and respect. How well have these complementary inspirations been achieved?

4. Some of the characters of the previous books have been brought forward, while new characters have been introduced. How well developed are the characters? Which ones could be developed further? Which ones could be developed less?

5. As in the previous books, characters are intended to be realistic. There are no stereotypes, and the characters are based on people I have known, directly or indirectly, mostly indirectly. How effective is the presentation of realistic characters?

6. Names of the characters are actual names I have encountered in various places, but with no known first and last name combinations. Some reflect a tendency of immigrants to give their children who are born in the U.S. names that reflect the ethnic identity of their homeland. Following generations often give children English-language given names with their ethnic surnames. How effective are the names selected for characters in this story?

7. Yet another inspiration is to illuminate and express the culture of locations that are not always well known. To what extent does the story allow you to get to know better the El Paso metropolitan area, along with suburbs and nearby communities in New Mexico? How effectively are places like Alpine, Texas; Ruidoso, New Mexico; and Albuquerque, New Mexico, presented?

8. As in the previous stories, actual commercial establishments are used whenever possible. Please feel free to do online searches for Faywood Hot Springs, Inn of the Mountain Gods, Jason's Deli, State Line restaurant, Cattle Baron

restaurants, and other business establishments mentioned in the book. To what extent does the use of actual businesses add to the authenticity of the story for you?

9. Romance and relationships between romantic partners have played important roles in subplots in this and the previous books. To what extent do the romantic activities in subplots in this story contribute to the overall story? How do you see the future development of relationships between Yusef and Nisrine? Between Khan and Otto? Between Brad and Jason?

10. The story was designed to present the U.S. federal judicial system in all of its elements, the courts and judges, U.S. Attorney General prosecutors, public defenders, private defenders, etc. How effective is this presentation?

11. The story was also designed to present the role and effectiveness of a free press and other news media. How effectively was this element accomplished?

12. Inspirations for story plots come to me from many sources. What would you like me to write about next?

THANK YOU FOR READING
DON'T FENCE ME IN

It was my pleasure to write it for your entertainment and enlightenment. Please let me hear from you about your thoughts and feedback.

Please consider writing a review for Amazon, Goodreads, newspapers, and wherever you go to find thoughtful reviews.

Please sign up to receive my periodic newsletter. Send your name and email address to the places below.

Blessings,

—Heath Daniels

HeathDanielsAuthor@gmail.com
HeathDanielsBooks.com
Facebook: Heath Daniels and Heath Daniels Books

ABOUT THE AUTHOR

Heath Daniels is semi-retired from a successful academic career as a professor and researcher in international business issues, writing and speaking professionally. He has lived in many countries and traveled to many other countries world-wide. These locations exposed him to many cultures and situations in which he developed appreciation, respect, and empathy for all persons everywhere, their cultures and traditions. His travels have inspired his fiction writing.

As indicated in the Afterword to Three Kisses, at New Year going from 2005 to 2006, thoughts and inspirations came into his mind and would not stop until he sat at the computer and started writing. Thus started a parallel career of being an academic living and working in various locations and writing action international intrigue novels under a pseudonym. Now that he has mostly retired from academia, he has continued through four novels with a fifth still developing in his head.

He grew up in a small city that would be considered the heartland of the US. During his academic career in the US, he lived in what would be viewed as a semi-rural area. While moving around the world, he lived in big cities, small towns, and in between. Upon semi-retirement. He moved back to his original home town which is now a larger, urban, cosmopolitan city that still has heartland roots. He continues to travel whenever possible, most recently returning from a four-week visit to southeast Asia.

Almost all locations in his books are places where he has lived or visited for a long enough time to be able to bring them to life through the books. All characters are fictionalized depictions of actual people with whom he has interacted, not always under pleasant circumstances. His novels feature current events, adventure, and intrigue that are designed to entertain, as well as inform and foster acceptance, tolerance, and respect. Many events that were written as fiction actually occurred later, as explained in the afterwords of the books published so far.

Made in the USA
Coppell, TX
01 September 2021